The Constant Rabbit

Jasper Fforde

The Constant Rabbit

HODDER &
STOUGHTON

First published in Great Britain in 2020 by Hodder & Stoughton
An Hachette UK company

I

A CIP catalogue record for this title is available from the British Library

Hardback ISBN 978 1 444 76362 1
Trade Paperback ISBN 978 1 444 76363 8
eBook ISBN 978 1 444 76365 2

Typeset in Bembo by Palimpsest Book Production Ltd, Falkirk, Stirlingshire

Printed and bound in Great Britain by Clays Ltd, Elcograf S.p.A.

Hodder & Stoughton policy is to use papers that are natural, renewable
and recyclable products and made from wood grown in sustainable forests.
The logging and manufacturing processes are expected to conform to
the environmental regulations of the country of origin.

Hodder & Stoughton Ltd
Carmelite House
50 Victoria Embankment
London EC4Y 0DZ

www.hodder.co.uk

It cannot be said too often: all life is one.
A Short History of Nearly Everything – Bill Bryson

To the human eye, each rabbit looks very much like the other.
The Private Life of the Rabbit – R.M. Lockley

Speed Librarying

Somebody once said that the library is actually the dominant life form on the planet. Humans simply exist as the reproductive means to achieve more libraries.

'Still on the Westerns, Baroness Thatcher?' I asked, moving slowly down the line of volunteers who were standing at readiness outside our library, a smallish mock-mock-Tudor building in the middle of Much Hemlock, itself more or less in the middle of the county of Hereford, which in turn was pretty much in the middle of the UK.

Much Hemlock was, in pretty much every meaning of the word, middling.

'Westerns are the best when they're not really Westerns at all,' said Baroness Thatcher, 'like when more akin to the Greek Epics. *True Grit*, for example.'

'*Shane* is more my kind of thing,' said Stanley Baldwin, who I think fancied himself as a softly spoken man of understated power and influence. Winston Churchill opined they were both wrong and that *The Ox-Bow Incident* was far better with its generally positive themes of extrajudicial violence. Neville Chamberlain tried to keep the peace and find some middle ground on the issue while David Lloyd George simply sat there in quiet repose, mentally preparing for the adrenaline-fuelled six minutes of Speed Librarying that lay before us.

Perhaps I should explain. The UKARP Government's much-vaunted Rural Library Strategic Group Vision Action Group had kept libraries open as per their election manifesto, but reduced the librarian staffing levels in Herefordshire to a single, solitary example working on greatly reduced hours – which meant that each of the county's twelve libraries could be open for precisely six minutes every two weeks.

And this is where my hand-picked team of faux politicians entered

1

the picture. Using a mixture of careful planning, swiftness of foot, a robust understanding of the Dewey Decimal Book Categorisation System and with strict adherence to procedure, we could facilitate a fortnight's worth of returns, loans, reserves and extensions in the three hundred and sixty seconds available to us. It was known to all and sundry as a *Buchblitz*.

My name is Peter Knox, but for the next six minutes I'll be your John Major.

'Ready, Stanley?' I asked Mr Baldwin, who oversaw returns and reservations but was actually retired Wing Commander Slocombe, a former RAF officer who famously lost an ear while ejecting out of a Hawker Hunter over Aden. Remarkably, a solitary ear was retrieved from the wreckage of the aircraft and reattached. Even more remarkably, it wasn't his.

'Three times ready, Team Leader.'

'Mr Major?' asked Mrs Griswold, who usually ran the Much Hemlock village shop, post office, gossip exchange and pub combined. 'I can't remember if I'm Winston Churchill or David Lloyd George.'

'You're David Lloyd George,' I said. 'You select the books from the shelves to be given to Mr Chamberlain, who takes them to the counter and to Mrs Thatcher, who offers them up to the Sole Librarian to be stamped. It's really *very* simple.'

'Right,' said Mrs Griswold, 'David Lloyd George. Got it.'

I had devised an Emergency Code system for Speed Librarying, and Mrs Griswold was definitely a Code 3-20: *'Someone who village diplomacy dictated should be on the Blitzer team, but was, nonetheless, useless'*. Sadly, no one but myself knew what a 3-20 was, as the system hadn't reached the levels of awareness I thought it deserved – a state of affairs that had its own code, a 5-12: *'Lack of enthusiasm over correct procedures'*.

The church clock signalled 10.45 and the chatter gave way to an expectant hush. We had seen the Sole Librarian rummaging around prior to the opening, and while she would permit us to reshelf, log reservations and even use the card index, her stamps were sacrosanct: hers and hers alone. Because of this it was Mrs Thatcher's responsibility to ensure that books and library cards were placed before the

Sole Librarian so that her stamping time was most effectively spent. The steady rhythm of rubber on paper was the litmus test of an efficient *Blitz*.

Speed Librarying was also fast becoming a spectator sport – no TV rights offers yet, sadly, but there was usually a group of local onlookers at every *Blitz*, eager to offer us moral support and ensure that tea and seedcake and a rub-down with a towel would be forthcoming once the *Blitz* was over. Not all onlookers were so helpful. Norman and Victor Mallett were the de facto elders of the village, and dominated every committee from Parish Council to Steeple Fund to coordinating Much Hemlock's entry in the *All Herefordshire Spick & Span Village Awards*. They were not themselves huge fans of libraries, regarding them as 'just one more pointless drain on the nation's resources'.

They had turned up ostensibly to support the current Neville Chamberlain, who happened also to be Victor Mallett's wife, to complain bitterly about anything that contravened their narrow worldview – and for Norman to take possession of his reserved copy of *The Glory and Triumph of the British Colonial System Illustrated*.

At two minutes to opening Mr Churchill – in charge of extensions, audiobooks and swapping tired periodicals for slightly less tired periodicals – indicated she needed a toilet break and would be unlikely to return within fifteen minutes. This was unfortunate but not a fatal blow, as Mr Beeton, a long-standing friend and next-door neighbour, was my all-parts understudy.

'Can you do Churchill?' I asked.

'We shall never surrender,' said Mr Beeton with a grin before coughing a deep, rattly cough.

'Are you sure?' said Stanley Baldwin to me in a low voice. 'He doesn't look very well to me.'

'Mr Beeton is the picture of good health,' I said in a hopeful manner with little basis in reality: Mr Beeton had so many ailments that he was less of an elderly resident and more of a walking medical conundrum, the only two ailments which he had not suffered in his long life being tennis elbow and death.

So Mr Beeton-now-Winston Churchill dutifully took his place

behind a wheelbarrow containing forty-six neatly stacked books all carefully sorted by shelf order for ease of return. I nodded to David Lloyd George to acknowledge the last-minute change in the team and she nodded in return as we saw the Sole Librarian approach the front door of the library and then check her watch to make sure she didn't open a second too early.

This was, in fact, crucial. There were two Herefordshire Library Opening Times Compliance Officers in attendance armed with clipboards and stopwatches, the pair funded at great expense by the Rural Library Strategic Group Vision Action Group, which now employed just under four thousand people, coincidentally the *exact* same number as the librarians whose continued employment had been deemed incompatible with UKARP's manifesto pledge.

I checked my watch.

'Little hand says it's time to rock and roll.'

The Sole Librarian threw the lock and the door swung open. We moved in with military-style precision, Winston Churchill pushing before him the wheelbarrow of books to be returned while Maggie Thatcher started the stopwatch.

'Good morning,' I said to the Sole Librarian.

'Good morning, Mr Major,' she returned in a sing-song tone. 'Will we hit our target today?'

'As easy as negotiating Maastricht,' I replied, trying to exude confidence when secretly I felt we would manage returns and loans, but fall short of our renewal and reserves target. The team swiftly moved to their allotted places: Mr Churchill, Mrs Thatcher and Stanley Baldwin went straight to the front desk and presented the books to the Sole Librarian. Within a few seconds a steady thump-thump-thump filled the air, demonstrating that work was very much in progress.

At the same time, David Lloyd George and Neville Chamberlain went rapidly down the aisles transferring the pre-ordered picks to a trolley ready to be brought to the front desk once the returns, extensions and reservations were completed – and once that was done, Mr Baldwin could reshelve the returned books, assisted by Neville Chamberlain.

'Time check,' I called.

'Ninety seconds gone, Mr Major,' replied Mrs Thatcher.

All seemed to be going well until the Sole Librarian's stamping abruptly ceased, suggesting a clog in the system, and Neville Chamberlain simultaneously announced that she couldn't find a copy of *Wind, Sand and Stars*.

'Try Aviation, three-eight-seven,' said the Sole Librarian, her deep knowledge of Dewey classification coming to the fore.

While Neville was dealing with the potential mis-shelving of Antoine de Saint-Exupéry, I went to see what the logjam was with returns. The problem was a Code 2-76: Mrs Dibley had kept her copy of *Henry Ford and Other Positive Role Models for Disaffected Youth* for eighteen weeks longer than the permitted time, and the Sole Librarian was filling out a form for an overdue fine.

'This lady was clearly not for returning,' said Mrs Thatcher, indicating the overdue book. I grimaced. The *Blitz* would be tight, but so far the situation was not irredeemable.

'How is it going with *Wind, Sand and Stars*, Mr Chamberlain?' I called towards the shelves as David Lloyd George pushed the trolley full of picked loans towards the front desk.

'I have in my hand this piece of paper,' replied Neville Chamberlain triumphantly, holding aloft the book.

The Sole Librarian shifted from returns to loans, and moved on to the rhythmic thump-*thump*, thump-*thump* of the 'double tap', one on the library card, one on the date return slip pasted in the front of the book. The next step was reshelving, and by the time Mrs Thatcher called out 'two minutes remaining' we were well ahead of ourselves and a sense of ease descended on the small group: we would clear this *Blitz* with time to spare. I was just placing a copy of the worryingly popular *Cecil Rhode's Greatest Speeches as Spoken by Oswald Mosley* in the Talking Book section when I heard a voice from behind me.

'May I ask a question?'

I stopped dead, for I recognised the voice. It was one I had not heard for a long time, nor had ever thought I would again. A soft yet very distinctive West Country accent, tinged with questioning allure. I turned slowly, unsure of quite what to say or do, and there was Connie, staring at me with the same intensity I remembered from our shared late-night coffees during freshman year at the University of Barnstaple.

'Sure,' I said, not knowing whether she recognised me or not.

'It's a book question,' she replied brightly, and seemingly without a flicker of recognition. Oddly, I felt relieved. I'd been very fond of her, although unwilling to show it, and I think she might have felt the same. But after a few dates – she never called them that although I did, secretly to myself – she was asked to leave the college following a judicial review of the legal status of her attendance, and that was that. I'd always wanted to see her again, and I would see much of her over the coming weeks. I'd be at her side three months from now during the Battle of May Hill, the smell of burned rubber and cordite drifting across the land, the crack of artillery fire in the distance. I had no idea of that, of course, and neither, I imagine, did she.

'Well, it *is* a library,' I said, hoping my sudden consternation didn't show. 'What do you want to know?'

By rights, she shouldn't have been there at all, and not because she was a rabbit. The public, although *technically* allowed to enter the library during opening hours, never did. We were, after all, simply doing our civic duty by way of the community, and the community, in turn, stayed away and allowed us to carry on the work on their behalf. I deemed Connie not just an old acquaintance, but a Code 4-51: *'Unidentified public in the Librarying area'*.

'I'm after *Rabbit and Rabbitability*,' she said. 'Like Austen's classic but more warren-based and with a greater emphasis on ears, sex, carrots, burrowing and sex.'

'You said sex twice.'

'Yes,' said Connie, blinking twice, 'I know.'

Rabbits aged better than humans so long as they got a chance to age at all, and she was pretty much unchanged in the thirty-odd years since I'd seen her last: smaller and slimmer than the norm, but Wildstock, the generic brown-furred variety. She wore a short spotted summer dress under a pale blue buttoned cardigan and her ears, long and elegant, carried four small silver ear-studs halfway up her right and three near the base of her left. Her most striking feature, then as now, was her eyes: both large and expressive, but while one was the brown of a fresh hazelnut, the other was pale bluey-violet, the colour of harebells.

'Are you OK?' she said, as I think I might have been staring.

Luckily, Neville Chamberlain chose that moment to interrupt.

'*Rabbit and Rabbitability* would be under six-three-two point six-six,' she said, referring to the Dewey categorisation number that related to: 'Technology/Agriculture/Pests/Disposal'. It was a predictably insulting response. She was, after all, married to Victor Mallett and the entire Mallett family's antagonism towards any social or species group not their own was well known. It was said Mallett children were encouraged to feed the ducks solely 'to see them fight'.

'Actually, Mr Chamberlain,' put in Stanley Baldwin, 'it's probably a six-three-six point nine-three.' This was a little less insulting as it referred to 'Technology/Agriculture/Domestic Animals/Rabbits', but was equally of little use. Connie wasn't after books *about* rabbits, but the range of British classics retold *for* rabbits, published when funding was more secure after the Spontaneous Anthropomorphic Event, when integration into society was still seen as guiding policy rather than the pipe-dream of idealistic liberals.

'Eight-nine-nine point nine-nine, Mr Major,' added the Sole Librarian, who didn't much care for rabbits either but hated misuse of the Dewey Decimal System a great deal more. 'Literature/Other Languages. Shelf nine.'

'Let me show you,' I said, handing the returned books to Neville, who hurried off to shelve them quickly so she could return, presumably, to air her anti-rabbit sentiments more fully. For my part I led Connie quickly towards the foreign language section.

'Hey,' she said with a giggle, 'isn't naming the team after former prime ministers a direct lift from that Kathryn Bigelow heist-gone-wrong movie?'

'I ... don't know what you mean.'

'Sure you do,' she said. 'The one with Patrick Swayze and Keanu Reeves. What's its name again?'

'*Point Break*,' I said, suddenly remembering that I'd seen it first with her at the Student Union cinema. We'd sat in the back row, a place usually reserved for lovers, but we weren't there for that reason. Rabbit cinema-goers, acutely conscious of how their often expressive ear movements can ruin a movie for anyone sitting behind, politely migrated to the back. Our upper arms had touched as we sat, which I remembered I quite liked; it was the sum total of any physical contact.

'And,' I concluded, 'it's more a homage, really.'

'That's the one,' she said with a smile, '*Point Break*. You could have disguised everyone in rubber masks, again, like in the movie.'

'Not very practical and we don't actually need to be disguised,' I said, 'and besides, while Mrs Thatcher and John Major masks are still obtainable, those of Neville Chamberlain and David Lloyd George are almost impossible to come by.'

'I heard you could paint William Shatner masks to represent almost anyone.'

I'd heard that too, but didn't say so.

'There's issues of being able to see out clearly enough,' I said.

'Ninety seconds!' called out Mrs Thatcher.

'You're in luck,' I said, picking a couple of dusty volumes from the shelves. 'Are either of these the ones you wanted?'

I showed her the covers, which were written in Rabbity script,[1] and unintelligible to me, or indeed any humans. Even after fifty-five years, no human had ever mastered anything but the most basic tenets of their language, verbal or written. Attempts by humans to converse in their mother tongue were usually met with peals of hysterical laughter, and remain one of the mainstays of rabbit comedy stand-up, along with jokes about ears, litter sizes, the broader etymological impact of 'cuniculus' and the hilarity that ensues when entering the wrong burrow by accident, at night, slightly drunk, during the mating season.

---

1. The script looks like 'scuffed mud', the sort of marks you get in the back porch after inclement weather. The Rabbity alphabet, incidentally, has only six letters: N, I, R, H, U and F.

'Oooh!' said Connie, grasping one of the books tightly. '*Planet of the Lagomorphs*. That's a find.'

I wasn't an expert on the whole Rabbit Literature Retelling Project of the early eighties, but I did know that out of the hundred or so titles, only one was ever banned. When you retold *Planet of the Apes* the dominant life form was the rabbit. It became something of a political hot potato, but not, crucially, amongst rabbits. The fledgling United Kingdom Anti-Rabbit Party declared the novel's central theme to be 'not conducive to good human/rabbit relations' – and lobbied successfully to have it withdrawn and pulped.

'Must have missed the dragnet,' I said.

'I'll give it a read to the family,' said Connie with a smile, 'might give us some ideas.'

Rabbits rarely read to themselves as they saw books more as a performance than a solitary occupation. Why, they asked, do anything by yourself that could be shared with others?

'Banned book?' said Neville Chamberlain, her shelving complete and now back on the scene. She clasped hold of the volume and tried to take it away, but Connie didn't relinquish her grip, and they both stood there, each with their hands/paws on the book, tugging backwards and forwards.

'It was on the shelf,' said Connie Rabbit, 'so free to be loaned. That's how libraries work.'

'Don't tell *me* how libraries work,' said Neville Chamberlain, who was now talking less like someone eager to appease, and more like the Mrs Mallett reactionary she was, 'I've been a library volunteer since before you munched your first carrot.'

It was a dumb insult, and they both knew it.

'Wow,' said Connie, 'you got me.'

'Forty-five seconds!' called out Mrs Thatcher, and I was now in a quandary. If Connie *now* was anything like the Connie I knew *then*, she wasn't going to take no for an answer, and if we overran it would be a Code 4-22: '*Opening Time Deficit*', which meant anything over the six minutes would be docked on the next library opening. I glanced towards where the two Library Opening Times Compliance

Officers were staring at us from the door, in the same manner vultures might regard an unwell zebra.

'Mr Major?' said Neville Chamberlain, using her Seventeenth-Century-School-Ma'am-That-Must-Be-Obeyed voice. 'Our library is a special place and not to be disrespected.'

'How is it being disrespected?' asked Connie in an even tone. 'Really, I'd like to know.'

'You have a *serious* attitude problem,' said Mrs Mallett, taking instant umbrage at being questioned directly by a lower animal.

'I'm so sorry,' said Connie, 'how is the library being disrespected – *ma'am?*'

There was a sudden unpleasant hush. Shock, anticipation of violence, confusion – maybe all three. I took a deep breath. Upset one Mallett and you upset them all. Mind you, the Malletts were always upset about *something*. Politics, local government, socialists, the price of onions. When *How to Cook a Wild Potato* went from the BBC to Channel Four they couldn't talk about anything else for months. Irrespective, I took my Librarying seriously and I'd never been a huge fan of the Malletts – and a chance to piss them off with the added bonus of plausible deniability should never be missed. I paused for a moment, then turned to Connie.

'Do you have a library card?'

'I do,' she said.

'Then the loan goes ahead.'

'Terrific,' said Mrs Mallett, shedding all vestiges of Neville Chamberlain completely, 'so we're just going to start handing out books to every bunny that walks in the door?'

'It's a library, Isadora,' I said, 'we loan out books. And "bunny" isn't really an acceptable term any more.'

She laughed in a mocking fashion.

'C'mon, Peter, it's only a name, a word, a label – like a hat or a car or an avocado or something. It means nothing.'

'What about "leporiphobic"?' I asked. 'I suppose that's just a word too?'

I felt Isadora rankle at the riposte. I shouldn't really have said it, but oddly, I think I might have been grandstanding in Connie's presence. But I was, in fact, correct. They were very hot on acceptable rabbit terminology down at the Rabbit Compliance Taskforce, and while RabCoT's relationship with the rabbit community was strained, we had to appear even-handed and without bias. Even referring to rabbits collectively as 'The Rabbit' was a little iffy these days.

'Twenty-five seconds!' said Mrs Thatcher with increased agitation. 'We have to be out of here, Mr Major.'

Before Mrs Mallett had time to argue, I beckoned Connie to the front desk. The Sole Librarian stared at her library card, then at Connie.

'Your name's Clifford Rabbit?'

'It's my husband's.'

'That's a Code 4-20 infraction right there,' said Mrs Mallett in a triumphant tone – it turned out she *had* been studying my codes after all – '*"Misuse of library property".*'

'The book's for my husband,' said Connie. 'Customers may collect books on others' behalf. True?'

She directed the last word at the Sole Librarian, who confirmed her agreement by stamping the library card and the book and handing them back.[2]

'Ten seconds!' yelled Mrs Thatcher, and we all hurried towards the door. The other members of the team had already made their way out, and as the door closed and the lock clunked, Mrs Thatcher and the Compliance Officers compared stopwatches. We had made it with only three seconds to spare.

'Well done, everyone,' I said, trying to inject a sense of cheeriness into the proceedings, but only Stanley Baldwin and Mrs Thatcher were standing beside me. The others had instead congregated around the observers outside, and in particular Norman and Victor Mallett, presumably to question them on how they let a rabbit slip past them

---

2. As a cost-cutting measure the old card system was reintroduced to Herefordshire libraries. Each user has a cardboard wallet held by the library, into which the card contained in a pocket on each book is placed. The book then has a stamp for its due return date, as has the card held by the library. The user wallets are stored in a large indexing system. It's a lot more simple than it sounds.

and into the library in the first place, and then figuring out the next move. Already I could see Norman's neck turning a nasty shade of purple, and several of the villagers directed frosty glances in my direction.

I looked around to see whether Connie was still about and caught sight of her as she leapt in a series of energetic bounds down the street towards the Leominster road, her library book in one hand and a mobile phone clamped to her ear in the other.

She hadn't recognised me at all.

'Why was there a rabbit in the village?' asked Mrs Thatcher, following my gaze.

'I don't know.'

'Well, it was a good *Blitz*, Peter,' she said, then hurriedly moved away as she saw Victor and Norman Mallett approach.

'Now then,' said Norman in the lofty tones of someone who believes, despite bountiful evidence to the contrary, that they have the moral high ground, 'let's have a little chat about whether bunnies are welcome in the library, shall we?'

But he didn't get to vent his anger. At that precise moment Mr Beeton gave out a quiet moan and collapsed in a heap. We called an ambulance while Lloyd George and Mrs Thatcher took turns in giving him CPR, but to no avail. We found out later he suffered a heart attack, which was the first and last time I'd had a Code 2-22: *'Unavoidable death while Librarying'*.

'I told you he looked unwell,' said Stanley Baldwin.

Toast & Two Legs Good

RabCoT or the Rabbit Compliance Taskforce was originally named the 'Rabbit Crime Taskforce', but that was deemed too aggressive, so was quietly renamed, much to Mr Smethwick's annoyance. He had wanted the original name to send a clear message that Cunicular Criminality would not be tolerated.

'So Mr Beeton just keeled over?' asked Pippa at breakfast on Monday morning. She'd been out all day and the night before and I hadn't heard her come in, but that wasn't unusual. I like to turn in early in order to read, and her bedroom was on the ground floor and she could totally look after herself these days. Sometimes it's better not to know when daughters don't come home for the night. She was twenty, but even so, still best not to know.

'Yup,' I said, 'went down like a ninepin. Mind you, he was eighty-eight, so it's not like it wasn't expected.'

I looked out of the kitchen window at Hemlock Towers opposite, where up until Saturday Mr Beeton had been a long-term resident. We lived in what had once been the stables to the old house, but unlike the Towers, it had been modernised over the years and was considerably more comfortable.

'I wonder who will take it over?' I mused – the impressively turreted building was the jewel in Much Hemlock's not inconsiderable collection of fine buildings. Parts of it dated back to the fourteenth century and some say that the pockmarks in the façade were the result of erratic musket-fire during the Civil War. The marksmanship of parliamentary forces, I figured, was little better than that of *Star Wars* stormtroopers.

'Someone like Mr Beeton, I should imagine,' said Pippa, 'lots of money, an imperviousness to cold.'

'... and insanely suspicious of modern plumbing,' I added, 'with a fondness for mice and rising damp.'

Pippa smiled and handed me a slice of toast with marmalade before pouring herself another coffee.

'I was over at Toby's yesterday evening,' she said.

'Ah.'

My relationship with the Malletts, always strained, had become immeasurably more complex since Toby Mallett, Victor's youngest, had been seeing Pippa on a regular basis. Despite his somewhat difficult family, Toby was handsome and generally well mannered, but I'd never entirely warmed to him. He'd professed vaguely liberal views, but I felt that was for Pip's benefit, as I knew for a fact his opinions were really more in tune with his father's. When the village put on a production of *The Sound of Music*, it was Toby who volunteered most enthusiastically to play Rolf. He told everyone it was so he could sing 'Sixteen Going on Seventeen' opposite Pippa's Liesl, but when in a less generous frame of mind I thought it was probably because he got a free pass to dress up as a Nazi.

My own feelings aside, she could do a lot worse. She *had* done a lot worse. But there was Daughter Rule Number Seven to consider: don't have opinions over boyfriends unless expressly asked, and then – well, play it safe and sit on the fence.

'Did you get any feedback over Mr Beeton's death?' I asked.

'No one blamed you,' she said, as the Malletts would often use Pippa as a conduit of information in my direction. 'He'd done the *Blitz* at least fifteen times and understood the risks of high-impact Librarying.'

'I hope everyone else thinks the same.'

'Aside from us, Mr Beeton wasn't particularly well liked,' observed Pippa. 'D'you remember when he scandalised the village by publicly announcing: "the poor aren't so bad"?'

'I liked him for that,' I said, chuckling at the memory.

'So did I. But he'll be forgotten in a couple of weeks. The village takes its grudges seriously. Remember when old Granny Watkins kicked the bucket? I'll swear most people in the church were only there to personally confirm she was dead.'

Pippa moved herself to the kitchen table and took a sip of coffee.

'The Malletts had a few choice words over what they saw as your overly generous treatment of the rabbit,' she added, 'and within earshot of me so they wanted it repeated.'

'Oh yes?' I said, having expected something like this would happen.

'Yes. Something along the lines of how they generally tolerated your left-wing views, but if you were going to start being "troublesomely ambivalent" towards undesirables there might be consequences.'

I turned from the window to face her.

'Would you describe me as left-wing, Pip?'

I considered myself centrist, to be honest. Apolitical, in fact. I had no time for it.

'Compared to the rest of the village,' she said with a smile, 'I'd say you're almost Marxist.'

Much Hemlock had always been a hotbed of right-wing sentiment, something that had strong historical precedent: the village had the dubious distinction of having convicted and burned more witches than any other English town in history. Thirty-one, all told, right up until a dark night in 1568 when they burned a real one by accident, and all her accusers came out in unsightly black pustules and died hideously painful deaths within forty-eight hours. Zephaniah Mallett had been the magistrate during the trials, but in a dark day for evolution he'd had children *before* dying so four centuries later Victor and Norman were very much in existence. They liked to keep family traditions alive, even if witch-burning was currently off limits.

'I'm not troublesome, am I, Pip?' I asked.

She looked up and smiled, and I recognised her mother. She'd been gone ten years but I'd still not really got used to it.

'You're not troublesome, Dad. The Malletts are troublesome. I think Victor thought you'd been unduly accommodating to the rabbit, and that kindness might be misinterpreted as welcoming, and you know what they think about preserving the cultural heart of the village.'

'Preserving the cultural heart of the village' was the Malletts' byline, mission statement, excuse and justification for their strident views all in one. Victor and Norman's 'cultural heart' speech was really more to do with justifying their desire to block undesirables, a definition that was so broad it had to be broken down into numerous subcategories, each of which attracted their ire in a distinctly unique way. It wasn't just foreigners or rabbits, either: they had an intense dislike for those whom they described as 'spongers' – again, a net that could be cast quite broadly but conveniently excluded those on a government pension, taken early – and other groups that they felt were deeply suspect, such as VW Passat drivers: 'the car of smug lefties'. Added to that was anyone who was vegetarian, or wore sandals, or men with 'overly vanitised' facial hair – or women who wore dungarees, spoke loudly and had the outrageous temerity to suggest that their views might be relevant, or worse, correct.

'I think I let Connie borrow the book to piss them off,' I said.

'And I applaud you for it.' She paused for a moment, then said: 'How did you know her name?'

'It was – um – on her library card.'

I managed to lie quite convincingly, although I wasn't sure why I was so quick to deny our friendship.

'Short for Constance, I imagine. They often have Victorian names. Part of the whole Beatrix Potter[3] Chic thing.'

Pippa nodded, and there was a double beep from a car horn outside. Sally Lomax had been Pippa's partner-in-crime since they first met in toddler group, and they were closer than sisters. Sally was at Nursing College too and could give her a lift – but was training in paediatrics, not management. Pippa finished her coffee and gathered up her stuff.

'I put in a good word for you with the Malletts,' she said, giving me a peck on the cheek. 'I told them your offensive level of toleration would have been solely due to Library Rules Applying, and you weren't a friend to rabbits any more than they were.'

'Thanks,' I said.

'See you this evening.'

And she was gone out of the door.

I tidied up, set the dishwasher, and at precisely nine o'clock

---

3. The blueprint for the way in which the rabbit had become anthropomorphised was generally agreed to be along Beatrix Potter lines. Why this was so it was impossible to say, but it was a look and a feel and a tone which the rabbit fully embraced.

gathered together my case, jacket and car keys and walked outside. Toby Mallett was waiting for me by the garage – we worked in the same office in Hereford and I often gave him a lift. Annoyingly – yet unsurprisingly – his father, Victor Mallett, was with him. We all wished each other cordial good mornings.

'Good morning,' said Victor.

'Good morning,' I said.

'Good morning,' said Toby.

Once this complex ritual was over, Victor said:

'Can I cadge a ride into the big smoke? The Zephyr's in the garage at the moment. Carbon on the valves.'

I agreed as I couldn't *not* agree, while knowing full well this was less about getting a lift into Hereford, and more about me copping a bollocking for the Connie incident. We hadn't got to the edge of the village before he began.

'Sorry about getting out of my pram at the library,' said Victor, 'what with the memsahib giving you the ugly prawn over that stray member of the public. You were right – the rabbit was allowed to be there.'

'That's OK,' I said, knowing this was usually how it worked. The charm, the flattery, the faux bonhomie – then the attempt to get what he actually wanted. Victor was as transparent as air, but nowhere near as useful. He'd probably ask me whether I knew who 'that rabbit' was next.

'So,' he said, 'do you know who that rabbit was?'

'Which one?'

'The one in the library.'

I'd been thinking about Connie most of the weekend. Back at uni we'd only met up for coffees and a few movies. Ten occasions, tops – and romance had never been mooted, much less acted upon – but she had made an impression on me, and I think, perhaps, I had a little on her. A demonstration had been planned when a review of university admission rules retrospectively forbade her attendance. The whole thing was precipitated by UKARP, when they were still agitators rather than serious political players. The anti-rabbit group had attempted to enrol eight goats, four earthworms and a pony named

Diddy into various university courses, arguing that if rabbits could attend then so, logically, could any animal – even dumb, non-anthropomorphised ones. A High Court ruling agreed with them and Connie, along with all rabbits in higher education, was out. We'd never said goodbye, and had not kept in contact. I'd thought of looking her up on the work database, but never had.

'I didn't catch her name.'

'Seen her before?'

'I … don't think so.'

'It helps,' said Victor, 'to better manage broad policy in the village if we know whether events are a one-off or part of a pattern, especially with the judges of the Spick & Span awards due any week now. I don't want what happened in Ross[4] to happen here. You can't move for bunnies, the whole town smells of lettuce and you barely hear English spoken at all.'

'I went into the Poundland there the other day,' added Toby, 'and it was stuffed with rabbits all chattering in Rabbity. I swear they were not understanding me on purpose, just to make me feel unwelcome.'

I made no answer, as there was no answer to make. What happened in Ross wasn't to everyone's liking, but it was all legal. I should know: it was a hot topic at work.

'Could you run a few enquiries for us when you get into RabCoT?' continued Victor. 'I heard the rabbit said the book was for her husband Clifford, and there can't be that many off-colony rabbits around here named Clifford who hold library cards.'

'I'm not sure that's an appropriate use of resources,' I said, not wanting to be a lackey of the Malletts, 'and we only work in the accounts office. If the rabbit or her husband are legally off-colony, then it's not a RabCoT matter anyway.'

I glanced across at Victor. He was staring at me in an empty, unblinking fashion – something that was usually the early portent of a lost temper.

'OK then,' he said, 'we can always ask TwoLegsGood to make some enquiries.'

---

4. Ross-on-Wye, the third-largest town in Herefordshire.

Of the three Hominid Supremacist groups currently active in the UK, TwoLegsGood were the largest, best organised – and most violent. I understood Victor Mallett's gambit.

'TwoLegsGood are thugs, pure and simple,' I said. 'Escalating the situation helps no one.'

'They're not thugs, they're patriots of their species,' replied Victor in a sniffy tone, 'and while we applaud their enthusiasm and politics, I do admit they need to show a little restraint on occasion. A jugging makes them look like right-wing reactionaries and leporiphobics,[5] which they're *not* – merely realists with a legitimate concern over multispecism.'

I sighed.

'I'll do what I can,' I said.

Victor Mallett smiled broadly. He liked it when he got his own way, and could do a passable imitation of a pleasant person once he did. It took a half-hour to get into Hereford, and I dropped Victor at Bobblestock.

'Well, cheerio, old chap,' he said once he'd climbed out of the car. 'You and Pip must come round for dinner one day.'

He didn't really mean it, and I said that would be very nice, again not really meaning it.

'Sorry about Dad,' said Toby as we drove the remaining short distance into town, 'but he only wants the best for the village.'

'I'm sure Pol Pot only wanted the best for Cambodia,' I replied, 'but it didn't really work out that way. *Joke,*' I added, as I could see Toby about to raise the curtains on some theatre of umbrage, something the Malletts often did when even mildly challenged.

'So,' I said, wanting to change the subject, 'who do you think's replacing Daniels?'

Daniels had been our Intelligence Officer, and about the most pleasant we'd had. But the job was stressful, and 'pleasant' wasn't really a winning strategy when it came to working in RabCoT.

'No idea,' said Toby, 'someone easy to work with, I hope.'

I parked up outside the regional Rabbit Compliance Taskforce

---

5. Those with a fear/mistrust/dislike of rabbits, but I figure you guessed that.

headquarters, a blocky building built in the thirties with half-arsed art-deco pretensions, and renamed the Smethwick Centre by Prime Minister Nigel Smethwick himself, who was very conscious of crafting his own legacy while he still wielded enough power to do so.

Smethwick had begun his steep political climb as the Minister for Rabbit Affairs fifteen years before, when UKARP were only a coalition partner, and to celebrate his promotion greatly increased the number of things a rabbit could do wrong. He personally drafted the 'Regularity Framework for Subterranean Construction' and 'The Orange Root Vegetable Licensing Act'. The new laws naturally increased rabbit arrest and incarceration rates, which Smethwick duly blamed on 'increased cunicular criminality', which was then, predictably and unashamedly, used to justify a greatly increased budget and workforce.

'Oh dear,' I said as I noticed a small crowd of people across the entrance to the Taskforce headquarters, 'looks like TwoLegsGood are upset about something again.'

There were only four of them, and the gathering seemed more of a presence than an active demonstration. Despite the Hominid Supremacist group's record of leporiphobic attacks, they generally stayed one step ahead of the law, and by a curious quirk of inverted stereotyping were not a bunch of semi-skilled neckless tattooed hooligans with IQs barely into double figures, but were predominantly middle class: retail, middle management, C of E fundamentalists, unemployed furriers and hatters, several doctors and barristers as well as a few strident environmentalists who saw the rise of the rabbit as 'a potentially greater threat to biodiversity on the planet than humans'.[6]

'Good morning, gentlemen,' said one as we walked past. 'Please don't waver from the bold and righteous anthropocentric path.'

Another was holding a banner exhorting that MegaWarren be opened sooner, and a third made some comment suggesting that the rabbit maximum wage was too high as it 'placed an unseemly burden

6. They often cited Macquarie Island, which is worth a read on Wikipedia, if you've got a few minutes.

on industry'. We said nothing in reply as Taskforce guidelines forbade membership of, or association with, any Hominid Supremacist group. To be honest, the Taskforce and UKARP and 2LG all pretty much had the same views: the difference lay in legality, accountability and sanity.

'Ah!' said another voice from a smaller group who had been until now hidden from view on the other side of the street. 'Can we speak to you about our work at the Rabbit Support Agency?'

They were a group of only two, and positioned a hundred metres from the Smethwick Centre, legally speaking the closest they could get. The human was Patrick Finkle, who had been a founder member of RabSAg and was currently the Regional Chief. He had a pinched, haunted look about him, as though the last twenty-five years had been spent waiting for a dawn raid. I knew of him, and had seen him around a lot, but we'd never spoken. We weren't allowed to chat to this bunch either.

'Can we talk to you about the Rabbit Way?' asked the second, a rabbit well known to the Taskforce named Fenton DG-6721. He was tall, snowy white and with piercing red eyes as befitted his Labstock heritage. He habitually wore dungarees and had half a dozen bullet holes in his ears. His charity work spoke volumes, and he would have been seen as the 'acceptable face of rabbit/human integration' if it wasn't for his propensity for speaking out over rabbit issues with visiting dignitaries, something which had him labelled 'troublesome'.

'The Rabbit Way is bullshit,' said one of the 2LG group from across the road. 'You can take your gimcrack religion, vegan funda-mentalism and lame idealism and poke it up your pellet slot.'

'That's what I enjoy most about Hominid Supremacists,' returned Fenton in an easy manner, 'their eloquence.'

'We believe in hominid *superiority* not *supremacy*,' he replied, parroting a legal ruling that had the latter deemed illegal, yet the former an acceptably realistic view, given the dominance of the species on the planet. 'It's an important distinction.'

'It's the same turd in a different wrapper,' said Fenton, 'but at least we have a workable policy regarding our sense of being, place within the biosphere and relationships with others of the same species. How's the Declaration of Human Rights working out for you?'

It had always been a contentious issue that one of the most lauded documents of the past fifty years was regarded with almost laughable derision by rabbits, whose own Way was based on a bill of responsibilities, whereby each individual was morally obliged to look after the well-being of others, rather than a bill of rights, where, the rabbit had decided, the onus was incorrectly laid upon the individual to demand that their rights were respected.

The comment was returned by the 2LG group's spokesman with an argument regarding primate hierarchy and the role of planet husbandry as a form of lofty paternalism, since it 'had worked so dazzlingly well in Victorian-era factories'. We didn't hear Finkle or Fenton's reply as we were soon lost to earshot. The argument, the demonstration, our emotional distance from both – very much business as usual.

'Did you see Finkle's hands?' said Toby.

'Lopped,' I replied, referring to the practice of voluntarily removing one's own thumbs to show unequivocal non-opposable unity to the rabbit cause. 'I heard he keeps them in a jar of vinegar at home.'

It was a controversial move and had been met with overwhelming surprise and revulsion, but achieved what Finkle desired: the ongoing trust of the Grand Council and rabbits in general. To UKARP, Nigel Smethwick, the Ministry of Rabbit Affairs and the Taskforce, he was entirely the opposite: the reviled poster-boy for dangerous human/rabbit relations.

'I once gave a thumbs-up sign to a bunch of teenage rabbits,' said Toby, 'before I understood how offensive it was. They caught me after a seven-mile chase.'

'Should have tried to escape in your car.'

'I *was* in a car. They can hop pretty fast when they want to.'

'What did they do to you? Ironic taunts, sarcasm, species-shaming?'

'No, more of a round-table discussion where they suggested I confront the shortcomings of my species, then told me how rabbit governance was not so much based on laws as we understand them, but a mutually agreed set of understandings and customs where non-compliance would be a suboptimal approach to peaceful coexistence.'

'How did you feel about that?' I asked, wanting to see whether Toby's politics had changed.

'Same old holier-than-thou rabbit bullshit.'

His politics, I noted, had *not* changed.

We accessed the building through the main entrance on Gaol Street, showed our IDs to the guard who diligently checked them as she'd done every morning, fifteen years for me, two for Toby, then opened the inner glass security doors, and we made our way past the Compliance Officers working on the large, open-plan ground floor. There were estimated to be just under a million anthropomorphised rabbits in the country, and only a hundred thousand or so had the legal right to live outside the fence. The rest, by well-established statute, remained inside the colonies, their rights to travel strictly controlled by a series of permits.

'Have you heard if the Senior Group Leader is due in today?' asked Toby.

'I heard not,' I replied, 'but the word will get around if he is.'

'He frightens me,' said Toby.

'I heard he even frightens Nigel Smethwick, and that must take some doing.'

This was indeed true. Even the most strident and voluble leporiphobics in the building regarded the Senior Group Leader as 'somewhat inclined towards uncontrollable anger'. It didn't seem to dent his general support, though.

Here at the Western Region Rabbit Compliance Taskforce we had responsibility for the 150,000 residents living on the hill above Ross, about twenty-five miles away. Rabbit Colony One was a large and sprawling warren of tunnels constructed beneath allotments, laundry rooms, sandwich-making factories and the ubiquitous call centres and assembly plants[7] for electrical goods, the whole encircled by a rabbit-proof fence which the Taskforce declared was to 'protect the most

7. Nothing was ever manufactured with components smaller than a marble. Dexterity could be challenging without opposable thumbs.

vulnerable rabbits from dangerous Hominid Supremacists'. No one believed them, least of all the rabbit.

We walked through the connecting corridor to the newer part of the building, up to the third floor and into our office, which was spacious and scrupulously tidy, walls painted a calming green shade, pot plants scattered about and a large framed poster of a mountain reflected in a lake in New Zealand that was meant to be 'motivational', but to me looked like a mountain reflected in a lake. Despite the large windows the office wasn't particularly bright and airy. The windows didn't open and the glass was semi-silvered to render us invisible to eyes outside. It was said they were bulletproof, too, installed when the concept of violent rabbit direct action groups had still been just about believable.

Agent Whizelle had not yet arrived but Section Officer Flemming was sitting in her office, one of the two glass-fronted cubicles that looked into the shared space, but which afforded her and Agent Whizelle privacy if required. Susan Flemming was smiley and good-looking, which made her *appear* considerably more pleasant than she actually was. Her strident views on hominid superiority mixed with an incurious intellect and moral detachment made her almost ideal for a long and successful career in the Rabbit Compliance industry. On her office wall was not a picture of family, but a picture of herself, Prime Minister Nigel Smethwick and the Senior Group Leader, presumably at the time Flemming was made Section Officer. But despite her good looks, Flemming had an expressionless demeanour and her one eye – she never explained how she lost the other – didn't blink much or seem to have free movement in its socket; she rotated her head to look about, which reminded me of a poorly operated marionette.

'Good morning, Mr Knox,' she said.

'Ma'am.'

'You're on Operations today,' she said, without preamble. 'The new Intelligence Officer is bringing an ongoing case with him. Whizelle and he have been planning it all weekend and I don't want you to disappoint.'

I didn't like the sound of this.

'I have an exemption from doing Ops on account of my fallen arches.'

I swayed a little on my feet by way of confirmation.

'Bullshit,' said Flemming.

'No, I really do. Signed by the Company Doctor.'

'I wasn't saying "bullshit" to you having the note,' explained Flemming. 'It's the fallen arches that's bullshit. Look, Toby doesn't have the experience or the training, and no one else is available. RabCoT needs field-worthy Spotters, not ones who spend their days cooped up like chickens.'

'Yes, but—'

'—you need to step up to the plate, Knox. Some of us have the distinct feeling your enthusiasm for the job might be waning. If you don't get out and about, we might decide on a performance review.'

'I had one not two months ago.'

'I was thinking more of a *personal* review from the Senior Group Leader.'

She tapped her long fingernails on the desk and cocked her head on one side.

This was different. A 'performance review' by the Group Leader was less of a cosy chat about one's work, and more a sustained and very personal profanity-laden rant.

'You wouldn't.'

'I would. He said you should drop by and discuss things if you refuse to go on Ops.'

I felt my palms go damp and a knot seemed to form in my stomach. No one liked to upset the Senior Group Leader. Operatives more senior than me had resigned rather than face a dressing-down, and bold men and women were known to come out of his office in a state of traumatic shock at his verbal threats and intimidation. Few but the brave even made eye contact, and I knew for a fact that Toby had taken a day off work after a particularly aggressive encounter in the elevator.

'I'll go on Ops,' I said. I needed at least another ten years' employment before I could even *think* about retirement.

'Good,' said Flemming. 'You can meet our new Intelligence Officer in the briefing room at midday; he'll tell you what he wants you to do.'

I sat down at my desk and was about to start work when Adrian Whizelle walked in.

The best you could say about him was that on a good day he was hardly obnoxious at all, which made him seem like Julie Andrews in comparison to the Senior Group Leader or Nigel Smethwick. He'd been co-opted into Rabbit Identity Fraud from the intelligence-gathering arm of RabCoT and had a useful coping mechanism in the often stressful compliance industry: a deep and very powerful loathing for rabbits.

'Good morning,' said Whizelle.

We returned his salutation, Toby more enthusiastically as the two of them played squash or racketball or something. Whizelle was tall and dark, as thin as a yard-broom with long arms and legs that gangled like those of a clumsy teenager as he walked. His pointed features gave little away and his small black eyes seemed to constantly dart about the room. He also had a massive twin-tracked scar down his cheek that ended in a wonky jaw, the result of a rabbit bite following a snatch squad op that went south; the rabbit's teeth had been scaled up during the Anthropomorphising Event and now had a sharpness and muscular strength that could go through flesh as though it were wet paper.

Whizelle, we figured, had been lucky to get away with only a scar.

'Anyone fancy a cuppa?' asked Whizelle, who understood the importance of office etiquette.

'I'll have one,' said Toby.

'Pete?'

'Go on, then.'

He made a 'T' sign to Flemming through the glass, who responded with a thumbs-up. Whizelle was about to go out, stopped, then said to me: 'You on Ops with us today?'

'So it appears.'

'Good man.'

And he wandered off.

'Bad luck,' said Toby, 'but look on the bright side: you're good at rabbit-spotting so they won't let you be compromised.'

'Maybe so,' I said, but I didn't voice my real concern: being on Ops carried a risk. Not just of personal safety, but of seeing and witnessing stuff I didn't really want to see and witness. If I'd had a mission statement for my employment at RabCoT, it would be: 'Keep your head down, blend into the wallpaper and never, ever, go on Ops'.

Spotters & Spotting

Rabbits always had trouble differentiating between humans. Hair colour, skin colour, clothes, gait, jewellery and voice all helped, but a lot of it was guesswork. In tests, eighty-two per cent of rabbits couldn't tell the difference between Brian Blessed and a gorilla, if dressed in similar clothes.

Individual rabbit identification had always been an issue, right from the start. Fingerprints didn't work as their paw-pads were hard and leathery, and DNA matching was pretty much useless as the rabbit gene pool was deplorably shallow. Mature bucks who'd been in several pistol duels could be recognised by the unique pattern of bullet holes in their ears – like an IBM punch card, as the joke went. But for the most part, juveniles, unduelled bucks and females looked pretty much identical. Any rabbit – of Wild or Labstock – who was detained by the police or Compliance Taskforce required a 'no mingling' protocol as, once they got mixed up, it was impossible to say which was which.

But crucially, not *all* human eyes were blind to the complexities of rabbit physiognomy. Toby and myself and others – how many, it was never quite ascertained – possessed a gene anomaly that allowed us to differentiate between rabbits almost as well as rabbits themselves. As you've probably guessed by now, Toby and I weren't lowly account-ants within RabCoT, we were a fundamental part of the Taskforce machinery. We were officially titled 'Rabbit Identification Operatives' but internally at RabCoT we were simply known as Spotters. Oddly, the skill was often discovered late: I only realised I had the talent when I noticed that the rabbit playing opposite Patrick Stewart in *Waiting for Godot* was the same one I'd seen playing Buttons to Les Dennis's Widow Twanky in 1982. Then, recalling an online advertising campaign that offered 'Dazzling Career Opportunities' for anyone who could tell rabbits apart, I contacted the Rabbit Compliance Taskforce, passed their rabbit comparison test and, following a rigorous background check to ensure I had 'no unhealthily positive attitude towards rabbits', my career changed from Post Office Local Sorting Office Manager (Parcels) to RabCoT Spotter within a fortnight. To be honest, I didn't really want a job in Rabbit Compliance as I'd never been leporiphobic, but was swayed by the good pay and final-salary pension options. Most of all, the work had job security. I could spot rabbits for as long as rabbits needed spotting, which as far as anyone could tell was, well, *for ever*.

So for eight hours a day, five days a week, Toby and I compared pictures of rabbits who for one reason or another – work, driving licence, detention, marriage, death, insurance claim, movement, prosecution, intelligence gathering – required confirmation of identity. For the most part it was fairly routine as rabbits either knew we were watching so didn't trouble to swap identities or were inherently honest. But occasionally we came across a rabbit who claimed to be a rabbit they weren't. Spotter slang dubbed them a *Miffy*.

I logged in and started to work, the 'target' and 'source' pictures coming up in pairs on my screen. I allocated a percentage likelihood they were the same rabbit: one hundred per cent for a certain match, zero per cent for a certain non-match and everything in between. I was quite good at it. In testing I could spot a Miffy with ninety-two per cent accuracy, up from sixty-six per cent when I started. But it wasn't an exact science. Any rabbit that got less than seventy-five per cent was referred to other Spotters and the scores aggregated using an algorithm to decide identity compliance.[8]

'There you go,' said Whizelle, who had returned with the teas. 'Keep a close eye on the screens, lads, there's been a lot of background chatter on Niffer, and while we've no idea what's being said, the increased traffic might suggest something is going on, so remain vigilant.'

We acknowledged the intel – and the teas – then resumed our

---

8. The algorithm was occasionally tweaked depending on whether arrest and conviction targets were being met.

work, which while seemingly easy, wasn't *totally* straightforward. Of the eighteen rabbits elevated to humanness at the Event, there were three distinct sub-groups: Wildstock, Labstock and Petstock. Petstock were the simplest to identify with their varied markings, easy enough for even a layperson. The brown-furred generic Wildstock variety were much harder – and Labstock harder still as they were always white with red eyes. Comparing the capillaries in the Labstocks' ears was a pet project of mine and had won me the Taskforce Adequate Conduct Award seven years previously along with a rare word of encouragement from the Senior Group Leader. Despite the benefits, Ear Capillary Identification had one major drawback: the subject usually needed a bright light behind them, which they almost never had.

'Shit,' said Toby, echoing my thoughts, 'these Labstocks are a bitch to tell apart.'

We continued working and for the next hour there was nothing but positive IDs, then a few around the fifty per cent mark. At a little after 11.30, I had my first Miffy of the day.

'Bingo,' I said as I stared at two pictures that were almost certainly not the same rabbit, 'there's a Petstock claiming to be one Randolph deBlackberry up in Berwick.'

There had been three Petstock rabbits anthropomorphised at the Event, house pets named Hercules, Blackberry and Buttercup. Only the last two still had clear and uninterrupted bloodlines. The 'Von Hercule' family died out during the Great Petstock Dynastic Exchange of Discourtesies[9] of 1980–88, and although several hundred carried the family's notable black fur either wholly or in part, none carried the name. The deBlackberrys won the struggle for aristocratic dominance but it didn't make them any more popular. Most Petstocks were greeted with suspicion by the Wild and Labstock members of the rabbit community – too cosy with humans in the past, it was said.

---

9. The closest thing to a war amongst rabbits. The high point of the hostilities was Anton Von Hercule's fourteen-hour 'less than polite' rant in July 1987, which was met by a barrage of sarcasm that is still talked about today, usually in hushed tones.

The all-white McButtercups, for their part, generally kept themselves to themselves, the way they liked it.

I gave the Miffy a four per cent, and Flemming asked Toby whether he concurred, which he did, so Flemming signed the warrant and Whizelle picked up the phone to coordinate the arrest of the rabbit on charges of identity fraud. Whizelle had done this before many times on my eye testimony, so the consequences of the unseen arrest and its aftermath were no longer something I worried too much about. The first month maybe, but not any more. Rabbits can be criminals too.

The excitement over, Flemming returned to her office and Whizelle busied himself with the paperwork, of which there was a lot. I took a break and then, out of a sense of curiosity regarding Connie rather than because of Victor Mallett's pleas, looked up 'Clifford Rabbit' on the RabCoT database. There were two thousand of them, so I narrowed it down to those off-colony and living in Herefordshire. This threw up three hits: one who was single, another who was currently doing time for 'insider trading on collateralised carrot obligations'[10] and one who lived in a temporary address for legal off-colony rabbits in Leominster. I discovered this last rabbit had been married almost exactly a year, and there she was: Constance Grace Iolanthe[11] Rabbit, and I double-checked to make sure it was her by accessing her mugshot from the Rabbit Employment Database.

Reading further I learned that she was two years older than me and second generation from the Event. She was a respectable eight short of the rabbit's ten-child policy, and was twice widowed, which was not unusual. The buck rabbit's propensity for duelling prior to the breeding season could often have fatal results.

'What you got there?' asked Whizelle, looking over from his desk. I explained that a rabbit had turned up in our village and I wanted to know who she was.

'Local village?' he asked.

---

10.   Your guess is as good as mine on this one.
11.   Rabbits were quite big into Gilbert and Sullivan operas, despite not having good singing voices. Few, if any, would even *attempt The Mikado.*

'Much Hemlock.'

He grunted.

'Multispecism never worked. Different agendas, you see. It's not leporiphobic to say they dislike integration – it's a fact. Does she have any previous you can use to move her on?'

'She's not resident in the village,' I said, then to add plausibility to the data search added: 'I was just making sure that she wasn't, um – y'know, on a recce.'

'Very wise,' said Whizelle, nodding in agreement, 'one can never be too careful as far as rabbits are concerned.' He looked at his watch. 'Time for the briefing, Knox. Toby, you've got two hours' overtime tonight to make up for Peter's absence.'

'No problem,' said Toby happily, as the Guild of Spotters had negotiated double-time overtime, with generous no-supper-break penalties.

'Flemming said you weren't keen on going on Operations,' said Whizelle as we walked down the stairs towards the briefing room, 'and even got a bogus note from medical. Any particular reason?'

Whizelle, like Flemming, spoke his mind.

'I was on Ops the night Dylan Rabbit was misidentified,' I said, attempting to gain some sort of sympathy, 'two years ago. The Senior Group Leader's last operation before promotion.'

'The whole Dylan Rabbit episode *was* unfortunate,' said Whizelle thoughtfully, I think meaning from a PR point of view and not from Dylan's point of view, as he wound up jugged, 'but to keep a high level of efficiency in Compliance there has to be a small amount of collateral damage. It's inevitable. Besides, Dylan Rabbit was probably guilty of *something* – or would be, given time.'

'The papers had a field day,' I said.

'No,' said Whizelle, 'the *Smugleftie* and *Headlights*[12] had a field day. The others barely covered it. Besides, you weren't lead Spotter. None of it came back to you.'

12. The most popular (and politically active) daily newspaper for rabbits. There is no online edition, and copies are banned off-colony owing to the ink 'falling short of industry standards'.

This was true. I'd been there on the sidelines only to verify the ID. The fallout over Dylan Rabbit was at least big enough to have Smethwick answer questions in Parliament and required RabCoT to 'seriously overhaul and thoroughly review their identification criteria'. This reached us as a single memo urging us to 'show a bit more caution for a few months' over identification. The thing was, I *knew* we'd got the wrong rabbit during the hard traffic stop and said so, but I'd been overruled. Not just by the Senior Spotter on duty who had retired once the mistake was made public, but by the Senior Group Leader, who threatened to 'punch my f★★★ing lights out' if I didn't concur with the identification. And I did.

'Identification is always a thorny problem,' said Whizelle, opening the door to the briefing room, 'and while the Rabbit Support Agency, Grand Council of Coneys and the rest of the woolly-liberal protest groups refuse to countenance RFI chipping or discreetly tattooed barcodes on the ears, we have to rely on Spotters who are only human and can and do make mistakes. Besides,' he added, 'if the perfidious bun didn't pull a Miffy every now and again, none of this would happen. They've only themselves to blame.'

Flemming was already there when he walked in the room. She was chatting amiably to five Compliance Officers. I knew them all by sight, but only three by name. Spotters regarded Compliance Officers as gung-ho thugs with only a badge and a union-appointed lawyer to separate them from TwoLegsGood, and COs regarded Spotters as overpaid milksops who had lucked out.

They all introduced themselves to me at Whizelle's behest, and they remained cordial, as did I, although I could see they were all deeply suspicious of my inclusion on the team. It wasn't just the Fallen Arches exemption that had kept me off Ops. If you're going to be part of a politically motivated team, you need a common goal, a common agreement, an *understanding*.

Our new Intelligence Officer was already there, but wasn't like any other Intel Officer we'd had, either permanent or loaned.

This one was a rabbit.

33

Fudds and Flopsies

'Fudd' – as in 'Elmer Fudd' – was the usual pejorative rabbit term for a human. There were also: Pinko, Fleshy, Homo, Bingo and Rupert. There were others in Rabbity, too, usually reproductive slurs regarding evolutionarily disadvantageous rates of ovulation and shockingly low litter sizes.

The new rabbit Intelligence Officer had a startled look which made it appear that he'd been caught in car headlamps some time in the seventies and was still suffering the trauma. He would have been Labstock owing to his white fur which looked matted and ill-kempt, and he was dressed in an embroidered waistcoat covered by a long duster jacket that had been patched several times with brown corduroy. Rabbits abhorred waste and would often use an item of clothing until it fell off them.

More shockingly, when he removed his battered brown derby hat, there were only two healed-over stumps where his long ears would have sprouted from his head. He'd been, in rabbit terminology, 'cropped'. His fellow rabbits had meted out the worst possible punishment for his unknown and presumably heinous crime and banished him from the rabbithood. Most rabbits took the honourable way out and dug themselves a lonely burrow in which to expire – but a few, consumed by humiliation and loss, wandered the country as outcasts, attempting to find absolution in any way they could. Some, like this one, flipped to the other side, knowing they could not be hated any more than they were already, but still knowing they would have to wear the burden of their sins for all to see, every day, *for ever*.

'A rabbit without ears,' a rabbit would say, 'is less of a rabbit than nothing.'

One of the officers might have stared for longer than was polite, for the earless rabbit said in a low and unusually threatening growl: 'What are you staring at, Fudd?'

'Nothing,' said the officer.

'This is Agent Douglas AY-002,' said Flemming, introducing the cropped rabbit warmly and to low gasps of recognition from the room, 'vouched for by the Senior Group Leader, no less, and transferred from the Swindon office. Treat him as you would a human,' she added, enthused by having a rabbit onside against the rabbit, 'his record is exemplary, his dislike of rabbits well known.'

I too had heard of this rabbit before, though I had not met him. All rabbits who had turned against their own were cropped, but that wasn't in itself enough. To be fully trusted, rabbits in the employ of the Taskforce would be expected to demonstrate their anti-rabbit credentials, and in this respect AY-002's reputation preceded him. It was said his usual method for extracting intelligence from any recalcitrant brethren was via a hammer – varying sizes, from toffee all the way up to claw, to match levels of coercion.

'Agent Whizelle,' said Whizelle, introducing himself, 'Intel, Identity Fraud. We met at the interrogation training weekend last year. I enjoyed your talk immensely – the one where you expounded on your "tie the suspect into a hessian sack and beat them with sticks" technique for extracting information.'

'Morris dancer's sticks,' corrected Douglas. 'It's an important point, and I thank you. I thought your talk with the Senior Group Leader about the MegaWarren project saving upwards of a hundred million a year by bringing all five colonies together was particularly enlightening, and not before time.'

'Kind,' said Whizelle, 'very kind.'

'This is Peter Knox,' said Flemming, beckoning me over, 'our Spotter today.'

Douglas AY-002 gazed at me suspiciously.

'I've seen your file,' he said after a pause. 'They say you're talented, but hobbled by an unwarranted sense of fair play.'

'I think it's important to play the safe game,' I managed to mumble, 'to stop RabCoT making a fool of itself.'

He stared at me for a moment.

'Is that all it is?'

'That's all it is.'

He paused again, then clasped my one hand in his two paws, the traditional human/rabbit greeting, as handshakes were tricky to accomplish without thumbs.

'I won't let you down, Mr AY-002.'

'I hope not,' said the earless rabbit, 'and you can call me Lugless; every other Fudd does.'

'I'd be happy to call you anything you want,' I said, trying to be accommodating.

'And I'd be happy if you didn't speak to me at all,' said Lugless, 'but I have a feeling I'm going to be disappointed. The Senior Group Leader told me to report directly to him if you get pointlessly sentimental over our little furry friends.'

'Lugless is a straight talker,' said Flemming in the awkward silence that followed. 'Agent AY-002, let me introduce you to the rest of team.'

'You come highly recommended,' said Sergeant Boscombe as they shook hand/paws. 'Your kind loathe you.'

'They *aren't* my kind,' said Lugless in a matter-of-fact tone. 'They took everything from me and I owe them nothing.'

'Good to hear,' said Boscombe, and introduced the others. Lugless greeted them all in a distant yet businesslike manner, but didn't direct any terse words towards any of the others. I had the sudden worrying realisation that I was on Operations today to be tested. If my loyalty to the department remained in question, I was probably finished, in spite of my skill at spotting.

'Take a seat, everyone,' said Lugless, switching on the overhead projector and pulling a bundle of acetate sheets from his case. Rabbits – all rabbits, not just ones who worked in Compliance – despised PowerPoint presentations, and not because it meant fiddling around with paw-unfriendly keyboards or pointers. No, it was rather the rabbit's wholly practical approach to technology. If something worked perfectly adequately and did not actually *need* to be replaced, they'd stick with it. Most of the colonies still used fax machines, printing presses and manual telephone switchboards, although this was probably not just a technological issue, but the fact that rabbits like to gossip, and manual switchboards made eavesdropping not only easy, but irresistible.

'An unidentified Labstock rabbit,' said Lugless placing the first acetate on the projector, 'similar to thousands like him. For the purposes of this operation, he'll be known as John Flopsy[13] 7770.'

We stared at the nondescript white rabbit that had come up on the screen.

'What's he done?' asked one of the compliance officers.

'It's not what he's done,' said Lugless, 'or about what he will do. It's about what he knows. Deep intel says the Bunty might be hanging out in Colony One, not twenty-five miles from where we're standing right now.'

The 'Bunty' to whom he referred would be the Venerable Bunty,[14] the rabbit's spiritual leader for the past decade and a rabbit of considerable influence. Her whereabouts were a closely guarded secret as Smethwick had once said in public that 'if we had Bunty in our hands, the rabbits would do anything we asked of them'. She remained a rabbit of great interest to the authorities, but had always evaded capture. Quite how she had done this was a mystery, as she routinely moved from colony to colony in order to offer spiritual and culinary guidance, as Lago, the Grand Matriarch, was as big on home cooking as she was on metaphysical well-being. It didn't help that no one knew what she looked like, and she usually gave sermons in disguise so few rabbits knew either – insurance against any rabbits who could be turned by the Compliance Taskforce.

'She has a pernicious influence on the rabbit,' said Flemming, 'and the Senior Group Leader wants her in custody to more fully ascertain her motives.'

13. 'John Flopsy' was the generic term to describe an unidentified rabbit, similar to 'John Doe' for humans. The female equivalent, logically enough, was 'Jane Flopsy'. The long-term usage of the word made 'Flopsy' slang for a rabbit of a criminal tendency, or often, any rabbit at all.

14. Her spiritual name was actually 'B'uuntii' but she was known by everyone, rabbits included, as 'Bunty'. The closest translation of her name would be 'I can see clearly now', which is also the first line of the rabbit's anthem and a Johnny Nash single, although it is not thought the two are related.

By this he probably meant that it was actually Smethwick who wanted her for questioning, but the PM liked to stay one step removed from anything too controversial.

'Are we thinking of snatching the Bunty from inside the colony?' asked Boscombe, seemingly quite excited about the idea as it probably involved several helicopters, lots of hardware and a totally knock-out cool code name.

'Eventually,' said Whizelle, 'but in truth it's only *rumoured* she's in Colony One, figuring out ways to "Complete the Circle".'

'What does that mean?' asked Boscombe.

'We *think*,' said Flemming in the manner of someone more comfortable with conjecture than truth, 'that it may relate to the rabbit's plan to weaponise their reproductive capabilities in order to overrun the UK.'

'Quite,' said Whizelle. 'The geographically restricting environment of MegaWarren is needed now more than ever to curb the ugly spectre of a sustained campaign of LitterBombing.'

Everyone in the room nodded sagely at this; it was an ongoing concern, but with little evidence to support it. The Council of Coneys branded the LitterBomb notion 'patently ridiculous', along with other leporiphobic conspiracy theories, such as a desire for 'Universal Veganism', a change to running the country 'the Rabbit Way' and a wholesale switch to the worship of Lago, the rabbit goddess.

'The point is,' continued Flemming, 'that there are at least fifty miles of warren inside the colony, and we need to narrow down the search. The Rabbit Underground Movement are doubtless in constant communication with the Bunty, and that's why we're eager to capture and interview this individual. Get to him and we get to her. Get her and we've got the rabbit where we want them.'

After we'd all stared pointlessly at the Flopsy for a few minutes Lugless replaced the picture on the projector with another, this time of the high street in Ross.

'Intel tells us Flopsy 7770 visits the post office in Ross-on-Wye every Tuesday to post letters to the other colonies. He uses the exterior pillar box and ensures he is there at the time of the four p.m. postal collection so he can add them to the mailbag directly. It's not exactly a freshly pulled carrot,[15] but I think Flopsy 7770 is acting suspiciously enough to warrant further investigation.'

'Labstocks are almost impossible to break,' murmured Boscombe.

This was true. When your kind were vivisected before the Spontaneous Anthropomorphising Event, it kind of made the 'continuous application of harsh coercive force' indistinguishable from 'last Tuesday'. Anyone in the Rabbit Underground who held sensitive material and had to go off-colony was usually Labstock for this precise reason.

'I haven't met a rabbit I couldn't turn,' said Lugless in an ominous manner. Gathering intel in the old days had been easy because rabbits were so trusting, but they had wised up over the years and now adopted a 'blank expression while blinking' approach to law enforcement questions which was devastatingly effective. But rabbits knew how to get to other rabbits, especially if they could feign dominance and had no ears, which was about as creepy and shocking to them as seeing someone with half a face might be to us.

'OK then,' said Lugless, laying another sheet of acetate on the overhead projector with his very precise plan on it, 'this is how we're going to do it.'

It was pretty much a standard sharp arrest. Always unexpected, always fast. An escaping rabbit might take three to five seconds to get up to a fast enough run to initiate the first bounce – and after that only an officer with a powerful net-gun could bring one down, and that was a weapon that had limited range and required the team to know in which direction the rabbit might go – an almost impossible task. 'Trounce before Bounce' was the guiding policy.

As Lugless outlined the plan everyone took notes. All the officers were to be in civilian clothes and ready to pounce on Flopsy 7770 the moment he posted the letters. There were questions and answers until most of the officers were satisfied. Whizelle wouldn't be coming as he was easily recognised, but Lugless would be present, coordinating the grab – but in disguise, he said, which I was intrigued about. Rabbits had a hard time looking like anything but rabbits.

15. Rabbit slang for a 'smoking gun', 'dead cert' or 'done deal'.

'What's my function in all this?' I asked.

'You're our plan B,' said Lugless. 'You're to get a good look at the Flopsy *before* the arrest, just in case he slips through our fingers. You can ID him later.'

'I can't guarantee that,' I said. 'He's a Labstock.'

Lugless stared at me in a dangerous sort of way.

'... but I'll do my best,' I added.

'I really hope so,' said Lugless, 'for your sake.'

The briefing broke up ten minutes later.

Ross & Rabbits

Rabbity was the English word for the rabbit language; the rabbit word was 'Niff', one of the few pronounceable words in the rabbit language. Dismayingly, Niff could also mean, depending on context: 'rabbit, life, wholeness, carrot (straight), warmth, sky, ratchet screwdriver, aeroplane, wagon, carrot (curved), Wensleydale cheese, hopscotch and sleeve-valve engines.'

Ross-on-Wye had a pre-rabbit population of eight thousand, all human. Today that had risen to twenty thousand, chiefly rabbits. Most were long-term residents, part of an early experiment in rabbit/human integration undertaken in the seventies by RabToil, which had initially been set up as an NGO to find employment for rabbits, but had grown and darkened over the years to control *all* rabbit employment and was now integrated into the Ministry for Rabbit Affairs.

The Ross integration experiment, while hugely successful at the time and still regarded as the gold standard for peaceful inter-species coexistence, was never rolled out further owing to a concerted smear campaign by UKARP, who despised the concept of integration and instigated numerous complaints about the rabbit's 'bacchanalian nature of rampant promiscuity that would surely corrupt the nation's youth'. Despite no evidence that the nation's youth needed any outside forces to help corrupt itself in the least, UKARP succeeded in casting doubt over further integration and were as surprised as anyone when their plan succeeded, and integration plans were abandoned. They used it as a springboard to further pursue their anti-rabbit agenda. No one could have foreseen that they'd actually lead the nation four decades later.

'Before Ross we had only failure,' said a spokesman for UKARP, 'afterwards, only success.'

Despite the leporiphobic rhetoric, the once sleepy market town of Ross was now a bustling centre of commerce which encompassed trade, crafts and literary and artistic pursuits, as well as two centres for higher learning that revolved around philosophy, high cuisine and sustainability. While a few residents initially complained about the rabbits, all were won over by the vibrant nightlife, friendly upbeat manner of the newcomers and, of course, the trading opportunities. Although rabbits were not paid well, they liked to spend what they earned quickly. The gourmet lettuce bars did particularly well, as did the numerous greengrocers, a thriving bookstore and several hookah dens where rabbits discussed politics, economics and carrot hybrid-isation issues while their hookahs bubbled and puffed with the aromatic scent of a variety of rabbit tobacco: dock leaf, catnip, burdock, celeriac and dandelion. Mornings in the hookah dens were reserved for performance readings: the one we passed had a reading of *The Hunchback of Notre Dame* going on all week.

More relevant to the Rabbit Compliance Taskforce, Ross was by local statute an 'Open Town' commercially, residentially and – crucially – for those on a day permit from Rabbit Colony One, eight miles to the east. Thanks to a well-intentioned by-law passed forty years before, busloads of rabbits could move between the two locations without identification checks, something of a headache for RabCoT as it made potential free movement of those in the banned Rabbit Underground that much easier. None of the other colonies enjoyed such freedoms, so it had long been assumed that Colony One was where the movement was based.

It was now half past three, and Lugless AY-002 and I were sitting in his Cadillac Eldorado on the opposite side of the road from the post office.

'Where are you now, Fudd One?' asked Lugless, who was wearing an eyepatch and a large tartan tam-o'-shanter stuffed with newspapers to disguise his earless state. The officer in question reported that he was across the street from the post office, standing in the doorway of a shop that repaired light bulbs. All the Compliance Officers were deployed in various places in the locale, either drinking acorn coffee at a sidewalk café, having an animated conversation on a mobile or simply waiting out of sight, ready to amble past and pounce when Flopsy 7770 made his move.

'Copy that,' said Lugless into his mic, acknowledging a message from Sergeant Boscombe that a Labstock carrying a briefcase was approaching from the north. Lugless checked his watch, then asked the officer tailing the post office van for an ETA. We received the reply that the van was still twenty minutes away. Having acknowledged both reports, Lugless then dug a carrot out of a brown-paper bag and crunched it up noisily.

'So,' I said, trying to ignore the carrot-munching, 'you're an AY-002?'

'Yup,' said Lugless, neither wanting nor expecting to expand upon the subject.

Since he carried the alphanumeric surname he would be descended from the three laboratory rabbits anthropomorphised at the Event. The DG-6721s were the most numerous with the MNU-683s not far behind. They all suffered ongoing health issues owing to experimentation pre-Event, aside from the AY-002s, whose ancestor, to their constant shame, had been a 'control rabbit' in the lab and subjected to no tests at all, something that gave them huge residual guilt that often manifested itself in antisocial behaviour. That, in itself, wasn't enough to justify cropping. Lugless must have done something seriously unpleasant. Either improper sexual conduct or doing what he was doing now. Rabbits despised a collaborator as much as they despised those who extracted favours by coercion.

We sat for another five minutes in silence.

'Am I here on some sort of test?' I asked.

'I don't know,' said Lugless without looking up from the crossword he was attempting. 'Are you?'

'I was on the Dylan Rabbit arrest detail,' I said. 'The Senior Group Leader wanted me to concur on an ID and I wasn't sure but was overruled. But I *was* right after all, and the shit hit the—'

'Is there a point to this story?' asked Lugless. 'Because you're getting kind of whiny and self-pitying in that uniquely human way.'

'I guess not,' I said, 'but an innocent rabbit was jugged because I didn't stand my ground, and I thought that was a good—'

'Look,' said Lugless, 'there are no innocent rabbits. There are simply those who have drifted into criminality, and those that will. You heard Whizelle and Flemming: there is an extremely good chance that the rabbit community might be planning to kick off a LitterBombing campaign that will outnumber Fudds in this green and pleasant land by at least three to one in under five years. Do you want to be outnumbered in your own country?'

'Well, no, obviously.'

'Right, then,' said Lugless, 'so why don't you shut your trap, do the spotting that a quirk of fate has bestowed upon you, and leave broad strategy to Nigel Smethwick and the Senior Group Leader?'

I fell silent. The notion of Reproductive Weaponisation had been the pet conspiracy theory of UKARP for over three decades, but given the rabbit had been here fifty-five years and barely numbered a million, 'commendable restraint' would be a more realistic appraisal of their reproductive habits.[16]

My earpiece crackled into life.

'Flopsy 7770 with you in one minute,' came the voice of Boscombe, followed by a report that the post van was heading into the town centre to do the teatime pick-up. Lugless shuffled in his seat and peered intently up the road, as did I, and within a short time a Labstock rabbit turned the corner and walked towards the postbox with the curious gait that anthropomorphic rabbits possessed – upright and on two legs but with an uncertain and almost comical waddle. He was holding a leather briefcase that was chained to his wrist and dressed in a practical tweed shooting jacket over a checked shirt and tie. Perched between his ears at a jaunty angle was a matching flat cap.

'Recognise him?' asked Lugless.

'No.'

'Me neither. Get out there for a closer look.'

Although Labstocks were the hardest to ID, up close it often

---

16. Given that rabbits can reproduce at age three with a potential litter of eight as many as six times a year, even a modest wastage figure of fifteen per cent would suggest their numbers could surpass those of humans in the UK in as little as four years.

became easier – the wrinkles on the nose, a distinctive mark on the iris, whisker placement. If I manoeuvred down-sun of him I could view the capillaries in his ears for later reference, but I'd have to be lucky with my timing – the sun had been in and out all day.

I swung a leather satchel around my shoulder and placed a flat cap on my head. Since rabbits were as poor at identifying humans as the average human was at identifying *them*, they took cues from clothing and manner, so RabCoT agents either affected an odd walk, or, more usually, disguised themselves as regional or cultural stereo-types. I had opted to pose as a Yorkshireman. For the next half-hour I'd be Eric Althwaite, a mill worker from Harrogate.

I climbed out of the car, popped the live whippet under my arm to augment my disguise and, clasping several postcards, walked across the road in a confident manner, telling random passers-by I was from Yorkshire.[17] Flopsy 7770 was already waiting at the postbox, and I wended my way through the pedestrians – nearly all rabbits – who were either lolloping, walking or half-hopping along the street. I was feeling nervous as perhaps never before, but knew I couldn't make it show. The future of my career and earning potential was weighing heavily upon me. I needed to get this right.

My timing was quite good because I could see the bright red post van driving down the road towards us. If Flopsy 7770 was nervous, he didn't show it. He didn't check his watch, didn't turn to observe the van approach, didn't seem to do anything at all, in fact – just stood there in a relaxed manner, his nose twitching, his expression blank. Annoyingly, there weren't enough distinguishing marks for me to recognise him if I saw him again, so I moved closer and bought some stamps from the vending machine, then nonchalantly stuck them on my postcards. At that moment the sun came out, and I turned to look at the Flopsy, thinking my luck had changed, but it hadn't – the post van had placed itself in between the sun and the Labstock. Unless he moved forward, I would not be able to see the fine network of veins in his ears. I could sense the other agents near by, too – dressed variously as a Village Person,

17. People from Yorkshire do this.

a Pearly King and a Scotsman – and ready to grab him the moment the postman unlocked the pillar box and the Flopsy made to deposit his satchel of post. But as I watched, something unusual happened. Three *more* Labstocks appeared from nowhere, all similar heights and build and dressed identically with briefcases also chained to their wrists. Lugless's plan had been compromised: the Underground had been taking precautions. They probably knew that a snatch squad typically had three agents – even if they *could* arrest three they'd not manage four – and all were Labstock to confound any potential Spotters.

I heard Lugless swear in my earpiece, and then the order:

'Take them. Take them all.'

The agents made to arrest the Labstocks, which could have a very different outcome if the rabbits decided to bring violence into the mix – a kick from the hind legs would be powerful enough to break bones and rupture internal organs, as well as catapult the victim at speed through a shop window, while a well-aimed bite would be fatal in as long a time as it takes to bleed out.

None of this happened because rabbits had a generally more robust relationship with consequences than humans, and the agents' commands to halt were met with a series of giggles from the Labstocks, who mingled briefly to confuse us before running off in separate directions as though it were some sort of jolly game.

'Don't just stand there like a twat, Knox,' came Lugless's voice in my earpiece, 'get after the fourth.'

I had until that time been stunned into inactivity by the sudden turn of events. I was, after all, a Spotter – not a Field Agent. This wasn't what I did. Even so, I looked around and saw the fourth Labstock walking in a relaxed manner towards the ancient Market House at the top of the main street.

'Look,' I said into my microphone while pretending to rub my mouth, 'I'm not trained for this. I'm not sure I even have the power of arrest.'

'I don't want you to arrest him, idiot,' came Lugless's voice, 'I want you to get a good look at him.'

This seemed reasonable so I walked up the road in the direction the Labstock had gone, lost sight of him as he walked to the right of the Market House, then caught another glimpse of him walking up the steps to the churchyard once I'd reached Rossiter's bookshop.[18] When I got to the churchyard I just caught sight of him as he vanished in through the door. I walked in an unhurried pace towards the church, acutely aware that the only people near me were rabbits. And although they weren't looking in my direction, the rabbit's peripheral vision was so good, it's safe to assume that if you can see a rabbit, they can see you.

I stopped to tie the whippet to the foot-scraper and took the opportunity to whisper into the microphone.

'Flopsy suspect in the church, but this could be a trap. The whole set-up might simply have been to bag a Spotter.'

This could indeed be true. Spotters were forbidden to go on-colony for that very reason, though my identity and job at the Taskforce were well guarded: hence the accountant cover story.

'Of secondary consideration,' came Lugless's voice. 'I want every single one of those fat furry bastards in the clink before teatime.'

I took a deep breath to calm my nerves, then pushed open the door and stepped inside the church. It was a good size, imposing but not overgrand, and boasted a double nave and tall stained-glass windows. A vicar was humming to himself while tidying the leaflets, postcards and guidebooks that were arranged on a small table.

I looked around to see whether I could spot my quarry. There were two rabbits inside, one Wildstock, one Labstock – and both were dressed in the sort of pale blue tabard that befits a church volunteer. I thought it was a different Labstock, but then I noticed an identical shooting jacket to the one 7770 had worn hung on a peg in the vestry, and it was still swinging from being hurriedly placed. I was just going to wander over to the Labstock on the pretext of studying several old tombs when the vicar caught my eye.

'Good afternoon,' he said.

---

18. It's very good, and now operates a book lease-back agreement with rabbits, to whom owning something that you might use once every six or seven years seemed a little pointless.

'Good afternoon,' I replied genially. 'I see you have our furry friends[19] as volunteers.'

Although the rabbit religion had no issue with where and when you worshipped, nor who, it was still unusual to see them in a church, probably because churches were as far from a cosy moss-and-fur-lined warren as you were likely to get.

'Yes indeed,' said the vicar. 'Saint Mary's is a church that accepts everyone through its doors, irrespective of taxonomic classification.'

I wasn't going to get any closer to the Labstock without conversing at least a little to allay suspicion, and the Labstock did not seem to be in a hurry to leave.

'Back home in Harrogate where I come from as I am a Yorkshireman, we have no rabbits,' I said. 'What is the Church's view?'

The vicar nodded his head thoughtfully.

'The Church's opinion is divided. Although we here on the ground consider rabbits as just one of many of God's blessed creatures, the official line is that they are a lower animal, and when they arrived they were viewed as an abomination – the sinful product of a satanic union. When that was disproved from the DNA evidence, our stance softened. I think the problem is that while human*like*, they are not actually human*ful*, and according to scripture and teaching, mankind was made in His image, as they were in their Grand Matriarch Lago's. Church policy is that we don't allow them to participate in church matters but we will not exclude them from our house – so long as there is no crunching of lettuces from the pews and pellets are kept to an absolute minimum.'

He paused for thought, then recited his next comment as though learned from a crib sheet.

'We must love *all* God's creatures, but allow change and acceptance to happen slowly and at a pace commensurate with acceptable norms and customs.'

'I see,' I said, and after making some excuse about wanting to view some particularly fine statuary, moved towards where the Labstock

19. A term used between pro-rabbit humans to describe rabbits. Although a positive term, it could also mean the opposite. Context is everything.

was still dusting. If he knew I was from the Taskforce he made no sign of it, and even nodded a greeting. But of distinguishing marks on his coat or whiskers or eyes – there was nothing.

'With you in five, Knox,' came Lugless's voice in my ear. 'Confirm to me suspect still in church.'

I tapped the microphone twice on my wrist, and stared with feigned interest at the impressive array of tombs, glad that the other agents would take the burden of action from me. I had done a fair job, and should not be poorly thought of. My career might very well still be secure.

I heard the doors to the church open on both sides, and turned, expecting to see the agents arrive. But it wasn't them, it was more rabbits – *and all of them Labstock*. Nine all told, and they hastily grabbed volunteer tabards that the vicar was handing out. Within a few minutes they would all be hopelessly mingled. I looked across at the target Labstock, who was staring back at me with a smile on his placid features. He was *definitely* the one we were after, and once the other Labstocks had moved in and around him, I would have no way of pointing him out, or even finding out who he was.

But I was wrong, for at that moment the sun came out, and shone through the church window, transfixing Flopsy 7770 in a shaft of white light that perfectly illuminated his ears. There, on his left, about two-thirds of the way up, was a unique pattern of capillaries that looked like a squashed Tudor rose.

I didn't have time to make comment as the influx of bustling Labstock church volunteers gathered in a clump around us, moving and whirling and mixing so that within a short space of time I had no idea who was who. I was impressed. 7770 had been smarter, and quicker, and one step ahead of Lugless. There was definitely a Rabbit Underground, and the Labstock – whoever he was – had been part of it. And if I saw him again I'd know exactly who he was.

So long as he had a bright light behind him.

Griswold & Gossip

_____

Because of their dislike of obsolescence, rabbits only chose domestic appliances that would last a minimum of half a century. Dualit toasters were favoured, as were Hoovermatic washing machines, vintage Kenwood Chef food mixers, seventies push-button phones, treadle sewing machines and large-format cameras. They loved wet-chemistry photography; the older the process the better.

'How was work?' asked Pippa when I got home after the debriefing. Even to my own daughter I had always maintained I was a low-level payroll accountant. I told someone I was a Spotter once, and there had been consequences. I didn't want that again.

So I couldn't tell her that of the three Labstock we'd arrested, all had cover stories and plausible IDs and no amount of coaxing would change their story. I couldn't tell her that their briefcases had contained sandwiches, nine yoyos, sachets of raspberry-flavoured Angel Delight and copies of _Rabbit Vogue_; couldn't tell her that Lugless had applied to the Senior Group Leader to use 'firmer methods' to get them to talk, but had been overruled on the grounds of operational secrecy. I couldn't tell her that my sighting was now the _only_ possible method of identification of Flopsy 7770, couldn't tell her that tomorrow I would be staring at the bunshot of every Labstock we possessed until I found the one they were looking for, couldn't tell her the reason I'd been delayed was because the person who had come to pick up the whippet had been late. I had to sit with it for an hour while it quivered and stared at me with its sad bulging eyes, like some thinned-down canine version of Peter Lorre.[20]

I could tell her only one thing:

20. Most notably, he played Ugarte in _Casablanca_. One of the now-forgotten stars of the silver screen.

'Work was … mundane, as usual,' I said. 'What about you?'

'I was doing a day course entitled "Why Spreadsheets Are Not Boring", so same as you, I guess.'

Pippa made supper after that, and, true to form, Victor Mallett dropped round to see whether I'd found out where 'that rabbit' had come from. I told him that as far as I could see, she was just passing through.

'Doubtless a scam,' said Victor with a grunt. 'Rabbits are always on the make.'

'Was any of that true?' asked Pippa once Victor had gone.

'No – she lives in Leominster with her third husband. Not a word to Toby.'

'Right you are.'

Over the next two weeks I spent all my office time trying to ID John Flopsy 7770, and by the end of a fortnight I had got precisely nowhere, and had exhausted only thirty-five per cent of the male Labstocks on record.

'7770 might not even be on the books,' said Flemming, eager to have me back on normal spotting duties, but Lugless spoke to the Senior Group Leader and had me continue going through the bunshots, and only rejecting those I was seventy-six per cent certain weren't him. Lugless took being hoodwinked by his own kind as a deeply personal affront, especially as, to add insult to injury, someone had tied two knee-length grey socks to the rear bumper of his Eldorado – an obvious jab at his earless state, and making a mockery of his attempt to disguise himself, although personally, I thought the eyepatch and tam-o'-shanter just bizarrely random enough to have worked.

At the *Buchblitz* that weekend we gave Mr Beeton a twenty-seconds pause, as befitted his status as a generally reliable member of the team. Norman and Victor Mallett kept a eager eye out for Connie's return while we were Speed Librarying, but she didn't turn up, so the brothers concluded I was right: just passing through.

While I spent another fruitless week searching for a hint of the squashed Tudor rose capillary ear pattern, Hemlock Towers opposite was being cleared of Mr Beeton's effects. The good stuff was taken by his closest relatives, his library sold to Addyman's in Hay-on-Wye.

His arguably worthless knick-knacks were picked through for value by his lesser relatives, and his meticulously researched twenty-year project on the development of Medium Density Fibreboard was taken away in a skip to be recycled, ironically enough, into Medium Density Fibreboard.

Hemlock Towers then stood empty once more, and gossip soon turned to who might become the new tenants. There were several false leads, of course – an Argentinian couple on the run from the police; someone who looked a lot like Rick Astley; a *National Geographic* photographer; a barrister convicted of embezzlement; a retired trapeze artist; someone else who looked like Rick Astley but did, in fact, turn out to be Rick Astley; another *National Geographic* photographer, unrelated to the first in an improbable coincidence. All came to nought, and it wasn't for another fortnight that word of the new tenants came to me by way of Mrs Griswold, who when she wasn't being a supremely lacklustre Stanley Baldwin ran the corner shop and post office. She was the village gossip but didn't relinquish her skilfully wrought intelligence for free, and had her own unique exchange rate. Something seriously juicy offered up to her altar of tittle-tattle could keep you in credit for weeks, but tired gossip already heard had no value at all. Luckily, I was in credit; I had overheard details of Mr Beeton's last will and testament, and it appeared that Mrs Silver the housekeeper was due for a considerable sum, something that gave rise to suspicion that her long-standing employment might have involved something more significant than just warm milk and dusting.

Once this piece of information was taken, digested, tutted about and then mentally filed, Mrs Griswold beckoned me closer and hissed: 'They're coming!' in a particularly unsubtle manner.

I looked out of the window to see whether the danger was imminent, but there was nothing to be seen. I concluded that the implied sense of threat was vague and intangible. The most dangerous kind, to my mind.

'Who?'

'Them,' she added, no more helpfully.

'Vegans?'

'No, not vegans,' she said, eyes opening wide, 'worse than that.'

'Foreigners?' I asked, catching sight of that morning's copy of *The Actual Truth*, whose leader column's outrage *du jour* was that unwashed foreign beggars were taking much-needed panhandling jobs from their hard-working British counterparts.

'Worse.'

'Vegan foreigners who are also … socialist?'

'No,' she said, lowering her voice, *'rabbits!'*

This startled Mr Wainwright, who was leafing through the magazine display, part of his one-man quest to read an eighteen-year run of *Champion Marrow Monthly* without once paying for a copy.

'What's that?' he said.

'Rabbits,' repeated Mrs Griswold, 'in the village.'

Mr Wainwright looked shocked and, I think, a little afraid.

'Better not be some of those modern, bolshie, in-your-face rabbits who like to cause trouble and have unrealistic views on equality.'

Actually, I thought to myself, *any* rabbit – even compliant, easygoing ones who kept themselves to themselves and didn't overbreed – would not find an easy home in Much Hemlock.

'They're off-colony legals,' said Mrs Griswold. 'Major Rabbit is retired ex-army. There are two children but I didn't hear what Mrs Rabbit did. I'm not sure she even speaks English, to be honest – they were speaking in Rabbity when they walked in.'

'What does this Rabbity sound like?' asked Mr Wainwright.

'Hnfffy noises, mostly,' said Mrs Griswold, 'hniff-niff-nfhhf-niffh, that sort of thing – and a lot of nose and whisker movements.'

And they both laughed at Mrs Griswold's impersonation of the rabbit: nose wrinkled, upper teeth on lower lip, hands masquerading as ears. Mrs Griswold was, however, quite wrong – all rabbits speak English and, owing to their traditional work in call centres, often three or four other languages[21] too.

---

21. Rabbits are good at languages as they are at much else – the average IQ of a rabbit is about twenty per cent higher than that of humans, an indication that the Event may have been partly satirical in nature.

'I heard they're moving into Mr Beeton's old place,' said Mrs Ponsonby, who had caught the end of the conversation as she arrived. 'Waste of a good house – but someone has to live in it. Hello, Peter.'

Mrs Ponsonby was my aunt, and had an odd habit of contradicting herself in every sentence. Pippa called it 'a demonstration of the duality of our species'. I called it 'just plain annoying'.

'They must have come into some serious cash,' said Mr Wainwright, 'to afford the old Beeton place.'

'If they have they'll probably blow the lot on lettuce,' said Mrs Ponsonby, adding: 'but that would be their choice.'

'I think Mrs Rabbit's name was Constance,' said Mrs Griswold.

'What?' I said.

'Constance,' she replied. 'I've never heard of a rabbit called Constance.'

I had, and it stood to reason Connie and Constance were the same rabbit, and I suddenly felt a little odd inside. A sense of interest, obviously, that I might be seeing her more regularly after all these years – but also a sudden paralysing fear that she might find out what I did for a job. But if I was having a conflicting moment right now, it suddenly got a whole lot worse, and very quickly.

'I heard she was the widow of that rabbit mistakenly jugged by TwoLegsGood,' said Mrs Griswold, and it felt as though iced water had been suddenly pressed into my veins. I had never connected the two. Why should I? But the truth was that I was partially responsible for Dylan Rabbit's death, even if the Compliance Taskforce was *not* the agency that killed him. He was released by RabCoT within twenty-four hours and dead in another five: TwoLegsGood activists dragged him from his house in the middle of the night and upended him in a forty-gallon drum of cheap gravy that had been seasoned with bay leaves, celery, thyme, juniper berries and red wine. The mistake was only discovered when the rabbit we were actually after died of myxomatosis three months later. Controversially, the BBC's *News & Views* had suggested that the Rabbit Compliance Taskforce had tipped off TwoLegsGood and had him released him only to be killed 'as a warning'. The Senior Group Leader vehemently denied the accusation as 'just another manufactured lie from the biased pro-rabbit media'.

As it turned out, Dylan's family – which I was now aware included Connie, obviously – were fully compensated and even given off-colony status. The Senior Group Leader remarked that: 'The whole debacle was probably the best result his family could have hoped for: a cunicular plumber could *never* have earned enough to buy his way off-colony.' But all that aside, Connie's and my shared university attendance was a long time ago, so there was a very good chance she'd have forgotten all about me: after all, she didn't appear to recognise me at the library. And even if she *did* remember me, she'd never know I was a Spotter, less so one who'd had a hand in the death of her second husband.

'Will they be trying to get the kids into the local school?' asked Mrs Ponsonby, adding: 'Waste of time, if you ask me – but everyone needs an education.'

'I think that's what they're here for,' replied Mrs Griswold, 'checking it out. Class sizes, vegan options, that sort of thing.'

'Carrot-munching pests who should have been smothered when they spoke their first word,' grumbled Mr Wainwright, whose social filters – if he'd ever had any – were now entirely absent. 'It's unnatural.'

He was right on that score: the Spontaneous Anthropomorphising Event was *completely* unnatural and totally unprecedented. On 12 August 1965 there had been an unexpected flurry of snow on the night of a full moon following the warmest of summer days, when the sunset glowed an eerie shade of green. Aluminium foil had inexplicably tarnished within ten miles of the Event, and glass had adopted a sheen like that of mineral oil on water. The eighteen rabbits of the Event morphed and grew into a semi-humanlike shape overnight, stretched, yawned – then asked for a glass of water and a carrot, adding: 'But really, only if it's no trouble.'

The fifty-fifth anniversary would be later on this summer, but it was unlikely anyone would celebrate, least of all the rabbits to whom the Event elicited mixed feelings. Some thought humanness a boon, others a lament. Most agreed on one thing, however: it was better to have a mind capable of philosophising over the question of their existence than not. And chocolate eclairs. They were *definitely* worth having.

'Well,' I said, taking a deep breath and making to leave, 'I dare say Mr Mallett and his brother have already formed an action committee.'

'Those Malletts,' said Mrs Griswold fondly, looking down and touching her hair absently, 'always *so* concerned about our welfare.'

Pippa & Pasta

___

'Rabbit Underground' was the broad term used to describe any clandestine rabbit direct action protest group. Many suggested it might not actually exist at all, and simply be an invention by the Minister for Rabbit Affairs to further demonise the rabbit – and to justify extra funding for the Taskforce.

'Is it the self-same rabbit who was so disrespectful to dear wifey in the library?' asked Victor Mallett when I found him handing out poorly photocopied leaflets in the public bar of the Unicorn.

'It looks like it.'

'I told you she looked like trouble – we should regard that library book she borrowed as stolen, and that clearly shows a pattern of criminal behaviour that we can only ignore at our peril. I thought you said she was just passing through?'

'I thought she was. Major Rabbit served with the British Army,' I added, in order to win Victor over, as I knew he was a supporter of the forces, but had not served himself. 'They both strike me as decent people.'

'*Obviously* we are grateful for his committed service in defence of our nation,' said Mr Mallett, 'and yes, they might be *individually* good neighbours and in time make a positive contribution to the community. There are always the good ones. But you're missing the big picture. Once you let a single family in, then the downward spiral begins. Other rabbits of less scrupulous morals move in – and following them, the criminal element.'

'Criminal element?' I asked. 'Like what?'

'Well,' he said, 'stealing library books, for one. But make no mistake,' he added with renewed enthusiasm, 'this is the thin end of the wedge. Let one family in and pretty soon they'll all be here, filling up the schools, attempting to convert us all to their uniquely aggressive form of veganism, undermining our worthy and utterly logical religion with their depraved and nonsensical faith – and then placing an intolerable burden on our already weakened infrastructure. Also,' he added as an afterthought, 'it could negatively impact on our chance to win a Spick & Span award.'

'And once they've established themselves,' added Norman Mallett, who had been sitting at the bar and up until now had remained silent, 'their friends and relatives start to swarm in. Pretty soon you won't be able to move in Much Hemlock for rabbits. House prices will tumble, and we'll be strangers in our own community. It will be like Ross-on-Wye all over again.'

'Aye,' said Victor, shaking his head, 'a plague.'

'Are you thinking of raising a petition?' I asked, fully aware of Mr Mallett's usual modus operandi.

'Already started one,' he replied cheerfully, waving one of the flyers at me, which screamed of a 'potential disaster of massive proportions' in the village.

'As a member of the Rabbit Compliance Taskforce,' I said, trying to de-escalate the situation, 'I should point out that legal off-colony rabbits have a right to live anywhere, and we could be making a whole heap of trouble for ourselves if we break the law. Harassing the widow of someone who was jugged in error by TwoLegsGood isn't going to play well if the newspapers get hold of it.'

'I fully appreciate what you're saying, Peter,' he said, which was Mallett shorthand for 'I would utterly reject what you're saying if I were listening, which I'm not', 'and all I want to do is raise awareness,' which was, again, Mr Mallett's shorthand for 'I think I'll stir up a whole heap of trouble and hope that in the ensuing scrum I'll get what I want but not be held accountable for it'. He went on: 'We must remain utterly vigilant at all times, and I'll be honest, Peter, I didn't have you pegged as a friend to rabbits.'

'I'm not,' I said, 'I just want to caution you against any extreme behaviour that might not reflect well upon the village.'

'But the good news,' said Norman, also not listening, 'is that MegaWarren is on schedule, and will give rabbits what they need most of all: a place of their own. With a bit of luck all the legals will want to go there too – rabbit nirvana, I heard someone call it. Freedom to burrow and grow lettuce and … do whatever it is rabbits like to do. I think you'll find that Rehoming them all in Wales is the best and most lasting solution to the rabbit issue. Besides, it was all agreed by referendum, then properly debated in the House. The nation has spoken.'

Mega Warren had always been controversial, but after the referendum never in doubt, even though the 'Rehoming rabbits in Wales' policy was won on a slender majority and with half the country not voting at all. But Norman was right. The ten-thousand-acre site located just to the west of Rhayader was nearing completion, although moving the regional colonies to one centralised home was decidedly *not* something the rabbits much liked the sound of, especially those with a grounding in human history, which generally presented a 'low to extremely low' expectation of anything turning out well where enforced removals were concerned.

'But,' said Victor, returning to the question of Hemlock Towers, 'we have one thing in our favour: the old Beeton place is only to be rented. If they move in, they can just as easily move out. Can I rely on your support to not support them? You'll be living next door, after all.'

'I'll take a leaflet,' I said diplomatically, 'but I have to remain neutral due to my work at RabCoT.'

'Stout fellow. Give my very best to Pip, won't you?'

'I shall.'

Pippa was at the kitchen table when I got home and had her nose in a book while at the same time eating yoghurt, texting someone – probably Sally – and keeping a watchful eye on a Netflix series on her iPad. When I was twenty I had trouble doing *one* thing at a time. I still do.

'Hey, Dad,' she said.

'How's it going?' I asked.

'I'm learning HR jargon and can't decide which phrase I dislike more: *Game changer*, *Onboarding* or *Going forward*.'

'*Blue sky thinking* was always the one I disliked most.'

'That became too clichéd even for management-speak,' she replied, 'along with *Thinking out of the box* and *We need a paradigm shift*. They were all officially retired last year. How was your day?'

'Usual fun and games. But more importantly: rabbits are moving in next door.'

'I heard something about that,' said Pippa, 'but if I was a rabbit family moving anywhere, it wouldn't be to the sort of village that sent troops to fight in the Spanish Civil War – on General Franco's side.'

'The village is not *that* bad,' I said, 'and I think mostly it's just bluster. How many residents do you suppose have even *spoken* to a rabbit who wasn't a barista, room cleaner or shelf-stacker?'

'Prejudice is best lubricated with ignorance,' said Pippa. 'What do you think the bigot-in-chief is going to say about it?'

I placed Mr Mallett's leaflet in front of her, then stared out of the window at Hemlock Towers opposite. 'I think he's going to whip up some anti-rabbit feeling and make life so unbearable they'll move out.'

'I dislike his politics but can't fault him on his use of the semi-colon,' said Pippa, scanning the pamphlet. 'It's a good job he rarely travels farther than Hereford. Containment is the best policy for people like him.'

'Yes,' I said. 'It also works wonders with Ebola. Did you hear anything else about the rabbits? Mrs Griswold's intel was pretty sketchy.'

'Mr Rabbit is a retired army major and Mrs Rabbit an actress,' said Pippa.

'Really? Was she in anything I might have seen?'

'I don't know – commercials, someone said, a small part in *Pulp Fiction* but she didn't make it to the final cut.'

'That's interesting,' I said, as I knew Connie had been keen on drama. She'd done a cracking audition as Shelley Levene in Barnstaple Uni's production of *Glengarry Glen Ross*, but was rejected as the director wanted someone 'more male and less furry'.

'And *Major* Rabbit, is it?' I added.

'Yup. Almost served in Afghanistan, they say.'

Next Sunday, Next Door

DNA testing revealed that the rabbits were not some weird human/rabbit hybrid but were, in fact, rabbits – genetically indistinguishable from their dim field-cousins. Whatever gives the humanlike rabbits their humanness, it isn't in their DNA.

The Rabbits arrived the following Sunday amidst the buzz of motor mowers and the snip-snap-snip of garden shears. Everyone was eager to have the village neat and tidy, shipshape and perfectly just-so on the off chance that the Spick & Span judges might drop by, as they had been seen mooching around Pembridge on Wednesday.

I was in the garage tinkering with my Austin-Healey when a 1974 Dodge Monaco[22] pulled up in front of Hemlock Towers. Rabbits liked large American cars as they were better suited to their physique and limited levels of dexterity. Bench seats, auto transmission, feather-light power steering and large pedals. They also took great care of the cars, as rabbits viewed obsolescence as the arrogant cousin of waste and thus incompatible with the fourth tenet of their faith: sustainability. There was a rabbit saying: 'Nfifnfinnfiifnnfifnfn', which roughly translates as: 'Only a fool buys twice'.

I hurried upstairs to see more easily over the dividing hedge. The kids got out first and, I noted, were traditionally dressed yet with modern trappings: the boy-rabbit was in a blue sailor-suit and Nikes, and listening to a cassette Walkman. He moved languidly as though either deep in thought or consumed by idleness, and was also wearing an ankle monitor of the type used by the probation services. The girl-rabbit was more animated, wore a flowery summer dress and

22. I didn't know that then; I found out later. The actual car is now part of the Event Museum near Rhayader. Coincidentally, it was the civilian model of the car that Jake and Elwood Blues drove.

bounced into the house with one or two excited hops while her father climbed out the driver's side. He was dressed in a green Harris tweed over a matching waistcoat, shirt and tie. Rabbits rarely wore any clothes from the waist down as it restricted movement and the ability to hop. This was of little consequence to the females, who routinely wore skirts, dresses and, if no bouncing was planned, culottes, but to the males, who in one very notable respect were extremely humanlike indeed, had to disguise their trouserless modesty beneath a series of discreet items of apparel whose ingenious complexity is not within the scope of this book.[23]

Major Rabbit consulted a fob watch that he kept in his waistcoat pocket and then moved to take the cases from the boot of the car. At the same time the front passenger door opened and Connie Rabbit climbed out, took a sniff of the air and looked around. She was wearing a leather jacket over a spotted summer dress and her ears were tied loosely at the base with a red bandana. Unusually, a small part of her tail peaked out from beneath her dress, the rabbit equivalent of a plunging neckline. Shocking in polite rabbit circles a decade ago, but mostly acceptable today.

The Spontaneous Anthropomorphic Event had taken place before I was born, so rabbits talking, wearing summer dresses or driving cars never seemed that unusual to me. Their appearance in 1965 had not been reported immediately as the whole thing was dismissed as an elaborate hoax, right up until the moment Franklin Rabbit chatted to Charles Wheeler live on the BBC's *Panorama Special*.[24] After that, every news station on the planet wanted to 'talk to the rabbit' and find out how this all came about, something which still remains elusive today. The initial scepticism and disbelief then turned to curiosity, celebration and acceptance before taking a downward spiral during the knotty issues regarding status and rights before changing, as their numbers rose, to suspicion, condemnation, hatred and fear.

23.   See Chapter 6 of Dr Sam Ingram's landmark work *Below-waist Costume, Modesty, and the Bipedal Post-Event Rabbit*.
24.   Mainly about carrots and fruitcake and his favourite Beatle, but Franklin was only young at the time. Interviewed later, he told reporters that he should have said something more measured and erudite.

The journey from celebration to rejection had taken less than two decades.

I was startled by the phone ringing. I picked it up too fast, fumbled, dropped, then answered the phone. It was Norman Mallett.

'*It's arrived!*' he said, as though announcing an outbreak of the bubonic plague. 'Can you see them?'

'Yes,' I replied, returning to the window with the phone. 'Two adults, two children. Why don't you come round and talk to them?'

'What? Don't be ridiculous. Do they look as if they'll be staying only a few nights?'

I looked out of the window as a large removals lorry reversed down the narrow lane, reverse warner beeping.

'No, I think they're here for a while.'

There was a pause on the phone and then the muffled sounds of people conversing. After a moment, Norman came back on the line, his voice sounding more strident.

'Listen here, Knox. We've had our differences in the past, but there is a moment in everyone's lives where they have to step up to the plate, be counted, grit their teeth and do the right thing for the community.'

'And what is that thing?' I asked, impressed he could cram five clichés into one sentence.

'You've got some seriously objectionable centrist views, Knox, so you'll be perfect cover. We need you to go in and ... talk to the Rabbits. Get their confidence. Make friends if such a thing is possible. And when you think the moment is right, tell them they can have five grand in cash to shove off.'

'She's already got a lot of money,' I said. 'Compensation from the Compliance Taskforce after they leaked her husband's address to TwoLegsGood.'

'Conspiracy theory, Knox – unproved and untrue.'

It was a well-known fact around RabCoT that not only was this *absolutely* true, but the Senior Group Leader was the one who did it – and even boasted about it at the Christmas party the same year.

'I really don't think,' I said slowly, 'a measly five grand would be nearly enough.'

'Bloodsuckers,' he muttered. 'Hasn't she milked enough cash out of the public purse already? OK, Knox, you drive a hard bargain. We can go all the way up to seven, but not a penny more – unless they turn you down, then get back to me ASAP. Will you do that for us?'

I didn't need to give it much thought. If there was a peaceful solution to the problem where everyone could be happy, I should probably try and make it happen. It wasn't the only reason I was content to go over there – I wanted to see Connie again. If I reminded her who I was, it was possible she might remember me.

'OK, then,' I said. 'I'll let them settle for half an hour and then go and say hello.'

'Splendid,' said Norman in a friendlier tone. 'I'll get a progress report from you later. Keep your eyes peeled and best leave your wallet and mobile phone at home. You know what they're like.'

I went down to the kitchen, dumped a bag of carrots into a wicker basket and then covered them with a gingham tea towel. I gave the Rabbits thirty minutes and walked across to the house, heart thumping, and knocked on the door. After a few seconds Connie opened it, and looked mildly shocked. She stared at me with her large, odd-coloured eyes for a moment then sniffed the air and looked at the basket. I noted that one of her ears – the top third of the left, actually – was tilted forward, and she smelled very faintly of warm, freshly turned earth.

'Oh,' she said with a timid smile, 'is this a moving-in Carrot-o-gram? If so, it's the first time I've seen a human do it. Are you really going to try and sing the Nhfiiihhnirff[25] song?'

'N–no,' I said hurriedly. 'I'm … your next-door neighbour. We met a few weeks back during the library *Buchblitz*.'

She stared at me for a moment, head sideways, one large eye faced towards me, the way rabbits usually did when scrutinising a person or object.

'Actually,' she said in a quiet voice, 'we met *before* that. A long time ago. It's Peter Knox, isn't it?'

25. Rough translation of first line: Your warren is my burrow / your burrow is my warren / veg we share / together for warmth / carrot Ho! / carrot Hah!

I suddenly felt an odd sense of warmth that she remembered me, mixed with a sense of what I'd felt towards her back then.

'Hello, Connie,' I said, feeling myself start to tremble ever so slightly, 'yes, it's me. How have you been?'

'Oh, generally favourable,' she replied with a smile. 'Lost a couple of husbands, gained a few children. Jobs here, jobs there – that sort of thing. Never did finish my degree, though. What about you?'

'I got my degree but never used it,' I said, trying to make my voice sound nonchalant and chatty instead of stilted and knotted. 'I got married, had a daughter, came back to the family home to look after Dad. Worked for a while with the post office. I'm now an accountant, Library Blitzing on the side. Y'know. Stuff.'

'I can see you live only for pleasure,' she said, smiling agreeably. 'Are you here to ask for that book to be returned? To be honest, I haven't even started it. I used to read a lot when younger, but, well, time just gets away from us, doesn't it?'

'I'm not here about the book. I came over to say ... welcome to Much Hemlock.'

'A welcome?' she said, staring at me intently. 'I thought everyone in this village would have pictures of Nigel Smethwick on their walls and stuff.'

'Some *may* do,' I said, 'but not all.' I paused for a moment then asked: 'Is a Carrot-o-gram actually a thing?'

'Oh yes,' she replied with a chuckle, '*totally* a thing.'

'Ah.'

'How did you recognise me from the library visit?' she asked suddenly, and I felt a flush rise in my cheeks. I was under express orders not to reveal my skill. Outed Spotters occasionally went missing. And not 'missing' as in 'went on a bender and turned up three days later', but as in 'missing and no one knows what happened to them'.

'Your eyes,' I said, 'and the West Country accent.'

'Oh yes,' she said, blinking so I could almost hear her long eyelashes swishing through the air, 'those *are* a bit of a giveaway, aren't they?'

We stood there for a moment.

'It's *really* good to see you again, Peter,' she said, breaking the impasse and holding my hand in both of her incredibly soft paws. 'A *lot* of catching up to do. Are those for me?'

She was pointing at the basket that contained the carrots.

'For *all* of you,' I said rather foolishly.

'How ... sweet,' she said in an uncertain voice. 'Really, you shouldn't have troubled yourself.'

There was another uncertain pause. I could have left there and then, but I was on a mission – and I admit I was curious, and not just about reacquainting myself with Connie: it's not often rabbits move in next door. I needed a conversation opener, so went for the most obvious.

'Will your children be going to the local school?'

'Not for a week or so,' she replied, I think also relieved by the mundane direction in which the conversation had headed. 'We need to speak to the headmistress Mrs Lomax about certain ... special requirements.'

I decided to tackle the elephant in the room.

'About being ... rabbits?' I said, in as matter-of-fact a tone as I could muster.

'No,' she replied innocently. 'Bobby has a potentially fatal allergy to peanuts.'

'Oh,' I said, feeling awkward now that the elephant in the room had denied its own existence, 'that must be very ... challenging for him.'

'Her. Roberta, but known as Bobby. Like in *The Railway Children*?'

'I don't remember that.'

'Jenny Agutter played her in the movie.'

'Ah, yes,' I said, but not really remembering.

'Who's at the door?' came a voice from inside the house.

'This is Peter Knox, our new neighbour,' said Connie, opening the door wider to reveal Major Rabbit hopping aggressively across the hall carpet. Since he was powerfully built and quite tall – at least six-four *without* the ears – I found him somewhat intimidating.

'He and I shared a few lectures at Barnstaple University.'

'Was he part of the *infinitesimally* small crowd that demonstrated against your expulsion?'

'Well—'

'I *would* have been there,' I said, 'but was away that weekend.'

'Oh yes?' said Major Rabbit.

'At my aunt's,' I explained, making it suddenly sound even *more* of a lame excuse than it was, 'she was ill.'

'Hmm,' said Major Rabbit, looking at Connie and then me, 'were he and you a thing?'

'Goodness me, *no*,' said Connie with a laugh, 'what an idea. No, we just did some coffee and films. Look,' she added, 'Peter brought over gifts.'

Major Rabbit took the basket from her, lifted the gingham tea towel, stared at the carrots for a moment and then scowled at me.

'What is this? Some kind of joke?'

'Clifford, *please*,' said Connie, 'you're embarrassing me. I'm sure Peter had no idea. Fudds are just *impossible* when it comes to following our ways and customs.'

Major Rabbit ignored her and continued to stare at me in a menacing fashion. I noticed that one of his eyes was slightly milky, and his ears had a dozen or so duelling bullet holes, evidence of loves lost and won. His left ear had a kink a quarter of the way up where a wound had healed badly, but Mrs Griswold and Pippa had been right: he *was* ex-military – his blood group, tissue type and favourite strain of carrot[26] were plainly visible, tattooed inside the right ear. Rabbits who had been marked in this manner never came up on our screens. No need.

'Listen,' I said, moving away slowly, 'I meant no offence. I thought rabbits liked carrots, that's all.'

'Of course we like carrots. We live for carrots. We'd die for a sodding carrot. But not like that. Not scrubbed ... topped ... and in a *basket*.'

He stared at me dangerously, awaiting an explanation that I couldn't give.

'Clifford,' said Connie more firmly, 'calm is as calm does, remember?'

---

26. One should never underestimate the recuperating properties of a favourite variety of carrot.

'Listen,' I said, 'I've no idea what I've done to offend you, but whatever it is, I apologise. I'm your neighbour.'

I pointed across the dividing hedge to my house and both Connie and Major Rabbit looked at my house for a moment, twitched their noses in unison, looked at each other, then back at me.

'It was simply a moving-in present,' I added, 'but I can see this is bad timing. I'll leave you in peace.'

I turned to go but Major Rabbit took a powerful bound and was instantly at my side. He laid a paw on my shoulder.

'You had no idea?'

'Listen,' I said, warming to my task, 'I'll admit there's been some negative sentiments about you moving here, but I'd thought and try and show you that despite the vocal minority, some of us are at least—' I tried to think of the right phrase '—harmlessly indifferent.'

Major Rabbit looked back at Connie, then at me, then smiled.

'If you're merely selling indifference, we'll buy that with cabbage. I think I owe you an apology.'

He slapped me on the back.

'I'm Major Clifford Rabbit, DSC, Powys Regiment.'

We shook hand/paws.

'Mr Knox,' he said after thinking for a moment, 'have you ever tried meadowfield stew?'

I had to admit that I hadn't.

'We shall deal with this woeful lapse in your life experience. Constance, my sweet? Are we busy tomorrow night?'

'Bridge club in Ross,' she said. 'No, wait, that's the night after.'

'Good,' said Major Rabbit, 'how about tomorrow night?'

'Thank you,' I said, 'I'd love to.'

'Excellent – and please, Mr Knox, bring your daughter.'

'How did you know I had a daughter?'

'From the size of her clothes on the washing line,' he said, seemingly without looking in that direction at all. 'She's probably nineteen or twenty, slim build. Working in management, I think.'

He leaned closer and sniffed at me delicately.

'But there's no scent of *adult* female on you,' he continued, seemingly quite carried away with his own precise observations. 'You are not partnered, but it's not by choice. I can smell emptiness, loss and a deep melanch—'

'That's enough, sweetness,' said Connie, walking up from the porch and taking her husband's arm. 'You can bring your elder brother, too, if you want, Peter. Have you had him tested? He looks a little simple.'

I frowned.

'I don't have a brother.'

'No? Then you have a burglar. I saw him nipping furtively into your back door while we were standing here talking. Had a sort of lumpy face that looked like a pothole repair done in haste and on a limited budget.'

'That'll be my gardener,' I said, realising she was describing Norman Mallett with alarming precision. He must be there lurking, wanting to quiz me. I looked at Connie and Clifford in turn.

'You seem very … *observant.*'

'Almost three hundred and ten degrees peripheral vision,' said Clifford, pointing at his large eyes. 'We can see front, back and top. In fact,' he added with a sense of pride, 'we can almost see better behind us than in front. If you were once prey, it pays to know what's going on around you at all times.'

'That must be very useful.'

'It certainly doesn't stink.'

'Sensing almost everything around us gives us an edge,' explained Connie, 'in a hostile environment.'

'Well,' I said with a smile, preparing to leave, 'I hope you don't find Much Hemlock too much of a hostile environment.'

But they didn't return my smile.

'I certainly hope that is the case,' said Major Rabbit evenly. 'Shall we say eight o'clock tomorrow, then?'

I had just got back to my own front door when the genuine Carrot-o-gram turned up – four rabbits dressed in stripy blazers and straw boaters. The Rabbity language in song sounded like a series of continuous delicate sneezes, but in four-part harmony.

'What a load of nonsense,' said Norman, who had indeed made his way into my house, and was now watching the Carrot-o-gram from behind the safety of the net curtains in the front room. 'What did you learn, Knoxie?'

'Not much. I'm going over there for a meal tomorrow evening.'

'Good man. But don't get *too* cosy. Just make friends and then persuade them that twelve thousand would buy an awful lot of carrots.'

'You said seven thousand earlier.'

'The vicar came on board – I think he must be raiding the church roof appeal or something. Actually, we could probably run to fifteen but keep that under your hat, yes?'

I told him I would then saw him out the back door.

'Act like you're my gardener,' I said.

'What?'

'They clocked you coming into my house, so it's your cover story.'

'Hell's teeth,' he said, 'can't a fella keep a close watch on stuff without nosy neighbours studying his every move?'

I closed the door behind him, not really thinking about the bribe and the task in hand, but about Connie. I knew what I had felt seeing her again, but wasn't sure whether she had felt the same – either now, or back when we were nineteen. I could recognise rabbits, but I couldn't *read* them. There's a big difference.

Searching in vain & Shopping in town

The United Kingdom Anti-Rabbit Party began as a one-issue pressure group in 1967 and morphed into a political party as their anti-rabbit message spread. Although it was dismissed as a joke in the early years, Nigel Smethwick's populist rhetoric, a polarised nation and a divided parliament led him to unexpected victory in the controversial 2012 snap election.

Lugless was in before Toby and me that morning, which was unusual. Rabbits, for the most part, were not early risers. When we walked in he was carefully tidying his desk, even though it wasn't cluttered. There was his nameplate, several hammers of varying sizes, a paw-compliant keyboard, his own dip pen and ink-pot, a citation of merit awarded him by Nigel Smethwick himself, and a single gourmet carrot in a terracotta plant pot. Behind him on the wall was a somewhat racy rabbit calendar displaying a Daisy Duke-wearing Miss April, even though it was well into July.

As soon as I walked in Lugless stopped what he was doing, sat back in his chair and crunched on a stick of romaine he had standing by in a jug of iced water.

He said nothing, so I logged in and began work, sifting through all the Labstocks on the database that were male, had no duelling scars and were six foot or taller.[27] I'd been quite close to the white rabbit in the church, and even though I was five foot ten, I barely came up to his shoulder. I'd made a rough sketch of the squashed Tudor rose pattern I'd seen in his ears and we'd dutifully shared it with other departments, but even the two probables they sent me were way off the mark.

27. Not counting the ears. Rabbits are measured to the space on the top of the head between their ears. As a curious aside, ears are *exactly* one third body height, irrespective of age. No one knows why.

Today I would be going through Labstocks who had died in case he'd faked his own death in order to avoid detection. There were several hundred of these, and since rabbits die frequently, on-colony deaths are not usually corroborated by sight, or pictures taken. After that, I'd have to start on the Labstocks based at the other colonies, which might, I estimated, take the best part of a month. And if he was unregistered – as would be likely – all my work would be for nothing. To be honest, if I were running the Rabbit Underground, I'd use unregistered Labstock rabbit as couriers for precisely this reason: a low to nil chance of identification.

'Any luck on the Flopsy?' asked Lugless, the '7770' suffix now redundant as he was all I'd been looking for these past weeks.

'Nothing,' I said, 'but there are plenty more bunshots for me to go through.'

'We really need a name, Knox.'

'I know that,' I said. 'I go the speed I can go.'

The day wound tediously around until lunch when I wandered off towards the Old Market precinct to buy some socks from TK-Maxx.

The air was warm but not sultry, the shoppers in a good temper, the town quiet as befits a Monday. As I walked past the car park outside the Odeon I noticed the Rabbits' Dodge Monaco. I knew it was theirs as, firstly, Monacos are not a frequent sight in Hereford, and secondly, there was a Playboy Bunny sticker on the back, something which was both iconic and ironic: iconic as the logo was the unofficial emblem of Rabbit Equality, and ironic because the Playboy Club had never permitted any *real* rabbits to ever be bunny girls.[28] I didn't know whether it meant Clifford was in town or Connie, but as I looked around I saw Connie hurrying into Waitrose, and Clifford nowhere in sight. All thoughts of birthday presents vanished from my head as I trotted into the store, grabbed a basket, hastily chucked five or six random objects inside for plausibility, then went to find her while wondering which 'accidental meeting' strategy

28. Not that any actually *wanted* to be bunny girls. It was more the principle of the matter.

would work best: to just bump into her, or amble past until she noticed me?

I found her in the magazine section, deep in conversation on her mobile. I nipped back into the next aisle and paused for thought, my heart thumping. I'd not seen her for over thirty years, and even way back then nothing had happened between us, nothing *could* have happened between us. What was I doing? I began to walk away but my quick exit was abruptly thwarted.

'So how did it go during dinner?' came a voice behind me, and I jumped. It was Victor Mallett. He always did his shopping in Waitrose, as it was 'a positive British experience generally unsullied by the presence of foreigners'.

'That's not until tonight,' I said.

'Ah,' said Victor, 'jolly good. The leaving fund is now up to twenty grand, but start low and haggle hard, yes? Make them think seven is our limit. Look,' he added, having another thought, 'we'd rather not spend the cash if we don't have to. The church roof isn't going to repair itself, and a financial hit of this size could impact on the next Royal Baby street party – so is there anyone at the Taskforce you could ask to pressure them into moving on?'

'That's not how it works.'

'Really? I thought that was *precisely* how it works. You're at RabCoT, for Christ's sake – hardly the bunny's best friend.'

'I'm only an accountant.'

It was the first time I think I realised how much of a massive lie it was. Victor Mallett, annoyingly, was right. If I'd been honest with myself, I could have easily seen that the Ministry of Rabbit Affairs – who oversaw the Rabbit Compliance Taskforce – were anything but congenial to rabbits. They had, up until we left the EU, been cited seven hundred and twenty-eight times by the European Court of Human Rights in Strasbourg. They'd ruled that since we were treating rabbits like humans – that they paid taxes, held employment, demonstrated free will, understood mortality and their place within society and the world – they were ipso facto human enough to be classed as such, with all the rights and privileges that went with it.

The UK government didn't see it in quite the same way, and legally defined rabbits on strict taxonomic grounds, which unequivocally had them classed as Oryctolagus cuniculus: rabbits. Emphatically not human. It was a decision that was roundly embraced by RabToil, as it meant that annoyingly restrictive employment laws could be usefully circumvented. Additionally, the government argued, giving rabbits equal rights was a dangerous precedence as it then made no legal sense not to give the same to chickens, cows and pigs. Accepting food as pay for being a dog or a horse could very well be defined as paid employment and require sick leave and other benefits, but it was the whole 'being murdered and eaten' issue that was so deeply problematic. The *Actual Truth* headlined the case as: 'Europe wants to take away your bacon rolls.'

I sighed, and a little bit more of myself crumbled inside. The really questionable work that RabCoT undertook was done on the floor below me, but even so, I enabled it. Even if I wasn't part of the problem, I was certainly not part of the solution.

Pippa's mum Helena had thought so too, and it was why she left me after a series of increasingly acrimonious arguments. I needed to provide for us and maintain the house, but she didn't think that keeping the family home in Much Hemlock was worth the price tag. She was the first and last person I told. No one else knew what I did. Not family, not friends, *definitely* not Pippa.

'I think you've got Major Rabbit and Connie all wrong,' I said in a quiet voice, hoping to smooth this over.

'Oh, "Connie" is it now?'

'She asked me to call her that,' I said, feeling hot and annoyed and wanting to be away from here. 'I thought you wanted me to get all friendly?'

'I did,' said Victor, 'but not familiar. And my point about criminality has been borne out: their son has a tag on his ankle – for burrowing, I heard.'

I'd seen the tag too.

'You see what I mean?' added Victor. 'Not content with decimating the countryside and taking away all the poorly paid jobs that no one wants to do, they've started undermining our towns and villages. Can't you see the metaphor? Their agenda is as clear as the nose on your face: Undermine and Overpopulate. Do you know how many buildings have been seriously damaged by Vandaburrolism?'

'I don't know,' I said, trying hard to remember even a single case.

'I don't know either,' said Victor, 'but it's dozens at least, perhaps more. The TwoLegsGood website is packed full of examples.'

'If you want to know about Kent, all you need do is ask.'

It was Connie. She stared at us both in turn, then blinked those large odd-coloured eyes of hers. I had no idea how much of our conversation she'd heard, but I hoped not the bit about how I worked in Rabbit Compliance.

'Have you met?' I said, swiftly defaulting to introductions. 'Mrs Rabbit, this is Mr Victor Mallett, chair of the Parish Council and long-time resident of Much Hemlock. Mr Mallett, this is Mrs Constance Rabbit, newly resident at Hemlock Towers.'

Mr Mallett faltered slightly, but then succumbed to Default Standard British.

'My pleasure,' he said politely, shaking her paw awkwardly, and with imperfectly disguised reluctance. 'Welcome to the village. The choir is always looking for new members, the knitting circle are a friendly bunch, and you'll find Peter and Pippa very generous neighbours.'

'We have found Mr Knox to be the *perfect* neighbour,' she said, smiling, 'but I'm not convinced of your sincerity. Is this pamphlet something to do with you?'

She produced one of the leaflets I had seen Mr Mallett distributing, warning all and sundry about the 'pernicious carrot-munching vermin in our midst'. Mr Mallett looked at it, then at me, then at Mrs Rabbit, who cocked her head on one side and stared at him impassively.

'Oh,' he said, looking like someone caught in headlights, 'I think perhaps our message might have been … taken out of context.'

'I see,' said Connie, 'and in what context would "pernicious carrot-munching vermin" be anything *but* grossly offensive and leporiphobic?'

'Well,' he said, suddenly recovering, 'now *you're* being offensive in calling *me* leporiphobic, which is a vicious and unwarranted slur of which you should be horribly ashamed – and which makes us all even. Goodness, is that the time? I am most hideously late for a meeting. So good to have made your acquaintance, Mrs Rabbit. Good day.'

And he walked away, wiping the hand that he used to shake Mrs Rabbit's paw on his trouser leg.

'Oh dear, oh dear,' said Connie, placing a paw to her mouth as she gave out a couple of chirpy giggles. 'I am *so* wicked. I really shouldn't have put him on the spot like that.'

'I tend to agree with you,' I said, 'as one of the few acquaintances you have in the village, I must tell you that Mr Mallett is the last person you should annoy.'

'If you stay acquainted with us, Mr Knox,' she said with dazzling directness, 'the only acquaintance you may have in the village is us.'

'I'll … take my chances,' I said.

She was now standing quite close, and I could sense her rich, loamy scent once more. It was the scent she'd worn all those years ago, something cooked up by the noted rabbit parfumier Gaston Rabbît. Whenever I'd smelled unwashed spuds it had put me in mind of her.

'*Jersey Royal Pour Femme*,' I said, suddenly recalling what it was called. She looked at me and smiled.

'You remembered.'

'I remember a lot of things.'

We stared at one another for a moment, until she suddenly switched her attention to the randomly gathered items in my basket. 'Well, well,' she said, 'incontinence pads, a tin of mushroom soup, Sun-Pat peanut butter and cocktail sticks?'

'It's for Mrs Ponsonby,' I said quickly. 'She's my aunt. I do her shopping.'

'The one who was ill the weekend I was expelled from uni?'

'No,' I said, 'that was another one. I have three.'

'I have sixty-eight aunts,' she said cheerfully, 'and forty-nine uncles, one of which was also my grandfather.'

'Really?'

'Yes,' she said reflectively, 'it always made things a little awkward at family get-togethers. Will you accompany me to fruit and veg?'

I could feel us being watched as we moved down the aisle. Shoppers suddenly needed to be somewhere else when we approached, and once, when Connie paused at the fussy-eaters section, the three shoppers already there hurriedly moved away while making clucking noises of disapproval.

'Someone said you had a small scene in *Pulp Fiction*,' I said by way of conversation.

'The high point of my lacklustre career,' she replied with a smile, 'was being edited out of a classic. The segment was originally called "The bunny incident". Quentin was pretty cool over the whole rabbit issue, but there was pressure from the studios and my small part was reshot with a human. They changed the "good carrot juice" dialogue to "good coffee". But if you run it again, it makes much more sense with Jimmy's wife being a rabbit. We could travel to the States in those days,' she added with a sigh. 'You had to carry a non-pregnancy certificate and any stay was limited to half a gestation period, but even so – happier times.'

'Missing out on the success of that movie must have been quite annoying.'

'All part of the fun and joy of being an actor,' said Connie philosophically. 'My work was mostly commercials, a guest spot in *Emmerdale*, *The Bill* and one hundred and eighty-three episodes of *How Deep Was My Warren* as midwife Rachel Rabbit. Have you ever watched it?'

'No,' I said, truthfully enough, as the multiple and intertwining plot threads were of such labyrinthine complexity that a single twenty-minute episode contained the same amount of drama as an entire season of *West Wing*. A few humans claimed to be able to follow it, but they were very likely lying.

'Not many humans have,' replied Connie, 'but here's a part of mine you might remember: do you recall the animated rabbit in the Cadbury's Caramel adverts?'

Oddly – or not so oddly at all, really – I had always thought of Connie when watching the adverts, even though the cartoon rabbit, while possessed of Connie's curves as much as my imagination allowed, didn't actually sound like her, despite sharing a similar West Country accent.

'That was you?'

Connie waved a paw dismissively.

'I was filmed so the animators could copy the movements, so yes, as a body and movement reference – *long* before the days of motion capture.'

'But not your voice, was it?' I said.

She smiled.

'Very perceptive of you. I didn't have an Equity card back then so Miriam Margolyes performed in my stead – but I was there in the recording studio to coach her. Lovely woman; her Nurse in *Romeo + Juliet* was the best ever.'

'Ever done any Shakespeare?' I asked.

'A two-week run playing Bottom in *A Midsummer Night's Dream* but I think I only got the part on account of my ears. Actually, do you know what?' she said as we reached the fruit and veg section. 'I don't really need to do any shopping.'

'No?'

'No. I'm having an affair and I wanted to make a call without Clifford overhearing. It's with Rupert Rabbit. He's a cousin on my father's sister's daughter's husband's mother's side.'

'I'm … I'm not sure you should be telling me this.'

'If you're a rabbit,' she said with a sigh, 'it's sometimes difficult to find someone who *isn't* your cousin.'

'No,' I said, 'I mean I'm not sure you should be telling me about your marital infidelities.'

She picked up a stick of celery and sniffed at it expertly.

'You were always someone I could trust, Pete. I told you stuff, things you might have repeated but didn't. Are you going to tell my husband?'

'No, of course not.'

'So that's why I'm sharing. Mind you, I'm not so sure about Rupert. Not quite rubbish enough.'

'Not rubbish *enough*?' I asked, taking an interest after all.

'Clifford is a wonderful husband. Upright, tall, intelligent, ambitious and driven – but if I'm having another litter, they probably shouldn't be his.'

I asked her why not, and she said it was 'a rabbit thing'. She lingered over the iceberg lettuce, then sniffed at some romaine before picking up a twin-pack of Little Gem lettuces.

'Technically they're actually miniature cos,' she said, something of an expert, 'and have a good resistance to root aphid. Did you know the ancient Egyptians considered lettuce a symbol of sexual prowess and fertility?'

'I know it now.'

'Is anyone watching?' she asked in a mischievous tone.

'What are you going to do?'

'Is there?'

I looked around.

'No.'

She took one of the Little Gem lettuces out of its cellophane.

'My second husband and I used to pop a Little Gem during … y'know. It increases the chance of ovulation.[29]'

Then, without pausing, she downed the Little Gem in a single gulp.

She closed her eyes, inhaled deeply, then shivered until her light brown fur stood out in a low ridge down her back. She held her breath, then exhaled a lungful of salady breath with a low sigh.

'Zowzer,' she said in a quiet voice. 'The Soil Association lettuces give the biggest hit. Look, you'd better have this.'

She handed me the remaining lettuce.

'If I come home with a Little Gem missing out of a two-pack, Clifford will be *insanely* suspicious. Oh-oh. Trouble.'

I turned to look behind me and could see the security guard deep in conversation with two of the disapproving shoppers, who were looking our way and pointing. I turned back to say something to Connie but she'd slipped away.

'Was that rabbit anything to do with you?' asked the store guard as he strode up.

---

29. Unlike humans, rabbits can become pregnant almost any time they choose. High reproduction rates can often be an engine of swift evolutionary change, and may account for forty per cent of all mammals today belonging to the rodent/ rabbit family.

'Which one?'

'The one who handed you the half-opened Little Gem – because it would make her husband jealous if she didn't.'

'That happens a lot, does it?'

'More than you might think. So: was that rabbit anything to do with you?'

'Well, no, not really – we'd just met.'

He grunted and moved away. I walked up and down the aisles trying to find Connie and eventually spotted her outside, walking briskly through the parking lot towards her car. I watched her climb into the Dodge, then reverse out of the car park and away. When at uni I'd liked her off-kilter character mixed with her utter directness, and I liked it now, too. I also knew that sooner or later, by accident or design, she'd find out about my role in the death of her second husband, Dylan Rabbit – and I wasn't looking forward to it.

Senior Group Leader

Myxomatosis was used as an anti-rabbit bacteriological agent from the early nineteenth century, most notably in Australia in 1950. The disease initially affects the eyes and genitals, which may grow tumours or *myxomata*. Secondary infections of pneumonia soon follow, and the rabbit is generally dead within two weeks of infection. There is no cure.

When I got back to the office I found Flemming and Lugless at my terminal, going through my semi-choices and rejections of the morning. Flemming had an Admin password so could access all my work, which didn't surprise me.

'Not much luck, then?' she asked.

'It's a long and tedious process,' I said, 'and can't really be rushed.'

'In that case,' said Lugless, 'I think what this project needs is an increased sense of purpose. We told him you'd drop in and offer up a progress report as soon as you got back.'

The warning bells started ringing.

'Drop in and see who?'

'Who do you think? The Senior Group Leader.'

I started. No one liked to meet the Senior Group Leader, *especially* if you were key personnel in an important investigation that had made no headway. I tried to think up a reasoned series of robust arguments that would bring everyone around to my way of thinking while also being cowed by my intellect and sharpness of wit, but all I could come up with was 'Do I have to?' in a whiny sort of voice.

'Of course not,' said Flemming, 'but you will because I'm ordering you to. Oh, and you're to drop into accounts on the way down. I think they have something they want taken to him.'

Flemming and Lugless both returned to their desks, the conversation over. I sighed, then walked slowly down the hall to where the head of Accounts was waiting for me with a bulging brown envelope attached to a petty cash form. I knew what it contained. The Senior Group Leader had many peculiar habits, and one of them was insisting on being paid cash for any 'special services'.

'Thanks for doing this,' she said nervously. 'I'd do it myself, of course, but I have a pressing dental appointment.'

She held her jaw and winced in a dramatic fashion to drive home the point, reminded me to get a signature for the cash and then vanished back into her office.

I made my way downstairs and into the main Taskforce office. The room was large, open plan and harshly lit by strip-lights. There were about sixty workers in the office, most of whom were either on the phone or hunched over their screens, figuring out movement orders, chasing up errant rabbits, keeping tabs on labour assignments, suspected spikes of criminality and rigidly enforcing the rabbit maximum wage.

As I walked slowly across the room, all eyes were upon me. It felt as though the entire office were heavy with doom-laden apprehension. No one liked the Senior Group Leader being here, and the arrival of someone with a fat brown envelope was good news all round. The sooner he was paid off, the sooner he would be away.

I didn't have to state my business to the Group Leader's assistant. He simply announced my arrival on the intercom and hurriedly waved me in. I stepped up to the door, took a deep breath, knocked and walked in.

The office was tidy and neat, the walls covered with photographs of the Group Leader along with mementos of his many achievements in vintage motor racing. There were trophies littered about, polished engine parts masquerading as clocks and ashtrays, and mounted on the wall was the spare bonnet of one of the Le Mans D-Type winners. The blinds were down so the interior was quite dark, and hanging in the air was a curiously fuggy blend of whisky, cigar smoke and Old Spice aftershave.

Sitting in the darkness was a figure only faintly illuminated by an orange glow as he pulled on a cigar. I cleared the nervousness from my throat and held up the envelope.

'Agent AY-002 suggested I give you an update on the hunt for

Flopsy 7770, and I've something for you from the accounts department.'

There was a pause, then:

'Top notch, old boy, top notch.'

His voice was smooth and low and sounded well educated. It put me in mind of my English master at school, whose mellow tones were nourished by a long-standing yet ultimately fatal relationship with Monte Cristo and Glenmorangie.

'*Bono malum superate*,[30]' he added. 'Be a good chap and leave it on the desk, hmmm?'

I bit my lip. I knew from office gossip that this was usually how it went down regarding the petty cash. Whoever delivered it tried to get the Group Leader to sign for it, and he always tried not to.

'I have to have it signed.'

'And you will, old boy, when I decide. Wait a moment, is that Mr Knox?'

I felt sweat prickle my back as he stood up and moved into the light.

The Senior Group Leader was impeccably dressed in a finely cut woollen three-piece suit of a handsome large check. He wore red socks inside brown leather brogues, and a scarlet tie was perfectly knotted and secured with a bejewelled tie-pin. He was a dark shade of orangey sandstone, over six feet tall, and his tail – sorry, *brush* – poked out from the back of his suit, where the white tip flicked the air in an impatient manner. There was also a lumpy hessian sack at his feet, which had dark stains in several places.

'Cat got your tongue?' he said. 'You are Mr Knox? I can tell male from female, young from old and dumb from not-so-dumb, but that's about as far as it goes.'

'Y-yes,' I stammered, and then watched with increased nervousness as he raised his lip to reveal a large canine that had been filed to a point. There seemed to be a clump of hair stuck between his fangs, to which there was attached a pink sliver of gristle.

'Yes … what?'

'Yes, sir, Mr Ffoxe, sir,' I said, 'that's my name – it's Mr Knox, sir.'

---

30. 'Overcome evil with good'.

Rabbits had not been the only animals caught up in the 1965 Spontaneous Anthropomorphising Event. There had also been six weasels, five guinea pigs, three foxes, a Dalmatian, a badger, nine bees and a caterpillar.

The badger and the Dalmatian, after numerous failed careers as chat-show hosts, royal reporters and pool hustlers, embarked on a career as comedy duo Spots and Stripes, whose routine, while variable in quality, was certainly unique.

The guinea pigs had all been male, which was problematic for any long-term survival possibilities. They were pretty much inseparable, and after a failed career in novelty cake baking had formed a crime syndicate dubbed 'Pig Iron' by the press. After a series of gangland-style hits, bank jobs and jewel heists, their luck finally ran out when their getaway car was boxed in by the police on the M4. But instead of going quietly, they elected to shoot their way out using an array of automatic weapons and even a rocket-propelled grenade launcher while yelling clichéd statements such as: 'No bastard copper's gonna bung me in chokey'.

The battle was described by a seasoned front-line firearms officer as 'the most terrifying half-hour of my life, and substantially worse than anything we faced in Iraq'. After a protracted gunfight, two car chases and a twenty-seven-hour stand-off in a KFC, the two surviving guinea pigs were arrested and eventually handed a twenty-six-year sentence each.

The weasels all worked in the intelligence community and in what could be described as either nominative determinism or simply playing up to their own stereotype were *weaselly* sorts of creatures. The only one I knew reasonably well was Adrian Whizelle, who had tried to sapienise his name[31] to appear less weaselly.

The caterpillar, in contrast, had taken to the Event badly and immediately formed into a chrysalis from which s/he was yet to

---

31. Until you actually met one in the flesh, you might never know they were a weasel – which surprises many a prospective date as they spend a disproportionate amount of time using dating apps. Inexplicably, with a young Anthony Eden or Unity Mitford as their profile picture.

emerge. S/he is currently hanging up in a large cupboard inside the Natural History Museum; you can view her/him on live webcam.

No one knows what happened to the bees.

'How's that delightful daughter of yours?' asked Mr Ffoxe, his comment relating to the 'bring a child to work day' that soured soon after his unplanned arrival in the office. Pippa had been fourteen at the time and became the focus of Mr Ffoxe's attentions, which were inappropriately suggestive and, had he been human, grounds for instant dismissal and possibly a criminal investigation.

'She's well,' I said, trying to seem cold and disdainful but actually sounding plaintive and apologetic.

'Is she still exceptionally pleasing to the eye?' he asked. 'We must reacquaint ourselves now those tiresome consent rules are past us.'

His small yellow eyes bored into me, and a dribble of saliva oozed from the side of his mouth. 'Repellent' couldn't even begin to describe him.

'I think I can speak for Pippa when I say she despises you,' I replied.

He grinned again.

'Quite the little minx. Well, her loss.'

Owing to small litter sizes and an impenetrably long and compli-cated mating ritual that required Michelin-starred dinner dates and visits to Glyndebourne, foxes had not reproduced nearly as well as rabbits. From the two vixens and a dog at Event Zero there were now a shade under six thousand individuals. They had become increasingly urbane over the years and insisted on sending their cubs to public schools, quoting Latin in a fatuous and pretentious manner whenever possible and respelling their surnames with a dazzling array of ridiculous affectations. There was plain 'Mr Fox', then about forty other permutations that included: Foxe, Ffoxe, Phocks, Phoxse, Forcks, Fforkse, Fourks, Fourxe, Foix, Fux, Foxx and Phourxes. All, without exception, were pronounced 'Fox'.

Unlike the rabbit, the foxes had secured British citizenship on the dubious legal grounds that the then Home Secretary liked 'the cut of their jib', but they also retained, in a unique legal ruling, dual taxonomic status. They were legally human but also allowed to be fox when the mood took them, or the job required it. They were also notoriously, painfully, *cunning*. There was a saying: you can never outfox the fox.

'So,' said Mr Ffoxe, 'let's have the cash.'

I handed him the receipt for signing and he withdrew an expensive pen from his top pocket and signed the docket before handing it back, and I passed over the cash.

'OK, then,' he said, stuffing the cash in his breast pocket, 'let's talk about the operation in Ross. Lugless tells me you haven't been embracing the sort of enthusiasm we like to see in our staff. With the Rabbit Underground threatening to upset the peaceful status quo of this green and pleasant land you need to try a little harder. Whizelle says you've been staring at pictures of Labstock for several weeks and haven't fingered a single one.'

I swallowed nervously.

'I haven't found him yet. These things take time.'

He moved closer, the heavy scent of Old Spice cologne suddenly filling the air like fog. Foxes used it to disguise their scent from rabbits as they moved in for the kill. And foxes *were* permitted to kill rabbits. At the High Court in 1978, *Fox* v. *Rabbit* established that a fox killing a rabbit – while taxonomically a fox – was legally defensible on the grounds of 'long-founded predation of historically natural prey'. It gave legality to their job as rabbit enforcers, and although it was legal for a rabbit to kill a fox in self-defence 'once all other avenues of escape had been exhausted and the law's definition of proportionality as it appertained to rabbits had been tested in the courts', rabbits rarely did, owing to ... reprisals.

Reprisals were seen less like mass murder and more a useful tool of deterrence, and began when a particularly unpleasant individual named Jethro Phox ventured on to Colony Five for 'a little sport' and was found face down two days later in a muddy ditch just outside the wall. The coroner found enough cocaine and alcohol in his body to kill a small horse, but the actual cause of death was asphyxiation due to 'a small carrot lodged in the windpipe'. While the coroner said this did not *immediately* suggest foul play on the part of rabbits, his brother foxes interpreted it differently. When the fur had settled, six hundred random rabbits had been killed, tortured and partially eaten in the most sadistic manner imaginable. It was so unpleasant that even then Prime Minister Tony Blair – a long-time supporter of fox rights – had to warn the fox community that any more 'overreach of this sort' would result in a repealing of *Fox* v. *Rabbit*.

This didn't stop the reprisals – the foxes just found the acceptable limits. A hundred dead rabbits per dead fox, as it turned out, effectively making foxes all but untouchable. But despite *Fox* v. *Rabbit*, foxes used right-to-kill sparingly to keep the culling fees disproportionately high.

'You haven't found him yet because *these things take time*?' he echoed. 'How much time?'

'Well, about as—'

'Give me some names,' said Mr Ffoxe, interrupting me. 'Labstocks who look a *bit* like Flopsy 7770 – even if nothing else than to sow a bit of discord amongst the cottontail.'

'I'm ... not sure that's a good idea.'

'Why?'

'We should try to avoid another Dylan Rabbit debacle,' I said, my mouth dry. 'It brings the Taskforce into disrepute.'

I could hear my voice crack.

'The public has moved on since then,' said Mr Ffoxe with a dismissive shrug. 'The whole Dylan Rabbit wrongful death nonsense lives on only in the deluded minds of the irredeemably self-righteous. To maintain the high efficiency of the Compliance Taskforce we are going to have to make a few mistakes here and there, and Mr Smethwick agrees with me that it is a price worth paying. Now: I want you to go back over your list of Labstocks and select four to be brought in for questioning.'

'I have no names,' I implored, 'not a single one.'

'That's not my problem,' said Mr Ffoxe, fixing me with a menacing look. 'It's yours. Four names. To show the Underground we mean business.'

'Then why not choose four from the Labstock community at random?' I said, a terrified warble in my throat. 'They'll be as guilty as any I can choose ...'

My voice trailed off as his small yellow eyes stared at me coldly.

'You're an excellent Spotter,' he said in a quiet voice, 'one of the best. Your strike rates are off the chart. But if you don't align yourself a little more with policy, we'll have to talk about letting you go.'

I swallowed nervously again. I needed this job.

'You can't fire me for not supplying you with random names.'

He smiled and patted me on the arm.

'My dear fellow, we're not going to fire you. Heavens above, no. It's just that there have been a number of intelligence leaks in the Taskforce, and those leaks can often have grave consequences.'

He stared at me with a faint smile and I felt hot and uncomfortable. Mr Ffoxe had leaked Dylan Rabbit's name to TwoLegsGood, who then jugged him. It was quite possible he could leak my name, too – but to rabbits with more on their minds than carrots, dandelion leaves and reruns of *How Deep Was My Warren*. He chuckled, and I knew he wasn't kidding. He placed his paw on my shoulder and spoke softly, close to my ear.

'Like it or not, Knox, you're one of us. You've taken the dollar, dipped your toes in the effluent. I'm not sure the rabbit would see your complicity in anything but a ...' he paused for thought '... unfavourable light.'

He was right. There were many incidents that, while seemingly accidental or unrelated, definitely benefitted rabbits. Like the sudden departure of Smethwick's deputy to a Buddhist retreat in Bhutan without explanation, or the higher-than-average fatal car accidents that involved foxes and weasels, or the Spotters who abruptly left the business, or just went missing without adequate explanation. There was a very good reason we kept our profession secret.

'Do we understand one another?' he asked.

I felt a cold sweat creep down my back.

'Yes,' I said, 'yes, we understand one another.'

This was typical of how foxes operate. Cajole, bully, threaten, diminish, divide, disseminate and eventually, as far as rabbits were concerned at least, murder. It was in their blood, it was in their DNA. More than that, they actually enjoyed it. Many of them considered inviting a fresh-found foxy friend on a rampage through the colonies as little more than a cracking first date.

It was time for me to leave. I mumbled that I was wanted else-where, and turned towards the door to find Mr Ffoxe *waiting at the door*. He had moved so blindingly fast it seemed as though there were two of him in the room, and I had to look back to check.

'Mr Knox, sir, not so fast, sir. Did I say that you could go, sir?'

'No, sir, no, sir, Mr Ffoxe, sir,' I mumbled. 'What else should I do, sir?'

He placed his muzzle close to me and inhaled deeply.

'Oh-ho,' he said, suddenly distracted, 'you've been near a female rabbit recently.'

I thought of Connie in Waitrose.

'I stopped at Ascari's on the way here,' I said, 'there was a rabbarista behind the counter.'

I stammered slightly as I said it, and Mr Ffoxe knew instantly I was lying.

'Well, how about that?' he said with a laugh. 'Little Knoxie's been beguiled. What was it? The eyes? The bobbling cottontail? The inexplicable and utterly inappropriate sexualisation of an other-wise unremarkable lower mammal? Who was she? Your new neighbour?'

'No—' I stopped as I realised what he'd said, then: 'How did you know I had rabbits as neighbours?'

He smiled.

'Don't let yourself be tempted by the bun's mild temperament and apparent peaceful nature,' he said without answering my question. 'That "cute and cuddly victim of human's domination" stuff they do? It's bullshit. It's not sunny meadows, warm burrows and dande-lion leaves they're after, it's majoritisation, assimilation and domination. And they could win out, if left unchecked. Promiscuity is not just their *raison d'être*, it's their secret weapon. A LitterBomb is a very real and present danger, and once the supply chain of stockpiled food is successfully coordinated by the Underground, the word will go out. Before you can say *Lapin à la cocotte* you'll be outnumbered, outvoted in your own nation, working for a rabbit, taking orders from a rabbit, worshipping at their altar and living the lapine way – it'll be lettuce for supper, dinner and tea. Do you want that?'

'Well, no.'

'Then we're totally together on this, because *that's* what Flopsy 7770 and the rest of those treasonous bunscum are up to.'

'Really?'

'You'd better believe it. So look, here's what you're going to do about your neighbours: be wary, but stay friendly. Do what you have to do to gain their confidence. We'll tell you what we want you to do in due course.'

'So I want to keep them in the village?' I said, thinking about the Malletts' moving-out fund.

'If you can. Infiltrate, make friends and report back. The Taskforce will be grateful. *I* will be grateful.'

Mr Ffoxe patted me on the shoulder in a patronising manner, and then, without me noticing, snaked a paw into my jacket and deposited a small yet very fresh fox turd in my inside breast pocket.[32] He then smiled.

'Oh yes,' he said, indicating the bloodstained hessian sack in the middle of his office carpet, 'want a couple of haunches for the pot? Tasty and nutritious.'

I finally found a voice.

'This isn't compliance,' I said, 'it's ...'

My voice trailed off.

'You can speak your mind here, Knox. I give you permission. This one's on me. A free pass.'

'It's ... *murder*,' I said, indicating the hessian sack.

He took a draw on his cigar and chuckled.

'Can you even begin to understand the level of that statement's hypocrisy coming from you? Cruel as we are, foxes are amateurs next to humans. I may be a little harsh on your furry woodland friends, but *exitus acta probat*,[33] Knox. But here's the thing: it's not me and my foxy chums currently and without even a flicker of collective guilt precipitating an unprecedented extinction event on the entire sodding planet.'

---

32. I only found this out the next time I put my hand in my pocket. It is a well-known fox joke, although only foxes find it funny.

33. The outcome justifies the deed.

90

He glared at me for a moment and I shifted my weight nervously.

'And don't say you're not personally responsible,' continued Mr Ffoxe, 'because you are. Your tacit support of the status quo is proof of your complicity, your shrugging indifference a favourable vote in support of keeping things *exactly* as they are. I'm not the murderer, Knox, you are – you and all your pathetic little naked primate cousins with their silly hairstyles and gangly limbs and over-developed sense of entitlement and self-serving delusion.'

I felt myself grow hot under his glare.

'And now,' he said in a low voice, 'you can piss off back to the upstanding and necessary work you are paid handsomely to do. Four names, on my desk, by sundown.'

I needed no second bidding and hastily left the room.

'Everything OK?' asked Toby when I got back to my desk.

'No,' I said, 'not really. In fact, not at all.'

Dinner & Dandelion Brandy

The most decorated service rabbit in history was RAF Navigation Officer Danielle 'Thumper' Rabbit, who ejected from a Tornado over Iraq when it was hit by a surface-to-air missile. She wrote about her time as a POW in *Bouncing Out of Tikrit*, and it was quite a good read, although critics did find fault with the overlong detail of Iraqi salad in the latter part of the book.

After prevaricating all afternoon on which Labstock names I should send down to Mr Ffoxe, I selected four who were already dead or long missing – but wouldn't be readily apparent as such. Someone would have to do some research, and that might give me breathing space for a couple of days.

The evening was warm and clear with white mares' tails flecking the sky as I drove back towards Much Hemlock. I said nothing to Toby on the way home, my mind full of spotting, LitterBombs, Mr Ffoxe, Connie – and, of course, the fox turd I found in my breast pocket when fumbling for my dark glasses. After I'd dropped Toby at his house, I drove home and had a shower, a shave, and went through the cupboard to find something to wear for my evening over at the Rabbits'. I eventually chose slacks, white shirt and casual sports jacket. I'd put on a few pounds since I'd bought them, and they felt a little tight, but were about the best threads I had. I didn't go out much.

Pippa had decided not to come with me as she'd half-promised to meet Toby at the new Welsh-Thai fusion restaurant that had opened in the village. She'd got wind of the leaving fund, too – the move to have them ousted was already known around the village as 'Rabxit'.

'Are you *really* going to ask them to shove off for cash?' she asked. 'I'm not sure being a mouthpiece for the Malletts can lead to anything but trouble.'

'I'll be diplomatic,' I said. 'After all, it's possible this might be the Rabbits' plan, and fleecing everyone who's put in some cash does have a sense of poetry about it.'

'Aside from the vicar who raided the church roof appeal.'

'Yes,' I said thoughtfully, 'maybe I could arrange some sort of ecclesiastical cashback arrangement.'

She told me to be careful, I said I would, and I walked across to their house.

Major Rabbit opened the door almost as soon as I knocked.

'Hello, Peter,' he said cheerfully. 'You don't mind if I call you Peter, do you?'

I said that he could, and he replied that I should call him 'Doc' because everyone else did.

He squeezed my hand in his two paws, then beckoned me in. Although it was still light, most of the curtains were drawn and what few lights were on had only low-wattage bulbs with an orange colour bias, so the interior appeared gloomy, yet warm. There was a rich, almost loamy scent of fresh earth in the air, and in a prominent place on the wall was a circle of delicately braided copper wire that represented the symbol of their faith, the five circles of lifefullness. We had a cross, they had a circle.

'The Circle of Lifefullness,' said Doc, following my gaze, 'and the circle of trust. It also represents home, the burrow, the bounty of ovulation, the birth canal from which we all emerge, and the mother earth to which we all return. It is incumbent upon us all to complete the circle.'

'What *exactly* does that mean?' I asked, as the term 'completion of the circle' had always remained ambiguous.

Doc shrugged and stared at the braided copper circle for a moment, deep in thought.

'The linguistic translation is easy, but the cultural translation much harder. It's ... the completion of an individual journey of one's own making. For some, it's simple, like seeing all the *Die Hard* movies in order, or collecting versions of Spider Man mini-figures. For others, it's harder, like attaining a truth, or bringing about a change in others.

For me and Connie, it's about leaving this world in a better state than we found it.'

'That sounds a noble cause,' I said.

'It's a noble *goal*,' he corrected me. 'Ninety-two per cent of circles remain broken – which is why some rabbits go for mini-figures and *Die Hard*. If you really want to achieve your life goal, it's probably best to keep it fairly simple.'

UKARP and Smethwick had long been worried about the whole Bunty 'Completing the Circle' issue, and always maintained – without evidence – that a noble goal in the rabbit's eyes might not be one that was compatible with humans. Bunty, as far as Smethwick was concerned, was not a spiritual leader at all, but a leader-in-waiting, poised to a seditious overthrow of the UK.

Doc had gone silent and was standing on one leg, as was the custom when venerating Lago, the Grand Matriarch, and I did the same. Doc looked at me oddly, so I put my foot down again.

'Connie has met the Venerable Bunty, you know,' he said quite proudly. 'Worked on her staff for a while – and was present when the Bunty performed one of her miracles.'

'Which one?'

'Number 16b: the reattachment of an ear following an unfortunate accident with a bacon slicer.'

Bunty's apparent ability to perform miracles confirmed her divine status to rabbits. Although it made her a powerful spiritual leader, there was no evidence to suppose she wielded that power for anything but good. The Taskforce had different ideas.

'Your bunch should do a few miracles,' said Doc. 'If your archbishop made someone's missing foot regrow, it would give the credibility of your church a massive boost.'

'I expect it would,' I said.

'It doesn't even have to be that dramatic,' he added more thought-fully. 'A vicar levitating would probably do the trick just as well. I mean, *something*.'

'I'm not sure miracles are really the C of E's thing.'

'No? Hmm. Look here,' he said, suddenly thinking of something else and leaning closer, 'can you and I have a word? Man to rabbit?'

'Of course.'

'Connie said you knew one another quite well at university and …
well, you're not planning any hooky-doo, are you?'

'We were just friends,' I said, suddenly feeling defensive, 'nothing
happened.'

'My dear chap,' he said with a laugh, 'I'm not suggesting it did.
But correct protocol is always observed in rabbit marriages, so if you
make a play for the missus either above or below the table, I will
probably have to kill you.'

'What?' I said, suddenly taken aback.

'Not for *real* obviously,' he said, giving me a friendly nudge,
'symbolically. In a duel. Or even in a *symbolic* duel, where you concede
your beta-male status in a meek and self-deprecating fashion without
a shot being fired.'

'How would I do that?'

'Rolling over and weeing on yourself is the most usual form, but
a written note of apology and a decent bottle of Chablis will probably suffice.'

I paused, trying to get my head around the complexities of rabbit
culture.

'I admit I liked her,' I said slowly, 'but not like *that*. Besides, I've
not seen her for over thirty years, and she's your wife.'

'She's only "mine" so long as that's what she wants,' explained Doc.
'I'm here more by permission than commitment. She's not mentioned
a change in husbands, so until she does, I'll warn off any newcomers.'

'O–OK,' I said, still a little confused, 'but I'm not going to make
a play for Connie.'

'That's great news,' said Doc, clapping his paws together happily
and seemingly satisfied. 'I'm glad to hear it – and I'm very happy
we've managed to have this little chat. Come into the living room,
why don't you?'

We walked across the large oak-panelled hall and then into the
front room, where Connie was working on a large jigsaw that
depicted, as far as I could see, a huge meadow covered by thousands
of dandelions.

'Good evening,' I said, her large and very luxuriant eyes staring back at me. I guessed she hadn't mentioned to her husband about our meeting in Waitrose that afternoon.

'Good evening, Peter,' she said, stepping forward to give me a light hug as Doc looked on. '*Nhfifh hi hniffr i hffnuh*: our burrow is your burrow. Was your daughter not able to come?'

'A prior engagement. She sends her apologies.'

'Another time, perhaps?'

'Yes indeed.'

'I *must* just go and stir the stew,' she said, pausing on her way out to momentarily adjust a picture of Dylan Rabbit that was displayed next to a battered guitar. She turned back.

'Make yourself comfortable, have a chat and … I'll be back in just a jiffy.'

I watched her walk across the hall and back into the kitchen, and my gaze might have inadvertently strayed to her cottontail. When I turned back Doc was staring at me and I suddenly felt acutely embarrassed.

'So, Doc,' I said, eager to move the conversation on, 'you're a medical man?'

He laughed.

'No, no. The "Doc" epithet was the result of barracks banter. There was a certain … hazing that I had to endure before being accepted in the army. Copies of *Watership Down* and heads of lettuce left on my bunk, taunts about Mr McGregor and the always hilarious "What's up, Doc?" I'm sure you can imagine it.'

'Well, no, not really – but then I'm not a military man. Or a rabbit.'

Doc shrugged.

'We can't all be so lucky. Anyway, I took this all on the chin except the lettuce, which I ate. But the good thing about the services is that you win or lose respect solely on merit. Show some steely resolve and the species barrier evaporates. I won the respect of my fellow soldiers during some fun and games in Kandahar, but the "Doc" name stuck, so I use it to this day.'

'I heard you almost served in Afghanistan.'

Doc laughed again.

'Not strictly true. I was almost served *up* in Afghanistan. I weighed two hundred and forty pounds then, and was unlucky enough to be captured. After interrogation and discussions over whether I was haram or not, they were going to make me into a hearty meal for at least thirty-two hungry mujahedin. No British officer had been eaten since Suez, so Command put on a bit of a show on my behalf – close air support, artillery, the works. Want to see a memento?'

Without waiting for an answer he hopped to the dresser, opened a drawer and pulled out a walnut case which contained a set of antique-looking percussion pistols, each one decorated with engraved animals, and both with a barrel about twelve inches long.

'Without opposable thumbs, operating any sort of weapon is tricky,' he said. 'These have been modified to work with a squeeze action rather than a trigger. Here.'

He handed me a pistol that was beautifully made, all wood and brass and blued steel with a crocodile inlaid in silver on the butt. It was surprisingly heavy, but quite well balanced. I'd shot a .22 target pistol at school, and had won several prizes.

'A handy last-resort close-combat weapon,' he said. 'Takes a whopping three-quarter-inch ball. With a double charge of powder, a round can go clean through two people and then at least as far as "plumbers" in the Yellow Pages. They're my family's old duelling pistols, but I took them with me – so they've seen action in combat.'

He grinned, retrieved the pistol and placed it carefully back in the box. Despite the mildly threatening tone engendered by showing me the pistols and his warning earlier, I was intrigued, as duelling was a part of rabbit culture that was rarely talked about.

'Have you used them?' I asked.

'More times than I would have liked,' he replied, nodding his head in the direction of the kitchen, where we could hear Connie singing softly to herself. 'Nothing of any value was ever easily gained. I've had a few losses, too, mind.'

'How can you lose a duel and not be dead?' I asked.

He pointed to the neat bullet holes in his ears which I'd noticed when we'd met the day they arrived. There were about nine obvious holes, then others partially hidden by fur and several more which were more like nicks off the top and sides – and might easily have been mistaken for general wear and tear. There was one very near the base of his left ear, too – two inches lower and he would have been dead.

'Closest to the head wins the bout,' he said, 'and a miss is a lose. Some serial rabbit Lotharios have ears like Swiss cheese, but if your aim is too low you might kill someone by accident – and that would entail a heavy financial penalty for the family. Did you know the biggest cause of male rabbit bankruptcy is accidental rabbitslaughter during a duel?'

'I did not know that.'

'You know it now. My goodness,' he added, 'I'm being a *terrible* host.'

He moved in a single bounce to the drinks trolley, narrowly missing the light fitting as he sailed elegantly through the room. 'Fancy a snifter?'

'Whisky if you have it.'

'Never touch the stuff. Have you tried dandelion brandy? Distilled from root. Makes you piss like billy-o and has the kick of a mule.'

I read something that described dandelion brandy as 'the diabolical three-way love child of methanol, crack cocaine and U-Boat fuel'. I'd been warned never to even go *near* the stuff, let alone drink it. So I said, without so much as a pause:

'Yes, I'd like that very much.'

Major Rabbit poured me a large measure of an oily liquid that had a vague pink sheen and smelled of rose petals. He then poured one for himself and another for Connie, who had just returned.

'Here's to new friends,' said Connie.

'New friends,' replied Doc and I together.

The brandy tasted of cough mixture mixed with summer harvest, bilberries and sweetened paint thinners. It slid down the throat easily and apparently without ill effect. Then, like a volcanic caldera that had been rumbling to itself for several millennia and suddenly chose an inopportune moment to erupt, the brandy kicked into life. The colour in my vision shifted from red to green with a sound like crinkly cellophane and I felt the sweat suddenly stand out on my forehead. A warmth coursed through my body as though I'd been given a blood transfusion with hot chocolate, I suddenly felt exceptionally amorous both mentally *and* physically, and the image of Helena, Pippa's mum, popped into my head – but not when we were married or just before I lost her, but just after we'd met and couldn't keep our hands off one another.

'Wow,' I said, to the evident amusement of Doc and Connie, 'any more?'

'Steady, tiger,' said Doc with a smile, 'best enjoyed in small amounts.'

'We distil it in the basement,' added Mrs Rabbit, 'but not a word to Customs & Excise. They want to slap a tariff on it to match that on cognac. Shall we sit down?'

The table was laid in the large dining room next door, the dark oak panelling hung with paintings of Connie and Doc's relations, each portrait looking pretty much the same as the next, with only variations of costume to give an idea of gender or age. The furniture was old, dark and well used; I guessed the house came furnished. The children were already seated, and politely stood up as we walked in.

'These are our two wonderful children,' said Connie, beaming. She indicated the male first. 'This is Kent.'

Kent was dressed in jeans and a T-shirt which featured Patrick Finkle and the Rabbit Support Agency motto *All Life is One*. His two-paw squeeze was a bit lacklustre, and his fur felt stiffer than Doc or Connie's. It would not have surprised me to learn that he used gel.

'Good evening, Mr Knox,' he said politely, yet with a certain degree of teenage reluctance.

'Hello, Kent,' I said, trying not to sound a little patronising and failing.

'And this is Bobby,' said Connie, 'who will take her Rabbalaureate next June.'

'It's Roberta, actually,' said Bobby with a toss of her head. She had large brown eyes, but was less elegant than her mother in manner, and somewhat sulky; I was amused to see that rabbit teenagers are not much different to ours.

'Hello, Roberta,' I said. 'Baccalaureate, eh?'

'A *Rabbalaureate*,' she corrected me. 'Much harder, and for rabbits. Physics, philosophy, horticulture, European languages, economics, botany, politics and mixed martial arts with an optional module on weapons training.'

'Thinking of the military? Officer training?'

'No – childminding. Rabbits make excellent childminders. We're cuddly, natural parents, and if required will fight to the death to protect our children.'

Doc and Connie laughed politely.

'The idealism of young childminders,' said Connie.

'I have a daughter,' I said, 'Pippa. She's twenty, training in hospital management.'

'You must have *hundreds* of grandchildren,' said Kent.

'Humans have far fewer offspring in a litter and breed only occasionally, if at all,' said Doc to Kent. 'And aside from very large asteroids, steep staircases, mosquitoes and themselves, have no natural predators.'

'No shit?' said Kent with some interest.

'We've had them in a single-species school,' explained Connie apologetically. 'We're hoping their move to a human school will teach them a little bit more about the Niffniff.[34] Perhaps Bobby and your daughter could go shopping together?'

'I could ask her.'

'Good. Shall we be seated? Peter, you can take the head as you are the guest, and I shall sit here, next to you.'

We all sat down, and once I had placed a carrot-embroidered napkin on my lap Connie lifted the lid from a large tureen. The smell of stewed vegetables filled the room, and the effect was mesmerising. The Rabbits arched their backs, lowered their ears and breathed in deeply.

'That's quite—'

'Shh!' said Connie, and after a few more seconds of silent contemplation, twitching limbs and rapt enjoyment, they all relaxed.

'Goodness,' said Connie, 'the scent of meadowfield stew always makes me feel a little frisky. Is it hot in here or is it me?'

---

34. Niffniff was the Rabbity word for human; the term 'Fudd' is colloquial.

And she fanned herself with her paws.

'Does vegan stew stir you somewhat in the nether regions, Peter?' asked Doc. 'It does us. Big time.'

'Well,' I said, trying to be as relaxed as them over matters sexual, something that I knew dominated a good deal of a rabbit's thought processes – if not *all* of them – 'a good meal can definitely be part of the romantic process.'

'How interesting,' said Bobby in a sarcastic tone, and Connie shot her a threatening glance.

'We shall say grace,' said Connie, and they bowed their heads for a moment and thanked Lago, who gave herself so that they could be saved, and for the bounteous wisdom that she had brought through the Way of the Circle. Doc and Connie said it in English, for my benefit, but Kent and Bobby spoke in Rabbity.

'Do you say grace at home?' asked Bobby.

'Not usually,' I said, meaning 'not at all'.

'In our faith we say grace quite a lot,' said Bobby, 'and on many different occasions. Eating, pulling up vegetables, having a shit. It engenders humility.'

'We even say it before sex,' added Doc. 'Quite aside from the spiritual aspect, it takes half a minute to say and must be said in separate rooms, which heightens the tension in a delightful way, and also gives the other party time to skedaddle if they have second thoughts.'

'Is it anything like the Lord's Prayer?' I asked.

'The first and last lines are broadly similar,' he said after a moment's thought, 'but the middle is *substantially* different.'

'So, Peter,' said Connie, placing her paw on my arm, 'hungry?'

She was becoming more tactile by the minute. Doc coughed politely and she removed her paw.

'Yes, very,' I said, suddenly realising that if they knew precisely *why* I was hungry and tired – a long and frustrating day at RabCoT – they would think considerably less of me, probably kick me out of the house and Connie would doubtless never speak to me again. I didn't really like the thought of that.

Doc ladled out the vegetable stew, which tasted every bit as good as it smelled. I told Mrs Rabbit that it was perfect, and she smiled pleasantly.

'Are you still in the army, Doc?' I asked.

'Semi-retired. I picked up some shrapnel, lost two fingers, a nut and partial sight in one eye during an overhead mortar burst during that Kandahar number I was telling you about. I'm a freelance security consultant these days, so now I sell deniability.'

'I'm not sure I follow,' I said.

'Modern warfare is quite different from the old days,' he said, 'and the ugly spectre of accountability can seriously hamper flexibility in a swiftly changing conflict.'

'Can we move on?' said Connie. 'I'm sure Peter doesn't want to talk military politics.'

'Governments ask us security contractors to do the shitty stuff they don't want to put their names to,' continued Doc, ignoring Connie's pleas, 'so if things go tits-up they can turn around and say it was nothing to do with them. It's very lucrative, I assure you.'

'I'm sure it must be,' I said.

'So, what about you?' said Connie brightly, touching my arm again. 'What do you do, Peter?'

'I'm an accountant for a small firm in town.'

'Chartered?' asked Doc.

'No, payroll,' I replied, having been coached on my cover story. I could talk payroll software quite convincingly for about three minutes – coincidentally, the longest anyone has ever been prepared to hear about it.

'That explains the precision of the Speed Librarying,' said Connie. 'Where is Pippa's mother these days?'

'She's no longer on the scene,' I said in a quiet voice.

'Cancer?' asked Bobby, without a hint of how inappropriate this might seem. It might have been easier to let it go there, and I could have sailed high on the sympathy, but Helena was emphatically *not* dead, and it seemed wrong to suggest that she was.

'No, she's still alive.'

'In prison?' asked Kent.

'No.'

'Appropriated by another male?' asked Doc with sudden interest. 'Like in a duel?'

'No,' I said, 'she just ... lost interest in me. I don't think I was charismatic enough.'

'I can see that,' said Doc, sizing me up. 'Went for someone younger, did she?'

'A documentary cameraman,' I replied, getting used to the rabbit's straight-talking ways. 'They live in a converted barn in Tuscany.'

'We tend to die quite often so marriage rarely lasts for long,' said Connie. 'Predation, myxomatosis, duels, cars. The words for death and divorce are often synonymous. I've been widowed twice already. My first husband died twenty-one years ago.'

'I'm sorry to hear that,' I said. 'Was that ... myxomatosis?'

I was hesitant as myxy was still a sticky subject with rabbits. Even though developed and used as a form of bacterial pest control *before* the Event, the effects and contagion had carried over into the anthropomorphised population. It accounted for almost forty per cent of all rabbit deaths, with no effective vaccine yet in sight.

'No,' said Connie with a thoughtful sigh, 'not myxy – a Toyota Corolla. They ran over his head so at least it was quick.'

I tried to figure out how this might have happened, and Connie, sensing my puzzlement, added:

'Grassy verges still hold a special place in our heart. Never did find the driver. Husband number two was Dylan. Sort of laid-back but played the guitar well and was unflappable, an easy rabbit to love. There was a case of mistaken identity; his name was leaked and he was jugged by those animals at TwoLegsGood. I'd have fallen apart if it hadn't been for Clifford, waiting in the wings to pick up the pieces.'

I hope they didn't see me take a deep breath, and a soft flush rise to my cheeks. If they could by some miracle overlook my work at the Taskforce, they'd *never* overlook the hand I had in Dylan's death.

'I'd fancied Connie for a while,' said Doc, 'so it seemed quite natural to ask her. I'm just sorry that our happiness came on the back of such loss.'

She put out a paw and Doc held it tightly. He lifted his glass.

'To Dylan,' said Doc.

'Dylan,' said Connie.

'Daddy,' said Kent and Bobby.

'As you can see,' said Doc, 'rabbits talk truthfully about most things. Life is too short for hidden agendas, vapid posturing and mendacity. Lago's third circle is about the truth which follows truth. Lies, conversely, make for more lies, one after another. It darkens the circle, and a circle that is dark leads to imbalance, and collapse.'

'Collapse,' echoed the others in unison.

'Truthful about everything?' I asked, thinking perhaps the question over Helena gave me a free pass.

'Yes.'

'Why is Kent wearing an ankle monitor?'

'Burrowing without due care and attention,' said Kent, quite matter-of-factly.

'Really?' I said, but Kent hadn't finished.

'Burrowing without a licence; going equipped to burrow; reckless burrowing leading to property damage; causing death by dangerous burrowing; burrowing while under the influence; incitement to burrow; burrowing while under a two-year burrowing ban; belonging to a banned burrowing organisation; and failure to stop burrowing when ordered to do so.'

'Wow,' I said, 'they really threw the book at you.'

'Every single one a bullshit charge,' said Bobby. 'That utter twat Smethwick has engineered the judicial landscape to be skewed against the rabbit.'

'The reason Kent's not banged up,' said Connie, 'is that there were many rabbits involved and Kent was a small cog, a bagman, removing spoil. Kent got two years supervised probation; all the rest got between three and nine years in jail.'

'Only six of the 5,672 rabbits currently incarcerated are in prison for violence,' said Bobby. 'Most are in for burrowing offences or theft of root vegetables, neither of which we consider a crime at all.'

'Anything that grows beneath the soil is a gift from Lago,' said Kent. 'Root veg can't be owned.'

'Kent might have got longer,' said Doc. 'It was a good job RabSAg lent us one of their lawyers.'

The Rabbit Support Agency had been formed only three weeks after the Event, and had worked tirelessly – and mostly in vain – to improve rabbit/human relations. 'Our work is finished,' their spokesperson Patrick Finkle said, 'when we see a female rabbit as prime minister.'

'So, Peter,' said Connie, 'more dandelion brandy?'

'Thank you.'

Connie poured me another tot and I downed it eagerly. It was powerful stuff, and I felt warm and tingly all over.

The conversation turned to education cuts and the NHS after that, and the differing ethical benchmarks between medical and veterinary science.

'We'd like to enjoy the ridiculous amount of attention you pay to minor ailments,' said Doc, 'and in return, you might think more carefully about the huge benefits of euthanasia.'

And then Connie served up a blackberry parfait for pudding that melted on your tongue. Once the meal was over and the children had been packed off to do homework, Connie shooed Doc and I into the living room and said she'd bring in some coffee.

'May I ask you a question?' I asked as Doc poked the fire.

'Of course.'

'Yesterday, when I gave Connie the basket of carrots, you seemed angry. I was wondering—?'

'You must excuse me my temper,' he said with a trace of embarrassment, 'scrubbed carrots given to a married doe can really only mean one thing: spouse appropriation.'

'Oh,' I said, 'hence your comments about a duel.'

'Pretty much. It's a good job for you it was only the Autumn King variant. If it had been a Cosmic Purple there would have been no room for ambiguity and I'd ask you to name your seconds[35] and we'd be standing back to back at dawn on a foggy heath somewhere.'

'Oh,' I said, realising how this might have been a hideous faux pas, 'sorry.'

---

35. During a duel, one always has appointed trusted 'seconds' to assist and ensure fair play.

'Don't give it a second thought,' said Doc amiably, 'but if you *do* want to make a play for Connie and she's up for it, it'll be pistols at dawn.'

'I'm not looking to appropriate your wife, Doc.'

'Good thing too, old boy. Cigar?'

'No thanks.'

I thought for a moment.

'So what's your explanation for how you came to be anthropomorphised?'

'Do you know,' said Doc with a frown, 'I'm not sure it's ever been fully explained – or even if it's relevant. Some say it was a *spontaneous* miracle performed by Lago the instant she died at the hand of man, or alternatively, a *retrospective* miracle performed by the Venerable Bunty, but I'm not sure that's possible. Bunty herself thinks that it might have had a satirical component—'

'Coffee!' said Connie as she bounded into the room with an energetic flourish, and placed the tray on the table.

The coffee was, again, excellent, and after challenging me to a game of Scrabble that I lost in a spectacular manner to Connie's placement of Poxviridae[36] across *two* triple word scores for a total of 257^{37} points, the evening was soon over and they saw me to the door. I had enjoyed Doc and Connie's company more than I had anyone else's in Much Hemlock – Pippa excluded – for at least ten years. I remembered more clearly what I'd liked about Connie, too. Her charm, her range of conversation, and her mixture of good humour and perceptiveness. I suddenly found myself feeling a little stupid that I'd never looked her up.

Connie and I paused in the porch as she saw me out, Doc having excused himself to set the VCR to record *The Great Escape*.[38]

36. It's the family of viruses behind Rabbitpox, just one of several viruses potentially fatal to rabbits.

37. She used up all seven tiles and got a bonus fifty, in case you're wondering how she did this. 'Rid' was already placed, although I have a sneaking suspicion that since Doc placed it, he might have been assisting his wife.

38. Rabbits are keen on any film involving tunnelling, and still embrace the retro tech of VCRs.

'It's been a very pleasant evening,' I said, 'thank you very much.'

'Likewise and really good to see you again,' said Connie, staring at me intently.

'Yes,' I agreed, suddenly feeling all hot and flustered, 'too long.'

She moved forward and gave me a hug. Her fur was as soft as the finest cashmere, and when her whiskers stroked against my cheek I twitched involuntarily. We released each other and then, catching me by surprise, she pulled me back in and gave me a *second* hug, much tighter yet briefer. I was going to ask her why, but at that moment Doc reappeared.

'Goodbye, Peter,' said Connie, 'pop by any time.'

'Yes indeed,' said Doc, 'always up for a game of Scrabble, or a gambol in the fields. Do you like gambolling? In moderation there's nothing better.'

Gambolling in the meadows was a pastime peculiar to rabbits which involved sporadic jumping around on turf, usually just after sunrise, and best enjoyed when little was on your mind. Sort of like mixing jazz dancing and yoga.

'I've not tried it,' I said. 'I think our version might be quite close to golf.'

'Ah!' said Doc. 'Do you play?'

'No.'

'Me neither. Rubbish game. What about rugby or soccer?'

'No.'

'Glad to hear it. We *abhor* gladiatorial team sports. Why are you still bringing up your young men to be warriors?'

'Are we?'

'Looks like it. You may want to address that, along with the mummying and princeling stuff. You should reappraise the "death as entertainment" bullshit, too – I'm sure it's not healthy.'

'We don't use death as entertainment.'

'Not *real* death any more, agreed,' said Doc, 'but enacted *unrelentingly* in the movies and on the TV, it's got to be sending mixed messages, eh? Death brings only bereavement and loss, and killing is only ever an option if it is the last possible resort.'

'Often it is,' I said, inexplicably defending my own.

'If you *really* believe that is the case,' said Connie, 'then I think your species' somewhat strained relationship with the beneficial powers of compromise and reconciliation could also do with a reappraisal.'

'Yes,' I said after a pause, 'I think that's quite a valid point.'

'Humans talk a great deal,' said Doc, 'and seemingly understand how they *should* behave – but rarely do. All that chat without positive action is nothing but hot air. It's a mystery to me how you managed to get this far without imploding. Well, pip pip!'

I moved to go. Given Mr Ffoxe's directive I'd not broached the subject of the 'shoving off' fund, and didn't quite know how to tell the Malletts that I hadn't. But as it turned out, we *did* talk about the fund – I just wasn't the one to raise it.

'How much are they offering us to leave?' asked Connie once I'd taken a few paces from their front door. I stopped and turned back.

'It was suggested I should start the negotiations at seven grand,' I said after a pause, feeling emboldened by my own honesty, 'but I think they'd easily go to twenty and perhaps more. How did you know there was a fund?'

'There's *always* a fund,' said Doc.

'Can I be honest with you?' I asked.

'We ask for nothing else.'

'Most of the villagers are not desperately leporiphobic, just ignorant and easily led. It's the Malletts you have to watch out for. They've already talked about getting 2LG involved.'

Connie and Doc looked at one another. I got the feeling that anyone who tried to put Doc head first into a forty-gallon drum of gravy would have a serious fight on their hands.

'Once you start running you never stop,' said Connie in a low voice. 'Spread the word: we'll be friends with whoever wants to be friends, and trouble to whoever wants to be trouble. And believe me, we can be trouble.'

I looked at Doc, who raised himself up to his full height. Even if I was eight inches taller, a lot fitter, twenty years younger and, most importantly, brave, I'd still think twice about tackling him.

'OK,' I said, the threatening tone seemingly at odds with the rabbit's generally peaceful demeanour. 'I'll make sure the message gets across.'

'Good man,' said Doc, suddenly amiable once more. 'Drop around any time – always an open door.'

Connie gave me a wave, and the door closed behind them. I walked back to my house, thinking deeply about the evening's events. Of duels, meadowfield stew, the massive differences between our cultures and being totally thrashed at Scrabble when I thought I was a good player. But most of all, I was thinking about that second hug from Connie.

Labstock Bunshot

Only Wildstock carried the surname Rabbit. The laboratory rabbit designated MNU-683 was being used to test the effect of cosmetics on skin when the Event occurred, and the following morning politely asked the life sciences technicians: 'I say, would you mind toning that down a bit?' She was released the following week, but her descendants retained her alphanumerical surname as a sign of respect.

When I came down the following morning, my head felt as though it had nine hyperactive hedgehogs inside, all doing a poorly coordinated line dance. Despite this, I could see a beautiful relationship developing between myself and the mind-altering charms of dandelion brandy. Pippa was already up and dressed, making breakfast.

'How was the Welsh-Thai fusion restaurant?' I asked.

'The Welsh rarebit lemongrass was intriguing but not much else,' she answered, passing me a cup of coffee, 'although the cockles and lava bread Mumbles-style noodles more than made up for it. More importantly, how was your evening with the Rabbits?'

'A bit strange. I wasn't quite sure if I was a friend, or a messenger, or perhaps a bit of both. Either way, they seemed pleasant enough – all in all, hugely enjoyable.'

'How did they take to you offering them money to leave?'

'That would have been ... impolite after their good company. As it turned out, they were the ones who broached the subject.'

'And?'

'I don't think they're leaving.'

'That'll make the fur fly in the village.'

'Not *literally*, I hope,' I said, getting the Shreddies out of the cupboard. 'Oh, and Connie asked if you'd like to go on a shopping trip with Bobby Rabbit.'

She stared at me, open-mouthed.

'You set me up on a date with their son? Why would you do such a thing?'

'No, no, Bobby is their daughter – Roberta, you know, like in *The Railway Children*?'

'The one played by Sally Thomsett?'

'No, the other one. Look, they're new in the neighbourhood. They need friends.'

'What if someone sees me?'

'What if they do? Have you got an issue with rabbits?'

'No,' she said quickly, 'not at all. I'm not leporiphobic. It's just that, well, I find their holier-than-thou attitude a little tiresome on occasion. You can't get one on the telly for more than ten minutes before they start banging on about our long history of culling, skinning, eating and rabbit-proof fences. I mean, that was our relationship with field rabbits, not the anthropomorphised bunch – it's really very different.'

'I think they see all rabbits as one.'

'Well, OK – but I wasn't *personally* responsible, was I? And to go on about it all the time just makes me think they're milking the issue for political gain.'

'All I know is that Doc and Connie didn't mention any of that once, and seem pretty friendly. I think they might be loaded, too – when I visited the downstairs loo there was a Kyffin Williams painting in there that I swear was an original.'

'Hang on a sec,' said Pippa, suddenly getting annoyed. 'It's a bit rich asking me if *I* have an issue with rabbits when *you're* the one working at RabCoT.'

I paused. She was right. It was a little hypocritical.

'I do payroll. I'd be replaced in a heartbeat and nothing would change.'

'You'd be not working at the Taskforce. That would change.'

We stared at one another for a few seconds, and right at that moment I really wanted to tell her what I actually did, and my justification for doing it – for her, for the house, to pay the bills, for the future. But I didn't. I said instead:

'So will you go with Bobby on the shopping trip? It might be fun.'

She took a deep breath.

'OK,' she said, 'entwined paws and fingers across the divide and so forth.'

A horn sounded outside and Pippa grabbed her bag and her lunch, dumped them on her lap and scooted out the door.

I tidied up, then went outside at the usual time and found Toby waiting for me. This time, he was with his uncle. I think I might have smiled.

'Share the joke, Peter,' he said, 'we could all do with a cheery morning.'

I was thinking about Connie's comment that Norman's face looked like 'a pothole repair done in haste and on a limited budget', but thought perhaps he didn't need to know that right now.

'Just ... something I heard on the radio,' I replied. 'Want a lift into Hereford?'

'Would you?' said Norman. 'The car's in the garage. Carbon on the valves.'

The Mallett brothers were never very imaginative when it came to making up excuses.

So he hopped into my car and we were soon driving out of the village. I thought he wouldn't broach the rabbit subject until at least Fillprington – and even then with preamble, to make me think he was dropping it into the conversation. But he didn't. He only made it as far as Squirmley, and didn't trouble with any preamble at all.

'So, did you offer them the cash?' he asked.

'It's sort of a work in progress,' I replied after a pause for thought. 'I need to get to know them better before they trust me. Once they do, I think I might be able to be a little more persuasive.'

'You seem to know them pretty well already,' said Norman. 'You were in their house for three hours and twenty-two minutes, and you seemed very chummy when you said goodnight. Mrs Rabbit had her paws all over you.'

'Rabbits are very tactile,' I said, 'it's a waking-up-warm-bundled-snug-up-in-the-warren kind of deal.'

'You could have pushed her away.'

'And upset them? And have no influence?'

Norman stared at me for a long time without speaking.

'Very well,' he said eventually, 'you've got one more chance – and after that I call the local chapter of TwoLegsGood and ask them for input.'

'Is that really a good idea?' I said. '2LG can be a little spring-loaded at times.'

'Oh, don't get me wrong,' replied Norman, 'I'm the least leporiphobic person you know. I've got *absolutely* nothing against rabbits. Fine upstanding creatures, many of them, I'm sure – just not around here. They burrow, you know. And if their lefty next-door neighbour – that's you, Knox – and forty grand can't make them see sense, then we have to take more strident measures.'

'I thought the leave fund was only at twenty?'

'The Rabxit campaign has gained a lot of support, and from as far afield as Lower Ballcock, Shatner's Polyp, Titson-under-Spatchcock and Little Kapok. The word is getting about, and this family could be the thin end of the wedge. Once they get a pawhold, there's no telling where it might end. And yes, TwoLegsGood can be a *little* extreme, but when a way of life needs defending, sometimes desperate measures need to be employed.'

The rabbit issue used to be friendly chat over tea and hobnobs in the old days, but the argument had, like many others in recent years, become polarised: if you weren't rabidly against rabbits, you were clearly only in favour of timidly bowing down to acquiesce to the Rabbit Way, then accepting Lago as your god and eating nothing but carrots and lettuce for the rest of your life.

'What about the Spick & Span awards?' I said, suddenly having a brainwave. 'The judges are due any day now, and a thuggy TwoLegsGood presence in the village wouldn't look very good.'

It was a good argument, but Norman, always apt to weigh arguments carefully, eventually remarked after a long pause:

'We can win the Spick & Span award next year or even the year after,' he said, 'depending on how damaged the wisteria and planters are in the town square. But if the village is overrun with rabbits, it'll *never* be ours.'

Toby and I said nothing, so he continued, this time his voice more threatening.

'You get one more chance to buy them out, Knox, then we go to TwoLegsGood. Rabxit is happening – no ifs or buts – and in whatever fashion we deem necessary. Be smart and do a good job with the bunnies. Forty grand is our final offer, but come in under that figure and we'll give you ten per cent. You can drop me here and I'll walk home.'

I stopped the car, let him out and we drove to Hereford in silence, arriving at RabCoT half an hour later. We picked up a coffee each from the canteen, then wandered up to the office and started work: Toby on his usual work-a-day spotting, and me trying to find our rogue Labstock 7770. Flemming said little to either of us when she got into the office, being busy, apparently, with an open day planned at the MegaWarren building site next week, and Lugless and Whizelle turned up at ten. Whizelle sat down at his desk and occupied himself with the endless form fillery that was part and parcel of Rabbit Compliance, but Lugless walked over to me.

'How are you getting on?' he asked. He seemed almost amiable, which immediately made me suspicious.

'Nothing yet.'

'Keep at it,' he said, then: 'Oh, I reviewed those Labstock names you submitted to Mr Ffoxe last night and made a few changes.'

I suddenly came over all cold.

'Changes? What sort of changes?'

'I hope you don't mind,' he said, knowing I would, 'but none of the ones you suggested were *remotely* suitable to be used as an example of what happens when you piss around with the Taskforce. Half of those rabbits haven't been seen at all for over three years, and are probably unregistered dead – and the other half haven't been off-colony for six months. No, I went for four who were happily living here in the city and would be easier to pick up for questioning. They're in the cells downstairs at the moment. They won't have anything to tell us, but we'll have a go nonetheless. The message to the Underground and to the rabbit at large will be abundantly clear.'

I stared at him coldly.

'But don't worry,' added Lugless with a grin, 'I won't steal your thunder – I made sure your name was still on the memo. Here.'

And he placed the new list in front of me, patted me on the shoulder and went back to his desk. I stared at the small group of Labstock that Lugless had chosen. The only name I recognised was Fenton DG-6721, who was the prominent charity organiser. The DG-6721s were the largest group in the Labstock community. Their ancestor had been used to study the effect of unsaturated fat on the liver prior to the 1965 anthropomorphising. A troubled pre-Event life had left all Labstocks with an indelibly etched propensity to devote themselves to the service of others. While I sat there, feeling hollow and sick, Whizelle looked up from his computer.

'Do you want to prepare a report on your dinner at Major and Mrs Rabbit's last night,' he asked, 'or go for a verbal debrief?'

'You know about that?' I asked with dismay. I had achieved relevance at RabCoT, but not the way I'd hoped.

'There's not much we don't know,' said Whizelle in a smug manner, 'so what about that report?'

'I'm still getting to know them,' I said, not wanting to talk to anyone about anything, 'there's nothing *to* report.'

'You should know that Constance Rabbit is flagged,' put in Lugless. I turned to face him. He had his rear paws up on the desk and was idly using the eraser end of a pencil to extract an ear-bogey. He stared at the jammy brown object for a moment, then ate it. Toby and I looked at one another. Rabbits have very few objectionable habits, but eating their ear-bogeys was definitely one of them.

'Flagged?' I echoed.

'Yup,' said Whizelle, 'as someone ripe for radicalisation by the Rabbit Underground. The Dylan Rabbit connection kind of makes her someone with a potential axe to grind, and those sorts of rabbits should always be watched very closely.'

It would have been cheaper and easier and better for human/rabbit relations for Mr Ffoxe *not* to have outed Dylan Rabbit to TwoLegsGood in the first place, but I didn't say so.

'This is important,' said Whizelle, walking over to sit on the edge of my desk, 'so we're keeping you in the loop: the Rabbit Hostility

Evaluation Action Team have declared the LitterBomb threat to have amplified from Amber, "Attack Probably Planned, We Think", to Red, "Attack Imminent, We're Guessing", and whilst we're not saying Constance Rabbit is involved, she's ripe to play a part. She's just rented a house with seven bedrooms and even the most cursory of glances at her Co-op loyalty card buying patterns reveals a strong propensity for two-for-one offers – an act that is long associated with stockpiling.'

'Really?' I asked.

'We have also observed Major Rabbit at B&Q,' added Lugless, mistaking my comment as interest rather than scepticism, 'looking at spades and forks and seeds and suchlike.'

'Right,' said Whizelle, as though their guilt had already been established, 'potentially growing extra food for those hungry, outnumbering mouths – the red flags are fluttering right under our noses and we'd be idiots to ignore them. Like the Senior Group Leader said, you're to keep your ear to the ground as regards your next-door neighbours and report back if you see or hear anything suspicious. Get it?'

'Got it.'

'Good.'

He returned to his desk to pick up a paper bag of sugared woodlice, something weasels found particularly tasty, then left the office. Lugless carried on staring at me for a while. It was one of those hard stares, the sort a hungry spaniel might use to bore holes in a fridge once known to have contained a single sausage.[39]

He only stopped staring when the phone rang. He picked it up and, after listening for a few seconds, told the caller he would be there presently, then chose the heaviest hammer from his desk drawer and trotted out of the office. I gave him two minutes, then left the office myself to see whether Fenton DG-6721 actually *was* in custody, and if so, whether there was anything I could do. I headed towards the canteen first, the most likely place to find someone 'in the know' regarding who was in custody, but I didn't need to go that far as the rabbit riot had already begun.

---

39. If you've ever owned a spaniel, you'll know exactly what this looks like.

Rabbit Riot

Rabbits are especially good at crowd-crunching calculations. Most of the team are used as memory, with key calculators doing sums, and three others dividing the mechanics of the calculation amongst the others. With a little practice, a team of two hundred rabbits can calculate the square root of any given four-digit number to fifty-four decimal places in under six minutes.

To be honest, it was only dubbed a 'riot' later, by the leader writer of *The Actual Truth*, UKARP and the Compliance Taskforce. To anyone else, the rabbit themselves and even a dispassionate observer, 'super non-violent silent protest with maths' would be closer to the mark. Outside the building were eight rabbits standing in a line and staring impassively at the Taskforce headquarters.

'What's up?' I asked someone in the lobby.

'Some complete and utter twat put Fenton DG-6721 on an arrest list, and it's kicked off a riot. Pisses me off totally. The building will be put on lockdown, and I have the finals of the all-Hereford bell-ringing competition this evening.'

'There's only eight of them,' I said, looking out of the one-way glass into the street, 'probably just a flash in the pan. No, wait, I can see some more.'

To the right and left more rabbits were arriving, alerted over the grapevine as to what was going on. They'd dropped everything, tied the traditional protest bandana loosely around the base of their ears and taken their place next to their colleagues.

'What's going on?' asked Whizelle, who had just appeared from the records office. The disappointed bell-ringer – I think he was from Ethics – told Whizelle what was happening and I decided to creep back to the office and keep my head down. My name was on this. I'd been stitched up by Lugless good and proper.

Toby was already watching the riot unfold when I got back upstairs as our office gave an unimpeded view down Gaol Street to the left and right. In ten minutes there were twenty rabbits and that doubled in another half an hour.

'It will be impossible to get a decent cup of coffee in town right now,' said Toby, who always thought of practicalities, 'let alone a sandwich.'

Within an hour there were certainly a hundred or so, all standing in the road outside, ears flat on their backs. I could hear them murmuring, too, but not words – *numbers*. Rabbits weren't fond of glib and pithy yet ultimately meaningless political slogans so used protest longevity as their chief tool. Since that could get very boring, they took to crowd-crunching extremely tricky mathematical calculations to pass the time, which was oddly disconcerting as the murmuring made little sense to non-mathematicians and at a distance sounded soft and restful, like falling water. The rabbits remained fairly motionless during a riot, but would eventually start to keel over from dehydration or lack of sleep after a couple of days. At which point they would be removed to a tent to be revived – and then replaced by a fresh rabbit, who would have been queuing patiently to have the honour of participation.

The longest riot in history took place in Runcorn over the arrest of two juvenile rabbits accused of stealing a packet of Ryvita, which might have ended without drama but for a stubborn regional commander who refused to give in. It lasted ninety-six days. Mass-arresting the rioting rabbits, waiting until they dropped or even using water cannon and tear gas made no difference – they were simply replaced by more rabbits. Even cordoning off the location of the riot didn't work as the rabbits just shifted the protest a hundred yards to the left, and carried on as before.

The Runcorn Ryvita Riot was a resounding win by the rabbits and, as a mathematical crowd-crunching side note, led to the discovery of a fifteen-hundred-digit prime number that someone had missed. More importantly, it made the authorities concede, with great reluctance, that any rabbit riot had to be dealt with using dialogue and compromise if any useful resolution could be achieved.

The first mass email arrived within the hour, informing the building what we'd already been told fifty-five minutes before: we were on lockdown. The despondency soon gave way to a cheery school-end-of-term atmosphere, with everyone gathering in the corridors to look out of the windows, knowing that since they were semi-silvered, none of the rabbits could see in. While I tried to get some work done, we were interrupted by Dennis, the Taskforce employee who always organised the office sweepstakes: pick a rioter and if your rabbit falls over first, you win the kitty.

'The only slots that are left are the fifth, ninth and seventeenth rabbit from the right,' he said, a bag of tenners in one hand and a clipboard in the other. 'Can I put you down for one each?'

Toby obliged but I didn't. I made some excuse about having no cash.

After an hour of tantalisingly complex three-body gravitational mathematics, Patrick Finkle turned up with a Labstock that I recognised as Ansel DG-6721, a cousin of Fenton and the local representative of the Grand Council of Coneys. They both came to the front door of the Taskforce HQ and demanded the release of the four prisoners. They were told that this was quite impossible as, firstly, they weren't 'prisoners' but 'guests', and secondly, the release would require confirming who was in custody – which would be a potential breach of the rabbit's data protection rights. Finkle replied that if the Senior Group Leader wouldn't negotiate within sixty minutes they'd have a thousand rabbits outside within twenty-four hours and five thousand within the week – and an unwanted and potentially embarrassing civil disobedience on their hands.

'Do you think Finkle is kidding?' asked Toby when the news filtered back to us.

'No,' I replied, having heard numerous tales of Finkle's unswerving dedication to rabbits. It was rumoured he was in a relationship with one, but if he was, he kept it secret. Not out of shame, but because his partner's liberty would rapidly become a bargaining chip. The Senior Group Leader was already on his way in, and arrived fifteen minutes after Finkle and Ansel's ultimatum. I got the call I was dreading ten minutes after that, demanding I attend a meeting in the fox's office.

Mr Ffoxe was already there when I arrived, still dressed in his Sparco overalls as he'd been track-testing his racing Bentley when he got the call. He didn't look very happy. Lugless and Whizelle had been called down to join us along with heads of departments, Legal, Sergeant Boscombe and the local representative of RabToil, the government-owned company that oversaw the many work contracts the rabbit fulfilled. Nigel Smethwick was also there – coincidentally, as it turned out. Although he was prime minister, his constituency had always been Hereford East, and he still liked to maintain strong links with his core supporters.

His physical appearance, I noted, was at odds with his power and influence. He was a small and ineffectual-looking man without height, charisma or any memorable features. The sort of person you'd fail to recognise if you met him out of context, the sort of person who was pushed around a lot at school and who classmates remembered – if they could at all – as 'the quiet one'. These days he was about as cold and calculating as anyone you would ever meet, and his quiet demeanour and outwardly vanilla presence hid a steely commitment to task. He spent years at UKARP in the policy unit and barely anyone knew his name until he'd wrested control of the party in a surprise coup.

'So what are the numbers?' asked Smethwick who was accompanied by a small retinue of staff which included Pandora Pandora,[40] the Taskforce's public relations guru. She was tall and thin, habitually dressed in black and with her blond hair pulled aggressively tight into a ponytail. She had the sort of cultured voice that can only be acquired through wise investment in parents, and her assistants – she had many – all looked pretty much the same: blonde, slender, dressed in black. I think they popped them out of a factory somewhere in Shoreditch.

'We've got about three hundred outside right now,' said Pandora Pandora, consulting an iPad, 'and with a disgustingly aggressive threat

40. Improbably enough, this was her name. No one knew whether it was the result of unimaginative parents, a foolish error during her birth registration or taking a partner's coincidental second name on marriage.

from the Grand Council of Coneys and that loser Finkle to mobilise a thousand of them within twenty-four hours if their demands are not met.'

'Can they do that?' asked Smethwick.

'Almost certainly, Prime Minister,' said Whizelle. 'From Colony One via the free movement rule. I think we'll have to hunker down for a long wait given Fenton DG-6721's popularity. Of all the rabbits to arrest, Fenton was probably the worst choice of all.'

'The way in which he was detained might be interpreted by an unsympathetic judge as illegal,' added the in-house legal representative, 'and to the left-leaning public at large as extrajudicial overreach. They're not human, which is legally useful, but they're cuddly with big eyes, something the otherwise apathetic general public often finds irresistible. We're keeping a careful eye on the platforms to see what develops.'

'Social media?' said Lugless with a sneer. '*Balls*. This morning it was something about a celebrity insulting another celebrity, at lunchtime it was a video of a piglet in gumboots. By this evening it will be someone you've never heard of saying something vaguely controversial on a subject that until now you knew nothing about. The hashtag #rabbitinperil barely trends at all these days, and every bunny outside on the street mumbling about standard deviation is one less bunny causing trouble.'

Smethwick had been staring at Lugless, probably because he hated rabbits and here, standing closer than he'd ever been to a rabbit, was a rabbit who also hated rabbits. I think it was kind of confusing for him.

'Why was he arrested anyway?' asked Smethwick. 'Even I'd think twice about having Fenton detained. Justin Bieber and the Dalai Lama follow him on Instagram for Christ's sake. None of this will play well with the leftie press, who are already winding themselves into a lather over MegaWarren.'

'It was part of an ongoing investigation into the Rabbit Underground,' said Flemming, who, like her or loathe her, looked after her team. 'The threat of a LitterBomb has been raised to Alert Red status, and Labstocks recently came under suspicion.'

'Whose investigation?' asked Smethwick.

Lugless put up his paw and Smethwick, who I think was about to hand out a serious bollocking, decided not to. I think it wasn't so much that he hated rabbits, than he was frightened of them.

'Oh,' he said instead, 'and what evidence do you have Fenton actually *is* involved?'

'He was identified by one of our Spotters as a rabbit of interest, Prime Minister. One who might have Underground connections.'

And Lugless turned to face me. All eyes swivelled in my direction and my mouth went dry. I wanted to make a run for it, but I didn't think I'd get very far. I'd seen how fast Mr Ffoxe could move.

'What's your name?' asked Smethwick. It was the first time he had acknowledged me, even though I had seen him on numerous occasions, and been introduced twice.

'Peter Knox – Spotter Grade V, fifteen years' service.'

Pandora Pandora tapped a note into her iPad.

'Oh yes?' said Smethwick, unimpressed. 'And just how sure are you that Fenton DG-6721 was the same rabbit as that involved with the Underground? Give me a figure,' he added, as he knew how Spotters worked, 'a percentage likelihood of identification.'

I paused, then:

'Less than two per cent,' I said, truthfully enough.

'Two per cent?' he echoed. 'That's it? We've arrested a prominent rabbit rights activist on a lousy two per cent? What other evidence do you have?'

The silence in the room was palpable, and I shivered as a cold sweat seemed to run down my back.

'None,' I said, hoping Lugless would say that *he* had put the name up, but knowing he wouldn't.

Smethwick stared at me for a moment then turned to Pandora Pandora.

'Can you think of a suitable term that I could use to describe Knox?' he asked.

'How about "a low-grade moron"?'

Smethwick snapped his fingers and smiled.

'Spot on. You're a complete moron, Knox. I don't give a tuppenny

shit about rabbits who think they can manipulate the liberal media
into making us look like a bunch of reactionaries, especially with
the Rehoming in the air, but we need public support, Knox, and
after all the careful PR work we've done over the past two years,
arresting Fenton is just *beyond* stupid. How many prominent rabbits
did we *not* arrest that we wanted to arrest, Pandora? Ones we let go
so as not to rock the boat ahead of MegaWarren?'

'Probably hundreds,' said Pandora Pandora while gazing at me with
a special level of deep loathing.

'Exactly. Hundreds. What in hell's name did you think you were
doing?'

'I ... don't know.'

'You don't know? You put the Rehoming in jeopardy and that's
the best you can do? Well, you're finished. Fired for gross incompetence, which we can bump up to criminal negligence and
contravention of Taskforce guidelines – which means we can save a
bit of cash on pensions, too. Hell's teeth, am I surrounded by idiots?
Now—'

'One moment, sir.'

It was Mr Ffoxe. He had moved to my side with lightning speed
and laid a paw on my shoulder. It couldn't possibly be friendly
consideration for a subordinate, so he clearly had a play to make.

'Yes?' said Smethwick, suddenly interested.

'I think this could work to our advantage, Prime Minister. I say
we leave the bunnies for twenty-four hours, then tell everyone there
has been a terrible mistake for which we are hugely sorry, then act
contrite and pretend we have fired half a dozen people for incompetence. The rabbits, hoping to gain a PR victory out of this, will
have the rug pulled from under their hind paws. The riot will be
seen as a knee-jerk reaction as befits a creature that wastes no time
in milking outrage by resorting to the aggressive spectre of civil
disobedience. I'll even lead the apologies, which should be worth a
few column inches, especially if I can squeeze out a tear.'

Smethwick stared at him for a moment, wondering whether this
was a good idea.

'I'm with the fox,' said Pandora Pandora. 'A climbdown now makes us look small, sitting it out makes us look weak, attempting to break it up makes us seem like bullies – but an apology in twenty-four hours will appear magnanimous and even-handed.'

'Sounds like a good plan,' said Smethwick at last. 'Without knowing it, Knox might have done us a favour. That's what we'll do. Twenty-four hours.'

'So … I'm not fired?' I asked.

'Far from it, old chap,' said Smethwick, 'you could be in for a citation. Just be a little more certain in future, hmm?'

And he clapped his hand on my back. The meeting might have adjourned there and then but for a voice.

'I need a word.'

It was the representative of RabToil, and he was holding a mobile phone to his ear.

'No, I think we're done here,' said Smethwick, eager not to prolong the decision-making process any more than he had to, and eager to get back to schmoozing his constituents.

'The CEO of RabToil wants you to halt the demonstration right now.'

I saw Smethwick blanch, and he swapped looks with Mr Ffoxe and Pandora Pandora.

'He does?'

'Yes. The potential loss of rabbit work-hours would not be conducive to productivity as there is a large order for electric foot spas that we need to fulfil. We currently have thirty thousand rabbits on our workforce at Colony One, and a riot will likely reduce that by seventy-five per cent.'

He paused to let this sink in.

'Do what you need to do by all means, but causing unnecessary distress to our manufacturing clients solely because RabCoT don't know what to do with a few recalcitrant bunnies might cause … *nervousness* amongst foreign investors eager to bring their manufacturing projects to the UK.'

Mr Ffoxe stared at the ground, and Smethwick looked at Pandora Pandora for support.

'We'll need to hear that from the CEO himself,' she said.

'Sure,' said the rep, 'he's on the phone right now.'

He held up the receiver, but no one took the call. Despite Smethwick's power and agenda, when it came to the bottom line, RabToil – and in effect, big business – called the shots. Commerce was everything.

'Do it,' said Smethwick, 'let them all out immediately and issue a press release explaining that the rabbits in question were arrested owing to a … regrettable and wholly avoidable administrative error.'

'Shall I add the empty platitude "lessons have been learned"?' asked Pandora Pandora. 'And: "we *can* do better and *will* do better"? Those lies always play well when the tech companies use them.'

'Sounds good to me,' said Smethwick. 'You could also put in something about how we are "reviewing procedures" – that's another massive porker that always goes down well.'

Everyone laughed. Mr Ffoxe asked Pandora Pandora to jot down her press release as quickly as possible, and picked up the phone to order the rabbits to be released. I had been slowly backing towards the door as this happened, hoping my fortunes would not once again be reversed, and once outside the door I slipped unseen back upstairs. Within half an hour every single rabbit had vanished from outside; the only evidence they had been there at all were seventy-six bandanas tied around a lamp-post and the cube root of nineteen chalked on the road – to twenty-eight decimal places.

Shopping & Sally Lomax

The more outlandish conspiracy theorists suggested the rabbit had ambitions for *galactic* domination. Exponentially increasing reproduction would, mathematically at least, cover the globe with rabbits, then eventually expand outwards from the earth, first beyond escape velocity and eventually towards the speed of light – presumably carrying a capsule in front of the mountain of ever-reproducing rabbits. It was dubbed 'HyperRabbitDrive'.

Despite my misgivings, there was no fall-out over the incident with Fenton DG-6721, and neither was I asked to present more random names to be detained. After two more days of fruitless searching for Flopsy 7770 I was returned to other duties, something that rankled with Lugless, who complained bitterly to anyone who would listen that his investigation had been 'cut off at the knees'. He tried several times to restart the enquiry, but by Friday his investigation was on hold, his superiors citing 'unwelcome scrutiny from the biased press on the MegaWarren project' as the reason.

The weekend break was therefore something of a blessing, and Pippa and Bobby's shopping trip on Saturday seemed to go pretty well. They were quiet on the way in, but animated on the way out. Pippa seemed delighted with Bobby, and despite the enormous differences between their species, they had a lot in common: career, food, political activism, taxonomy (both belonging to the class *mammalia*), and feminism – the latter a subject upon which Bobby had some interesting thoughts.

'Before the Event we were a matriarchy, and as far as we were concerned everything worked really well. Males were basically body-guards, with payment in mating rights. The problem,' continued Bobby, 'was that the Event gave us not just some of the *physical* attributes of your species, but many of the social ones, too – including a switch to the patriarchal system. Almost immediately the bucks realised that under this new system they could do what they did before *and* hoover up some fringe benefits at the same time. Simply put, they wanted us all to embrace some of the more egregious male-centric bullshit you guys seem go in for.'

'How did you deal with it?' asked Pippa.

'Well,' said Bobby with a smile, 'for a rabbit, the power lies in the workers who control the means of reproduction, so we told them that unless they agreed to a nine-point gender equality constitution, it was strictly no sex of any sort.'

'How long did that last?'

'A seventeen-day shutdown was all it took, as it turned out.'

She laughed.

'Before my time, of course, but by all accounts they were climbing the walls. Mind you, so were the females, but when you feel that strongly about something, I guess sacrifices are always worth it.'

'What were the nine points of the constitution?' asked Pippa.

'Oh, the usual suspects,' she said, 'all the stuff you Fudds bang on about but are slow to implement. Strict gender split in governing bodies both on the institutional and corporate level was the biggest, as I recall. Simultaneously, we also formulated a long-term plan to water down the seemingly innate sense of male hierarchy entitlement, and head towards a goal of hard-wired pluralism.'

'By education?' asked Pippa.

'No,' replied Bobby. 'We decided to tinker with toxic masculinity at the evolutionary level, where we can make a lasting difference. Simply put, we're sexually sidelining the Byronic male rabbits with looks, aggression and drive in favour of breeding with the also-rans. The nice-enough, good-enough bucks who are – shall we say – less impulsive, less exciting, less willing to take ridiculous risks. Boring even. Evolutionary biology is a fascinating subject, but if you want to use it to bring about meaningful societal change, then you have to play the long game – I reckon we might see some results in a couple of thousand generations.'

'So some time next year?' I said somewhat daringly, but she took it in good humour, and laughed out loud.

'Or sooner. Exploiting unity and focus in the quest to effect change should never be underestimated.'

Pippa and I fell silent, pondering Bobby's words. The human version of unity and focus was probably more akin to vague agreement and self-serving muddling.

'So what do the males think about having their mysogyny being bred out of them?' I asked.

'We thought it best not to tell them. Not a word now, especially to Doc. He's a terrific stepfather – ambitious, fun, a born leader and with a never-ending supply of bawdy limericks – but Mum will have to head for someone less dynamic to father her next litter if she's fully committed to the machismo dilution plan.'

I thought about Connie and her talk of Rupert being 'not rubbish enough'. That must have been what she was up to.

'What if it doesn't work?' I said. 'What if it turns out you actually *need* your bucks like that for broad societal advantage, even *with* the pitfalls?'

'Then we'll reverse the policy,' she said simply. 'But look, if you don't try these things, you'll never know if they'll work or not.'

'Wow,' said Pippa, 'you really take your social issues seriously.'

Bobby smiled.

'It's a rabbit thing.'

'You are *such* a sweet darling!' said Connie when I saw Bobby to their front door at Hemlock Towers. Mrs Rabbit smiled and blinked her large eyes, and I could detect that warm earthy scent again.

Bobby asked Pippa whether she wanted to see her collection of Rick Astley memorabilia, and Pippa said, 'That would be totally awesome' and they disappeared into the back of the house somewhere. Where possible, rabbits avoided heights, and that included going upstairs. The rabbit version of the Extreme Sports Club centred around daring each other to climb to the top of a stepladder.[41]

'I think they got on quite well,' I said.

---

41. Oddly, they *could* deal with heights – but just didn't like to. Rabbits serving in the RAF saw it as their duty and soon got used to it.

'Seems so,' she said, and then, voice lower, added: 'Look, thanks for not mentioning to Doc we bumped into one another in Waitrose. Did I *really* pop a Little Gem in the fruit and veg section?'

I nodded, and she grimaced.

'A woeful reversion to stereotype – *most* regrettable. Sorry I legged it; there was a family emergency.'

'About Rupert?'

She looked at me quizzically.

'Who's Rupert?'

'The cousin you were having the affair with?'

She thought hard.

'I know thirty-four Ruperts, all are cousins and I've had affairs with nine of them. Could you narrow it down a bit?'

'On your father's sister's daughter's husband's mother's side?'

'Oh, *that* Rupert. No, it wasn't working out. I was sleeping with him but thinking about someone else. That never really works, does it?'

'I wouldn't know.'

'In any event,' she said, moving swiftly on, 'the family emergency was Diane Rabbit, who is my twelfth cousin on my father's aunt's sister's daughter's boyfriend's father's aunt's side. She was caught off-colony without a pass and I had to stand her bail. Have you ever been into the colonies?'

The colonies were mostly an underground warren: dark, warm, labyrinthine and a place where humans were traditionally not welcome unless expressly invited. I would visit, eventually, on the day of the Battle of May Hill, my first and last time. But that wouldn't happen for another two months, and I would see little except the basement of the meeting house and the spinney of trees on the summit.

I'd be there when it all ended.

'No,' I said, 'I've never been.'

'You should. They do tours now, y'know. Peek behind the species curtain, try some carrot gin, smoke some dandelion root, watch a live multiple birth, that sort of thing.'

Her voice trailed off and we stood in silence for a moment, staring at one another. I was thinking of the conversations we'd had back at uni, and I think she was too. We'd found there was little we couldn't talk about, and our conversations ranged far and wide. Sometimes political, sometimes about movies, sometimes about nothing at all. But for me at least, there was always something more to it than just chat and social intimacy. I had grown fond of her, no matter how ridiculous and impossible that sounded, and I always wondered whether she had felt the same.

'Well,' she said, breaking the awkward pause, 'you and I must have a catch-up some time.'

'Yes,' I said, 'I'd like that.'

And there was another long pause. I think she wanted me to suggest something, but again, I couldn't be sure, and felt sort of tongue-tied and stupid.

'What happened to Rosalind?' I asked, referring to the only other rabbit on campus. She'd been big into X-ray crystallography.

'Her co-researchers took a Nobel prize for physics,' said Connie, 'as animals weren't eligible for the prize at the time. She then worked at B&Q for a bit, and brought up eight children while deciphering Linear A[42] for fun. Last I heard she was fitting micro-wave doors for RabToil. What about your friend Kevin? Did he ever graduate?'

'No,' I replied, 'dropped out in the second year, bummed around for a decade, then got lucky, fell in with some whizz kids and made a killing just before the '08 crash. He lives in Guernsey these days.'

'Ah,' she said, and we fell silent again.

'Has it risen?' she asked.

'Has what risen?'

'The leaving fund.'

'I think you could almost name your price.'

She laughed, then told me she needed to marinade the carrots for supper, and I smiled politely and turned to go. I was about twenty

---

42. 'Linear A' is a Minoan writing system used between 1800 and 1400 BC, and was generally thought to be undecipherable.

paces away when I heard the front door close. She must have been watching me walk away.

Pippa returned three hours later, and vanished into her bedroom.

'Bobby must have a lot of Rick Astley memorabilia,' I said as she scooted past, thinking myself a lot funnier than I actually was.

She said 'Ho ho' and returned thirty minutes later in trousers, a plain blue blouse and a pair of Timberlands.

'Going out?'

'A party, with Bobby.'

'A rabbit party?'

'Yes,' she replied with a grin, 'a *wild* rabbit party. We're picking up Sally on the way. She's been very curious about rabbit parties but never had an invite.'

'Well, text me if you're going to be later than midnight,' I said, then added: 'Kind of plainly dressed, aren't you? For a party, I mean.'

'Bobby said you always dress down,' she said. 'Ostentation is frowned upon, and besides, it can get a little dusty in the warrens.'

'Wait, wait,' I said, suddenly worried. '*Warren*? You're going on-colony?'

She didn't seem put out in the least.

'Bobby will be there to look after us. *Tons* of people I know have done it. You're kind of a loser if you haven't.'

I said nothing for a moment.

'Loser means "uncool" rather than "idiot",' she said, trying to be helpful.

'I know what loser means. But the warrens, are they, y'know – suitable?'

'Hard-packed earth,' Pippa said, 'no stairs, smooth as asphalt. I can look after myself.'

'I know you can – it's just, well, I forbid it.'

She looked kind of puzzled. I'd always had a policy of allowing her to do whatever she wanted, try anything and be anything, so she was surprised at my attitude, rather than shocked by the order – which we both knew she could and would ignore. She was an adult, after all.

'Why ever not? Paws and hands across the divide – you know the score.'

Actually, she was right: going on-colony to a bunny bop was quite a common occurrence amongst youth, and you would be perfectly safe – Lago's fifth circle related to hospitality, which itself begets hospitality, completing the cycle of respect, understanding and tolerance. But my concern was different. If my name *had* been leaked to the Underground, they might try to get to me through Pippa. Paranoid delusion perhaps, but when it comes to being a father, paranoid delusions really hold sway.

'I can't tell you why you can't go, you just can't.'

'Dad,' she said, giving me the look Helena gave me when I had not the slightest chance of winning an argument, 'parental orders worked when I was thirteen. They don't any more. If you have a genuine grievance, I'm all ears – if not, I'm going.'

I thought for a moment.

'OK – but if asked, use your mother's surname.'

She paused for a moment, then said:

'If it makes you happy.'

'It makes me happy.'

A car horn sounded outside, and Pippa gave me a cheery wave, dumped her coat and bag on her lap and was out of the door in a flash. I followed her outside, where Bobby was standing beside another large American car that I learned later was a Chevy Impala, probably from the seventies. It was a licensed RabCab in the usual orange and green livery, and the uniformed driver, I noted, was a male Labstock, features partly hidden behind dark glasses. He climbed out to assist Pippa into the car, and as I stood there feeling worried and silly and fathery, the low sunlight caught his long and elegant ears, and my heart missed a beat.

He had the pattern of capillaries in the shape of a squashed Tudor rose in his left ear.

He was John Flopsy 7770. There, in the fur, right in front of me. Living, breathing.

Shit.

While I was rooted to the spot wondering what to do, he returned to the driver's door, then turned and, seeing me staring at him, lowered his dark glasses and winked at me with the click of his tongue. He then climbed into the car and a few seconds later they were off in a sedate manner down the lane.

I took a mental note of the number plate as they drove away, then waited until the car was out of sight before hurrying indoors. *Always assume that if you can see a rabbit, they can see you.* I ran into the kitchen, picked up my mobile and dialled the RabCoT Crisis Room, which was on Speed Dial One disguised as 'Aunt Vera'. All I needed to do was to pass them the details of the car and the duty sergeant would be on to it. Given the importance of this particular Flopsy, there would doubtless be a hard stop before they even got as far as Hereford.

I gave the controller my name and employee number, and they asked me, as was standard practice, to answer 'that's right' if I was being coerced or had in any way been compromised. I told them I wasn't and hadn't.

'Pass your message.'

I opened my mouth to speak, then shut it again. Since Flopsy 7770 had been flagged by Lugless as 'seditious', 'highly wanted' and a 'serious bounce risk' there would quite likely be weapons involved in the hard stop – and Pippa was in the car.

'Oh,' I said, trying to think quickly, 'wrong number. I actually need to speak to Human Resources. I'm not going to be in work tomorrow.'

'It's Sunday tomorrow.'

'Monday, then,' I said. 'I'll call them in the morning. *Monday* morning.'

The duty officer asked me again whether I was OK, then, satisfied I was either an idiot or drunk or quite possibly both, rang off.

I put the phone down and leaned on the edge of the kitchen table, trying to calm down. Pippa was just going to a rabbit party with Bobby and Sally. She'd been to dodgier parties with worse people. Pippa was sensible. She'd text me if she needed anything. And as for Flopsy 7770, he was a RabCab driver. All journeys were logged. I'd have his name first thing Monday.

I wandered into the living room and watched *Mastercook* on the telly, which featured, unusually, a bright-eyed Wetstock named Sue

Patton Rabbit. She apparently ran a fashionable bakery in Brick Lane called *Empire of the Bun*, although I hadn't heard of it until now.

'Well, Sue,' said Greg, 'what will you be cooking for us tonight?'

'I thought I'd start with carrot three-way,' she said a little nervously, her ears covered by a tall chef's hat, 'with a carrot jus, carrot crumble and quintuple fried baby carrot.'

'OK,' said Greg, 'and for the dessert?'

'Carrot soufflé,' said Sue, 'with a caramelised carrot sauce and crumbed carrot sprinkles.'

'Hmm,' said Greg, 'you don't think that the taste of carrot might dominate the meal?'

'I'm counting on it.'

'OK – you've got sixty minutes to make your dream a reality.'

Sue carefully chose her ingredients from nineteen separate carrot varieties, and then started chopping.

'You don't wash off the earth?' asked Greg, peering over her shoulder as she prepared the carrots.

'It adds a little frisson to the three-way,' said Sue. 'My sister likes to throw in an earthworm or two for good measure but she was always a little bit crazy like that.'

Just then, the doorbell rang. Not on the telly, obviously, but for real. It was Toby.

'She's out with Sally and Bobby,' I told him when he asked whether Pippa was in.

'Sally and *who*?'

'Bobby Rabbit,' I said, 'who lives next door. They've gone to a party.'

'She's gone to a bunny bop with Sally and a buck rabbit?'

'Bobby's a girl,' I said, 'short for Roberta. Like in *The Railway Children*.'

'Ah – Jenny Agutter.'

'That's the one. And look, even if away from work, we should actually say *rabbits* these days. "Bunnies" isn't—'

'Yeah, I know. Political correctness gone completely bonkers. They *are* bunnies in the same way that we *are* humans. Besides, they call us "Fudds", which is equally offensive and basically just reverse specism.'

'I'm not sure that it is.'

'What isn't? The offensiveness or the reverse specism?'

'Both. I think it's a false equivalency.'

He shrugged.

'Whatever. I never knew Pippa was friendly with rabbits.'

There was a perjorative lilt to the 'friendly with rabbits' comment. It was one of those British phrases, along with 'May I help you?', that can be either exceedingly polite or hugely aggressive.

'Pippa is friendly with anyone who wants to be friendly with her,' I said.

'She might have told me she was going out,' he said. 'I'd turned down several parties to be with her.'

There was a sense of Pippa ownership about him that I suddenly didn't much like. His politics had always been suspect, and he wasn't much fun as a co-worker. Actually, he was a pain in the arse. Rarely got the teas, endlessly cozied up to Whizelle and Flemming and never did a Danish-and-decent-coffee takeout run to Ascari's. In an instant, I decided that I no longer wished to give him the benefit of the doubt in the likeability stakes.

'I'll pass on your comments,' I said, now wondering when Pippa was going to dump him, and whether I could devise any strategies to assist in that direction. He paused for a moment, jangling his keys in his pocket with indecision.

'Is there anything else?' I asked.

'May Hill, right?'

He didn't really need to ask. The next-closest colony would be Bodmin. So after bidding me good evening, he departed.

When I'd made some coffee and got back to *Mastercook*, Greg was trying out Sue Rabbit's meal.

'I'll be truthful,' he said, 'I'm not a big fan of carrots, but there are a host of warm subtleties that play off one another in an unexpectedly exciting way.'

All the guest chefs had similar comments, which were delivered in a state of shocked bewilderment. I got the impression that Sue Rabbit had been brought in to tick some boxes somewhere, and wasn't expected to go anywhere in the contest.

'That is quite, quite brilliant,' said Greg, tasting the carrot soufflé, which collapsed beneath his spoon with a contented sigh, 'although perhaps a little more sugar.'

Sue Rabbit easily made it through to the next round, and I then fell asleep while watching the director's cut of *While You Were Sleeping*, and was woken by a car door banging and the unmistakable burble of a large V8 engine. I looked at the clock. It was two in the morning. The front door creaked open; we never locked it.

'Still up?' asked Pippa once I'd walked to the hall.

'I fell asleep in front of the TV.'

'Sorry,' she said, realising I'd stayed up for her. 'I would have texted but my phone got stolen.'

I leaned down to give her a hug. She smelled of soil, brandy and dandelion tobacco.

'Not a problem,' I said. 'Hello, Sally.'

'Hello, Mishter Knoxsh,' slurred Sally, who was leaning against the door frame, much the worse for wear and with her skirt on backwards.

'So,' I said, 'anyone want tea?'

'No thanks,' said Pippa, and made for her room, pushing Sally in front of her with a foot. 'Sal needs a shower and then we're going to bed. We'll tell you all about it during breakfast.'

'I'd like to pre-order a bucket of coffee,' mumbled Sally, 'and a paracetamol the size of a dustbin lid.'

I waited until I heard the shower turn on, then called Mrs Lomax to tell her Sally was OK and she could pick her up tomorrow. We'd actually spoken three times that evening already. She'd suggested coming over with a Lancashire hotpot that was 'way too much for one'. This wasn't the first time she'd proposed a cosy late-night tête-à-tête since Mr Lomax passed away, and it wasn't the first time I'd quietly refused, even though Pippa and Sally had both suggested on numerous occasions I invite her around. 'You won't be disappointed,' Sally had told me in a comment not really awash with ambiguity.

'Colony One?' Mrs Lomax had said when I'd told her where they were going. Traditionally, she had little to no idea of what her daughter got up to. Sally was the same age as Pippa, and Mrs Lomax, like me, often had difficulty coming to terms with the fact that the little girls we remembered so fondly were now fully grown-up women who did fully grown-up woman things.

Tittle-Tattle and Toast

Buttons are tricky for rabbits to manage with paws; zips ditto. Velcro would be usable, but is regarded by rabbits as: 'a hideously inelegant method of clothes fastening'. Buttons *can* be done up by them, but it's a two-rabbit job and requires specialist tools. The human equivalent would be 'trying to mend an aneroid barometer in boxing gloves'.

The following morning over coffee they told me about the previous evening. Rabbit parties, I learned, were pretty wild. There was loud music, booze, fights, impassioned political discourse, more fights, more music, more booze – and a lot of sex, usually in cosy side burrows at regular intervals. But it was the music that impressed Pippa the most.

'It's kind of like swing and jazz and mambo all at the same time,' she said, 'and played with such gusto. The trombonist actually *died* of a brain haemorrhage during his solo and the next number was dedicated to him – then everything just carried on as before. They have a zest for life that we don't possess; as though they need to pack as much fun and good living into their lives as possible.'

'Rabbits have high mortality issues what with disease, foxes, industrial accidents and trombone solos,' said Sally, who was now wearing dark glasses, avoiding all sudden movements and speaking in a quiet voice, 'so have to live life to the full, just in case.'

'Makes sense, I guess,' I said. 'What's it like inside Colony One?'

'Like you see on the documentaries,' said Pippa, 'centred around May Hill but mostly below ground, and highly ordered. Tidy, neat, zero crime and not a speck of litter anywhere. We were in a subterranean club called The Cottontail Club. While everyone danced bits of dry earth fell from the ceiling. I asked Bobby about whether there were ever any collapses, and she said there were – frequently – but they just burrowed themselves out, and to keep close to her, just in case.'

'So she looked after you?' I asked.

'She was great. Sally and I were being given some verbal over the ecological impact of our toxic anthropocentric agenda, and Bobby led a robust discussion group in which we concluded that the notion of "ownership" needs to give way to "custodianship", and that individuals *must* shoulder responsibility for groupcrime – even if they do not know they are doing it or even agree with it – and should atone for their de facto complicity by working ever harder to effect change, and consider restorative justice options. It was quite humbling, but empowering, too.'

'Can you stop talking so loudly?' said Sally. 'Or just stop talking? I'm really not feeling so well.'

I poured her a glass of water and put it next to her. She groaned, and took the tiniest of sips.

'Who drove you in?' I asked as casually as I could. 'Was that a RabCab?'

'An ex-boyfriend of Bobby's named Harvey,' replied Pippa.

It was the sort of information I really didn't want to hear. A rabbit's social circle was immensely strong, inclusive and supportive. If Harvey was an ex of Bobby's, he'd know Doc and Connie well, too – and I knew how the Taskforce worked, and how everyone could be implicated.

'Bobby and Harvey are still good friends,' said Pippa, 'Harvey was there at the club with us.'

'Really?' I said.

'Yes. He and Bobs and two others were talking about how they could suspend the Rehoming of Rabbits Act until a Pan-European Humanlike Rights panel can discuss and advise on the Rabbit Equality Issue.'

'Sometimes I think that was why Nigel Smethwick was so glad for us to leave the EU,' I said, trying hard not to think about Harvey, 'so no one could legally challenge the UK's record over rabbit rights and the introduction of the maximum wage.[43]'

'Give equal rights to rabbits and it makes no sense not to give it

---

43. For a group so reviled, the rabbit's cheap and skilled labour force was essential as an economic safety net after Brexit. 'Without the rabbit's good nature and industry,' said Finkle, 'the UK would be on its knees.'

to cows,' murmured Sally, face firmly planted on the tablecloth, 'or horses or bats or sheep. That's the bigger issue here. The inherent rights of *all* life to enjoy the bounteous fruits of the biosphere – and not in a shared, abstract sense – but as a unifying concept for sentient life.'

She then groaned and said she felt she wanted to die, but somewhere glamorous, like Powys.

'Why Powys?' I asked. 'It's a pretty county, but I'd hardly call it glamorous.'

'Not *Powys*,' said Sally, face still flat on the tablecloth, '*Paris*. Excuse me.'

And she got up and fast-staggered out of the room in the direction of the toilet. I turned back to Pippa, who was staring at me.

'Dad?'

'Yes?'

She looked down and traced the pattern on the tablecloth with her finger.

'You, working for the Taskforce. Do you really think that's a good idea?'

Conversations about the Rabbit Equality Issue always led to discussion of the Compliance Taskforce. She'd probably talked about it a lot with Bobby and Harvey the previous evening.

'I'm a junior accountant, darling, an infinitesimally small cog. I'm not leporiphobic; my employer is irrelevant to me.'

I got up and walked to the sink with my empty cup in order to hide the hot flush that had risen in my cheeks. There was another pause and I heard Pippa take a deep breath.

'Dad,' she said, 'you don't know the first thing about accountancy. You can barely add. You're a Spotter. You ID rabbits for the Taskforce. I've known for years.'

'What? Oh – well, yes,' I said, then to cover for the lie, I lied again: 'We're forbidden to tell family members for security reasons.'

The hot flush in my face deepened, and I stood there at the sink, my back to Pippa, speechless. I felt ashamed of working there and of lying, but the short exchange also made me feel, well, *relieved*.

'I don't guide policy,' I said, still with my back to her, 'or undertake any anti-rabbit activities personally. I just recognise rabbits for forty hours a week, and check they're being honest. If they were honest to begin with, I wouldn't have a job. Besides,' I added, trying to normalise my position through repetition, 'given that I'm unusual in wanting to do my job properly, I'm actually a net *positive* to the whole issue. If I didn't do it, there'd only be someone far worse in control.'

'Hmm,' said Pippa.

'It helped with you, too,' I added, 'we always needed a little extra. Putting in a wet room and your bedroom downstairs, that sort of stuff.'

'Don't put this on me,' she said, her temper rising. 'I can do stairs if I want – and a bath too, at a pinch. Is Toby one too?'

I paused, then nodded.

'Well,' she said, 'that makes it easier to dump—'

'You need more toilet paper,' said Sally, lurching back into the room, 'and you may want to put the hand towel in the laundry.'

'Don't worry about it.'

With Sally present the conversation moved on, and she was picked up by her mother soon after. But instead of the usual touching of her pearls, shy smiles and oblique references to her underused time-share in Palafrugell 'with a view of the sea from the bedroom', Mrs Lomax glared at me savagely – as though it were entirely my fault that Sally was in a state.

After that, Pippa went to do an online training course on how to spot evidence of radicalisation amongst rabbits in the workplace, and I, since it was a Sunday, to wash the car and mow the grass. I did both on autopilot, wondering whether I should tell Lugless about Harvey's identity. The only really good news about recent events was that Toby now had a greatly reduced chance of becoming my son-in-law. But if Pippa had known for years I was a Spotter, it wouldn't take Connie too long to figure it out.

The rabbits were also out in the garden. Major Rabbit had his jacket off and was digging the lawn into neat furrows. Every now and then he would stop and mop his brow with a red-spotted handkerchief, which was pretty pointless as rabbits, being fur-bearing, don't sweat. Connie, by contrast, was sitting on a sun lounger in the tiniest bikini imaginable while reading a copy of *Ludlow Vogue*. Her figure, like those of nearly all female anthropomorphised rabbits, was very humanlike, with bulges and curves in all the right places. By the way in which the post-church-service pedestrians slowed down as they walked past, I wasn't the only one who thought this. It wasn't long before the Malletts turned up.

We nodded greetings, then Norman lowered his voice and began:

'I'm not sure this is the sort of village where rabbit females should disport themselves almost naked,' he said, his eyes not leaving her form for one second. 'Flaunting herself in that manner is unhealthy for our young men – might give them ideas.'

'Semi-nudity encourages unsound moral behaviour,' agreed Victor, also staring, possibly to make *absolutely* sure he disapproved. 'Women should be chaste and demure, lest they lead men into temptation and precipitate their fall.'

The brothers nodded their heads vigorously, unaware they were talking crap, while still staring, eyes like organ stops.

'Hell's teeth,' said Norman, suddenly noticing Doc, 'is Major Rabbit digging up the lawn? Mr Beeton spent thirty years cultivating that piece of turf into the finest slab of green this side of Mansell Gamage, and what's more, it was going to be one of our major selling points to the Spick & Span judges: "so smooth we could play snooker on it – and have".'

'I'm not sure why you're telling me all this,' I said. 'Why don't you take it up with the Rabbits?'

They looked quite taken aback.

'What's the point? So long as you do your job and persuade them that Rabxit benefits us all, the problem will be over. Have you mentioned the leaving fund?'

'Not yet.'

'Well, don't dally. Wait a moment: what's that indentation on your lawn?'

I'd noticed it earlier: there was a mild dent in my garden only ten feet from where it shared a common boundary with Hemlock Towers.

'It's been there for a while,' I lied, 'the remains of a garden pond.'

'Ah,' said Victor, 'love a garden pond, me. Restful. Takes one's mind off the pressures of life.'

I wondered what possible pressures Victor Mallett could have to contend with. Cosy retirement, enviable social position, a compliant wife who cooked and cleaned, and, as wagging tongues had it, an extramarital love interest over in Bobblestock.

'Yes indeed,' he continued, 'life can be tough, but thank God I have the strength of character and humility to endure. Have you seen Toby, by the way? He wasn't at church and Granny Mallett had to give the lesson on forgiveness and tolerance on her own.'

I told them I hadn't, and they stared at Connie in her tiny bikini one last time – then made disapproving noises and moved off.

Once they'd gone, Doc sauntered over.

'Trouble?' he asked.

I decided not to mention their comments about Connie, so instead repeated their remarks about digging up the lawn.

'I think you'll find,' said Doc, 'that fresh veg in neat lines, bean poles tied with natty green twine, cloches sweating with early-morning dew, seed packets on lolly-sticks in crumb-crisp soil, and all weeded to perfection, has a simple elegance that the judges will find hugely attractive. Veg is the thing, Pete. Exquisiteness merged with edibility, form merged with function. Consider,' he said, eyes half closed, 'the taut skin of a ripe courgette, the rough hardiness of an unearthed spud, the reassuring yet somehow saddening *snick* one hears when snapping the tap root on a carrot when pulled.' I nodded, but he wasn't done. 'The thud of a windfall apple against mossy ground, the colour of peas as the pods ripen to burst. The furry lining of a broad bean pod, the way raindrops settle on a ripening lettuce head.'

He sighed deeply, then turned to me with a smile.

'OK, I'm done.'

'I agree with you veg-wise,' I said. 'It's just that the village take the awards very seriously; in thirty-six years the closest to a Spick & Span we've ever got was a "Merit" due to Mrs Ponsonby's wisteria in 1997 – and even then, I think they only gave us the award to annoy the village of Mansel Lacy. And look, what's this?'

I pointed at the indentation in the grass on my side of the hedge, and he bounced clean over the hedge to have a closer look.

'Subsidence,' he said after thumping a rear paw on the offending dip. 'Probably a sinkhole or something.'

'We're on gravel,' I said, 'I don't think that's very likely. That fence post looks a bit squiffy too.'

I pointed at a fence panel that had fallen out of skew. It was on a direct line between the dent and the Rabbits' house.

'I'm not sure what you're driving at,' said Doc, drawing himself up to his full height. 'Do you think *we're* involved? Tell me what you're thinking. We like to be straight about things.'

'I'm thinking ... perhaps ... burrowing?'

Doc showed me his paws. His nails were in pretty good shape.

'Do I look like a burrower?'

'I'm only trying to help you,' I said. 'The villagers are looking for any excuse to complain.'

'Let them,' he said, 'and just so we're clear: we're here to stay, Peter. Only a fox or a gun will get us out of here.'

'A fox?' I asked.

'Where?' said Doc, suddenly looking around nervously.

'No, I mean have you seen a fox around the village?' I asked, suddenly worried that the Senior Group Leader might escalate his interest in Doc and Connie.

'Not seen or heard or smelled,' said Doc, 'they switched from Hai Karate aftershave to Old Spice when we figured out that's what they were using to mask their scent. Cunning, you see, always ahead of the game.'

And we were both silent for a few moments.

'Well,' I said at last, 'you've every right to live where you want. Just don't tell anyone I said that. And for goodness' sake, be careful.'

'Rabbits are born careful,' said Doc, patting me on the back, 'it's our edge. That and large litters, early sexual maturity, a short gestation period and an easily exploited niche in the ecosystem.'

He took out his pocket watch and stared at it for a moment.

'How about that,' he said. 'The cricket's just started. Nothing like the crack of leather on willow to round out a Sunday. Rabbit 1st XI versus the MCC: should be a corker.'

'I thought you didn't like gladiatorial contests?' I said.

'Nothing even *remotely* gladiatorial about cricket,' he said with a snort. 'It's a craft, not a sport. See you later.'

And with a single hop he bounded across the hedge into his garden, and then into the house by way of an open window. There was a crash as he landed on some furniture, followed by some choice words and an admonishment along the lines of 'what damn fool left that bloody table there?' to which I heard Constance reply: 'You did.'

I went inside once the lawn was mowed, meaning to tell Pippa the latest on the Malletts, but she had something unusual of her own to contend with.

'What do you make of this?' she asked, handing me the phone. 'I lost my mobile and this is all I get when I ring my own number.'

I listened intently down the line to a series of softly spoken squeaks and sniffing noises, interspersed with short gasps.

'It sounds like Rabbity,' I said. 'You could ask Bobby to translate.'

'I know,' said Pippa. 'I asked her over, that's probably her now.'

There was, indeed, the sound of thumps growing closer from outside, and true to rabbit form – they regarded doors as less of an aid to privacy, and more as something that simply stopped draughts – Bobby bounded into the kitchen.

'Good morning, Mr Knox,' she said with a grin, clearly unaffected by the previous night's revelry. 'Hello, Pip. What's the problem?'

Pippa handed the phone to Bobby, who listened intently for a few moments, then broke into peals of squeaky laughter.

'What's so funny?' I asked.

'It's *Madame Bovary* being read out loud in real time,' said Bobby. 'Rabbits are very into French literature at the moment, and phones are often hijacked to help rabbits on the production lines deal with boredom through the injection of a little Flaubertian virtuosity. There'll be an announcement by the reader at the end asking if you'd like to pledge a few pounds if you liked it. They'll do anything to make money in the colonies. *Madame Bovary* is a firm favourite – kind of racy, you see – Emma would have made a fine rabbit. Best of all, it pisses off UKARP – they're not fans of any literature that isn't British.'

'OK,' I said, 'but what do we do about Pippa's phone?'

'Just tell your provider. They'll soon shut them down. Hang on a second.'

Something on the telephone had just caught her attention. Her ears twitched and she grimaced.

'Oh-oh,' she said, 'Rodolphe's left a note in a basket of apricots. Will he? Won't he? Will they? Won't they? Oh … *dang*. Never saw that coming.'

She pressed the *off* button and handed back the phone.

'Flaubert never gets boring, does he? 1 hope for your sake they haven't been calling the other colonies on your mobile. Rabbits have lots of cousins, and they do like to chat.'

She looked around, then expertly scratched her ear with her left foot while balancing on her right.

'I can smell coffee,' said Bobby, 'any going begging?'

So I poured her a cup of coffee as Pippa called Vodafone Customer Support, who suddenly became *really* interested when she explained that rabbits were involved.

'They're connecting me to the Fraud Department,' she whispered, hand over the mouthpiece.

'Are you going to see Harvey again?' Bobby asked Pippa once she'd had a sip of coffee. 'You and he seemed to hit it off *really* well together.'

Pippa glanced at me then glared hard at Bobby, who said: 'Whoops', and her ears went flat on her back with a faintly audible *whap*.

'Nice decor you've got here, Mr Knox,' said Bobby, looking around at our unremarkable kitchen in a ploy to divert attention from her last remark. 'Did you design it or was it your wife who left you because you were boring?'

'Don't take this the wrong way,' I said, 'but if you want to be amongst humans, you've got to understand what makes us angry or upset. Saying my wife left me because I'm boring, well, it's just … rude.'

'Your great-grandfather wore my great-grandfather as a hat,' she said, 'that's hardly polite − and nor is the denial of citizenship, despite us being resident here since Roman times.'

It was a good point. I was of Maltese descent, and Pippa's mum was Polish. Bobby was probably more British than almost everybody I knew. Even the Malletts were descended from the DeMalet family, who arrived from France in the fourteenth century.

'Well, OK,' said Pippa, who sounded as though her conversation with Customer Support was just ending, 'I'll await your call.'

'Right, then,' said Bobby, preparing to leave, 'I'll be off. Pop round later, why don't you, Pip?'

Pippa said she would, and Bobby bounced clean from the kitchen across the hall and out of the front door in a single hop, a distance of about fifteen feet.

'They don't close doors much, do they?' I said.

'They have an odd relation with barriers,' said Pippa, once I'd shut the door. 'They like to roam. I think it's why they find the rabbit-proof fences so iniquitous. Did you know the concrete foundations of MegaWarren extend seventy feet below the surface?'

'Who told you that?'

'Harvey.'

'Oh, yes,' I said, pleased that she had raised him as a topic of conversation, 'tell me all about him.'

'Harvey was kinda cute and *real* smart,' she said, and I spotted a gleam in her eye that had the warning flags suddenly waving. 'Labstock by coat and appearance but carries the McButtercup surname so he's actually a Petstock.'

I mentally kicked myself. No wonder I couldn't find him. He wasn't Labstock at all. Mind you, Lugless hadn't suggested it either, so I felt slightly better about it.

'Best of all,' continued Pippa, 'he didn't try to hit on me and knew some seriously cool dance moves.'

I didn't like the sound of this. Harvey McButtercup was probably connected to the Underground, and if that was so, then Pippa could be at serious risk.

'Listen: you mustn't …'

My voice petered out. Since the accident, I'd never told Pippa there was anything she couldn't do and couldn't be, and I really didn't think I should start now. If she fancied a suspected member of a banned rabbit direct action organisation, then I couldn't stand in her way – no matter how daft that might seem.

'Mustn't what?' she asked.

'Mustn't ... be *imprudent*. Extra–species[44] romances are still frowned upon.'

Rabbit/human couplings raised eyebrows at best, and were met with utter revulsion at worst. While technically illegal, prosecutions were becoming more rare, owing probably to Lord Jefferson, who gave a passionate defence of his relationship with Sophie Rabbit during his resignation speech as Attorney General.

'It's *not* a romance,' she said in the sort of way that meant it was *totally* a romance. 'Besides,' she added, chin held high, 'coming from you that's a bit rich. It's not like you don't fancy Connie.'

'I most certainly do *not*. Besides, we go back a way – she and I spent some time together at uni.'

She stared at me.

'You never told me that.'

'Didn't I?'

'No, you *totally* missed out that little snippet. Anyway you go all mushy when she's around, and you've become very pro-rabbit recently.'

She paused for a moment, then asked: 'How well, *exactly*, did you know her at university?'

'We were just good friends.'

'Hmm. Like me and Harvey?'

I sighed.

'OK, point taken.'

There was a pause.

'Would you like to see him again?' I asked.

'Yes,' she said, 'yes, I would.'

---

44. Technically I was incorrect: since mammalia is the last taxonomic classification that rabbits and humans share and we differ firstly by order, not species, any contact should really be termed 'extra-order', and as the Venerable Bunty was heard to say, 'We should celebrate the extraordinary'.

All Saints, All Spite

Fox and Friends is published monthly and caters for the witty and urbane fox-about-town. It contains news, reviews, fashion – and tips on more efficient ways to kill rabbits. It's sort of like *GQ* meets *Horse and Hounds* meets *Soldier of Fortune*.

Toby was a no-show the following morning. By long-standing agreement, if he wasn't there by 9.05 a.m. sharp he'd be making his own arrangements.

When I got into the office Flemming and Whizelle were both out but Lugless was already there and ignored me when I wished him good morning. I was obligated to tell him about Harvey but had decided I wouldn't. As far as I was concerned, Harvey was just a white rabbit driving a taxi.

Nothing unusual in that.

I made some tea, settled down to my spotting, and had my first Miffy within an hour. I thought of saying they weren't the same rabbit solely because it would put a spanner in the works, but spotting skills were always under scrutiny; I wasn't the only one seeing these images. And if another Spotter fingered a Miffy that I didn't, someone would get suspicious I was developing a conscience and I'd be out of a job. It suddenly occurred to me that the Spotters who claimed to have lost the skill probably hadn't lost anything at all – just had a daughter like Pippa, or had met some rabbits like Doc and Connie.

I looked across at Lugless, who was reading in silence. I wasn't a big fan of Toby but we did talk to relieve the monotony of the day. After another half-hour of silence with Lugless making notes, shuffling papers and sniffing, I finally said:

'Where's Whizelle?'

'Out,' he said, without looking up.

'Yes, I can see that. What about Flemming?'

'Which one's Flemming?'

'The female with the eyepatch? Your boss?'

'Ah, *her*. No, she's out too.'

'Do you know where?'

He stopped, dropped the file he was reading heavily on the desk, then turned to stare at me. His eyelid twitched.

'Is that all you do here?' he asked. 'Talk?'

'It relieves the tedium of the day,' I said, 'and builds rapport amongst team members.'

'I prefer it when you just do as I say,' he said. 'Teams work best with a strong leader.'

And he carried on with his paperwork.

After I'd reviewed another twenty rabbits, all of whom were exactly who they said they were, Lugless suddenly said:

'Section Officer Flemming, Whizelle and the rest of senior management are at a MegaWarren site meeting. I would have gone but it's barred to all rabbits, irrespective of security clearance.'

He was right. Rabbits had been banned from seeing their new home on the grounds that it might 'spoil the nice surprise'.

'The official visit for staff that includes me is tomorow,' said Lugless. 'You going?'

'Probably.'

'Actually, I don't care a mouldy carrot if you do or don't,' said the earless rabbit. 'Is that enough rapport and comradeship for you?'

'Yes, thank you.'

And he went back to his work. The phone rang ten minutes later. He waited for it to ring six times – he always did that, I'd noticed – and after listening to the caller for a few minutes, said: 'The fat furry bastard. Don't let him talk to anyone until I get there.'

He put the phone down and in an unhurried manner chose a hammer from his desk drawer and departed, doubtless on one of his 'no rabbit I can't turn' quests. I quickly went over to his desk. It was a long shot but rabbits were notoriously lax at computer security, and it was possible that Lugless had been given the usual default password, and hadn't yet changed it.

I was in luck, and quickly logged in to the Working Rabbit

Database. The reason was simple. I wanted to look at Harvey's details, but didn't want anyone to know that I was the one doing it. Lugless looked up rabbits all the time; it would be just one more search of many. Since Harvey was a Petstock, a McButtercup and a licensed RabCab driver, it took me less than a minute to find him. His full name was Harvey Augustus McButtercup, age twenty-six, resident in Colony One and a cabbie for six years. I went through his record, which revealed nothing more exciting than a series of minor traffic offences dotted around the country – either close to other colonies, or en route from one to another. If the Underground needed a courier moving around without restrictions, they'd choose a cabbie. It wasn't a smoking gun, but factoring in his politics and his work as a courier in Ross made it pretty clear he was Underground. I logged out of Lugless's computer, and returned to my own desk and worked non-stop until lunch.

For a change I decided to use the café in All Saints church so sauntered over there, ordered a coffee and panini and sat down. I opened my copy of the *Smugleftie*. Most papers relegated rabbit news to page five or six if they covered rabbit stories at all, and today, I turned there first. The articles mostly covered overcrowding in the colonies, the ballooning costs of MegaWarren and the worryingly broad remit of Rehoming legislation.

'Panini and a coffee?' said the waitress, placing the items on my table. I thanked her and she hopped back to the kitchens.

I read on and learned that Smethwick was already six months ahead of schedule with MegaWarren and the planned Rabbit Rehoming Initiative. The site, after protracted and delicate negotiations with the Welsh Assembly, was just south of the Elan Valley and sandwiched between the reservoir complex and Rhayader itself, an ideal location as the disused railway from Builth could be easily relaid to allow ease of transportation for the million or so rabbits who would live there. At close to ten thousand acres and with a seventeen-mile perimeter fence – or wall, if they could get the rabbit to pay for it – MegaWarren would be large enough, Smethwick said, 'to provide a lasting, workable and cost-effective answer to the pressing rabbit issue once and for all, but not so large as to encourage irresponsible levels of reproduction'.

I was interrupted in my paper-reading reverie by a high-pitched peal of laughter that I recognised instantly. Connie Rabbit had just walked into the café with a friend. They were both carrying shopping bags, and were dressed in the 'Moneyed Outdoor' look of Hunter wellies, tweed shooting jackets and flat caps precariously perched between their ears. The conversation in the café muted for a few moments as they entered, then started up again, but in a lower tone, most likely commentary on their attire and overtly strident speech and manner. Connie and her friend seemed not to notice and ordered a skinny chai latte and a green salad each, then sat at a newly vacated table. I hunched lower and raised my newspaper. I'd be happier not to be recognised by her, not here in All Saints.

Connie and her friend spoke loudly and not at all guardedly, and at one point described their recent sexual exploits in perhaps a little too much detail for the clientele. Several couples near by moved away, and after a few minutes the manager appeared and had a quiet word. To their credit, both Connie and her companion complied, and just as the room had got used to their presence she noticed me.

'Yoo-hoo, Peter!' she said in a loud voice. 'Over here!'

The room turned to see who they might be talking to. I tried to hide behind my copy of the *Smugleftie* but the newspaper had moved from broadsheet to tabloid format, which made it difficult to hide behind. Providence is guided by such quirks of fate. After realising that hiding was useless, I looked up, pretended to recognise her and strode over. Connie rose rapidly and hugged me fondly then planted a kiss on both cheeks, right there in front of everyone. While I confess being hugged and kissed by Connie Rabbit was not wholly unwelcome, I would have been more comfortable with no one watching.

'This is Peter,' said Connie to her friend in a loud voice, 'about the only human I've ever really liked. We go back a ways. Peter, this is my twelfth cousin on my father's aunt's son's daughter's boyfriend's aunt's daughter's side: Diane Rabbit. We grew up in adjoining burrows in Colony Three.'

'We shagged our way off-colony,' said Diane, who seemed to be drunk.

'Oh, Diane,' said Connie with a mildly embarrassed laugh, 'you are a one.'

'Pleased to meet you,' I said, offering my hand for her to shake. She looked me up and down as you might regard a haunch of meat.

'You're right,' said Diane, who smelled strongly of dandelion brandy, 'this one is quite good-looking in a small-eared sort of way.'

The café was listening to every word, and I could hear the other diners making derisive comments to one another about *me*, which somehow seemed manifestly unfair – I was getting more flak for being friends with a rabbit than Connie and her noisy friend seemed to be getting for actually *being* rabbits. I suddenly felt very uncomfortable, and I didn't like it.

'I'm trespassing on your time,' I said, and made to leave.

Connie didn't answer and instead suddenly stood stock-still, whiskers trembling.

'Diane,' she said between clenched teeth, 'oxfay at the oorday.'

'What?'

'*Oxfay at the oorday*,' she repeated, then, because Diane wasn't getting it: 'Fox – at the door.'

I turned and noted that Mr Ffoxe, the Senior Group Leader, was indeed at the door, holding a copy of the popular periodical for foxes, *Fox and Friends*. He walked over to the counter to order and it didn't look as though he'd noticed us.

'I'm so outta here,' said Diane, ears completely flat on her back. She turned to walk away and in her panic momentarily lapsed to lolloping on all fours like a standard rabbit, before she managed to regain her dignity to stand on two feet and then walk briskly away.

'What's the panic?' I asked. 'You're legal.'

'Foxes don't give a limp lettuce for legality,' whispered Connie. 'The government putting foxes in charge of rabbits is like – I don't know – putting a fox in charge of a henhouse.'

She paused.

'That idiom doesn't really quite work, does it?'

She indicated the table and asked me to join her.

'I should be getting back to—'

'Please?'

She looked sort of desperate, so I sat down opposite. Diane had spilled a milk jug on the table earlier, and it had dripped on the chair, so I suddenly had a damp behind.

'So,' I said, 'is that the Diane who was caught off-colony and you had to bail out?'

'That's the one,' said Connie, keeping a watchful eye on Mr Ffoxe. 'She's just been appropriated by a better husband. The duel was this morning, so we've been celebrating since then. I'm not sure duelling with pistols is the best way to sort it out, but they *are* quite fun – one of the odder things carried over from you after the Event.'

'What do you think caused it?'

'Diane's appropriation? Boredom, probably.'

'I meant the Event.'

It was an oft-asked question, but instead of the usual shrug, she thought for a moment and said:

'Since there were dramatic portents before the Event occurred – snow flurries, power surges, green sunsets, electrical storms, a full moon, dogs howling for no reason – perhaps scientists should reframe the question from *how* it happened to *why* it happened.'

It was a good point. Behavioural psychologists had recently suggested that because the consequences of the Event seemed to highlight areas of the human social experience that perhaps needed greater exploration, understanding and some kind of concerted action, it was possible that searching for a physical reason for all of this was actually missing the point. Although once a fringe idea, the notion that the Event might have been *satirically* induced was gaining wider acceptance.

'The Event does have all the trappings of satire,' I said, 'although somewhat clumsy in execution.'

'We live in unsubtle times,' said Connie. 'I think—'

'Well, well,' came a low voice close at hand. 'May I join your cosy little tête-à-tête?'

It was Torquil Ffoxe. His copy of *Fox and Friends* was folded open at an article entitled 'The lightning neck-break: your questions answered' and he was holding a large cappuccino. I couldn't be sure but he looked as though he were inhaling deeply to take in Connie's earthy aroma. If so, it was to his liking, as his lips were wet with saliva. The neighbouring table found him repulsive and hurriedly left, but other diners found his politics sound enough to stay. They were curious, too. Foxes and rabbits were rarely seen together without some kind of conflict taking place, and I think a couple at the back were secretly taking bets with the diners next to them as to how many minutes before Connie's skull was crushed.

'Why don't you join us?' said Connie in an even tone, although I could feel her leg under the table shake nervously. Mr Ffoxe looked at me, then Connie, then sat down in the chair I had recently vacated to make room for him.

'Oh,' he said, 'I appear to have sat on something wet.'

'Diane spilt the soya milk,' I said.

'Who's Diane?' asked Mr Ffoxe.

'Mrs Rabbit's twelfth cousin on her father's aunt's sister's daughter's … Nope,' I said, 'I've forgotten the rest.'

'I wasn't interested anyway,' said Mr Ffoxe. 'Now Peter, aren't you going to introduce me to your little bunny friend?'

'I'm not sure "bun—"'

'Your *bunny* friend,' said Mr Ffoxe again, 'introduce her to me.'

I swallowed nervously. Even having a passing acquaintance to a fox spoke bundles about a person – and it was rarely, if ever, a proud boast.

'Mr Ffoxe, this is Mrs Constance Grace Rabbit, my next-door neighbour. Mrs Rabbit, Mr Torquil Featherstonehaugh[45] Ffoxe, Senior Group Leader, Colony One.'

Mr Ffoxe narrowed his eyes.

'Have we met?' he asked.

'No,' she said in a loud, clear voice, 'but you told that scum at TwoLegsGood where they could find Dylan Rabbit, my husband. They came round and jugged him in front of the children.'

He stared at her for a moment in silence, then said in a measured tone:

45. It's pronounced 'Fanshaw'.

'That is a disgusting and baseless accusation which does you no credit and for which you should be ashamed. Besides, it was never proven, and neither were any of the others.'

'Others?'

'*Alleged* others. *Nemo sine vitio est.*[46]'

I saw Connie narrow her eyes and a sense of hardy resolve seemed to fall across her like a shadow.

'It's not the only time you and I have connected,' she said. 'Four years ago you murdered my niece for being caught off-colony two minutes before curfew and four miles away.'

'She never would have made it home in time, and I'm sure you have many, many nieces. What's the big deal?'

'This: you crushed her head in your jaws, but didn't finish the job. It took her nine hours to die.'

'I don't recall the incident,' said Mr Ffoxe, 'but then I retire a lot of rabbits so it's tricky to remember individual cases. Most shiver with fright and shit themselves before I deal with them – and none try to resist. What evolutionary value is there in a species that won't lift a paw to defend itself? There's hunter, and there's hunted. It's the way of things.'

Connie said nothing and instead picked up Mr Ffoxe's cappuccino and then, slowly and deliberately, poured it out on to the floor next to us. The entire café was staring at us in horrified silence by now, and the expectation of sudden violence seemed to fill the air like a damp fog. When she was done, Connie placed the cup gently back on the saucer and stared at Mr Ffoxe defiantly.

'Happy?' he asked.

'No, but it'll do for now. Say, is that a little bit of mange on your neck?'

The café, which I thought had already taken about as sharp an intake of breath as possible over the spilled coffee, took another. It was a grossly inflammatory comment, and one that I had not thought that anyone would ever dare make. The thing was, Mr Ffoxe *did* have a patch of mange on his neck, half covered by his silk cravat. We'd

46. 'No one is above fault'.

known about it in the office for a while, but foxes, notoriously sensitive over their orange fur and oddly small paws, usually took badly to anyone raising the subject. This time was no exception, and he lunged forward, mouth open, teeth bared. In my eagerness to get away I instinctively pushed away from the table and went sailing over backwards to land entangled with my chair in a painful heap on the floor. I struggled to my feet, expecting to find Connie's neck limp and broken, but instead she'd produced a large pearl-handled flick-knife and had it pressed against Mr Ffoxe's throat.

While this was an interesting impasse and doubtless not seen before in All Saints, Mr Ffoxe had the legal upper hand. He could kill her now using the 'natural prey' defence and just go and order another cappuccino. On the other hand, Connie would have to cope with serious reprisals if she harmed him. She'd certainly be dead – and probably tortured[47] first – and after that, not the usual hundred rabbits would lose their lives, but *ten times that* given his seniority. It would be friends and relatives and certainly include Doc, Kent, Bobby and any rabbit whom she knew particularly well. Violent reprisal was a strategy that worked well; not a single rabbit had killed a fox for nearly twenty-five years. Foxes were bad news and rabbits hoped them dead – but not at any price. You couldn't, once again, outfox the fox. But oddly, there was a factor in Connie's favour: most foxes were loath to kill a rabbit if there wasn't a fee involved. 'It would be like Tom Jones singing in the shower,' quipped one fox, 'a waste of money.'

'You know what?' said Mr Ffoxe. 'I'm finding you curiously appealing.'

'The feeling's not mutual,' said Connie.

The fox's eyes flickered dangerously and several drops of saliva fell from the tip of his canines and dripped on to the tablecloth. I knew I had to say something. Foxes never backed down, and Connie, well, I think she was made of pretty stern stuff too – and had a flick-knife. Foxes don't like blades any more than they like foxhounds and shouts of 'tally ho!'.

---

47. Foxes called it 'playing', claiming euphemistic linguistic precedence, as when a cat 'plays with a mouse'.

'Well, this has been fun,' I said in a trembling voice, clapping my hands together loudly. 'I must get back to work, and Mrs Rabbit – weren't you going to meet Diane at the cathedral to show her the Mappa Mundi?'

I think they were both relieved at my intervention. Connie slowly withdrew the knife and folded it up without taking her eyes off Mr Ffoxe, then gathered up her bags and mobile phone.

'Another time, Fox,' she said.

'Oh, for sure,' he replied. 'We'll meet again – and what's more, you'll beg me to make it quick. Your defiance will make the chase that much more enjoyable, the struggle so much more alluring, the defiling and death that much sweeter.'

Connie stared at him with cold defiance, then walked to the door with a slow, confident stride. She'd not blinked in the presence of a fox, and I couldn't help but feel there was a sense of the warrior about her. I'd seen it before, years ago – her unyielding strength of purpose – but never quite been able to articulate what I'd felt.

The café, for its part, breathed a sigh of relief and turned back to whatever it was doing. Coffee, I think, and banal chit-chat not *quite* so banal as before.

'We'll talk about this later, Knox,' said Mr Ffoxe, glaring at me. 'No rabbit is going to call me mangy and get away with it – unless,' he said, having a sudden thought, 'she had amorous intentions. You know what they say, how every rabbit secretly wants a fox?'

'It was probably more to do with you leaking her husband's name to the 2LG and murdering her niece.'

'Oh, yes,' he said reflectively, 'that might make her a little miffed, mightn't it?'

'I think so. Why didn't you kill her?'

'Oh, I will,' he said airily, 'as sure as night follows day. But there's a time and a place for everything – and while All Saints would *probably* tolerate a killing, the dismembering I had planned might not go down too well, and having one without the other is like a Spice Girls reunion without Posh. Besides, I've just had this suit dry-cleaned.'

He smiled and gave me a wink.

'Oh, and thanks for your intervention, old chum. Well timed.'

He picked up his copy of *Fox and Friends* and went to get another coffee.

'Nice friends you have,' said the couple next to me.

'At least I have some,' I replied, failing utterly to think of a suitably sarcastic retort.

'The only safe fast breeder is a nuclear reactor,' said a young man on another table, parroting a favourite slogan of Hominid Supremacists – an intellectual step up from the usual rallying cry of 'Where dat pesky wabbit?'

I was still trembling when I got back to the office. I found Lugless in the kitchenette, where he'd just made a cup of Ovaltine and was adding a slug of Jack Daniels. He didn't hear me at the door – owing to the lack of ears, I guess – and I heard him muttering to himself: 'Keep it together, Douglas, keep it together.' I stopped, then very carefully moved away, just in case he reacted badly to me catching him in a state that presumably he did not wish to be found. I returned to my desk in the office and he rejoined me soon after, speaking on his mobile.

'The suspect was working as a researcher for that turd Finkle over at RabSAg, Group Leader,' he said, 'but had something to impart: the Bunty is *definitely* in Colony One. Yes,' he said, after a pause, 'I will keep on trying, but the ones with good intel rarely come off-colony. We need to do a crime sweep, or simply pull them out during the Rehoming process … I will, sir. Thank you, sir.'

He hung up, glared at me, then started to write out a report. If the Venerable Bunty was confirmed as being in Colony One, then that would be a matter of considerable interest. With her in custody, the Rehoming could go very smoothly indeed.

'How was lunch?' asked Lugless. 'My therapist says I need to engage socially whether I like it or not.'

'Eventful,' I replied.

'Is that good or bad?'

'Bad.'

I wasn't kidding. Of all the thoughts churning around inside me – from having seen a rabbit momentarily better a fox, to Connie revealing that I was one of the only humans she ever liked and Mr Ffoxe's admission that he routinely murdered rabbits or leaked their details to TwoLegsGood – there was another, more relevant fact dominating my concerns: Doc and Connie might be wondering who their next-door neighbour actually was, and just why, *precisely*, a Senior Group Leader knew me by name. Discovering my part in Dylan Rabbit's death would surely not be far behind, and I didn't think Connie would take kindly to me being complicit in her second husband's death. Worse, Mr Ffoxe's run-in with Connie and his request for me to keep them under observation indicated that Connie and Doc were rabbits of interest. If I'd been a rabbit, I'd work hard to ensure I wasn't *remotely* interesting to a fox – especially one like Ffoxe.

Cops & Kitten

'Gregors', 'Greggs' or 'The Maccy-Gs' are all rabbit slang for law enforcement agents, named after Mr McGregor, the villain in the Beatrix Potter Peter Rabbit books. In the dubbed-into-Rabbity version of *Star Wars*, Darth Vader is literally translated as 'Mr McGregor'.

The Rabbits' Dodge Monaco wasn't in their drive when I got home, and Hemlock Towers looked empty. I let myself into my house, made a cup of tea and put the washing on the line. When I walked back indoors, Sally had dropped Pippa off and she was on the phone to Vodafone Customer Support.

'Hey, Dad,' she said once she was done, 'how was work?'

She said it in a semi-sarcastic tone that I didn't much like, but understood.

'There's something you need to know,' I said, getting straight to the point, 'about Harvey.'

I sat down at the kitchen table and I told her everything I knew. That I'd been on Ops and seen him work as a courier, and while he was as yet unidentified as a rabbit of interest, that probably wouldn't last for long. I told her I'd seen his record, and his movements around the country coupled with the sighting in Ross suggested that he was heavily connected with the Underground.

'His politics would indicate the same,' she said, 'but it doesn't change anything. He and I just … *connected* in a way that's difficult to describe. We talked about, well, everything, and he listened and responded and made me think about stuff, and I then made observations that he'd not thought of, and he liked that. Welcomed it. I really want to see him again.'

'I know,' I said, 'and I'm going to quit the Taskforce.'

She smiled, took my hand and squeezed it.

'What will you do for a job? We need money, Dad. I'm training,

161

but there's no guarantee I'll be selected for a job at the end of it. It's better out there, but it'll never be a level playing field.'

'I've got it all figured out,' I said, in the way people do when they've not really figured anything out at all, not even a little bit. 'I'll just make more and more mistakes until I'm deemed unreliable and they'll have to let me go. I've been there a while, so I may even get a payoff.'

It was probably the least likely scenario I could think of, given that Mr Ffoxe had already threatened to leak my name to the Rabbit Underground, but delusive hope seemed to currently be my best plan of action. Pippa told me she was proud of me, which was about the best thing I'd heard from, well, anyone.

We heard the sound of a car pulling up outside.

'Are you expecting someone?'

She shook her head and I walked to the kitchen window.

'That's odd,' I said, 'it's the cops.'

'Taskforce?'

'No, HPD: Hereford Police Department.'

Expecting this to be a complaint regarding the rabbits, I opened the door warily. The ranking officer was DI Eastman, who had been in the year above me at sixth form college. Her number two looked more experienced than her by about ten years and thirty bar fights. Eastman introduced her as Sweet, but said it in the sort of way that made it sound as though she *were* sweet, rather than that simply being her name. But they weren't here to speak to me or discuss the Rabbits next door. They had come to talk to Pippa – about Toby Mallett.

I invited them in.

'Missing?' I said once they'd explained. I'd noticed he wasn't at work that morning, and come to think of it, the Malletts had mentioned something about it on Sunday. So far he'd left no trace: they hadn't found his car, mobile phone – nothing.

'I last saw him Friday,' said Pippa, 'and haven't spoken to him since, although I may have texted him a couple of times before I lost my phone. He didn't reply, but that's not unusual. In fact, I was going to break up with him.'

'Any particular reason?' asked Eastman.

Pippa shrugged.

'He's a Mallett,' she said, 'and something of a massive tit.'

'I see,' said Eastman in an understanding manner. She'd been at school with the Malletts too, and knew them well enough. The cops might have left after that, but then, really without thinking, I said:

'I saw him Saturday. He came round here looking for Pip.'

'He did?' said Eastman and Pippa at the same time.

There was a long pause in which I suddenly realised the implications of what I'd just said. I related my conversation with Toby as Sweet took notes. About how Toby had appeared, asked about Pippa, and I told him that she was at a rabbit party in Colony One. DI Eastman listened carefully, asked a few more questions, then said in a kind of weirdly accusative way that I was the last verified sighting. She then turned back to Pippa.

'So you went to a rabbit party at Colony One?'

Pippa shot a daggerish glance at me then raised her chin in defiance.

'It's not illegal.'

'No,' said Eastman icily, 'not illegal. Would Mr Mallett have come looking for you?'

Pippa shrugged.

'He *might* have done, but I couldn't say for sure.'

The questions went on for another twenty minutes and, finally satisfied, they left, but only once DI Eastman had imparted some advice to Pippa: about while the rebellious spirit and animalistic attraction of the rabbit is well known, fraternisation can have a devastating effect upon one's social and professional life.

'Thanks for the advice,' she said.

Eastman ignored Pippa's sarcastic retort and departed, and I shook my head at my own crass stupidity. It wouldn't be long before the Taskforce got wind of all this, and if they thought rabbits were involved with his disappearance – as they surely would – there would be consequences.

'Will they do a crime sweep of the colony to try and find Toby this close to the Rehoming?' asked Pippa once the door had closed.

'If they've got an ounce of sense, no,' I replied, realising I shouldn't have said anything at all, 'but Mr Ffoxe might think it a useful justification to sow some terror – and get his hands on the Venerable Bunty, who's in Colony One right now.'

The house phone rang and Pippa answered it, talked for a few minutes and then hung up.

'That was Vodafone Technical Support,' she said. 'They're reporting my phone is currently pinging from the local mast. Suggested I'd simply mislaid it.'

'Have you?'

'No.'

I looked out at Hemlock Towers opposite. The Dodge Monaco was still absent from the drive.

'Wait here,' I said, but she didn't, of course, and followed me as I walked across to the Rabbits' place. The curtains were drawn, the lights switched off, and the front door swung open with an ominous creak when I knocked. I stepped in, and Pippa followed, heaving to bump herself over the weather strip. Her tyres squeaked on the polished wooden floor of the hall.

'Hello?' I said.

Nothing.

'Downstairs?' whispered Pippa, gesturing towards where a sliver of warm light emerged from the partially open cellar door. Intrigued, I moved across, opened the door and a waft of cool air swept up from below, along with the smell of damp earth and dandelion brandy.

'Hello?' I said again.

I opened the door wider, glanced at Pippa, then walked slowly down the steps and on to the stone-flagged floor of the cellar. The large chamber was held up by stone vaulting. Evidence, apparently, that Hemlock Towers was built on the site of an abbey.

'What's down there?' called out Pippa.

'A home distillery for dandelion brandy,' I called back, looking at two trestle tables that were covered by an array of glass retorts, beakers, empty bottles of surgical spirit, various vegetables, cough mixture, red ink and, disturbingly, a kitten pickled in a jar. I picked a bottle out of a crate that was on the floor near by, uncorked it, had a sniff – and the world seemed to reel about me.

'Wow,' I said, 'the Excise office would have a field d ...'

My voice trailed off as I noticed that on the far wall the stones had been removed and stacked neatly on the floor. Beyond them an earth-lined tunnel lit by low-wattage light bulbs was leading out from the cellar, the tunnel walls scalloped and grooved by the committed industry of busy paws. They'd not been here long, so it was an impressive feat. I stepped closer and peered into the gloom. The tunnel seemed to go straight for about sixty feet or so, then turn abruptly to the right. As I was about to step inside and see where it led, a figure turned the corner in the tunnel. He was short, wore an ankle tag and carried a bucket in each paw.

'Ah,' said Kent, looking at me, then at the buckets of soil he was carrying, 'would you believe me if I told you I was doing a soil survey as part of a school biology project?'

'No,' I said.

'Then you've got me bang to rights. You won't tell Mum or Doc I'm burrowing, will you?'

'They don't know?'

'They *pretend* not to – but I think they probably do,' he said in a reflective manner as he walked towards me, 'just in denial. Before the Event teenage rabbits weren't much of a handful, but post-Event the problems reflect your own: when it comes to burrowing, I just can't seem to help myself. I've been on countless rehab courses, but within a couple of days all I can think about is my next hole. Still, at least I don't have a gambolling problem – that leads only to ruin.'

Compulsive gambolling in meadows could lead to excessive fatigue and a narrowing of career and social focus. Third to gambolling and burrowing as a social ill was 'tripping the orange fantastic', the slang for over-consumption of carrots.

'Burrowing is actually a lot of fun,' said Kent, who seemed to have suddenly warmed to me. 'Do you want to have a go?'

'I'm not sure I have the nails for it. But if the village finds out it'll just give them another reason to hate you all.'

'I'm not sure they need any more reasons than they have already,' said Kent as he reached up to pull down his left ear. He sniffed at it absently then released it; the ear shot back up with a *twang*. 'Just

165

being different is enough. Will you tell them about the burrowing? The village, I mean?'

'No,' I said, after a moment's thought.

'Well, that's a relief,' he replied with a smile, and stepped forward to select a bottle of dandelion brandy.

'Have a bottle, but be careful – it's concentrated so has a specific energy potential equal to rocket fuel. Top fuel dragsters use it as an alternative to nitromethane. Dilute one part to nine with water, unless you want to go blind.'

'Does it really have pickled kitten in it?' I asked, pointing at the jar on the desk.

'No – I just needed some formaldehyde, and you can't buy it neat as a rabbit. What are you doing here anyway?'

'We came over to look for Pippa's mobile phone.'

'Ah,' he said, 'that makes sense. Let's go up top.'

We climbed back up the steps to where Pippa was waiting for us.

'Hello, Kent,' she said.

'Hello, Pip,' he replied, pushing the door closed with his hind paw. 'Bobby put the word out that you were a friend of hers and someone pushed the phone through the letterbox this morning. Bobby's like that. Sort of popular. Can't see why; she seems a bit of a bossy twit to me. There you go.'

He retrieved the mobile from where it was lying next to the coat rack by the door and handed it over.

'Thank you,' said Pippa, wiping off the dried earth.

'So,' said Kent, 'what did the Maccy-Gs want?'

'When?'

'Just now. Over at your place.'

'Oh – a missing person,' I said.

'What's going on?' asked Bobby, pulling out some tangerine-sized earpods as she bounced out of the living room. We told her about Toby.

'We're of the opinion he might have followed Pippa into Colony One,' I said, 'and he's not been seen since.'

'He'll be fine,' said Bobby without any sort of urgency in her voice. 'Rabbits go missing all the time. They're usually seeing an aunt.

166

We have a lot of aunts and all need visiting. Your Toby was probably doing the same. He'll turn up.'

This was tricky. I took a deep breath.

'You don't get it,' I said. 'I think – *we think* – Toby's a Spotter for the Taskforce.'

Her sunny disposition vanished and she looked at both of us in turn, then pulled a mobile phone from the front of her pinafore and dialled a number. The inference wasn't lost on her: with a Spotter missing in Colony One, the Taskforce would be going in – no matter what.

'I know a rabbit who knows a rabbit who knows a rabbit,' she said, waiting for the call to connect. 'How do you know he's a Spotter?'

'Loose talk on the pillow,' said Pippa before I had a chance to say anything dumb. 'He might not be Taskforce at all, of course – Toby is a Mallett, and they all like to brag.'

'Ah,' she said, then, on the phone: 'It's Bobby ... Roberta ... Like in *The Railway Children* ... no, the other one ... I'm fine, thank you. Looks like we've a potential shitstorm on our hands. Wait one.'

She put her hand over the mouthpiece.

'This'll take a while,' she said to Pippa, 'and, look, Doc's off in the Middle East right now, so do you want to come to the flicks tonight to see the latest Dwayne Johnson film? He has a big following in the colonies.'

'Why?' I asked.

'He just does,' said Bobby with a shrug. 'How about it?'

Pippa said she wanted to get an early night, but then Bobby gave her a broad wink and said it might be a *really* good idea if she came, and Pippa got the message and changed her mind.

'Good,' said Bobby, 'pick you up at seven.'

She then started to chat on the phone, but this time in Rabbity.

'Well,' said Kent with a broad grin, 'this has been fun. Drop around to have a scrape if the mood takes you, but not a word to Mum and Doc, yes?'

'So long as you don't dig out anyone's foundations.'

'On my honour,' he said, making the sign of Lago by hopping on one foot. It was an unusual gesture of veneration, but not illogical: rabbit scriptures report that Lago, the Grand Matriarch, died when caught in a snare leading her warren to safety – that was the reason their faith used the sign of the circle.

The Thespian Talk-Through

Rabbits never drove fast. They liked to enjoy the view, didn't much care for speed and besides, it was wasteful of fuel. If you want to get somewhere a long way away, just leave early. Days, if that's what's required. Or, as Samuel C. Rabbit had it: 'nhffnfhfiifhfnnffhrhrfhrf' or 'to travel joyously is better than to arrive'.

The Toby issue now out of our hands, Pippa went off to read about the Rabbit Way, presumably to be better informed when she next met Harvey. For my part, I wheeled the Austin-Healey[48] out of the garage to rectify a fault with the brake lights and tinkered for an hour before deciding to go for a walk. I told Pippa to have fun at the cinema, while privately thinking she was probably far safer in Harvey's company than she ever was in Toby's. I then wended my way up the pyon[49] to the brick octagonal building that sat on the summit. It had been derelict for a long time, and the walls were daubed with graffiti. Discarded cans of Stella Artois surrounded an old sofa that someone had lugged up there, and the location, which once had been mysterious and magical, now seemed shabby and sad.

I returned by way of the church. The vicar was in the graveyard with Mrs Pettigrew, and although I had known them both for over twenty years, they were suddenly in haste to be somewhere else, gave me a curt 'good evening' and hurried off.

Pippa had gone by the time I got back, but had sent me a text saying not to worry about her, which had the entirely opposite effect – who tells you not to worry about anything unless there is something to worry about? I shrugged, then went through to the kitchen and was

---

48. Not the 3000, obviously – quite out of my price bracket. No, this was a Sprite Mk1, known affectionately as the 'Frogeye'.
49. The name for a hill in this corner of Herefordshire.

staring into the fridge for some sort of dinner-for-one inspiration when I heard the front door open. I walked through to the hall, thinking that perhaps the film was booked up and Pippa had returned early, but she hadn't. It was Connie, and she was carefully removing her outdoor shoes and placing them neatly by the grandfather clock. She was dressed in a pale blue summer dress with a crocheted button cardigan. She spoke without looking up.

'Bobby bumped into some friends of hers and they went too,' she said. 'I gave them some vouchers to eat at Vegamama's[50] afterwards,' she added. 'Bobby's pals were colony, so barely have two carrots to rub together.'

'Was one of them Harvey?' I asked. 'I think he and Pippa might have a thing going.'

'You may be right,' she said with a smile, 'but don't fret. Harvey's a nice lad – for a Friend of Starsky.'

'Friend of Starsky' was one of the politer names Wildstock used for Petstock, the less polite ones being 'Petters' and 'Bottle-Lickers'.

'Oh, and listen,' she added, sucking her lip, 'sorry about the scene in All Saints Church. I hope it didn't cause you any trouble at the Taskforce.'

I had kind of expected this, but even so was unprepared.

'You knew that I worked at RabCoT?'

'Yes, of course,' said Connie with a smile. 'I got the lowdown on you from Mrs Griswold at the newsagents soon after we arrived. When it comes to trading salacious gossip of a seriously hanky-panky nature, rabbits have a lot of ammunition. Mind you, I was surprised that Mr Ffoxe knew you by name. Are you important there?'

'No,' I lied, 'I'm just a junior accountant. I – ah – bring Mr Ffoxe his petty cash.'

'That's odd,' she said. 'I thought you'd be a Spotter. You recognised me the first time in the library, although I think you were pretending you hadn't.'

---

50. A popular vegan chain of restaurants run entirely by rabbits, something that TwoLegsGood and UKARP describe as 'the disgusting spectre of food fascism laid bare for all to see'.

She said it with her head cocked on one side, and staring intently into my eyes.

'Junior accountant,' I reaffirmed.

'Well, someone has to do these jobs. Our beef is with head office, Nigel Smethwick and the Regional Fox, not rank-and-file officers trying to earn a crust to feed their families.'

'Oh,' I said, 'that's good. Did you think it was wise,' I continued, wanting to move on, 'threatening Mr Ffoxe in that manner?'

She shrugged.

'I don't know, but if you let people – foxes, politicians, media outlets, platforms, whatever – get away with unacceptable behaviour, then it emboldens them and others to greater and more extreme conduct. Besides, he knew I wouldn't have harmed him – I'd be killing my own if I took him out. No, I just wanted to make my feelings known.'

'They're an unlikely ally of humans,' I said. 'Before the Event we used to hunt them on horseback and shoot them on sight.'

'It's a shame you still don't,' she said. 'It's a your-enemy-is-my-enemy-you-must-be-my-friend deal. Now,' she added, giving me a twirl there in the hall, 'what do you think?'

I didn't know what she was referring to: her figure, her clothes, or even her general demeanour. They were all pretty much perfect. I stammered for a moment, and she helped me out.

'It's called Flopsy Chic by Stella Rabbit,' she said, indicating the clothes. 'Very *in* at the moment. A sort of Beatrix Potter juvenilia mixed with practicality, and of stretch fabric so bouncing is unencumbered.'

'It's very nice,' I said, still unsure why she was in my front hall, but very glad she was.

There was a pause.

'Actually,' she said, 'I came over here to ask a favour, but if this is a bad moment I can leave.'

'N-no,' I said, perhaps a little too quickly. 'I mean, no, it's fine, really – I was just wondering what to do with myself for the evening. There's always *Casualty* on the telly, but it's not been the same since Brenda Fricker left.'

'That was *years* ago,' said Connie. 'Have you really been watching it all that time hoping it will get better?'

'No,' I said. 'Well, maybe now and again. Please, come in.'

I led her into the living room and she draped herself over the sofa.

'Nice curtains,' she said, stretching her toes out over the arm of the settee. 'We don't have carrot patterns on ours, by the by, that's a myth. It would be like you having bacon sandwiches on yours.'

We both sat in silence for a few moments.

'You don't mind me popping round, do you?' she asked, blinking her large eyes. 'I don't have many friends in the area, rabbit or otherwise, and I always thought you and I got on well, y'know, back in the day.'

There was a pause, and to fill the empty air I asked whether she'd like a drink.

'Thought you'd never ask. Any dandelion brandy?'

'A friend gave me some earlier today.'

I poured two small measures, stopped, then made them larger.

'Bobby said Doc was on assignment in the Middle East,' I said over my shoulder.

'Yes,' she said, 'something regarding security but I didn't ask. It's best not to know in his line of work.'

I told her I understood, and handed her the drink.

'Bottoms up,' I said.

'Cottontails to the ceiling.'

I sipped mine but hers went down in a single gulp.

'Hmm,' she said, 'very good – maybe a little "kitteny" for me, but heigh-ho: are refills free in this house?'

We both laughed even though it wasn't funny, and I went and fetched her another.

'So what's this favour I can help you with, Connie?'

She produced two scripts from her bag.

'I've got an audition on Monday and was wondering if you could run some lines with me?'

'Of course,' I said, and sat down beside her. 'But I'm not an actor.'

'We are all actors,' said Connie. 'Our true feelings and desires hidden behind masks carved from the trammels of accepted social norms. Wouldn't you say so?'

She didn't wait for me to answer and instead passed me one of the scripts.

'There's no acting required. I just need someone upon whom to project, and to feed me my cue lines. This is the scene I want to run,' she added, placing her warm paw on my hand and moving closer. 'I'm a manipulative *Lapin fatale* who is trying to ensnare a social inferior in order that she can use him to murder her husband in a duel. I wrote it myself.'

'Oh,' I said, 'a thriller?'

'Domestic drama. We're very social creatures, and the close proximity in which we live our lives has engendered a strong tradition of family drama. The last remake of *The Flopsy Bunnies* was three hours long and sort of like *Neighbours*, *Amadeus* and *Fast & Furious* all rolled into one.'

'Sounds complex.'

'Not to us. Our version of *The Comedy of Errors* has nine sets of identical sextuplets. It's much funnier. Shakespeare really missed a trick on that one.'

'Rabbit society seems quite full on.'

'I'd agree with that. We like to enjoy the fruits not just of being rabbits, but being partly human, too.'

'Such as?'

'Speech is super-useful, along with reason, free will and abstract thought. Appreciation of literature, music and the visual arts is also a winner. We especially like Barbara Hepworth and Preston Sturges' films – plus anything with Jimmy Stewart or Dame Maggie Smith.'

She sucked her lip and thought some more.

'But there are drawbacks, too: the knowledge of one's own demise is a bit of a downer, like a massive spoiler alert, and your spiteful sense of illogical hatred does take a little getting used to. It's just all so, well, *pointless* – and such a waste of spirit, especially when you think what could be achieved with a little more unity and focus.'

She fell silent for a few moments.

'But oddly, hate's counter-emotion does ameliorate the sense of waste. We had a *serious* amount of sex when we were rabbits – still do – but it brings everything to an all-new high when love is brought into the mix. It's like – I don't know – listening to a six-year-old attempting "A Spoonful of Sugar" on a kazoo for your entire life, then discovering Puccini.'

'It's a winner,' I agreed, 'but only if the object of that love loves you back.'

'True,' she said, 'and we are often surprised when love strikes in a sometimes illogical and arbitrary fashion.'

Her voice had been becoming gradually softer as she spoke. I shifted my weight on the sofa.

'I'll be honest,' she said, staring intently into my eyes. 'From the moment I first saw you I knew that we would be together, no matter how insane that was. That love would find a way. That love will *always* find a way.'

I stared at her, not quite believing what I was hearing. I'd felt the same, too, all those years ago, and still felt it now. Had *always* felt it. And just as I was wondering *how* you kiss a rabbit – or even if you kiss a rabbit at all – she suddenly recomposed herself and said in an abrupt fashion: 'Line.'

'I'm sorry?'

'It's your line. In the script.'

'Oh,' I said, and in something of a panic looked down and simply read the first line I could see.

'I've been impregnated by your uncle,' I said, 'and it feels like it might be octuplets.'

'I think we've missed a page,' she murmured, taking my script and flipping back a leaf and tapping the first line. 'Here we are.'

'You're very attractive,' I said, reading the script, 'but this won't work.'

'Yes, you *say* that,' she said, 'but it can't have escaped your attention that there has been something between us, something stronger than both of us – a mutual attraction that transcends the tiresome normalities of everyday life.'

I didn't say anything, and she blinked at me.

'I don't know what to say,' I said.

'Say whatever you feel,' she whispered, closing her eyes and leaning forward.

'No,' I said, 'I *really* don't know what to say. I think your ink cartridge ran out.'

I held up the script by way of explanation.

'Oh!' she said, looking flustered. 'Kent must have been using the printer again. Drat that boy.' She then added: 'Is it hot in here?'

'It *is* quite hot,' I said.

'Then you don't mind if I remove my cardig …'

She'd stopped speaking because there was a knock at the front door.

'Shit,' she said. 'It's Doc.'

'Isn't he in the Middle East?'

'Oh, yes,' she said, 'then maybe Rupert.'

'Isn't that affair finished?'

'No, no, not that Rupert. *Another* Rupert. He told Doc he'd keep an eye on me in case I was planning to initiate a spousal appropriation. How are you with a duelling pistol?'

'What?'

'Just my joke,' she said. 'Actually, since they've knocked on the door, they're not likely to be a rabbit at all, are they?'

'Unless,' I said slowly, 'they're a rabbit *pretending* to be a human in order to put either you or me off guard?'

'Good point,' she said. 'Do you have a cupboard in which I could hide?'

'Really?'

'Yes – hiding in cupboards from suspicious partners has a strong tradition in rabbit culture. Really, Peter, this is all *totally* normal.'

I opened the broom cupboard, and then, after picking a copy of *The Count of Monte Cristo* out of her bag along with a torch, Connie stepped elegantly inside.

'Oooh,' she said, looking around, 'you have a Henry vacuum cleaner. Any good?'

'Very good. Not a word now.'

She sat down on the Henry and opened the book, then flicked on the torch. I had the feeling that she might have done this before – many times.

I walked through to the hallway and opened the front door. But

175

it wasn't a rabbit, or a rabbit pretending to be a human. It was a human: a Toby Mallett sort of human.

Toby's Torn T-shirt

Traditionally, carrots were a treat, not a staple, and aside from garden raids and compost heaps, unknown to Wildstock before the Event. While they are harmless in small amounts, overindulgence can lead to issues very similar to alcoholism in humans.

Toby had a lost and empty appearance about him. His T-shirt looked as if it had been pulled through brambles with him still inside as it was badly ripped and his torso was criss-crossed with scratches. His face was streaked with dried dirt, the mud in his blond hair made it look brown, and there was a large and very purple bruise on the side of his head which had partially closed his bloodshot left eye.

'Toby?' I said. 'Are you OK?'

'I have never been better,' he said, holding on to the door frame to steady himself.

'You don't look it. How did you get that bruise?'

'I walked into a tree,' he replied unconvincingly.

'And the scratches?'

'A … *thorny* tree.'

'You know everyone's looking for you?'

'I guessed they might be,' he muttered. 'Is Pippa in?'

'She's gone to the flicks.'

'Oh,' he said, then: 'Will you tell her that I'm sorry and that I'm not worthy? Despite strict RabCoT employment guidelines I've been a paid-up member of TwoLegsGood for the past seven years. I've hounded twenty-eight rabbits out of their houses and I am most definitely leporiphobic. I've also cheated on Pippa several times, usually with Arabella down at the pony club, but there were others.'

None of this was hugely surprising, but it was important he'd been returned. For Toby, obviously, but more importantly, it meant Mr Ffoxe had no justification for initiating a crime sweep through

Colony One – and that Bobby *definitely* had connections to the Underground. I asked Toby whether he wanted to come in and sit down.

'Better not,' he said, glancing at the Rabbits' house next door. 'I've got to go home and explain where I've been.'

'And where have you been?'

'Oh. Er … on a monumental two-day bender. And visiting my aunt. Nowhere near Colony One, if I knew where it was – which I don't.'

'Everyone knows where it is,' I said. 'It's been there *years.*'

'Has it?' he said unconvincingly. 'Just goes to show.'

He looked around nervously and lowered his voice.

'They know my every move. They have watchers. Even in the dark. *Especially* in the dark. It's those carrots, you know. Will you tell Pippa it's all over and I'm not worthy? It was one of the conditions of my release that I say that.'

'I'll tell her. What were the other conditions?'

'That I resign from RabCoT, donate my worldly possessions to rabbit charities and then join a monastery and devote my life to prayer and silent contemplation.'

'Very worthy,' I said, not imagining for one minute that Toby was monk material.

Relieved at this, he staggered back to his car, which was so muddy it looked as though it had been buried, abandoned, then dug up and hastily cleaned with a yard broom. He fumbled with the key and then fell over, so I walked across, hauled him to his feet, pushed him into the car and drove him the half-mile back to his home, a large Elizabethan half-timbered house, one of the finest in the village.

I rang the doorbell while Toby sat dejectedly on the seat inside the porch. As soon as Mrs Mallett opened the door Toby went into a long and borderline coherent explanation of the 'bender' he had allegedly been on, interspersed with sobs and apologies and declarations of how much he'd missed them all, and how he was quitting the Compliance Taskforce and renouncing his membership of TwoLegsGood, even if that meant returning the funny hat and two-handled paddle used in his initiation.

The second Mrs Mallett was clearly relieved her stepson had reappeared, but without a huge amount of enthusiasm. After a few moments Victor Mallett appeared and demanded to know where I'd found him. I explained what I knew, and he looked at Toby, the state he was in, then the state of his car.

'Kidnapped by friends of yours?' he demanded. 'Those sodding rabbits?'

'I don't know anything more than what I've just told you.'

Victor took a step forward. He was taller than me, a lot stronger and very intimidating.

'If I ever find out you had a hand in his kidnapping, Knox,' he said, 'my revenge will be terrible. Do you understand me?'

'I had nothing—'

'Do you understand me?'

'Yes,' I said, 'I understand you.'

'Good.'

And he slammed the door in my face. There was a pause, the door reopened, they bundled Toby inside, then slammed the door again. I waited for the door to reopen for the third time and then handed them Toby's car keys.

As soon as I got home I went immediately into the kitchen.

'It was Toby,' I said outside the cupboard door, 'and he looks as though he's been beaten up and held captive by rabbits before being released, probably because they found out he was with the Taskforce, and they didn't want a colony crime sweep.'

Connie didn't answer.

'What troubles me,' I continued, 'is that we mention to Bobby that Toby is missing and a member of the Taskforce, and she makes a phone call and all of a sudden he's apologising to Pip and confessing he'd slept with Arabella from the pony club, and he looked frightened. *Really* frightened.'

I leaned closer to the cupboard door.

'Is your family involved with the Underground?'

I paused.

'You're not in there, are you?'

I opened the cupboard door to find I was correct. Connie wasn't there, and neither was the Alexandre Dumas novel, the torch – nor, oddly, the Henry vacuum cleaner. I shut the door, sighed, made myself some tea and sat at the kitchen table, wondering whether Harvey had a hand in Toby's condition, whether he had been at the movies too – and whether they had even been going to the pictures at all. I reminded myself that Pippa was her own person then walked towards the living room, meaning to watch something – *anything* on the telly. I didn't get that far as something in the hall caught my eye. Connie's shoes were still parked where she'd left them near the grandfather clock. It had rained briefly that evening, and I knew that rabbits had a peculiar dislike for getting their paws wet.

She was still in the house.

I looked in the living room, then the utility room, where I could see Connie's floral-pattern dress going round and round through the viewing port of the washing machine. Now more flustered, I checked the conservatory, my study and the dining room, but she was nowhere to be seen. I returned to the hallway, then heard the sound of the shower running upstairs.

'Mrs Rabbit?' I called up the stairwell. 'Are you up there?'

She didn't answer, and instead I heard her singing in a rather lovely voice. I stood there for a moment, undecided as to what to do, but then told myself that this was *my* house, so I padded slowly up the stairs.

The shower in use was the en suite in my bedroom, and the door was open. I could see her reflection in the mirror. With wet fur and discounting her tail and powerful thigh and calf muscles, she had a body that was almost identical to a human's. I looked away, paused for a moment, looked back and then looked away again. *If you can see a rabbit, they can see you.*

'Connie?'

'Oh, hello, Peter,' she sang out, seemingly unconcerned by my presence. 'I didn't know how long you were going to be so I took the opportunity to wash some things and have a shower – we can't seem to get the hot water to work over in Hemlock Towers. You don't mind, do you?'

'Well, no,' I said, which was kind of true.

'I've used all your shampoo,' she said, 'all two litres of it. I have a lot of fur. But I couldn't find any conditioner.'

'I don't use it.'

'Maybe just as well,' she said, 'as I tend to go a little fluffy. Would you pass me a towel?'

So I did so as best I could without looking as though I shouldn't be looking, but not wanting to appear prudish, I made sure I did look at her, but just her eyes.

'Thank you,' she said, wrapping herself and stepping out of the shower. 'You don't have a hairdryer, do you? Fur takes an age to dry and can get a little spiky if not brushed immediately.'

'I'll get you Pippa's,' I said, and went downstairs to fetch it. When I got back Connie had dispensed with the towel and was staring at her naked self in the full-length mirror on the cupboard door.

'Bunty teaches us that mirrors, endless selfies and self-aggrandisement on social media are the gateway to narcissistic self-absorption,' she said, turning this way and that to get a better look at herself. 'There are no mirrors in the colonies, we don't have one in the house, and car mirrors are always reduced in size to avoid unseemly self-regard. What do you think?'

'I think you are … very lovely, Connie.'

She smiled, took the hairdryer and started to blow-dry her fur, which, being quite fine, seemed to dry quite fast. She started on her hind paws and then worked upwards, all the time seemingly unconcerned by my presence.

'They returned Toby,' I said.

'I know,' she said. 'Bobby knows a rabbit who knows a rabbit who knows a rabbit.'

'Are you with the Underground?'

'All rabbits are with the Underground,' she replied after a pause. 'It's an understanding rather than a recruitment. You get a nod or a tap on the shoulder or a phone call and you have to do the right thing, no matter what the personal cost. Unity and focus. Here, dry my back, would you?'

She turned round and I directed the hairdryer at her furry back. She passed me a soft brush and I brushed the fur at the same time.

'Do you remember all those terrible films we went to see?' she said over her shoulder. 'And we sat in the back row because of my ears and we didn't hold hands or anything, but the seats were small so we were touching?'

'I remember that very clearly.'

'I liked that,' she said after a pause. 'A sort of understated intimacy. I always felt that we kinda just clicked, you and I. Never had that since. Not with a rabbit, not with a human, not really with any of my husbands.'

'Yeah,' I said, 'I felt that too. OK, your back's dry.'

She turned round, took the hairdryer from me and then started to dry the fur on her arms and torso.

'Listen,' I said, 'I'm sorry.'

She turned the dryer on to her ears, which flapped in a comical manner.

'About what?'

'You know when I said I wasn't a Spotter for RabCoT? Well … I lied. I am. For the past fifteen years.'

I looked down and saw that my fingers were knotted together in a telltale fidget. My heart was thumping and it felt as though there was a tight band of steel around my chest.

'I knew you had the gift thirty years ago,' she said in a soft voice, 'when you could pick me out of a crowd of rabbits back at uni. I often wondered if you'd realise you had the skill, and what you'd do with it. I accept your apology for lying earlier. The Rabbit Way allows one to quash the stain of an untruth so long as one makes good within the hour and there was no advantage. I think you just squeaked through.'

And she smiled.

'Nothing's changed, Pete. Not between us.'

I took a deep breath.

'That's not *really* what I'm sorry about.'

'Ah,' she said, suddenly looking more serious, 'then what?'

I stared at her for a moment, opened my mouth to tell her about how I was the secondary Spotter the night Dylan Rabbit was arrested and that I was pressured to confirm the ID. That I should have done more, that I *could* have done more. But what came out was:

'Not being at the demo when you were asked to leave the university. My aunt wasn't *that* ill – and eventually pulled through. I should have been there, with you.'

She shrugged.

'I'd have been chucked out irrespective. Your aunt needed you. I have no problem with any of that; it was UKARP policy to change the university's admissions policy, not yours. And Peter?'

'Yes?'

'I'm sorry too.'

'What about?'

'You'll see.'

I was going to tell her that I'd always regretted not getting in contact, even after Helena had left, probably out of fear. Fear of seeing a rabbit, fear of me being wrong about what I thought we'd felt. But I didn't get to say any of that, because Connie's long and very elegant ears, which up until then had been draped in a relaxed fashion down her back, suddenly popped vertically upwards and she listened intently for a few seconds.

'*Bother*,' she said, 'I just heard a car door slam.'

'It won't be Pippa back yet – probably a neighbour.'

'It was the Dodge. A *highly* distinctive sound. Doc probably came back for the night. Rabbits become uneasy when not in their own bed at night.'

'But … but the Middle East is a ten-hour flight away.'

'No, no,' she said, 'not *that* Middle East – Nottingham.' She pulled the sheet from my bed and wrapped it around herself while I went to the bedroom window and looked out. Sure enough, Doc had parked the Dodge and was hopping towards the front entrance of the house. Even though evening, being summer it was still quite light.

'Well?' asked Connie.

'He's gone into the house. No, hang on, he's come out again.'

Doc stood there, sniffed the air and then began to stride in our direction.

'He's walking over here,' I said, a tremor of fear in my voice.

'Does he have a purposeful stride in his walk?'

'Yes.'

'Oh dear,' she said. 'It's just possible he'll get the wrong idea about this.'

'No,' I said, 'he will *definitely* get the wrong idea about this. What are we going to do?'

'Well,' she said, looking thoughtful, 'he's already suspicious, so he'll interpret this as an appropriation and challenge you to a duel.'

'That's fine; I can just refuse.'

'Not really,' she said, shaking her head. 'If he challenges you then it's a goer — only a spineless reptile of the very worst sort would try and back out.'

'A spineless reptile?'

'Of the worst sort.'

'I've a better idea,' I said. Her Dumas novel and torch were lying on the bed, so I handed them to her and opened the wardrobe door. She half climbed in, then stopped and turned back to me.

'Doc is very big on honour and duelling and you may have no choice in the matter, so this is something you need to know: his set of duelling pistols is decorated with animals, and you'll be given the choice of which to use. The one that has a picture of a lark tends to shoot off to the left, while the one with the engraving of the crocodile on the handle is pretty much straight on the money.'

'I'll never remember all that.'

'It's easy: the shot hits the spot if you've a croc on the stock, while the mark of the lark shoots wide of the mark.'

'The shot hits the spot,' I repeated slowly, 'if you've a lark on ... no, wait, a *croc* on the stock, while the lark with the mark ... er, *mark with the lark* shoots wide of the mark.'

'Don't forget that,' she said, 'it could save your life.' She smiled, gave me a kiss and closed the door.

The doorbell rang. Doc, it seemed, had a better idea of front-door etiquette than Connie or Bobby. I ran downstairs mumbling the rhyme, then composed myself for a few seconds, and opened the front door.

Connie & Caution

Rabbit playwrights have rewritten Shakespeare to appeal to more rabbit audiences for a long time. The performance of *Seven Thousand and Eighty-Three Noble Kinsmen* was met with great acclaim in 1973, and 1982's *A Comedy of Ears* is considered a benchmark adaptive literary work. Not all were so successful: *A Winter's Cottontail* was panned by rabbit critics, all of whom thought it was simply an 'excuse for a feeble pun'.

'Oh,' I said, feigning surprise, 'hello, Doc. I thought you were away?'

'I was,' he said, gazing at me dangerously, 'and now I'm back. Kent said the increasingly poorly named Constance was over here running some lines from her new play or something.'

'Oh yes,' I said, 'she was. But then she left.'

'Really?'

'Yes,' I said, a hot stickiness starting to crawl up my back, 'really. Something to do with Diane.'

'Is that her new play there?' he asked, pointing towards where the script was still lying on the hall table.

'Yes,' I said, 'we were going to do some more later. Tomorrow, I think, or the day after.'

I thought about having to face Doc in a duel.

'Or if you'd prefer it, never.'

I suddenly realised that her shoes were still where she'd left them, right there in plain sight, barely a yard from where we were standing. Although rabbits had outstanding peripheral vision for signs of movement, peripheral *relevance* was harder for them – one of the reasons they drive slowly. In high-rabbit-concentration driving areas, road signs have a small logo of a fox in the bottom left-hand corner to ensure they are noticed.

'You'd better take the play with you,' I said, reaching for the script while at the same time pushing her shoes underneath the umbrella stand with my foot. He didn't take the proffered script and instead leaned closer to me.

'I wasn't sure if they were her shoes or not,' he growled, 'until you pushed them under the stand.'

'Did I?'

'You did,' said Doc in a threatening murmur, 'and if I know Connie she'll be hiding in a cupboard somewhere with a Victor Hugo novel. Am I right?'

'Not at all,' I said with perfect deniability. She was hiding in a cupboard, sure, but with a novel by *Dumas*, not Hugo.

Irrespective, he pushed past me into the hall.

'I know you're in here!' he yelled, lolloping through to the kitchen. I was going to follow him in but was distracted by two people outside, strolling towards me from the direction of the lane. It was Victor and Norman Mallett, and this was exceptionally bad timing.

'Good evening, Peter,' said Victor with thinly disguised aggression as soon as they were standing in my doorway, 'we'd like a word.'

'Can't it wait?' I said. 'This is really not the best time.'

'*Line of Duty* ended twenty minutes ago,' said Norman, 'so what can you be doing that's so important—'

Norman abruptly stopping talking as Connie, still wrapped only in my bedsheet, ran down the stairs. She gave me a smile and a shrug but then slid to a stop on the hall rug when she came face to face with Victor and Norman, whose eyes opened wide in surprise.

'Back to the burrow!' yelled Doc, who had seen her from the kitchen, 'I'll deal with you later!'

'*No!*' she said defiantly, her voice rising. 'You can take your "back to the burrow" alpha-buck anthropocentric possessive misogynistic honcho machismo bullshit and shove it right up your pellet slot. You got a problem with me, you tell it to my face.'

'Problem?' he yelled back as they squared off to one another in the hall. 'I'll tell you the problem. You shagging the next-door neighbour is the problem. He's a *human*, for Lago's sake – have you not even a single shred of decency?'

Victor and Norman turned to stare at me with a look of utter revulsion etched on their features.

'I can explain,' I said.

'Don't tell me what I can or can't do!' yelled Connie as I saw two *more* people appear behind the Mallett brothers outside. They looked vaguely familiar but I couldn't at first place them. They were immaculately turned out, held a clipboard each and in their free hand expensive pens poised mid-air in a dramatic fashion.

'Can't we all just keep our voices down?' I said.

'Is this what you usually do?' said Doc, turning to me. 'Take advantage of vulnerable does when their husbands are out of town?'

'I'm *anything but* vulnerable,' yelled Connie. 'I'm quite capable of making up my own mind, and let me tell you, Major Clifford Rabbit, Peter here gave me twice as good a time as anything you've ever handed out.'

'Disgusting,' said Victor.

'Reprehensible,' said Norman.

'But—' I said as Doc made a lunge towards Connie. She ran off with a giggle but Doc — maybe accidentally, maybe on purpose — stood on the bedsheet and she was suddenly completely naked, right there on the IKEA rug in the hall. In front of everyone.

There was a sudden hollow and very empty moment in time that seemed to hang for an eternity.

'Whoops,' she said with an embarrassed grin, then bounced out of the door past the Mallett brothers to spring with the utmost of elegance over the dividing fence. Within two more bounds she was back inside her house, her husband close behind. There was a crashing of furniture, some breaking of crockery — then silence.

I looked back at Victor and Norman. They were all staring at me in shocked silence, mouths open.

'This isn't what it looks like,' I said.

'It seems abundantly clear to us that this is *exactly* what it looks like,' said Victor.

'Is this how Much Hemlock disports itself?' said one of the people holding the clipboards, who I now recognised as Reginald Spick, one half of the Herefordshire Spick & Span award team. 'As a hotbed of base, lewd and depraved behaviour?'

'You would come around right *now*,' said Victor, who had also just recognised him.

'The judges appear randomly to maintain fair play,' said Mr Spick in a haughty manner.

'For a *very* good reason,' said Mrs Span, Mr Spick's partner.

'Can't you just pretend this never happened?' said Norman. 'Just go away and come back later?'

'Nothing *whatsoever* happened,' I said, partly for the judges, partly for me and partly for the Mallett brothers, 'and even if it did, what is it to you?'

'Quite a lot, actually,' said Victor. 'This is a good village, and we have a respectable way of doing things – and that generally excludes lying down with vermin.'

'Connie's not vermin.'

'Not to you, obviously.'

'I think we've seen enough,' said the judges, making to leave. 'This sort of thing *never* happens in Pembridge. Winning a Spick & Span award is not just about a fine herbaceous border, roses to die for and local honey of impeccable quality, it's about cultural propriety. Why do you think Slipton Flipflop has never won a prize, when they have the finest hanging baskets in the county?'

'But just a minute,' said Norman, the issue over Connie and me momentarily forgotten, 'this is emphatically *not* what we discussed – and considering the sum we paid you, we expect at the very least a fair shake of the stick.'

'We're bribed by *everyone*,' said Mrs Span in a tart manner. 'Don't think we owe you any special treatment because of it.' She paused. 'But I suppose we *could* be persuaded to rejudge so long as your current issues have been ... dealt with. Do we understand one another?'

Norman said that they *definitely* understood, thanked them for their patience and forbearance and Spick & Span made their exit as Victor and Norman turned back to me.

'I think the course of action is clear,' said Norman. 'The well-being of the village comes before you and your little bunny chums. But since you were once a friend and we are reasonable people who embrace proportionality and fair play, we'll throw you a bone. Forty-eight hours to get out, and you can take your fickle daughter and long-eared chums with you. It's non-negotiable, Knox. And if you can't persuade the Rabbits to go, then we will – using whatever means at our disposal.'

Since I now knew Toby was TwoLegsGood, it stood to reason that his father and uncle were too. This wasn't an empty threat.

'Look,' I said, 'perhaps we can start a dialogue or—'

'Forty-eight hours,' said Norman, glaring at me in the sort of way I imagine a psychopath might do, just *after* they unchain you from the radiator, but just *before* they remove your liver with a spoon, 'is that enough dialogue for you?'

'Yes, OK,' I said.

And they left. I thought of going over to the Rabbits' and warning them of the impending shitstorm, but instead locked the door, waited until the wash cycle finished, then put Connie's dress in the tumble dryer. I waited until midnight for Pippa to come home, but when she didn't, I turned in.

Morning Mood

At the last count there were eight hundred and seventy-two rabbits living in the Isle of Man safe haven. All had been granted full UK residency by the Tynwald and seventeen applications for passports were being considered at the time of the Battle of May Hill.

I woke to the sound of the doorbell. I rolled over in bed, caught a whiff of Connie's scent on the sheet and stared at the clock. Half past six. I pulled on my bathrobe and walked slowly downstairs. Pippa's keys and bag were on the kitchen table so I was relieved at least that she'd made it home safe and well. I approached the front door and, without opening it, said:

'Who is it?'

I was hoping it was Connie, calling round to assure me she'd tell everyone that her comment that I'd 'given her twice as good as her husband' was to goad Doc, nothing more. Even if it *was* her and she wanted everything to be made right, somehow I felt the damage was already done.

'Who is it?' I said again. Silence.

There was no one outside when I opened the door, and I stepped out into the early-morning light. It would be a hot day later, but for now, a low mist hung in the trees. Seeing no one, I turned to go back indoors and then noticed someone had spray-painted 'Bunnyshagger' on the garage door. I stared at the graffito, first thinking that it was outrageous, then thinking it was probably small beer to what the rabbit had to contend with on a day-to-day basis. I looked over the fence to see whether the Rabbits' house had been similarly defaced, but it had not.

'Probably because Hemlock Towers is Grade II listed,' said Pippa when I told her two hours later over breakfast. 'Remember that 2LG's core demographic is middle-class professionals who would be more likely to have a subscription to *Radio Times* than be a member of a far-right gang.'

I outlined what had happened the previous evening. I told her about Connie, the script, Toby's reappearance and the shower, the bedsheet, the Spick & Span judges and finally Norman's forty-eight-hour ultimatum. I decided *not* to tell Pippa that Toby had slept with Arabella at the pony club.

'What are you going to do?' she asked, taking a slurp of coffee.

I sighed. Although I'd never consciously discriminated against rabbits, read a single issue of *The Actual Truth* or considered myself leporiphobic in the least – I was. As a young man I'd laughed at and told anti-rabbit jokes[51] and I never once challenged leporiphobic views when I heard them. And although I'd disapproved of encroaching anti-rabbit legislation I'd done nothing as their rights were slowly eroded. My words and thoughts had never progressed to positive actions. No rallies, no angry letters, no funds to RabSAg, nothing.

'Dad?'

'I'm still thinking.'

But even if I *had* made a stand, my long-term and sustained employment at the Rabbit Compliance Taskforce would have negated everything. My most pressing emotion right now was not a sense of righteous indignation, frustration at the unfairness of my situation or even a courageous sense of justice that a fight needed to be fought and won. No, what I truly felt was a sense of deep and inexcusable *shame*.

'I have no idea what to do,' I said finally. 'What about you?'

'I don't know,' she said. 'How bad do you think things might get?'

'Oh, I don't know. Worst-case scenario: petrol through the letterbox, a broken jaw and TwoLegsGood run the Rabbits out of the village. Best-case scenario: no one in Much Hemlock talks to you or me for the next six to eight decades.'

---

51. Why don't Petstock and Labstock mate? Because the offspring might be too lazy to steal. When are rabbits really good mothers? When they eat their own young. What looks best on a rabbit? A pie crust. What's the difference between a rabbit and a bucket of turds? The bucket.

'That sounds quite attractive,' she said.

'It does, doesn't it?'

'I'm staying,' said Pippa. 'They're not likely to attack me, are they? Even 2LG losers draw the line *somewhere*.'

'That's true,' I said with a smile, 'and if you're staying, so am I.'

We fist-bumped nervously and sat in silence for a few moments. I don't know what Pippa was thinking about but I was wondering what a broken nose felt like.

'So,' I said finally, 'how was your evening?'

'Harvey was there,' she replied, glad too of the conversational change. 'We went to Vegamama's afterwards with Bobby. Had a good chat over dinner, mostly about MegaWarren. They're all extremely suspicious of the Rehoming, and feel that this might be the last chance rabbits get to make a stand before losing any of their hard-won rights for ever. There's talk of the Venerable Bunty issuing an edict about a refusal to be rehomed, but Harvey is worried that rabbits, naturally polite, compliant and disliking of confrontation, will not be able to refuse the order – and with Senior Group Leader Ffoxe and fifteen hundred foxes assisting with the Rehoming, restraint isn't likely to be on anyone's agenda, especially as foxes can use what force they wish with impunity.'

This didn't sound at all good.

'Are they thinking of another demonstration?' I asked.

'I think they're beyond that. Harvey said that any attack on the colony permits the Grand Council to invoke Bugs Bunny Protocols – namely, that almost any behaviour is permissable once a rabbit is pushed into a corner – even violence.'

There was a pause.

'I think Harvey and I have a chance together,' said Pippa, looking me straight in the eye, 'and yes, I will be careful and I do know what I'm doing.'

Despite Lord Jefferson's celebrated proclamation of love for Sophie Rabbit, mixed-species relationships remained illegal and open to prosecution. When outed, most couples simply took up residence in the colonies. At the time of the Battle of May Hill, an estimated four thousand humans were living on-colony, eight hundred of them lopped to show thumbless allegiance to the Rabbit Way. Smethwick regarded them as 'traitors to our species' and 'beneath contempt'. Rabbits regarded them as 'welcome guests'.

'You know what, Pip?' I said. 'I really hope it works out.'

Sally called to say she wasn't going into college that day, and since I guessed Toby would not be going to work either – if ever again – I decided to take Pippa myself.

'It was Toby,' she said, looking at the graffito once we were outside. 'I recognise his handwriting. I can't imagine what I saw in him.'

We also noted that the Rabbits had not been *entirely* unmolested overnight: sitting on their lawn was a forty-gallon oil drum, the usual receptacle for a jugging. Although the unspeakably cruel act was mercifully rare, the very threat was usually enough to have a rabbit family packing their bags and gone within the hour. I was confident it would have little effect on Connie and Doc.

'Good morning!' came a voice, and Doc bounded in from the direction of the lane, presumably back from his usual five-kilometre early-morning bounce, as he was wearing a tracksuit top and a Nike sweatband around the base of his ears.

'Good morning,' we said.

'Looks like 2LG have been busy,' he said, staring at the forty-gallon drum. 'With a lick of paint it will make a nice planter for my aspidistra.'

'You don't seem very worried,' I said.

'I've had death threats before,' he said. 'At our last place someone daubed *kill dat pesky wabbit* on our drive and sub-standard photocopies of rabbit pie recipes were pushed through the letterbox. The work of sad little cowards, trying in vain to staunch a losing battle with irrelevance. But you know what?'

'What?'

'If I was going to kill someone, I wouldn't warn them first.'

'Ah,' I said, as Doc had said it in a particularly menacing fashion, and I wondered whether that was what he had planned for me.

'Look,' I said, 'about last night—'

'Water under the proverbial bridge, old chap,' he said with a grin.

'When one is married to a doe as dazzling as Constance, one must expect to have to fight suitors off every now and again.'

'I'm not a suitor,' I said hurriedly, 'and nothing happened.'

'And I will do all I can to ensure it stays that way,' he replied evenly. 'Mind you, if Connie gives you the nod and you want to challenge me to a duel I'm totally up for it. Pistols, mind – my swordsmanship is a little rusty.'

'No challenge from me,' I said hurriedly, 'truly.'

'As you wish.'

And without another word he bounced clean over my car, the garden fence, *his* car – and went back indoors.

Pippa and I were on the road five minutes later. It was a delightful morning, sunny and bright, but neither of us was feeling that comfortable. Worry has a way of sitting on your chest like a baby elephant. Of the forty-eight hours we'd been given, we now had thirty-seven left. It felt good that Pippa and I were going to make a stand, but I couldn't helping thinking that however the Malletts expressed their displeasure, it would be neither pleasant nor proportional, and that our stand, with all the human privileges defaulted to us at birth, would probably not be a stand at all. We were human. Ultimately, we'd be just fine.

'You're visiting MegaWarren?' said Pippa when I'd told her what I was doing that day.

'It's part of management's efforts to make the move as easy as possible.'

'For the rabbit?'

'No – for the staff at the Taskforce.'

There seemed little point in secrecy now. Today's tour, I told her, was for staff at RabCoT to see first-hand just what the new facility was all about. How RabToil would manage the workforce and manufacturing areas, the living facilities, security, that sort of thing. She asked about the timescale, and I said it would certainly be this year, 'perhaps just months'.

'Did anyone ever ask the rabbits what they thought?' she asked.

They *were* asked, but only in a roundabout way. The Grand Council of Coneys was part of the consultation process and was assured that 'every opportunity would be used to ensure that the best interests of all the UK residents would be foremost in the Rehoming Committee's thoughts'. It didn't help that there were no rabbits on the committee, and that Nigel Smethwick had chaired the proceedings.

I dropped Pippa at college then went on to the Taskforce offices.

Since we were going on the MegaWarren tour that day I didn't go to my office, just had my name ticked against a box and was given a lanyard with a visitor's pass and allocated seating on the coach. We waited in the canteen for half an hour, then were addressed by Taskforce PR guru Pandora Pandora.

'Good morning,' she said, her dress and demeanour seeming somehow darker than usual this morning, 'and welcome to the MegaWarren tour. You're going on this trip because you have been selected to be part of the Advance Rehoming Implementation Team. Look upon this as early orientation.'

There were murmurings at this, mostly because this was the first indication that the long-expected redundancies were actually going to go ahead – and who might be staying on. Needless to say, my colleagues were looking quite happy. Rehoming work, because of the greater responsibilities and potential for stress, would be carrying generous bonuses.

'I've only one major point to make this morning,' she continued, 'and this is it: six members of the press will be accompanying us, and we need to keep a firm control of the way in which MegaWarren is perceived by the public. There are some deluded Social Justice Warriors out there who do not have a clear enough understanding of the issues involved to be a meaningful part of the dialogue. I have my people embedded near the press corps, but if any of the hacks go rogue and ask you anything at all – *anything* – you are to say nothing and send them over to me or a member of my team. Speak out of line and you will have to explain yourself. Not to me, not to a disciplinary panel – but to the Senior Group Leader *personally*. Have I made myself understood?'

We all grunted our agreement, and half an hour later we were in the coach heading west. I was next to an empty seat, presumably Toby's. We'd got as far as Llandrindod Wells when I noticed Lugless get up from his seat at the front and lumber back through the coach. He was dressed in his usual grey duster coat, the stumps of his cropped ears covered by a flat cap. I noticed that he wore a shoulder-holster containing his largest hammer. I ignored him, hoping he wouldn't join me, but he did.

'Is that Knox?' he asked – since I was out of the office and thus out of context, I was not wholly recognisable to his rabbit eyes.

'Yes,' I said without looking up, and he sat down next to me.

'Where's Toby Mallett?' he asked.

'Resigned,' I said, still staring out of the window.

'Do you think he was compromised? Think the Underground got to him?'

'You'd have to ask him that.'

I turned to face Lugless and almost gave out a cry. The rabbit sitting next to me wasn't Lugless at all. He was definitely missing his ears but was subtly different in many other ways. I was about to ask him who he was, but he put out a paw to quieten me and made a familiar gesture – a wink and a click of his tongue, the same gesture I had seen when he had arrived to pick up Bobby and Pippa in the RabCab.

It was Harvey.

MegaWarren

Finkle had been arrested dozens of times, usually on account of some obscure medieval law that could usefully be modified as required. When escorting his then partner Debbie Rabbit to dinner, a contravention was found in the 1524 statute that disallowed 'the carrying of live game in a tavern or eating house'.

'What are you staring at?' he asked.

'Nothing,' I said, my mind in something of a whirl. I was on the coach that day, and Toby wasn't – the only two people in the Compliance office who would have seen the Lugless/Harvey switch immediately. I suddenly wondered where the real Lugless was, and marvelled that Harvey had wanted access to MegaWarren so badly he had cropped his own ears. Only a rabbit like Lugless could hope to gain access: one who had been given security clearance by a fox.

While Harvey stared at me, presumably trying to gauge my intent, I noticed a small trickle of blood creeping down from his cap. If he'd cut off his own ears, the wounds would still be raw and freshly stitched. To uncover the impostor, all I had to do was to flick off his cap. It would be that easy.

But I didn't. Instead, I simply touched my head in the place where I could see the blood on his. He got the message, touched the area with the tip of a claw and stared at it for a moment. He said nothing, got up and walked towards the back of the coach, where there was a toilet.

'Oi,' I heard a human voice say, 'humans only. Tie a knot in it, Hoppy.'

'Really?' came Harvey's voice. 'Want to see me tie a knot in yours?'

There was silence, and I heard the toilet door close and lock.

Now thoroughly unnerved, I looked out of the window, and noted we were driving through a cordon where a group of protesters – humans and rabbits – were holding banners at the side of the road.

Several yurts had been set up, and a couple of fresh burrows in the verges had been repurposed into pop-up cafés offering cappuccinos and sandwiches free of charge.

'Ten-mile exclusion zone for protesters,' I heard one of the other passengers say. 'The Taskforce don't want to deal with the added burden of protesters above the complexity of the Rehoming. Anyone in the zone without a legitimate reason for being there can be prosecuted for criminal trespass.'

I looked about at my fellow passengers, mostly Compliance Officers who worked on the main floor, and all seemed to be in something of a party mood, buoyed by the attraction of a new workplace and the bonuses. Near the front were the journalists, each of whom was accompanied by their own dedicated Pandora Pandora PR clone – all pencil-thin, all blonde, all dressed in black, all supremely confident.

From their conversation, none of the press seemed unduly concerned over the Rehoming. 'Not before time' was a comment I heard, and a well-known TV anchorwoman two rows up referred to it as 'the best thing for them'. As we drove along, I could see that the main road to Rhayader had been greatly improved in terms of access, all paid for by the Rehoming Commission – there were several billboards proclaiming such – and on the opposite bank of the River Wye I could see where the railway tracks had been relaid, again at huge expense, to facilitate the transportation of the rabbit.

We drove into town, turned left, crossed the bridge and then parked up. I surrendered my mobile phone, stepped from the coach and had my first view of the MegaWarren complex.

It was, firstly, huge. The main gates were set into a brick-built gatehouse of baroque design, and from both sides of this central tower a wall at least thirty feet high stretched off to left and right, changing to a double-layer fence after about 250 yards. We were parked at the railway terminus, which had one long platform and a siding; built around it were office blocks, presumably for Compliance staff.

We obediently followed Pandora Pandora to the main entrance, the access road lined by raised borders which had been recently planted with bedding plants. It all looked extremely twee and friendly – the sort of thing the Spick & Span judges might go for.

We continued on to the main gateway, had the barcode on our passes scanned and moved into a large open area surrounded by smaller admin buildings, the higher doorways indicating they were designed for rabbits. I could see four large factory units behind this emblazoned with the RabToil logo, at least an acre of greenhouses, a Lago meeting house and what looked like a funfair beyond.

Dotted around were dedicated MegaWarren security officers, who all seemed to be keeping a careful eye on us. I was aware of an altercation behind me so turned to see several of the security staff talking to Harvey at the entrance. One was looking at his ID and a second was talking on his radio. I stopped in my tracks, took a deep breath and walked back towards the main gate.

'Problems?' I asked. The two officers looked at me suspiciously, then grunted. Harvey/Lugless was staring at them, presumably awaiting whatever the situation might bring.

'We need secondary identification for non-humans,' said the first, 'Mr Ffoxe told me personally we were to triple check for infiltrators.'

'Isn't the lack of ears something of a giveaway?' I said.

'Mr AY-002 filled out his birthdate wrongly on the security confirmation form,' said the second, 'and the secure link to the Spotting server is down.'

'I got my birthday *right*,' said Harvey/Lugless in a sniffy tone, 'it's your records that are wrong.'

'Regulations,' said the second officer, who seemed more bored than officious.

'I'm a Spotter from RabCoT in Hereford,' I said in a low voice. 'Just don't yell it out. Lugless here works out of our office.'

'That's good,' said the second officer, who then made a phone call to check out my credentials, and once this was done he let us both in.

'Thanks for that,' said Harvey once we were out of earshot. 'Our faith in you was justified.'

And we parted, Harvey walking off towards one of the factory units, and me to where everyone was congregated around Mr Ffoxe, Pandora Pandora and, in an unexpected personal appearance, Prime Minister Nigel Smethwick himself.

I entered the back of the crowd, where Pandora Pandora was giving an address.

'... the building you saw outside is the centralised head office of the Rabbit Compliance Taskforce, and will be featuring impressive IT capabilities to safely administer to the million or so guests we are expecting, and to ensure that legal off-colony movement is both efficient and easily enforced. I would also like to point out that the presence of the Taskforce will bring much-needed jobs to the area, and will continue to do so for the foreseeable future, one of the many ways in which the presence of MegaWarren is benefitting the local community.'

She went on to talk about how the 800-million-pound project was completed in under two years, thanked the Welsh government for their support, and especially the two hundred or so residents who were relocated to make way for the facility. She then handed over to Nigel Smethwick, who had been eager to receive the microphone for some time. He started off by saying what a pleasure it was to see so many journalists and dedicated Taskforce professionals, and how MegaWarren would offer something that all the residents of the United Kingdom wanted: a safe place for rabbits from which they could use their many skills to usefully contribute to the UK's economy. He talked about himself and his achievements quite a lot, and eventually said that we could go wherever we wanted. He then asked, somewhat reluctantly, whether there were any questions.

'When do the rabbit arrive?' asked a journalist at the back.

The Senior Group Leader answered the question.

'We will expect,' said Mr Ffoxe, 'to start inviting early beta-tester rabbits to move in in about two weeks. Travel will be free to all voluntarily participating rabbits, and generous early relocation payments will be forthcoming at a level which is yet to be decided. The first to arrive will be given the best homes and plots.'

'The Grand Council of Coneys have long insisted,' said a BBC journalist at the front, 'that the colonies are little more than gilded workhouses, and have vowed to resist a move to MegaWarren. Do you have any comment on that?'

'*Timendi causa est nescire*,' he replied; 'the cause of fear is ignorance.

The old colonies are currently unfit for purpose. They are crowded, unsanitary and often situated in places where the soil is sub-standard and burrow collapse a very real and pressing problem. MegaWarren has been *specifically* designed with the well-being of the rabbit in mind, and as soon as word gets out about how wonderfully fabulous it is, the rabbit will be heading over here in droves.'

'I've heard the speeches,' said the same BBC reporter, 'but what about the Grand Council's reservations?'

The fox looked testily at the reporter, but he smiled broadly and brought his considerable charm to bear.

'It is indeed a great shame that the Council of Coneys have decided to be so pointlessly obstructive over the issue,' said Mr Ffoxe, 'but you must understand that the rabbit does not reason in the same way as the human. They have a simplistic, childlike approach to politics, and reluctantly we have decided that it is necessary to undertake changes for their own good, either with their agreement or not.'

'It looks like a prison to me,' said another journalist, who had sounded more pro-MegaWarren on the bus, but may have been doing so, it seemed, to actually get an invite, 'and rabbits are known to be stubborn and will, if pushed, invoke their "Bugs Bunny Protocol" and meet force with force. What if they refuse to be moved at all?'

'They won't,' said Nigel Smethwick, taking the microphone. 'A recent poll conducted by UKARP indicates that ninety-seven per cent of rabbits will be overjoyed to move here. The three per cent of troublemakers whom it will be impossible to convince of our magnanimity may have to be re-educated to persuade them that a non-compliant stance would not be in the best interests of rabbit/human relations. The Rehoming policy is not leporiphobic, it is simply in the best interests of all our species groups. We *like* rabbits,' he added, 'but we like compliant rabbits the most, in a homeland that best suits their needs.'

'We should add,' said Mr Ffoxe, 'that rabbits are currently not legally defined as human, so it must be appreciated that what we are doing shows an unprecedented level of compassion and understanding of animal rights. We would like our good intentions to be noted, and at the very minimum, repaid with simple gratitude as good manners dictate. Goats, sheep, chickens, ducks, cows and pigs – actually, most other animals, I hardly need point out – have never, and will never, receive a similar level of care.'

Oddly, there was a murmuring of agreement at this. There were more questions over cost overruns, and whether the site could be expanded, all of which were expertly evaded or obscured by either Smethwick, Pandora Pandora or Mr Ffoxe. Finally, someone asked the question that I would have asked, if I'd been permitted, or braver.

'What about the hundred thousand legal off-colony rabbits?'

It was a tricky question, and Ffoxe and Smethwick looked at one another, then passed the microphone to Pandora Pandora.

'MegaWarren is available to all rabbits, irrespective of status,' she said, 'and we are fully confident that all off-colony rabbits will be only too happy to relocate here once they see just how wonderful it is.'

'What if they don't?' asked someone.

'If there are no more questions,' said Pandora Pandora, 'please feel free to wander around the facility and ask as many questions as you like – lunch will be served at 1 p.m. in the Palace of Creative Joy.'

The group broke up and I made to move away but Whizelle caught my eye and walked over.

'Hello, Knox,' he said, 'what do you think of it all?'

'Impressive, sir,' I replied, as weasels, like foxes, were never ones to cross.

'Attractive to rabbits?'

'Definitely.'

'Conducive to happiness and high productivity?'

'I hope so.'

'Good. Listen, have you noticed anything odd about Lugless this morning?'

I felt my heart start to beat faster and resisted a temptation to scratch my nose or look away.

'What do you mean?'

'Odd. Different. Seems … distracted. I went to speak to him about a case we were discussing yesterday and he kind of looked through me.'

'I've known him less than a month,' I said, 'and he seems as unpleasant now as when I first met him.'

'Humph,' said Whizelle, then thanked me and moved away. I made a quick exit too, just in case he wanted to question me further.

I wandered into the Palace of Creative Joy, which was actually one of the factories in which the rabbits would build vacuum cleaners, microwave ovens, kitchen appliances and car engines. There were four of these buildings, all huge, and subcontractors from RabToil were busily installing the moving assembly lines. I could see CCTV cameras everywhere, and knew that this alone could be a deal-breaker. None of the colonies had a single camera. Rabbits hated being surveilled. I suddenly had the strongest feeling that for all the planning and money and effort, not a single rabbit would ever move here. Or at least, not by their own choice.

I left the Palace of Creative Joy and walked across to the Lago meeting house. The circular building was of tiered seating on six levels that surrounded a central area where a large circular void in the roof bathed the interior with natural light. I paused for a moment, having never been in such a place before, then stepped back outside and looked around. Beyond the admin blocks, factory units and large multilingual call centres, the land stretched away to the steep hills opposite, four or five miles distant. I could see the perimeter fence undulating softly with the contours of the land, and a river wended its way out from the hills through a narrow gorge and what looked like productive farmland, criss-crossed by hedges, spinneys and the odd oak tree in cheerful abundance. It was, I had to admit, a very lovely area of the world. The soil good, the climate pleasant. If you took away the sense of menacing coercion, it was somewhere any rabbit might want to live.

'Hello!' said a young woman, one of the Pandora Pandora clones – dressed all in black, with an aggressive attitude of chatty bonhomie and the mandated blond hair, 'I'm Miss Robyns. Want to see the burrows?'

'OK,' I said.

We walked down one of the access roads while Miss Robyns regaled me with all the high points of the facility. About how beautiful it was, how clean, and how there was space to roam and even a sixteen-mile perimeter bouncing track for early-morning jaunts and for beta-bucks to 'blow off excess humours during the inevitable disappointments of the mating season'.

We stopped where a six-foot-wide concrete pipe was sticking out of the ground with 'Section 87D' stencilled on the side. She led the way into the ground by way of some steps but the tunnel soon levelled out and after fifty feet or so made a sharp right turn.

'Although no ferret was anthropomorphised during the Event,' said Miss Robyns, 'the rabbit still like to have defensible bends in their burrows.'

As we walked, I noted that every ten feet or so a panelled wooden door complete with doorknob, brass knocker and letterbox slot was set into the wall of the concrete pipe. We stopped opposite one marked '87D-237' and I opened the door to find that it led nowhere – facing me was a wall of soft earth, with the imprint of the back of the door neatly impressed upon it.

'The rabbit like to dig their own home,' explained Miss Robyns, and I closed the door.

'There must be a lot of doors,' I said.

'Yes,' said Miss Robyns, suddenly looking bored, 'thousands.'

We turned the anti-ferret corner and could see the long tunnel stretch out in front of us, doors off to left and right. We also surprised Harvey, whose hearing, I thought later, was probably greatly diminished. He was staring into one of a series of ventilation grilles set into the tunnel wall, each one above a telephone point, postbox and WiFi transmitter.

'Very interesting,' he said, secreting in his coat what looked like a camera. I was walking in front, so Miss Robyns didn't notice.

'Oh!' she said, startled by his appearance. I told her who he was and how he disliked rabbits more than almost anyone I knew, and she shook hands with him, but was at pains to point out that she was only doing this job because it *was* her job, and not because she was leporiphobic.

'I believe you,' said Harvey/Lugless in an ambiguous manner, and he joined us as we viewed the communal kitchens, rest, play and nursery areas. We then retraced our steps to the entrance and blinked as we came out into the warm sunshine. Almost immediately we noticed some sort of commotion near by, where Mr Ffoxe was talking to Whizelle and Section Officer Flemming.

'... when did you hear about this, Weasel?' asked Mr Ffoxe.

'Just now, and it's pronounced "Whizelle".'

The fox then caught sight of our small group.

'You!' said the Senior Group Leader, jabbing a paw in our direction. 'You're in some big f★★★ing trouble.'

The game, it seemed, was up, and I think Harvey knew it too as I heard a faint 'pop' as he dropped a pellet.[52]

If Mr Ffoxe knew Harvey wasn't Lugless he'd be tortured and killed at the hands of the Senior Group Leader – probably here, right in front of us. But to my shame, I wasn't really thinking of that. I was thinking that they'd figure out that I knew too – I'd vouched for Harvey's identity to get him in here. But things didn't quite turn out that way. As the fox, weasel and human drew closer I realised that the focus of their anger was not Harvey/Lugless at all – but *me*.

'That's right, Knox,' said Whizelle as they encircled me, 'we've heard about your lewd and unnatural associations with your rabbit next-door neighbour. Taskforce guideline 68/5b forbids it. You're suspended from work and will have all security privileges withdrawn pending an internal investigation.'

'Well now,' said Mr Ffoxe with a chuckle. 'I know I asked for deep infiltration, but this is *definitely* not what I had in mind. *In partibus lagomorphium*, eh? Mind you,' he added with a smile, 'anyone who threatens a fox with a flick-knife does show spirit.'[53]

And he turned to Whizelle.

'Weasel, have Knox debriefed back at the office. Tease out the truth, but courteously – Knox remains a valuable asset and one that we would wish to be able to re-educate.'

---

52. Up until that moment, I thought this was a leporiphobic slur. Apparently it wasn't.

53. Literally 'among the rabbits', but I'm not sure where the quote came from, nor who he was paraphrasing.

'Certainly,' said Whizelle, 'but you pronounce my name "Whi—"'

'So, Tamara,' said Mr Ffoxe, cutting Whizelle dead and taking Miss Robyns by the arm in a courteous manner, 'been working for the Taskforce long?'

'How did you know my name?'

'My dear,' he said, 'aren't you *all* called Tamara?'

'Personally,' said Whizelle to me, 'I don't give a monkey's what you get up to in your spare time, but rules are rules. Lugless, find a car and get Knox back to the Hereford office. I'll be a couple of hours behind you, and just in case: no phone calls, no visits, no solicitor.'

'Why me?' said Harvey, remaining in character.

'You'll do as you're told,' said Whizelle, and Harvey shrugged and flicked his head, indicating I should follow him.

'Bother and blast,' he said once we were safely out of earshot. 'That didn't go as planned. I got barely an hour inside. Even so.'

He looked at me.

'You want to know what's going on, don't you?'

'No,' I said, 'I do *not* want to know what's going on. I didn't see anything, I don't know anything, and as far as anyone is concerned, for now and ever more you *are* Lugless AY-002.'

'Probably quite wise,' said Harvey as we walked towards where Lugless's car was parked, the same late-seventies Eldorado Lugless had used while on Ops in Ross-on-Wye. I started to ask Harvey how it came to be here, but he silenced me, took the keys from where they had been hidden on the top of the rear tyre, unlocked the doors, and told me to hop in the back. He then started the car and reversed out of the parking lot. He drove quite fast – for a rabbit – but I didn't want to ask him anything because I didn't want to know anything. I wanted to resign, go home and devote my life to Speed Librarying – a life choice that I made official by designating it with a code: 12–345.

We took the main road back towards Hereford, picked up some more speed and as soon as the road was clear in both directions, Harvey hauled hard right on the wheel and the car swerved and left the road. There was a double thump as the wheels struck the verge and then everything felt smooth and quiet as we became airborne.

There was a steep escarpment beyond the verge and I watched the litter and discarded junk food cartons inside the car suddenly become weightless as we gracefully went into a brief free fall that ended with a teeth-juddering thump, a cracking of wood and the soft implosive noise that toughened windscreens make when they burst. I was thrown hard forward into my seat belt, bounced back into the door pillar and everything went black.

Car & Custody

Ninety-seven per cent of all rabbit internet traffic was colony-to-colony. Within the warren and burrow, nearly all conversation and gossip were undertaken nose to nose, and a recent survey found that, given the levels to which rabbits like to gossip, news and views within the colony could travel faster than broadband, and were a lot more fun.

I came to my senses with a shocking headache, the taste of blood in my mouth and the smell of burning in my nostrils. The car had landed upright and was facing backwards at the bottom of a steep wooded slope. The burned-out Eldorado – much scavenged by tourists – remained in situ for a decade until removed for inclusion in the Event Museum at the repurposed MegaWarren Induction Centre. I visited this site a lot when I ran tours after the publication of my book, eight years after the Battle of May Hill.

The windscreen had vanished, the car's bonnet had been folded up almost to the scuttle by the action of a large tree that had fared better than us in the altercation, and a wisp of smoke was rising from under the bonnet. I looked out of my window and could see that the car was resting in a cow pasture; three Friesian heifers stared at us with a look of extreme indifference while solemnly chewing the cud. Harvey was conscious and having trouble opening the car door, so he lay on his back on the front seat and gave the door an almighty kick with his powerful hind legs. The door was wrenched off its hinges and landed two dozen yards away.

'What happened?' I said, but Harvey just glanced at me and walked around to open the boot of the car.

'C'mon,' he said, 'it's time.'

He wasn't speaking to me. He was speaking to another rabbit, who climbed out of the boot. He was identically dressed and, like Harvey, earless. But unlike Harvey, whose ears had recently been cropped – I could now see the stitches, which were of string – these were long-healed. It was Lugless.

'Change of plan?' said Lugless in a surprisingly meek tone. 'That was never eight hours.'

'There was an unforeseen hiccup,' said Harvey, 'but a deal's a deal.'

Small tongues of flame were now visibly curling around the crumpled bonnet, but I think I was too confused by the turn of events to assess the sort of danger I was in. As I watched from the back seat, Lugless climbed into the car and placed himself behind the wheel.

'You have them?' he asked.

'Here,' said Harvey, and handed him what looked like two short and very withered scrolls tied up with red ribbon. Lugless took them with the greatest of reverence and held them tight to his body.

'By the power vested in me by the Venerable Bunty,' said Harvey, 'and in deference to the indulgence bestowed upon you, I declare upon the name and spirit of Lago, the Grand Matriarch, that your mortal sins are expunged. You go to your maker as pure, and complete, as the circle of trust that binds us all, which took our saviour, and the unbreakable bond that joins all rabbits.[54]'

I saw Lugless take a deep breath, and bow his head, and Harvey made the sign of the circle on his forehead. The flames were quite high now, and Harvey bowed again, took a step back, coughed and looked at me.

'Are you staying in there or what?'

I rapidly came to my senses and clambered out of the car, relieved to find I had no broken bones – just a twisted knee.

'Is he staying in there?' I asked.

'He's at peace,' said Harvey, 'and whole. I have to leave now, but you and I will meet again, at the place and time the Venerable Bunty completes the circle.'

'How do you know I'll be there?' I asked.

54. I am to this day confused as to why Harvey didn't speak to Lugless in Rabbity. Either he was speaking for my benefit or Lugless wasn't considered rabbit enough to be treated as such. There may have been another reason. I will never know.

'Because Bunty has foreseen it. She foresees *everything*. When you feel the time is right, tell Pippa that what happened between us was real, and she knows where to find me if she can love a half-rabbit.'

And he then made the circle of trust on my forehead, smiled and vanished off across the fields in a series of rapid bounces, each covering a good twenty yards. I meant to ask him what the two dried scrolls were that he'd handed to Lugless, but I think it was fairly obvious. They were Lugless's ears.

I turned back to the Eldorado, which was now well alight. Molten plastic dripped from the engine bay as little smoking raindrops of fire, and the heat was blistering the paint on the bonnet.

'I always knew I'd eventually find a rabbit I couldn't turn,' Lugless said, staring straight ahead, 'and there would always be one who would eventually turn me. But everything comes to an end.'

I put up one arm to shield the heat from my face and stepped forward, stretching out my other hand for him to take.

'Join me out here,' I said, 'you don't need to do this.'

He smiled as the flames started to lick around him, the smell of singed fur now in the air. Douglas AY-002 turned to me and gave a wry smile.

'Humans,' he said, 'so little time – so much to know.'

He turned back towards the steering wheel and held his newly returned ears closer to him as the flames consumed him.

He didn't make a single sound. Not a squeak not a whimper – nothing.

Help was not long in arriving owing to the telltale pall of black smoke and the gap in the fencing. I was still trembling when the ambulance took me to Hereford General, accompanied by a Taskforce officer whom I didn't recognise. They kept me in overnight for observation given the clout on my head, but aside from a few cuts and bruises and the twisted knee, I was unhurt. I was supervised throughout, even my phone call to Pippa, who expressed concern and offered to come and visit, but I told her she shouldn't.

No one had noticed that Harvey had been a Miffy, except me. As far as anyone was concerned, the earless rabbit who visited Mega Warren was the same one who had died transporting a compromised Taskforce employee back to base.

I was allowed a shower without supervision and driven the following morning to the Nigel Smethwick Centre and given some breakfast in the canteen, again supervised, then told to wait in one of the interview rooms. It didn't occur to me until later that Connie would have been hauled in for questioning too, but she was.

I sat there for maybe an hour, conscious of not only my predicament here, but also that the clock was ticking – the Mallett brothers had given Pippa, myself and the Rabbits until this evening at ten to leave Much Hemlock – and they'd probably worked out none of us were playing ball. Tonight would be the night I made a stand – and I wasn't looking forward to it.

The spartan interview room was clean and warm but otherwise unremarkable. The table was bolted to the floor, but the plastic chairs could be moved. In the centre of the table was a large brass ring for potential restraint, but it seemed little used. When it came down to it, rabbits just weren't violent unless pushed into a corner, and even then were far more likely to use reasoned debate than tooth and claw.

The door opened at a little after eleven, and Whizelle walked in accompanied by Flemming. They sat down opposite me and placed a mug of coffee on the table. It was the good stuff, not RabCoT canteen or chain muck. I was being schmoozed.

'How are you feeling, Peter?' asked Flemming.

'Bruised, but OK, thanks.'

'We're glad of that,' said Whizelle. 'The loss of Douglas AY-002 is a serious annoyance as he was one of only three rabbits the Taskforce implicitly trusted, and "tragic car accidents" always need to be viewed with a degree of suspicion, especially on clear roads, in good weather.'

'What do you mean?' I asked.

'We think it might have been a hit,' said Flemming, 'on him, you – or both of you. Following on from Toby Mallett's unexpected resignation and utter failure to give a plausible account of why he did, we're inclined to think that the Spotters' office here in Hereford has been targeted by either rabbits, rabbit sympathisers or rabbit sympathiser-sympathisers.'

'Oh,' I said.

'So before we even *begin* to talk about the allegations regarding you and your next-door neighbour, tell us about the accident.'

I told them everything I knew, and tried to stick as much to the truth as I could. I'd be questioned about this again, and if I was inconsistent over my story, I'd be more stuffed than I was already. I told them Lugless steered purposely off the road, no other car was involved, and that I scrambled out of the burning car when I came to. Lugless, I told them, was either dead in the crash or unconscious. Either way, I couldn't get to him.

'So you have no idea why he swerved off the road?' asked Whizelle.

'None. One moment we're driving along the road, the next I'm waking up in a blazing car.'

Whizelle looked at Flemming, who nodded, and the weasel opened a file and placed a picture of a white rabbit on the table. Now I'd seen him up close, I could recognise him better and the name on the picture confirmed it – he was Harvey Augustus McButtercup, aged twenty-six, a RabCab driver, resident in Colony One. I also knew he was now earless, a prominent member of the Rabbit Underground, had successfully infiltrated the Taskforce – and was in love with, and loved by, my daughter.

'Have you seen this rabbit before?' he asked.

'No. Spotting isn't an exact science. Who is he?'

'We think he's Flopsy 7770,' said Whizelle. 'Lugless looked him up on the Rabbit Employment Database before he died. But he didn't tell anyone. You and he were in the office alone that morning – did he share with you?'

'Lugless shared little with me,' I said, now extremely glad I had searched for Harvey's details on Lugless's computer, but realising that I had led them directly to Harvey's identity. I thought momentarily of asking whether I was detained and requesting a solicitor, but I got the feeling that this would only increase suspicions, not allay them.

They moved on to the allegations I had been suspended about, and the mood in the room seemed to darken. Flemming and Whizelle had been work colleagues for many years and we'd got on OK, but right now that counted for nothing. There followed a long and very detailed account of what 'four plausible witnesses' had seen outside my house the night before last. Unlike the Harvey/Lugless issue, where I had to lie convincingly several times, this was a testimony I could actually give from start to finish fairly truthfully – from when the Rabbits moved in, to the incident in All Saints with Mr Ffoxe, and then to the evening when we ran through her lines, the farcical hiding in the cupboards with the Dumas novel, and Connie and Doc's argument in the hallway.

'Nothing happened,' I said.

'Let me spell this out for you,' said Whizelle in a more serious voice. 'Right now we can charge you and Constance Rabbit with offences contrary to the Unnatural Associations Section of the Anthropomorphised Animals Limited Rights Act of 1996.'

I didn't know the act word for word, but knew that the law was tactically enforced by the authorities as they saw fit. In the current climate, it seemed that they wanted it enforced. Friendship with rabbits, as far as the Rehoming was concerned, was to be discouraged.

'With four eyewitnesses all happy to testify,' he continued, 'you both go to the clink – not a lot, two years, out in one, but with that on your files, I'd like to think that life will never quite be the same. Y'know how everyone believes they're broad-minded and open? Well, spoiler alert: they're not. And,' he added, 'along with your criminal record and time served, your pension can be cancelled on the grounds of "gross professional misconduct".'

'You can do that?'

'We can do that,' said Flemming. 'All we want, Peter, is a teensy-weensy little confession implicating Constance Rabbit in intimate entrapment. You can say it was an accident or a dare or you were beguiled or were drunk or something. You'll still lose your job but you'll keep your pension and there's nothing on your record. Back to Much Hemlock and your uneventful life.'

'What will happen to Constance?'

'We'll plea-bargain it down to surrender of her off-colony status on grounds of "demonstrable moral turpitude". She'll be back in the colonies by next week, and probably a great deal happier for it. She wasn't really what we'd call trustworthy off-colony material.'

'Best of all,' added Whizelle, 'it will send a clear message to female rabbits everywhere that beguiling humans into depravity can and will have dire consequences.'

I stared down at the table in silence.

'So what do you say?' asked Whizelle.

'I—'

But I didn't get to answer. The door opened, and in walked Mr Ffoxe.

The Art of the Deal

Weasels still turned white for the winter, even though there was no reason to do so. They can get very crotchety either side of 'the change' but were actually a lot more agreeable as ermine. Most weasels took the winter off, and headed to the slopes, where they were competent – though not highly visible – skiers.

I say 'walked' but 'burst' might be a better term. I saw Flemming blanch and make a reflexive move to run away, but she checked herself and stayed put. Whizelle didn't flinch, but instead looked annoyed. The timing was poor, and things can get badly out of hand when foxes take control.

Mr Ffoxe looked at everyone in the room in turn.

'You can piss off,' he said to Flemming, 'and you, Weasel, can *definitely* piss off.'

'It's pronounced "Whi-zelle".'

'Whatever. Tamara, get in here.'

Miss Robyns stepped in, armed with a clipboard and holding three mobile phones.

'Hello!' she said in a chirpy fashion. 'I work for Torquil now.'

'Congratulations,' I said.

'What is this?' said Whizelle, who I think was about the only operative in the Taskforce who could stand up to Ffoxe. '*I* am conducting this interview.'

'Not any more you're not. I have some new information that elevates our enquiry beyond a little bit of furry slap and tickle.'

'I'd like to be briefed on this,' said Whizelle.

'And I'd like to share a glass of Pinot Grigio with Tilda Swinton,' replied the fox, 'but life is full of disappointments. Close the door on your way out, old boy.'

'No,' said Whizelle. 'Knox might be weak-willed and a rabbit-fancying turncoat, but he's a human, and we know what happened the last time you interviewed a human, don't we?'

'That is a disgusting and unfounded accusation,' said Mr Ffoxe, 'but when you run with the bun, you are scum like the bun.'

'Look—' began Whizelle, but Mr Ffoxe simply lifted a quivering lip and gave a low growl at the back of his throat. I felt the hairs rise on the back of my neck and Whizelle's ears flicked back as he suddenly became utterly submissive.

'I'm so sorry for my outburst,' he said quietly, 'I don't know what came over me.'

And he left the interview room with his tail firmly between his legs.

'Well now,' said the fox, seating himself opposite me, 'tempers are a little fraught today, aren't they?'

He leaned back in the chair while his small yellow eyes peered at me with an appearance of ... actually, I'm not quite sure what. Disdain, I think, mixed with quiet confidence and a sense of arrogant superiority. He said nothing, removed a cigarette from a silver case, tapped it on the box and then lit it from a large gold lighter that Tamara held out for him. He took a deep breath, then exhaled the smoke in my direction and said nothing – for quite a long time.[55]

'You're not going to harm me,' I said, unable to stand the silence any more. 'And as I said to Whizelle and Flemming, nothing happened.'

The fox looked at me coolly.

'Whether you did or you didn't, old boy, it doesn't really matter. And you know what? I believe you. But since we are so close to the Rehoming, I don't think it's in anyone's best interest to be making waves. What's more, because of your unique circle of friends and intimate associations, I can offer you a deal whereby all this goes away, you get full pension rights, a fifty-grand cash bonus and not a blemish on your record. How does that sound?'

'It sounds like it has strings attached.'

'Astute of you. Here it is: we have reason to believe Constance Rabbit has connections to the Rabbit Underground, and we think

---

55. It felt like half an hour but was probably less than a minute.

she is a bunnytrap, simply there to gain access to the Taskforce's mainframe through you, the dupe.'

I'd not thought about this before. It didn't *sound* true, and for one good reason:

'I don't have access to the Taskforce's mainframe.'

'The Underground don't know that. I want you to work for us, working against them, together. They want to make Britain into a rabbit nation, with their laws, their heathen god, their aggressive veganism and quasi-rodent way of doing things. This sceptr'd isle, this green and pleasant land, is reserved for humans and a few foxes, not for a plague of vermin. And they can do that, they can make that happen, just by doing what they like to do best. They're planning on outnumbering us. The LitterBomb. It's on the cards, I *know*.'

It was all UKARP conspiracy-theory nonsense. Nigel Smethwick had been spouting similar stuff for years, and none of it remotely proven.

'They're just *rabbits*, sir. Herbivores. Compliant, trusting, hardworking. I've spoken to them, I think I kind of *know* them. I don't believe they have any agenda at all. They simply want … to *be*.'

Mr Ffoxe laughed.

'Knoxie, my old chum, that's *exactly* what they want you to believe. The truth, my friend, is far bleaker: all that cute cuddly stuff – don't be fooled. You saw Mrs Rabbit with that knife against my throat in All Saints?'

'You crushed her niece's head in your jaws.'

'Well, woop-woop,' he said, 'one rabbit down is not any kind of a loss. It was just my very good fortune that I didn't become another victim of rabbit-on-fox violence.'

It was a stretch that even Smethwick would have been hard-pressed to make.

'She wouldn't have killed you,' I said, 'not with the likely reprisals.'

He stared at me coldly.

'Reprisals are *vital* to maintain order,' he said. 'Besides, sixty seconds of what the rabbits jokingly call passion would soon make up those losses. Now: I can make everything go away and give you your pension and some cash, or we can bump the charges up from simple association to lending material support to the Rabbit Underground – which is a banned disruptionist movement. It's a minimum ten years.'

'Wait, wait,' I said, 'material *support?*'

'Sure. Were you paid to get Harvey McButtercup into the MegaWarren, or were you simply pulling a solid for your furry woodland friends?'

'I ... I don't know what you mean.'

'Sure you do. How do you think Lugless managed to leave his car in the car park when he arrived in the coach? The rabbit masquerading as Lugless was with you when we spoke at MegaWarren. I smelled the fear on him. I'd met Lugless before and he didn't fear me at all. I liked him. The best kind of rabbits are furry on the inside.'

'That's the evidence of your nose against my eyes, Mr Ffoxe,' I said, feeling braver externally but not within, as a nasty churning feeling seemed to be going on inside, and my mouth felt dry.

'There's more,' said Mr Ffoxe. 'When Lugless was cropped they would have kept his ears. They always do. It's a religious "going to rabbit heaven complete" sort of deal. Trouble is, they preserve them in hot sand which tends to turn them into hard leather.'

Tamara chucked an evidence bag on to the table containing Lugless's rolled-up ears, badly charred but more or less still extant.

'If we had the forensic boys unroll these I'd bet my foxy left nut we'd find a pattern of duel-holes that exactly matched AY-002's. He fought a lot of duels. Liked the ladies. A little too much, as it turned out.'

'Perhaps he carried his ears with him, as, I don't know – a memento?'

'Cropped rabbits are denied their ears. That's the point. No, I think Lugless swapped with Harvey in *exchange* for his ears and an honourable death. I think you were the one who used Lugless's computer to look up Harvey McButtercup, and you vouched for Harvey when he inveigled his way into MegaWarren. You've seen him out there in the real world. Where, I don't know. But I'll find out.'

This was all annoyingly excellent detective work. You can't outfox the fox.

'Conjecture,' I said.

In an instant I was on my back with Mr Ffoxe on top of me. He had moved so quickly it seemed like someone had snipped two seconds out of time. While Tamara moved to the door to ensure no one entered, Mr Ffoxe stared deeply into my eyes, and I felt fear. Not your ordinary run-of-the-mill worry about being late for an important meeting, or a funny lump that turns out to be nothing at the doctor's. This was pure, unadulterated, mortal fear of one's imminent demise. And what's more, that one's end is inescapable, inevitable and will be protracted, and *painful*.

Mr Ffoxe said nothing and slowly pressed the point of a single claw into the side of my left eyeball. My vision blurred and greyed out, and the pain was intense – yet I hardly dared breathe lest my added movement caused my eyeball to burst.

'Now listen,' he said in a soft whisper, his breath reeking of rancid meat and claret, 'I'm going to ask you once again, and if you don't tell me the full and complete truth first time out, I'm going to take out your eye, and then I'm going to eat it.'

'You wouldn't do that,' I whispered.

'Ever wonder how Flemming lost hers?' he asked. 'We had a disagreement a while ago. I think it was over company policy – or who was the best Batman. I forget which, but she's totally on board now.'

I think I started to sob then, quietly and without moving.

'That's right,' he said, 'it's all fun and games until someone loses an eye. Now: are you going to be a good little human and tell me what I want to know? In return, you get a pension, fifty K, and you get to keep both your peepers.' He paused, then added: 'This is where you say, "Yes, Sir, Mr Ffoxe, sir, Mr Knox agrees with the fox, Sir".'

'Yes Sir, Mr Ffoxe sir,' I whispered.

'Close enough.'

And in an instant, I was suddenly alone on the floor with Mr Ffoxe back in his seat. I climbed shakily to my feet, sat down and placed the monogrammed handkerchief the fox handed me to my eye.

'So,' he said in a quiet voice, 'talk to me.'

And I did. I told him *everything*.

Bunnytrap Trap

After the Battle of May Hill and as part of the government inquiry, it was found that Mr Ffoxe had plucked out and eaten eighteen human eyes in total, and the ensuing compensation claims were estimated to have cost £17.4 million.

I explained pretty much everything about me and Connie and the Rabbits as accurately as I could while the vision slowly clouded in my right eye, the action of the blood seeping into the eyeball. He wanted to know every word Harvey uttered, every exchange we made. 'What did he mean by that?' 'What was your impression of him as he looked in the ventilation ducts at MegaWarren?' 'Have you ever spoken to Patrick Finkle?' 'Do you think Constance Rabbit works for the Underground?' 'Do you think you'll be seeing Harvey again?'

'Actually,' I answered in response to the last question, 'I think I might. He said we'd meet again, at the time and place where the Venerable Bunty completes the circle.'

For the briefest moment I saw a flicker of consternation pass over the Group Leader's face. His eyes, I think, although small at the best of times, opened just a little bit wider – but then it was gone, and he was as poker-faced as ever, giving nothing away. He sat and stared at me again for some time, Tamara rubbing his shoulders.

'OK,' he said finally, 'with the Rehoming imminent, the biggest fly in the ointment is the Bunty false prophet and the Underground. I need you to work for me. Be my eyes and ears.'

'The deal was to tell you everything I know for my pension and fifty K.'

The fox said nothing, pointed at my eye and grinned.

'Let's just *suppose* I agree,' I said after a pause; 'what would you have me do?'

Mr Ffoxe outlined his plan. I was to keep office hours but sit them out in an interview room – bring crayons and a colouring book, he told me – and let my relationship with Mrs Rabbit develop; she would be released without charge. If she asked me to access the Taskforce's databases, I was to report back and hand over the intel that Mr Ffoxe permitted. I was basically to report everything I heard, and especially the time and place I would meet with the Venerable Bunty.

'I might not meet her,' I said.

'If she has foreseen it,' said the fox, giving more credibility to Bunty's powers than I thought possible of him, 'then it will happen. And I want to be there to stop it.'

Within ten minutes I was outside, blinking stupidly in the sunlight. I took a deep breath and made my way into town, gathering my thoughts. I was working out a plan of my own: to never speak to Connie again and avoid her at every opportunity.

But that didn't happen, of course.

I texted Pippa as soon as they returned my phone and met her in the café at All Saints.

'Shit, Dad,' she said, 'what happened to your eye?'

'Mr Ffoxe threatened to take it out and eat it.'

She winced and stared at me for a moment.

'You're not kidding, are you?'

I told her how I was now acting as a bunnytrap trap for Mr Ffoxe and that both Bobby and Harvey were prominent members of the Rabbit Underground. As I spoke, her demeanour changed from simple concern to the panicky realisation that this was bigger and deeper and more serious than she might possibly have imagined.

I also told Pippa that her relationship with Harvey was something I hadn't mentioned, but given Mr Ffoxe's powers of deduction, he either already knew or it wouldn't be a secret for long – and that it would be a really good idea if she were to lay low for a while.

'The last time Harvey spoke to me it was about you,' I added. 'He said to tell you it was real – and I don't think he was lying.'

'Rabbits rarely lie,' said Pippa. 'They take their greatest pride in preserving most strongly the parts of them that aren't us.'

I thought about her words carefully, and also about Connie. If rabbits rarely lied, then it stood to reason they didn't misrepresent what they felt, either. If Connie was a bunnytrap then she might have been selected precisely because she *did* like me. One less subterfuge.

Pippa departed within ten minutes after giving me a long hug. I asked her where she would go, and she said 'she had somewhere safe in mind', but I didn't ask her any more questions. Best not, really. Once she was gone I sat there for an hour, then headed home. As I was passing the village of Slipton Flipflop I had a sudden thought that if Connie *was* a bunnytrap then she'd have probably guessed that I'd tell Mr Ffoxe everything – and I half expected them to be gone by the time I arrived home. Indeed, I was actually hoping they *would* be gone. It would give me licence to do nothing, and I so wanted to do nothing.

I didn't get my wish. Their Dodge was in the driveway and Major Rabbit was clipping the privet hedge while smoking his pipe. It was a warm afternoon, so he had draped his jacket over a garden fork and was working in his waistcoat. He gave me a cheery wave as I climbed out of the car, and I noticed that Connie was watering the large vegetable patch that had now replaced most of the lawn. If she was worried about being arrested and questioned all day, she wasn't showing it. Connie's apparent normality wasn't the only surprise in store. Toby Mallett was busy repainting my garage door.

'I'm ever so sorry, Mr Knox, for daubing obscenities on your garage door the other night,' he said in an obsequious tone as soon as he saw me, 'but I was very drunk and wasn't fully in command of my senses. Papa told me the error of my ways, so I'm here making amends.'

'Really?' I said somewhat doubtfully. Apology and contrition really weren't in the Malletts' range of character traits. 'Are you wanting to see Pip again?'

'No!' he said, eyes open wide in shock and making one of several nervous glances towards the Rabbits' house. 'I mean, no, *thank you* – that's all past history. Has she found out about me sleeping with Arabella down at the pony club?'

'Has she beckoned you down to her level and then thumped you in the eye?'

He shook his head.

'Then that'll be a no.'

After discussing what colour to repaint the garage door over the primer he had already applied, he hastily departed with another nervous glance towards Hemlock Towers. Something was going on.

I unlocked the door and went into my house, checked the post in the hall – bills and circulars, mostly – and then jumped in fright when I found Doc waiting for me in the kitchen.

'I do wish you wouldn't do that,' I said, 'popping up like a jack-in-the-box. It's very disconcerting.'

'Sorry,' he said, 'but I need to talk to you about the trouble and strife.'

'The what?'

'The ball and chain. She-who-must-be-obeyed. Y'know, the missus.'

'Look,' I said, expecting trouble, 'it was all a huge misunderstanding.'

'Oh, I know,' he said with a smile, laying a powerful paw on my shoulder. 'Connie explained to me what happened and we had a good laugh about it. Can I speak candidly?'

'Sure.'

He looked down and absently clicked his claws against the linoleum.

'My aim with a pistol is not as true these days, and sooner or later I'm going to find myself at dawn on a foggy heath somewhere, staring down the barrel of a pistol held by some know-it-all young buck with a steadier hand while my seconds assure me everything will be all right when I know that it won't.'

He sat down at the kitchen table.

'I don't want to end up as one of those sad ex-alphas who live alone, their ears so full of holes you could use them to strain cabbage, each puncture a constant reminder of a love hard fought and eventually lost.'

'I'm not sure I follow.'

'You and Connie seem to be quite chummy, and I'd like you to keep me in the loop about any affairs she's having that you think might be *truly* serious. I know it's a long time till the spring mating season, but spouse appropriation starts earlier and earlier these days, and if forewarned, I could chase off the competition with some hard-hitting rhetoric, cash or a pantomime display of male aggression – and in that way avoid a challenge.'

'I get what you're saying,' I said, 'but I'm not totally happy spying on your wife.'

'It's not spying when you love someone. I'd ask Bobby but those two are thick as thieves, and Kent, well, that boy is an inveterate burrower. Do you know I have to keep all the shovels hidden when he's about?'

'Shocking.'

'Yes indeed,' said Doc, getting ready to leave and seemingly quite chirpy again, 'shocking. You will tell me about Connie, though, won't you? I need to keep my marriage together *without* having to fight any duels.'

'I'll do what I can.'

'Stout fellow,' said Doc. 'By the by, you haven't seen Bobby, have you? She packed her bags and left when I was in Hereford picking Connie up from the clink.'

'No,' I said, figuring that if she knew Harvey had been identified, she would probably be in for questioning next. It seemed odd that both our daughters were on the run from the Taskforce.

'Jolly good,' he said, gave me a smile, bounced clean out of the back door and was back gardening in under ten seconds.

I heard the news of the TwoLegsGood demonstration over at Colony One just as I was making a casserole for supper. About two hundred Hominid Supremacists had converged at the entrance to the colony, angry that ordinary hard-working humans were being denied basic benefits while rabbits were being rehomed in 'the lap of luxury'. While the demo was aggressively voluble it was not illegal, and the police and Taskforce seemed unwilling to move them on. Given Mr Ffoxe's connections to TwoLegsGood, I couldn't help wondering whether this was a lockdown by another name – to keep the Venerable

Bunty from moving around the country, spreading, as Smethwick put it, 'her dangerous message of insurrection'.

I'd just popped the casserole in the oven when the doorbell rang. I thought it might have been Connie – ringing so as not to appear too forward – but it wasn't. It was Victor and Norman Mallett.

'Ah,' I said warily, 'good afternoon.'

'Good afternoon, Peter. What happened to your eye?'

'I caught it on a nail.'

'Oh. May we come in?'

'Actually, no. You told me I had forty-eight hours to leave the village and then shopped me to the Taskforce. I've still got eight hours until I default on your request, so you can leave me alone until then.'

Victor and Norman looked at one another.

'I think our comments might have taken been out of context when we gave you forty-eight hours to leave,' said Victor. 'I think what we *actually* meant was that you had forty-eight hours to stay.'

'That explanation makes no sense.'

'Yes – we came over to clarify.'

'OK, so let me ask you something: what was the context when your son daubed "bunnyshagger" on my garage door?'

'He did apologise and paint over it,' said Victor. 'If you look on the plus side you've got a repainted garage door.'

'You're right,' I said, 'I really should be thanking you. Look, I've lived in this village for fifty years. I was born here. I know everyone who lives here, and everyone knows me. And while Much Hemlock is a little right-wing, I thought we could all get along irrespective of political affiliation. But add a family of rabbits and everyone goes nuts.'

'Well, yes,' said Victor, 'that's what we were thinking. Norman and I feel we might have been … in a rush to judgement over you and the Rabbits and we'd like to make amends.'

'Would that be word-amends or actions-amends?' I asked suspiciously, as the first was abundantly common, and the second almost vanishingly rare.

'Action-amends, naturally.'

'OK, then,' I said, eager to see how this might pan out as the Mallett brothers were famed throughout the county for their false platitudes. 'A full apology to the Rabbits, a dropping of all hostilities, if anyone from UKARP or 2LG turns up you tell them to go home – and a position for Major Rabbit on the Much Hemlock Parish Council.'

It was a ridiculous demand, and I fully expected them to laugh in my face. But they didn't.

'We can do that,' said Victor, who'd controlled the council almost since the dawn of time.

'And,' I continued, wondering how far I could push this, 'Mrs Rabbit is to cut the ribbon at the Much Hemlock Village Fete next weekend.'

'Impossible,' said Norman. 'Mrs Griswold and the vicar *always* do the opening. But while cutting the ribbon is plainly an insane suggestion, I could probably have Mrs Rabbit put in charge of the bottle stall.'

'I was thinking of something more prestigious,' I replied, as the bottle stall was by long tradition the entry point for volunteers, lunatics or people out of favour in the village. Less well thought of, even, than the shove ha'penny and whack-a-mole. 'How about if she runs the tombola?'

Victor and Norm laughed – the idea was, we all knew, preposterous. Mrs Fudge-Rigby had overseen the tombola at least since the sixties, and physically attacked the last person to suggest she might want to 'take a break'.

'OK, then,' I said, having a bright idea, 'what about judging the vegetables in the home produce tent?'

Victor and Norman looked at one another.

'Deal,' said Victor.

We shook hands on it and Victor and Norman, a day ago my mortal enemies, were now once again my friends, presumably courtesy of a discreet call from Mr Ffoxe, requesting them to leave us alone so my bunnytrap-trap efforts could continue unimpeded. I shut the door behind them, then watched out of the window as they walked away, patting each other on the back, a job, they thought, well done. They'd been like this from the moment I became aware of them aged eight, and they'd not changed one iota over the years: always trying to play people for their own advantage – and never once any good at it.

Bouncing with Constance

Bouncing was the sport of rabbits, and the mainstay of the Rabbit Games: Long Bounce, Vertical Bounce, Marathon, Sprint and Synchronised. It always looked unusual as rabbits before the Event never really did this – the bouncing they expressed now was more akin to kangaroo motion, and was a quirk of the process that brought them from all rabbit to mostly human.

I rang in sick the following morning as my eye still hurt badly. My sleep was punctuated by nightmares – mostly about Mr Ffoxe clamping his jaws around my throat and squeezing so hard I couldn't breathe.

Once I'd made the coffee and put on the toast, I tuned into the news on the radio to see what had happened in Colony One overnight. The answer, as it turned out, was 'not much'. TwoLegsGood had stayed outside the gates until 2 a.m., shouting their trademark anthem: 'Run, rabbit, run, rabbit, run, run, run, here comes a farmer with a gun gun gun'. While clearly offensive and an incitement to violence, an earlier court hearing had decided the words were from a 'humorous ditty predating the Event' so had historical precedent – and was thus allowable. The upshot of all this activity was that Colony One remained closed to all movement and would remain so, a Compliance Taskforce spokesman said, 'until the safety of the rabbit population can be assured'.

At about nine, the doorbell rang and there was Connie, bright as a button, all smiles and wearing a sports crop top and short skirt, brand new Nikes and a sweatband looped around the base of her ears.

'Hello!' she said in a chirpy voice. 'Fancy a bounce?'

'I'm sorry?'

'A bounce. I'm in training for the Herefordshire double marathon bounce next month, and I'm a little rusty on pace and rhythm. If

228

you bounce too high on each cycle then you tire too quickly, and if you try to overstretch a bounce, the landing can be awkward. I need a safe twenty-four-mile-per-hour bouncing average to beat my PB, or even to have a hope of finishing in the top five.'

'OK,' I said.

'But I need to tell you something first. You remember the duelling pistols I was telling you about?'

'Yes, but it's irrelevant – I'm not going to duel with your husband.'

'The Venerable Bunty thinks you will,' she said, 'and she's rarely wrong.'

'Why is she suddenly so interested in me?'

'She's interested in everybody. So, you remember the rhyme I told you?'

'The one about how "the shot hits the spot if you've a croc on the stock, while the mark of the lark shoots wide of the mark"?'

'Yes, but here's the thing: he doesn't use the pistol with the mark of the lark any more.'

'He doesn't?'

'No – he replaced it with one that has an engraving of a rabbit.'

'A gun with a bun?'

'Yes. But you don't want that.'

'I don't?'

'No. The gun with the bun has the aim that is lame.'

'What does the lark have?'

She sighed deeply, as if I were an idiot.

'I'll go through it once again, so listen very, very carefully: the gun with the bun has the aim that is lame, but the shot'll hit the spot if you've a croc on the stock.'

I repeated it back more or less correct, then said:

'But look, I can't duel him unless you give our union your permission.'

'I know,' she said, 'the Venerable Bunty has foreseen that, too.'

'Does she predict useful things, like the 4.15 at Kempton Park?'

'All the time – but it would be unethical to use that information for material gain. Now: to bouncing. Since you're a human and thus hobbled with the puniest of leg muscles, you could not possibly hope

229

to keep up – so I suggest you drive alongside me. I've drawn a route that's almost exactly eight miles. If I can do a lap in under twenty minutes, then I'm in with a chance of beating Penelope Rabbit, who's way too full of herself and really needs to be taken down a hop or two.'

'Is Doc OK with this?'

'If he knew I'm sure he'd be totally fine about it.'

'Really?'

'Sort of.'

'OK, then.'

I opted to take the Austin-Healey as it was a convertible, and once I'd reversed out, Connie laid a map on the bonnet to brief me. There was a long straight road between Much Hemlock and Squiffton Coachbolt that she suggested taking, then a left by the church of St Julius of the Swollen Glands, then following the disused railway along a three-mile stretch of road before arriving in Syon Kapok, where a left past the old tithe barn would return us to Much Hemlock via Slipton Flipflop.

'I'll give you a head start,' she said. 'Keep to a steady twenty-four if you can.'

I had an accurate speedo on the car, so set off in the direction she had indicated, holding as steady a speed as I could. She soon caught up with me and managed to hold station with the car using a series of powerful leaps in the field next to me, expertly negotiating walls, fences, a small spinney, a sheep and the occasional cow. When she was mid-leap it looked as though she were hanging in the air next to me, then she would land and in a burst of energy and a sharp cry that put me in mind of tennis players during a rally, she would launch herself into the air and was once again momentarily airborne, at which point she had a second or two to speak.

'I'm really sorry for what happened,' she said, sailing over a dry-stone wall. 'I didn't plan for you to get hauled up in front of the Taskforce. You told them nothing happened, right?'

'Nothing *did* happen,' I said, having to shout to be heard in the breeze. 'What did you tell Doc?'

'The same,' she said, taking another leap. 'He's *insanely* suspicious, gets very stressed in the pre-mating season and has a temper, so I just said that you and I were out of the question because you were, well—'

'Uncharismatic?'

'My word was boring, actually.'

'Thanks. He wants me to spy on you.'

She landed just before a row of trees, jumped, then expertly tucked herself into a ball and passed through the foliage with a crack of broken twigs and a burst of leaves.

'He's frightened of losing you to another buck in a duel,' I said. 'He told me he doesn't want the only memento of you to be a hole in his ear.'

This, I think, was news to Connie.

'He said that?'

'More or less.'

She landed, gave out a cry and leapt clear across a small herd of Friesians, who looked as though they'd suddenly realised that it was a Tuesday and would have to reconfigure their plans. We took a left by the church in Squiffton Coachbolt, which Connie undertook by a series of bounds around the graveyard, then she disappeared behind the tea rooms and caught up with me, bouncing along the relative flatness of the disused railway. I told her how Flemming and Whizelle had initially tried to make me testify against her but that the Senior Group Leader had intervened.

'It was Mr Ffoxe who made the charges go away.'

She looked at me, grimaced, then landed, gave another sharp cry and cleared a carelessly abandoned combine harvester with inches to spare. She then slowed her pace and eventually came to stop beside a small clump of trees that bounded a field of ripening wheat.

'How did I do?' she said, wrapping her ears with a cold towel from a cooler she'd placed in my car.

'Twenty-two minutes and eighteen seconds,' I said, studying my stopwatch.

'It's a work in progress,' she said with a shrug as I switched off the engine. She then turned to walk along the edge of a field bounded with silver birches. It was an invitation to join her, and after looking around and seeing no one, I climbed out of the car and followed. She brushed her paw against the wheat that was dry-rustling in the breeze as we walked along, following the footpath that took us towards the distant spire of Clagdangle-on-Arrow by way of Kintley barn, a dilapidated brick-built affair that in days gone by was a favourite hangout for teenagers: just far enough to be away from adults, but not so far away that it couldn't be easily reached on bicycles. I had my first kiss there – with Isadora Fairfax, now the second Mrs Mallett – and it was also the place where Norman, in a furious rage, hit James Bryant with a length of scaffolding, something that we always believed was behind Jim's onset of seizures and early death at twenty-two.

'So,' said Connie, 'why did Mr Ffoxe make the charges go away?'

'He wanted you and I to carry on exactly as we are. He said you were a …'

'A what?'

'A … bunnytrap. That you had moved in opposite to entice and entrap me, probably to gain access to the Taskforce servers via my security clearance.'

She stopped walking, turned to me and cocked her head on one side, her ears falling forward quizzically.

'Is that what you think?'

'I don't know what to think. I've got clearance, you're a rabbit, the Rehoming begins in a month—'

'I've always thought we might be together, Peter, right from when we first met at university. Don't know how or why or even whether we can, but always felt it, kind of deep down.'

I'd felt that too, but didn't know whether risking death in a duel would be worth it. Doc was military, and I'd spotted several prizes for marksmanship in their front room. I'd shot .22 pistols at school, but duelling with a heavy smoothbore was something else entirely. It wasn't likely I'd win. Perhaps that was the plan.

'What else did Mr Ffoxe say?' she asked.

'That I was to let the relationship take its course and see what I could find out about you, the plans for civil disobedience against the Rehoming, and about the Venerable Bunty in particular. He said that if I didn't play ball he'd take my eye out. I agreed to help him, but I'm telling you now so you know I'm no snitch.'

'I'm glad,' she said. 'Thank you.'

She stopped at the entrance to the barn. The oak lintel had rotted and was partly collapsed, and several bricks hung precariously above the doorway.

'Come on in,' she said.

'Do you know what,' I said with great difficulty, 'I'm really not sure that's a good idea.'

'I respect you for it,' she said, 'but it's not for what you think. I want you to meet someone.'

'Who?'

'Trust me.'

A human male and a doe rabbit were waiting for us inside, both seated on the remains of a haywain that was now just a partially collapsed chassis, but had been almost intact when I'd played here as a child. As I drew closer I could see the man was Patrick Finkle of the Rabbit Support Agency, and he stood up as we approached, smiled and stepped forward to shake my hand. The rabbit with him was snowy white, wore thick horn-rimmed glasses and was dressed in Potter chic, a light blue flowery dress with a pinafore, and a large matching bow between her ears. They were both wearing hiking boots, and two knapsacks were on the ground beside them.

'Hello, Mr Knox,' said Finkle, 'good to meet you at last. I see you quite often on the way to work at RabCoT.'

He squeezed my one hand in his two; I could feel the lack of opposability and it sent an odd chill up my back. Finkle had been the first to voluntarily remove his thumbs in order to show oneness with the rabbit cause, and given that one might argue opposability and tool use were as indicative of our species as ears are for a rabbit, there was something more than just a levelling of the dexterous field – it was a comment about our humanness, and the rejection thereof. In an instant my odd sense of revulsion turned to understanding and, in some measure, admiration. I took a deep breath and stood up straighter.

'Call me Peter,' I said. 'I face instant dismissal for even talking to you.'

He gave me a half-smile.

'I won't tell if you won't. You want to stare at my absent thumbs, don't you?'

'Is it that obvious?'

'I'm afraid so. Don't feel bad – everyone wants to.'

He held up his hands so I could look and get it out of my system. These days the surgery could be done so precisely a lopped human would appear as if they'd *never* had thumbs, but Finkle had used a bandsaw on himself, so the stumps were ragged and mismatched. There must have been a lot of blood.

'Miss them?' I asked stupidly, not knowing how to open a conversation with a lopped.

'Every day,' he said evenly, 'but sacrificing something you don't need isn't a sacrifice.'

At the last count there were eight hundred others who had lopped themselves, all living in the colonies or in the Isle of Man safe haven, having adopted rabbit ways. It was a controversial move: a few had even been snatched back by the same companies that did cult interventions, but every individual returned to the colonies as soon as they could. Once you were lopped, you'd made your choice and would stick by it.

'And this,' said Finkle, turning to introduce his female rabbit companion, 'is the Venerable Bunty Celestine MNU-683, my mentor, spiritual guide and romantic life partner.'

'Oh!' I said, suddenly taken aback, not just at meeting her, but at the trust in which I must have been held to be allowed to do so. 'Hello.'

If I had been expecting some sort of mystical experience upon meeting her – an aura of righteousness or spirituality or something – I was disappointed. She looked just like any other Labstock rabbit, although the spectacles were a giveaway as to her heritage: the test animal known as MNU-683 from the tag on her cage had been used for shampoo eye irritation tests before the Event, and her descendants always had poor eyesight, although I wasn't sure how this was heritable.

'Hello!' she said with a bright smile as she held my hand in her paws. 'Pleased to meet you. Goodness: what happened to your eye?'

'Little bit of foxing,' I said, 'nothing serious.'

'Did he threaten to take it out and eat it?'

'He did.'

She grimaced, then made the circular sign of Lago around my eye and laid her paw upon it for a couple of seconds. I thought this might have been a miracle or something, but it wasn't. When she lifted her paw, my eye seemed no better than before.

Once all the introductions were over we perched on the remains of the haywain while the bees buzzed merrily around, the morning beginning to heat up. The Venerable Bunty passed round tin cups[56] of Vimto and offered us a cucumber sandwich.

'I could so murder a whopping great carrot right now,' said Connie, who had just done the equivalent of fifteen one-hundred-metre sprints.

'I've taken a vow of abstinence,' said the Venerable Bunty, 'so didn't bring any. Sorry.'

'Oh yes,' said Connie, mildly embarrassed that she'd forgotten rabbit clergy denied themselves 'the pleasure of the orange' to detach themselves better from the distracting indulgences of the material world.

'Aren't there some peaches?' said Finkle. 'And I think I've got a bar of Fruit & Nut somewhere.'

'Hang on,' said the Venerable Bunty, rummaging in her knapsack, 'there are some banana sandwiches, but they got a bit squashed – and some walnut cake, I think…'

'Well, Peter,' said Finkle once we'd had something to eat, 'tell me about the deal you made with Mr Ffoxe.'

'I've only just told Connie about that,' I said. 'How did you know?'

'It was pretty obvious as soon as Constance was released,' said Finkle. 'I can't see why else they'd be so generous.'

---

56. Rabbits routinely avoided single-use plastics. Knowing that rabbits adored their tea cakes, Tunnock's – in an inspired move – shipped their goods to rabbits in wooden crates of two hundred.

I told them everything I knew, and they both listened quietly, speaking only to ask a question or to clarify a point. The Venerable Bunty asked me to describe the layout of MegaWarren, which I furnished as best as I could, and what sort of security clearance I had on the Taskforce mainframe.

'One up from the lowest,' I said, 'but I won't be able to access it. Mr Ffoxe and the weasel will simply want to know what you'll ask me to find out, and use that to figure out your plans.'

'Hmm,' said Finkle, 'we should accept that Mr Ffoxe assumed you would tell us everything, so it's difficult to see his *precise* play.'

'He was very eager to find out your whereabouts,' I said to the Venerable Bunty, 'and was very interested in the subject of "completing the circle".'

'Ah,' said the Venerable Bunty, 'that's very interesting.'

'It is?' I asked.

'Yes,' said Finkle, 'it is.'

I looked at Connie, who was, I think, still musing about the 'whopping great carrot' she wanted.

'Ultimately,' I said, 'Mr Ffoxe wants leverage to move you all to MegaWarren without any trouble, and thinks that with the Venerable Bunty in custody it will be a lot easier.'

'Even with the VB under lock and key, he'll still have trouble,' said Finkle. 'The Grand Council of Coneys have ratified the plans for civil stubbornness, so each rabbit will have to be carried all the way to Wales one by one, which will be prohibitively expensive, not to mention a PR nightmare.'

'Since Smethwick and Mr Ffoxe have staked their reputations on the Rehoming,' added the Venerable Bunty, 'they'll want to have it completed in whatever way they can – and with over fifteen hundred foxes and ten thousand Compliance Officers at the Taskforce, it might all turn rather unpleasant.'

I knew this too – it wasn't really news. I think UKARP suspected that when push came to shove, the rabbit's innate dislike of confrontation and the Taskforce's innate *propensity* to confrontation would win the day.

The conversation stopped for a minute or two while the Venerable

Bunty cut the hardly-squashed-at-all walnut cake, but soon picked up again as we learned that the Venerable Bunty was brought up in-colony and had been doing miracles since passing her GCSEs, so had been a shoo-in to take over as spiritual leader when the previous Bunty died, herself the fifth since the Event. Our meeting seemed chatty rather than focused, and at one point I asked Finkle whether he wanted me to do anything.

'Not really,' he said. 'I just wanted to meet you. Get the measure of Connie's neighbour, see what he has to offer. Now that I have, I'd like you to play along with Mr Ffoxe. You can tell him about this meeting if you like. There's been no breach of the law, just a minor employment infraction on your behalf for talking to me.'

'Are you sure?' I asked, disappointed that I wasn't going to be of more use.

'We're sure,' said Finkle. 'You can tell him about Bunty, too. Just give us four hours to make ourselves scarce before you do.'

'That's it?' I said.

'That's it.'

So while we ate the excellent walnut cake that the Venerable Bunty's mother's sister's daughter's husband's son had baked, Venerable Bunty and Connie told us about life inside the colonies, which despite the lack of freedom and limited space were the only areas within the United Kingdom that ran themselves entirely on rabbit socio-egalitarian principles.

'It's occasionally aggressive and often uncompromising,' said Finkle, 'but from what I've seen of both systems, a country run on rabbit principles would be a step forward – although to be honest, I'm not sure we'd be neurologically suited to the regime. While most humans are wired to be reasonably decent, a few are wired to be utter shits – and they do tend to tip the balance.'

'The decent humans are generally supportive of doing the right thing,' said the Venerable Bunty, 'but never take it much farther than that. You're trashing the ecosystem for no reason other than a deluded sense of anthropocentric manifest destiny, and until you stop talking around the issue and actually feel some genuine guilt, there'll be no change.'

'Shame, for want of a better word, is good,' said Finkle. 'Shame is right, shame *works*. Shame is the gateway emotion to increased self-criticism, which leads to realisation, an apology, outrage and eventually meaningful action. We're not holding our breaths that any appreciable numbers can be arsed to make the journey along that difficult chain of emotional honesty – many good people get past realisation, only to then get horribly stuck at apology – but we live in hope.'

'I understand,' I said, having felt that I too had yet to make the jump to apology.

'It's further evidence of satire being the engine of the Event,' said Connie, 'although if that's true, we're not sure for whose benefit.'

'Certainly not humans',' said Finkle, 'since satire is meant to highlight faults in a humorous way to achieve betterment, and if anything, the presence of rabbits has actually made humans worse.'

'Maybe it's the default position of humans when they feel threatened,' I ventured, 'although if I'm honest, I know a lot of people who claim to have "nothing against rabbits" but tacitly do nothing against the overt leporiphobia that surrounds them.'

'Or maybe it's just satire for comedy's sake and nothing else,' added Connie, 'or even more useless, satire that provokes a few guffaws but only low to middling outrage – but is coupled with more talk and no action. A sort of … empty cleverness.'

'Maybe a small puff in the right moral direction is the best that could be hoped for,' added Finkle thoughtfully. 'Perhaps that's what satire does – not change things wholesale but nudge the collective consciousness in a direction that favours justice and equality. Is there any more walnut cake?'

'I'm afraid I had the last slice,' I said, 'but I did ask if anyone else wanted it.'

'Not to worry,' said Finkle, looking at his watch. 'I think we should be making a move anyway. Tell me, Peter, do you like owls?'

'Owls?'

'Yes, the bird, y'know, large eyes, fond of mice, not that smart?'

'Yes, I suppose.'

'It's an abiding passion of mine and I need someone to look after Ollie until the Rehoming is over.'

'I don't have an aviary.'

'I have a portable one on a trailer. I'll send it round. Well, goodbye, Mr Knox – very pleased to have met you. And Constance? Send my very best to Doc and tell him that he still owes me a rematch for that ping-pong trouncing he gave me.'

Connie said she would and we all clasped hands again. The Venerable Bunty said a few words in Rabbity and after a blessing in which we all stood on one foot for a half-minute, we parted in opposite directions: the Venerable Bunty and Patrick towards Clagdangle-on-Arrow and Connie and I back to where I'd parked the car.

'What was that all about?' I asked once we back at the Austin-Healey.

'Finkle and the Venerable Bunty said they wanted to meet you. Get your … measure.'

'For what reason?'

'Tell you what,' she said, suddenly animated, 'I'll race you back home on the Slipton Flipflop road. Ready?'

I jumped in the car and yelled 'ready', and we were off with a screech of tyres and a grunt of effort from Connie. The trip home took ten minutes, and while the Austin-Healey was faster then her, she had the height-and-sight advantage around corners where I had to slow down. I made some headway on the road to Flipflop but had to slow down through the village. Connie didn't. She went straight through the small hamlet in a series of increasingly reckless bounds, once bouncing into the open top-storey window of Mr Gumley's house before emerging from the French windows on the other side and intercepting the road back to Much Hemlock. I caught up with her about halfway there but she pulled ahead when I had to slow down for some cyclists and a pony.

The door to my house was open when I got home and I found Connie in the utility room with her ears draped inside the chest freezer.

'Overheated,' she explained. 'That sweating thing you do is super-useful. If I was a member of a species eager for world domination, it would be first on my list, along with sensible footwear, literacy and double-entry bookkeeping.'

'Connie, can I tell you something?'

'You disagree about the importance of double-entry bookkeeping?'

'No, I think that's irrefutable,' I replied, taking a deep breath and suddenly feeling the urge to stare at my feet. 'It's about your ... second husband.'

'Dylan?'

'Yes. I was ... there the night he was mistakenly identified.'

She stopped and gazed at me intently, her head cocked on one side.

'I was wondering when you were going to tell me.'

'Wait, what – you *knew*?'

She nodded.

'We knew you were a Spotter, and knew what you'd done. But I said I knew you, and you weren't all bad. That you were weak, that's all – and easily led.'

'Then all this friendship stuff is a sham? You really *are* a bunnytrap?'

'No,' she replied, 'it's not a sham. Everyone is capable of reform. It's quite possible to do bad things and find some kind of restorative justice – personally, and for those you've wronged. I knew you before you made poor choices, when you could have done anything you wanted. I'd like to think that there are parts of *that* Peter Knox still around.'

I stared back at her, unable to think of anything to say.

'Really, I'm totally OK with it,' she said, as I must have looked unconvinced. 'We know you pleaded with Mr Ffoxe that it wasn't Dylan, we know that you were overruled. You could have done more and think you still might. You can help us, and by the same measure, we can help you. This isn't a bunnytrap, or an exploitation – it's an intervention. Do you understand what I'm trying to say?'

'That I'm repairable?'

'Yes,' she said, laying a paw on my arm, 'you're repairable.'

'So,' I said after a pause, 'you were close to killing Mr Ffoxe at All Saints simply for revenge?'

'Nope,' she said, 'not with the risk of reprisals. Killing such a prominent fox would be ten times the usual penalty for rabbit-murder. No, that was just to get him interested.'

There was another pause.

'How did you know all that?' I asked. 'About me and Dylan and stuff?'

She smiled.

'You'd be surprised how many people are friendly to rabbits. And you see these?'

She pointed at her long and very elegant ears, which were covered with the faintest wisp of downy fur.

'Yes?'

'They're not just for decoration.'

Bugged Bunny

Rabbity glossary: Hiffniff. The direct translation is an 'edict' but 'a suggestion to undertake a unified act of benefit to the warren' would be closer, albeit more verbose. An emphasis on the last 'f' would, however, change the meaning to 'any item of apparel worn by women on a hen night'.

I didn't know it at the time, but Pippa – with Bobby's help – made it into Colony One at about the same time as I was talking to Finkle and the Venerable Bunty. She met up with Harvey but I didn't see them again until I too was inside the colony, the same day as the Battle of May Hill. I'd see Pippa and Harvey leave me as I stood beside Connie and the Venerable Bunty, the artillery shells falling, the sharp barks, yelps and cries of excited foxes mixing with the frightened cries of rabbits. But all of this was in the future, and unknowable. Or at least, unknowable to me.

I slept unusually well the night after the meeting with Finkle and Bunty, and the following morning my eye, which the day before had been bloodshot and sore and gave only hazy vision, was almost healed. I had breakfast feeling oddly quite good about myself, took delivery of Finkle's owl and the portable aviary and then called the Taskforce HR department to say that I would be doing half-days until further notice for 'personal reasons'. I then spent the next week pretending that Connie and I had a thing going. It was her idea in order that Mr Ffoxe waste valuable resources which would otherwise have been spent preparing for the Rehoming, and I happily went along with it, as spending time with her was always pleasant.

On the first day we met in the lobby of the Green Dragon Hotel and went to a shared room, stayed for an hour to play Scrabble, then unsubtly departed, ten minutes apart. We met at All Saints for lunch on more than one occasion, took the train to Birmingham to see a

Vilhelm Hammershoi retrospective, and on the day after that, I called in sick and hid in my spare room while Connie sent our mobiles in a RabCab all the way to Liverpool's Tarbuck International Airport. She didn't say why, but I guessed to give the impression we were doing a recce for a possible escape to the Isle of Man. I even asked her to shadow Stanley Baldwin during that Tuesday *Buchblitz*, where she showed considerable flair for reshelving.

Whenever I got into the office, usually afternoons, I spent the time in Interview Room One, reading a copy of *Madame Bovary* that Connie had lent me.

'Anything?' asked Adrian Whizelle on the afternoon of the sixth day. It was always Whizelle.

'Nothing yet,' I said.

'The Senior Group Leader is becoming impatient,' said Whizelle. 'The Grand Council has announced that the colonies won't be moved, and that witch Bunty has issued a *hiffniff* telling all and sundry to hold fast, not be moved and to offer passive and polite resistance to anyone who tries to rehome them.'

'I heard,' I said, 'it was on the news.'

'Mr Ffoxe and Smethwick have taken advice from the Attorney General, and since the removal is legal owing to the Rehoming Act, the rabbit's frontal incisors have been designated offensive weapons. "Being cornered in possession of teeth" is now the legal equivalent of "attack with a deadly weapon", and we are permitted to counter that threat with any force deemed necessary – even pre-emptively. So tell your little bun-chums that.'

The statement was so manifestly unjust I wasn't going to validate it with a comment.

'I don't have any sway with the Venerable Bunty, the Council of Coneys or any of the on-colony rabbits,' I said. 'If Connie asks me for information or tells me anything, I'll repeat it back to you. That was the deal.'

'The deal was you'd help us,' said Whizelle, 'and I haven't seen—'

He stopped talking as the door to the interview room opened and my heart sank as Senior Group Leader Ffoxe walked in. I suppose I should have guessed he'd be listening in to the conversation, but up to now I'd not really appreciated how I was not just one strand of enquiry – but the main one.

'Hello, Peter,' said the fox.

'Look, I'm doing what you asked me,' I said, perhaps a little bit too defensively.

'I know, I know,' said Mr Ffoxe in a semi-soothing manner. 'I'm not here to make threats. No one's eye is coming out.'

And he then sat down and stared at me for a long time without blinking, while I sat there fidgeting. I'd told him all about my meeting with Finkle and the Venerable Bunty four hours after I'd met them, which gave me credibility for at least a couple of days.

'It's been almost a week,' he said finally, 'and you've been making the job of my boys really difficult.'

'I'm doing the best I can. If Connie doesn't tell me anything, I can't repeat it.'

Despite my outwardly timid manner, which I was exaggerating at Connie's suggestion, I was actually feeling a little braver, probably because I sensed the fox still needed me. Mr Ffoxe opened his mouth, removed a piece of gristle from between his teeth, stared at it for a moment, then said:

'Whose idea was it to send your mobile phones in a cab all the way up to Tarbuck International?'

'Connie's.'

'Have the Rabbits asked you to do anything for them?'

'No.'

'Have you heard anything that you feel might be useful?'

'No.'

'Then we'll have to up our game. Will you be seeing the Rabbits later today?'

'Almost certainly. It's Doc's first Parish Council meeting and they've invited me to supper afterwards.'

'Perfect. I want you to wear a listening device. Ask them about Bunty, the Rehoming, Finkle, RabSAg – anything you can. I want to hear them talk, get an idea of their mood. Quiz them, but I also want to hear you make some sort of effort on our behalf, because I really don't think you're trying hard enough.'

'I'll … want something in return,' I said, scratching my nose nervously. 'If they find out I'm wearing a wire, they could do what they did to Toby but without the "returning safely" part.'

'We're listening,' said Whizelle.

'My daughter is in Colony One, which is currently encircled by TwoLegsGood and Taskforce personnel. I want her and an unnamed rabbit to be given safe passage to the Isle of Man.'

Mr Ffoxe smiled.

'OK,' said Mr Ffoxe, 'you got yourself a deal. Pippa Knox plus one rabbit. Make a note, Weasel.'

'It's *Whi-zelle* for the hundredth time,' I heard Whizelle mutter under his breath.

There was no doubt in my mind Mr Ffoxe would not lift a paw to help Pippa or her significant rabbit. To him, my daughter had already crossed the species divide and would be treated accordingly. The only reason I asked was to make him think I would not wear a wire lightly. Mr Ffoxe walked around the table and made to shake my hand, but instead grabbed my head and thumped it painfully on the interview-room desk. Then, after a pause, he did it again, harder, then once more, harder still. I felt a tooth break in my jaw.

'Shit,' I said, 'that *really* hurt.'

'The first was to make the point,' he said, 'that if you double-cross me I will find you, wherever you are, and make good on the whole eye-coming-out-and-eating-it scenario. The second was for betraying your own species.'

'And the third?' I asked.

'That one,' he said, leaning closer to whisper in my ear, 'was simply for pleasure.'

Dinner & Deity

Thumping the hind leg upon the ground was a good method of non-verbal communication with a range of about four hundred yards, sort of like rabbit WiFi. Using Morse code, entire books could be transmitted to a large group of rabbits while occupied on assembly-line work. It is the origin of the phrase 'a thumping good tale'.

I drove straight home, my head still throbbing. The bugging device that Whizelle had given me was a plain Parker ballpoint that required me only to click it once to switch on, once to switch off. The battery, he'd said, would last for six hours and transmit up to a mile away.

The thing was, I was under no illusion that I was fooling Mr Ffoxe. He'd know I'd tell them I was wired, so he'd also know they'd only give up intel that they *wanted* him to hear. Was I a bunnytrap-trap trap, or a bunnytrap-trap-trap trap? It was impossible to know. I gave up on trying to figure it all out and instead went and fed Finkle's owl, who stared back at me blankly.

The clock was indicating six when there was a knock on the door. It was Doc. He was returning the Henry vacuum cleaner with an apologetic 'sorry, don't know why she keeps pinching them when I'm the one that does the cleaning' and also wanting to know whether I fancied watching him make a fool of himself at the Parish Council. I told him I wouldn't miss it for anything as council meetings were often closer to live cabaret than the first tier of democracy. We walked the short distance to the village hall, talking about how all of his security consultancy contracts had been withdrawn or cancelled without explanation.

'The Rehoming is putting a spanner in the works for legal off-colony rabbits,' he said. 'I have a feeling we won't be off-colony for long.'

Doc's initiation into the Parish Council all seemed to go fairly well. Victor had been the chairman for decades, and although Norman was not on the council he was there with the public, sitting next to me, and I saw him nod imperceptibly while listening to Doc's robust arguments regarding the best strategy to improve traffic calming, and how the local playground could be upgraded with minimum outlay. There was an embarrassing moment when Article 15 on the agenda was read out, which related to the council contributing to the 'leaving payment' the village had been gathering to buy the Rabbits out. With true professionalism Doc recused himself from the argument and went to smoke his pipe outside until recalled to discuss allocating more funds to tidying up the churchyard for when the Spick & Span judges returned – something Councillor Wainwright thought would be next Tuesday at three, although when pressed he gave no answer as to why he should think that. When the meeting finished and the usual post-meeting talks were going on, Victor had a call on his mobile and rapidly departed, along with his brother.

I would find out why later.

'I think that all went fairly well, don't you?' said Doc as we walked back from the village hall an hour later.

'They're being pleasant because they've been told to,' I said; 'it won't last.'

'True,' said Doc, 'but let's enjoy it while we can, eh?'

I'd had a brief call earlier from Pippa saying she was fine and that Bobby and Harvey had been looking after her at Colony One, and not to worry about her as she had found the place and the person she wanted to be, and the rabbit who she wanted to share that with.

I asked Doc whether Bobby had been in touch with her or Connie, and he said she hadn't.

'Constance always remarked that Bobby was a little headstrong,' he said, 'and watched a lot of *'Allo 'Allo* when she was young, so I suppose it was inevitable she'd end up doing all the cloak-and-dagger stuff. Her Underground name is Bridgette, apparently.'

'Do you think she's in any danger at Colony One?' I asked, more out of concern for Pippa.

'Who knows? It's really down to whether Smethwick and Mr Ffoxe order the enforced clearance of the colonies and exercise all their powers to do so. I know the citizens of the UK are not wildly pro-rabbit, but oddly, they can become very interested – albeit for a short period of time – if there is any cruelty to animals involved. It's always been their soft spot.'

He stopped walking at the bus stop, turned and looked at me.

'Look here, Peter, old chap,' he said, 'I think we need to talk. Cards on the table and all that. I think you and Constance are having an affair, and unless you can give me a solemn promise to keep your grubby paws off my wife, I'm going to have to challenge you to a duel.'

'I can assure you we are not,' I said.

'That's what she says, and I gave her the benefit of the doubt during that incident with the bedsheet, but, well, I asked Kent to put a tracker on her phone and she's been to the Green Dragon Hotel a couple of times, and I saw you both in All Saints.'

'We just met up for coffee,' I said.

'That's how it always begins. Coffee, dinner, going out for a bounce, basket of scrubbed carrots, Scrabble. What were you two doing in that dilapidated barn? I was watching for an hour and you didn't come out – I would have stayed for longer, but I had to get home to watch the cricket.'

'We were meeting with Patrick Finkle and the Venerable Bunty,' I said.

'Oh, *sure*,' said Doc, 'and I suppose Victor Lewis-Smith and the Pope were there too? If you want to be together, Pete, then do the decent thing, stop inventing silly stories and make a challenge – waiting for me to challenge *you* is really the coward's way, how weasels would do it.'

'Weasels fight duels too?'

'No, but if they did.'

'We're not having an affair, Doc, I promise you.'

He stared at me and blinked.

'I wish I could believe you,' he said with a sigh. 'Why don't we have a pint after dinner at the Unicorn and thrash it out there?'

'OK,' I said, glad to move away from the subject for a couple of hours.

We walked the rest of the way in silence, and inside my pocket I clicked the Parker pen to activate the listening device.

'Two more in the burrow,' called out Doc as we walked in the door, using a traditional rabbit greeting.

'Hello,' said Connie, popping her head round the kitchen door. 'How did the council meeting go?'

'They were eating out of my paw,' said Doc.

'Really?'

'No, not really – it was a charade. They despised me with a vengeance.'

'Same old same old,' said Connie.

While Doc went off to lay the table, I went into the kitchen and passed Connie a note I had prepared. It was written in block capitals because their visual cortex was not so attuned to reading as ours, but was absolutely clear:

I AM WEARING A WIRE

She pointed to a message on the fridge constructed out of magnetic letters:

I THOUGHT YOU MIGHT BE

She smiled, winked at me and squeezed my hand.

Once we were all seated and grace had been said – in Rabbity this time, as I think they thought I was a good enough friend not to take offence – Connie ladled out the stew and we ate, the Rabbits making slurpy noises with the occasional clinking of spoons against teeth, as cutlery and their dentition didn't really work very well together. During dinner we spoke briefly of the latest episode in *The Archers*, the first time a storyline had featured rabbits, with the Grundys employing a rabbit stockman named Tim who was embroiled in some off-colony politics. Kent said that Rabbit TV was a lot better, even though *How Deep Was My Warren* had recently been plunged into controversy.

'A recent shake-up has reduced the ensemble cast to barely six thousand,' explained Connie, 'which makes it all a little easy to follow.'

'Dumbing down for a young rabbit's short attention span,' added Doc in a huffy manner. 'Kids today can barely follow six hundred simultaneous storylines. I blame the fad for board games, personally.'

Connie, in what I realised later was an effort to steer the conversation to where she needed it, mentioned that *Fortean Times* had reported that a moose shot dead by a hunter was later found to have amassed a considerable library of George Eliot novels, critical appraisals, biographies and poetry, and had been attempting to write a dissertation on how Eliot's life could be viewed from the viewpoint of even-toed ungulates singled out for their lack of apparent good looks.

'I think moose are rather handsome,' said Doc thoughtfully, ladling out seconds. 'They just need to keep their chins up a little.'

'It's the weight of the antlers,' said Kent, who had taken on the young male human trope of being an expert on absolutely everything.

'Probably a sense of low self-esteem,' added Connie. 'Maybe that's why they always look so gloomy.'

'Was it *really* another Event?' I asked. 'One hears stories like this, but it might simply have been another hoax.'

'Goulburn,' said Connie and Doc together.

It had been a contentious subject since the stories first emerged, but the Event in the UK was decidedly *not* the only one. They were either rare or commonplace, depending on your interpretation of events, and how open to evidence of conspiracies you were. Eleven years after the UK Event and near a town called Goulburn in Australia, there were reports of the usual overly dramatic conditions that presaged all of the alleged Events across the globe: power surges, electrical storms, dogs howling, showers of fish, a full moon. There had also been talk of a mobilised armed fast-response team appearing in the area within two hours, leading to questions in the Australian parliament to determine whether the government, in line with many others, had a covert 'Extermination at First Discovery' policy towards potential Anthropomorphic Eventees. The government denied a cover-up, so what had occurred remained in the sphere of conjecture, but urban legend told of 'a dozen or so man-sized wombats wearing singlets and shorts' being bulldozed into a mass grave with a shed-load of empty beer cans. The apparent sole survivor was a merino ram named Rambo, who gave several lengthy interviews over the phone, interspersing what he knew of the affair with exhortations to drop in and visit Goulburn, which was 'really jolly nice'. The interviews abruptly stopped the same day a ram was found shot dead behind the bandstand. There was no evidence that he *was* the Eventee, but the townspeople, annoyed at the government intervention and pleased by the publicity, put up a statue in his honour anyway.[57]

'Stories come out from time to time,' said Doc, 'but the only places we *know* that have entertained an Event are the UK, Kenya and Oregon. But we think there might have been more.'

Only Kenya had accorded the Eventees full human status. But since they were elephants and had a gestation period of two years, their numbers were never likely to be high and they were entirely unthreatening – and, as it turned out, very funny, charming and good on wind instruments. Firyali Elephant, the spokesphant of the group, now worked as the minister of the interior, and was tipped as a possible PM, even after the scandal involving the bootlegged copies of *Dumbo*.

The bears in Oregon generally kept to themselves, but had recently been given Second Amendment rights, so were legally allowed to shoot hunters in self-defence – and did so quite frequently, much to the annoyance of hunters, who considered it 'manifestly unfair' because the bears, now suitably armed, were actually better hunters than they were.

'The unspoken policy is eradication at first appearance,' said Connie. 'No one wants what has happened here to happen anywhere else.'

'Has anyone looked for a link between the Events,' I said, 'to get an idea of what is causing it?'

'Nothing concrete so far,' said Kent, 'just bundles of speculation. In that manner it's a little like trying to explain *Lost*.'

'There could be another reason for the move to MegaWarren,' mused Connie, 'that is nothing to do with incarceration, population control or the exploitation of the rabbit workforce.'

'Such as?' I asked, playing my part as best as I could, given that we were being listened to by the Taskforce right now.

'Clearing the colonies will flush the Venerable Bunty out, but they don't want her so the other rabbits will fall into line – they suspect the Venerable Bunty might be *behind* the Events. That she's a physical

57. It is still there, by the side of the road as you drive into town having left the Hume Highway from the Canberra direction.

251

manifestation of the Ancestral Earth Mother Gaia, here to cause trouble for the dominant species, who, let's face it, have been getting a little too big for their own frontal lobes recently.'

We all fell into the sort of silence one adopts when a friend previously thought of as sober and clear-headed suddenly announces that the world is flat.

'I don't think that's very likely,' said Doc in a scoffy sort of voice. 'Gaia is a myth, sweetheart, like Zeus and Bacchus and Loki and Yoda and—'

'And Lago?' said Connie.

Doc fell silent.

'Faith and religion and spiritual belief are one thing,' I said, 'but creating anthropomorphised animals out of thin air is quite another. You think all this was somehow divinely inspired? It doesn't seem very likely.'

'Actually,' said Kent slowly, 'if you think about it, talking rabbits spontaneously anthropomorphised have a chance–factor ratio of around 1×10^{89}, which, while not *totally* impossible, is about as likely as the universe spontaneously turning into cottage cheese. The fact that we're here suggests that tremendously unlikely things *can* happen – which would make Gaia reappearing to tweak a few things for the better not so very daft at all.'

'You're formulating a mathematical proof for the existence of the primordial earth mother based on talking-rabbit probability?' I said. 'Wouldn't that make *everything* possible?'

'Within the multiverse,' said Kent, 'everything *is* possible.'

'That … is … enough!' said Doc, jumping to his feet. 'This conversation is just getting, well, too, too … *metaphysical*.'

And he stormed out of the room, muttering something about the standard model.

'Doc is more of an empiricist,' explained Connie, then added: 'Kent, darling, would you put on the kettle for coffee?'

Kent dutifully went off to the kitchen.

'Listen,' said Connie in a quiet voice, 'the Venerable Bunty is key to the Rehoming. With her at liberty, a stand-off between the rabbit and the Taskforce would be a long and torturously expensive affair.

There's lots of food: half of the colonies are laid to market gardening, and the growing season is only half done. We can keep the Bunty moving around, but ultimately they'll find her — which is why we have formulated ... a plan.'

'A plan?'

'Yes.'

She didn't elucidate further as Doc had walked back in, his half-finished apple crumble a greater draw than talk of impossibilities. Connie didn't mention the Venerable Bunty again, but didn't need to. I think she'd said what she wanted, and to the audience she wanted to hear her — not me, but Whizelle and Ffoxe and Smethwick and anyone else who was listening.

'Well,' said Doc, once the dinner things were washed up and I had said that I should probably make a move, 'it's still early. Do you want to have that swift bevvy in the Unicorn so we can talk about ... y'know?'

I was hoping he'd leave the subject alone for longer, but pre-mating season wife appropriation issues were a big thing to rabbits.

'Are you sure you want to go to the Unicorn? Despite indications to the contrary, we're still both social pariahs in the village right now.'

'And a swift bevvy with the locals,' replied Doc cheerfully, 'will be just the ticket to change it. Wait there and I'll get my coat.'

Cordiality Collapse

… Even after eight years, I am still undecided whether the rabbit were the instigators of the Event, victims of it or simply part of a larger plan laid by a higher power. Even now, there are more questions than answers …

The sun had long sunk below the horizon when we stepped out of Hemlock Towers, and the skies were a deep navy blue, the stars bright, the air clear – a perfect summer's night. We walked down the lane in silence, took a left and then a right into the main street. Doc chatted amiably about how when in the forces he was always popular on forward operations as he could bounce vertically upwards about twenty feet, good for reconnaissance, although not without mishap as it made him a target – albeit a brief one – for enemy snipers.

'See that one here?' he asked, pointing at a bullet hole in his ear that was smaller than the others.

'Tikrit?'

'Kidderminster. Saturday nights can get pretty insane. Hang on.'

His mobile phone had just rung.

'That's odd,' he said, staring at the screen, then putting the mobile to his ear. 'Yes, Honeybounce?'

He listened intently for a while, looked at me, then hung up.

'You go ahead,' he said, 'mine's a pint of Rancid Bishop,[58] and get me some Tyrrells – sea salt flavour.'

And he bounced back off in the direction of his house. I stood there for a moment, hesitant, but carried on since I'd come this far already. A few minutes later and I was in the lounge bar of the Unicorn, all seventies decor, beer-stained carpets and Constable prints on the walls faded to pallid variations of the colour green.

---

58. It's a popular brand of real ale. Still available, I believe.

Worryingly, it all went quiet as I walked in. If someone had been playing the piano, it would have stopped. There were about a dozen people present. Victor Mallett was sitting with his brother and a couple of others I only vaguely recognised. The room was staring at me silently. The recent *entente cordiale* seemed to have evaporated as swiftly as it had arrived.

I walked up to the bar.

'A half of Guinness and a pint of Rancid Bishop, please, Janice.'

'Right-o.'

She began the slow pour of the Guinness and then started to pull the Rancid Bishop.

'Who's the Bishop for, Peter?' asked Norman from the other end of the bar.

'Your new parish councillor,' I replied.

'That post was rescinded eight minutes ago,' said Victor, 'as was minding the bottle stall at the village fete.'

'We negotiated up from bottle stall to judging the vegetables,' I pointed out.

'Whatever. It doesn't matter, Peter old chap. I could have promised her the tombola and the opening ceremony – she was never going to do any of it.'

I felt the chill in the room. Villagers stuck together; it was what they did. That would have been all well and good if it was about the church roof fund appeal or the Spick & Span awards, but not if you were the recipient of their combined outrage. I took the bugged Parker pen out of my pocket and placed it on the counter.

'Major Rabbit won't be joining you,' said Norman. 'Pour the ale away, Janice.'

Janice looked at me. She and I went back a long way. I'd let her copy my schoolwork when we were nine, because I knew she was having a rotten home life.

'Pour it, Janice.'

Janice continued to pour the ale, and a dull, portentous silence filled the room.

'Look here, Peter,' said Victor, 'we were once good friends and we'll be good friends again. There'll be a place in the village for you, once everything's back to normal. Sit down and drink your Guinness, and … take your time.'

I didn't at first understand what he was trying to say, but then my eyes fell upon the table in the far corner, the one where Dicky the drunk had sat before his life hobby finally caught up with him. There was an unfinished glass of whisky on the table, a smouldering Sobranie in the ashtray and a folded-up copy of *Fox and Friends*.

I stood up, but so did Victor.

'Peter,' he said more seriously and, oddly, it was about the only time he had shown me a shred of empathy or concern, 'don't get involved. Not with this. You can look the other way.'

I headed towards the door but found my way blocked by Norman, who pushed me hard in the chest. He was a heavy man, and while tall, I'm not that weighty, and he easily put me off balance and I found myself sprawled on the floor, to several shocked intakes of breath from the people in the bar. Bullying coercion was one thing, physical violence quite another.

Before I knew it I was on my feet and made a wild sprint towards Norman. I put out a fist where I thought his face might be and placed my full weight behind the blow. I surprised myself by actually connecting with his chin in a quite forceful manner – fluke, I think, as I'd never fought anyone, not ever – and we both went rolling out of the door into the street. I picked myself up and made off towards Hemlock Towers, the sound of Victor saying 'Let the silly sod go, Norm' echoing in my ears as I ran.

I took a leaf from the Rabbits' book and ran straight into the house without knocking, reasoning to myself that Mr Ffoxe's actions might be postponed or at least softened into mere threats by my presence. I stumbled into the oak-panelled hall to find Doc and Connie standing there, seemingly unconcerned. Of Mr Ffoxe, there was no sign.

'Hello,' said Doc with a smile. 'What do I owe you for the Rancid Bishop?'

'Mr Ffoxe is in the village,' I said, breathless after the run.

'D'you know, I thought I could smell Old Spice on the air,' said Doc, apparently with little concern.

'You're not worried?'

'Constance told me everything. She's a member of the Underground, y'know.'

There was a hint of pride in his voice.

'And Bobby and Harvey,' I said, 'and now probably Pippa, too. Look, I saw some unfamiliar cars parked up on the way here. I think there might be other Taskforce officers about, and the faces I didn't recognise in the Unicorn looked blandly middle-class enough to be members of TwoLegsGood. You're in a lot of danger and you need to get out. I never thought they'd act *this* fast.'

'We're not running,' said Connie. 'It all ends here and now. He'll ask me what I know of the Venerable Bunty's greater plans and movements, I'll tell him nothing, and that will be it.'

'You don't have a chance,' I said, 'he's a *fox*, for Christ's sake, a four-legged multi-fanged rabbit-killing machine.'

Doc and Connie's ears popped up as a rapid series of thumps were heard on the upstairs floor.

'In the back garden between the runner beans and cabbages,' said Doc, reading Kent's lookout thumps perfectly. 'They like to sneak up in an unannounced assault so they can paralyse us with fear before they pounce. I think it excites them. The vixens too,' he added. 'In fact, I think they're worse.'

'Please,' I said, 'you've got to leave. He'll kill you all. Kent and Bobby and everyone you ever knew.'

There was another series of rapid thumps on the floor upstairs, and Doc and Connie moved so they were with me, at the far end of the hall facing the door to the kitchen. Connie's hind leg quivered anxiously. As we watched, the door to the kitchen opened a crack and a whiskery snout sniffed the air cautiously. We were about twenty feet away, with Doc taking up a defensive position a couple of yards in front of us and to the right.

'Hello, Doc,' said Mr Ffoxe.

'Hello, Torquil.'

'Been a while.'

'Never long enough. Haven't seen you at any regimental get-togethers.'

'I've moved on,' said Mr Ffoxe. 'Dwell in the past and you're stuck

257

in the past. Your wife has some intel about the Bunty that I want, and she's going to give it to me. We can do this the easy way, or we can do this the exceptionally unpleasant way.'

'Far as I recall there's only ever an unpleasant way between your kind and mine.'

Doc's voice sounded confident. I guess he'd faced dangers as great or greater than this in the armed forces. But I don't think he'd seen the speed at which Mr Ffoxe could move. The fox could be across the room, snap both their necks and have them half buried behind the compost heap before they'd even realised he was through the door.

I could feel Connie trembling as she moved closer in behind me and wrapped one arm around my waist. I could smell her earthy scent once again, her whiskers tickling the back of my neck.

'Mr Smethwick says the whole ripping-to-pieces thing is bad PR,' said Mr Ffoxe, still with only his snout showing through the kitchen door, 'so I'm willing to forgo the good sport that is my right and simply give you a deal: I get to question Constance at my leisure, and you and the boy upstairs go free.'

'I've a better deal,' said Doc. 'You take your mangy ginger butt out of our house right now, and we'll forget this ever happened.'

Mr Ffoxe gave out a raspy chuckle.

'There's only one deal on the table,' he said. 'Mr Knox, are you there?'

'I'm here,' I said.

'You've been a fool, Mr Knox, but at least you've got to see rabbits for what they truly are: vermin, eager only to invade, dominate and then assimilate us all to their ways. I will spare you, Knox, but you should leave unless you've got a strong stomach, which I doubt.'

'I'm staying,' I said, not *quite* in the brave voice I'd intended.

Mr Ffoxe's snout sniffed the air again.

'You were warned. When the orange mist comes down I rarely show restraint. Final offer, Doc: give up the wife or I'll take out every last one of your friends and relatives. There'll be no rabbit left alive who even *knew* you.'

I looked at Doc, who was swaying on the spot, readying himself for the attack. He was the biggest and most powerful – Mr Ffoxe would kill him first. Connie was still behind me, holding on tight. I could feel the warmth of her body, her heart thumping rapidly beneath her soft fur.

'You want to know my answer, Torquil?' said Doc. 'Here it is: your wife, mother, sister, aunt and grandmother … *all mate out of season.*'

There was a shocked intake of breath from Connie.

'Is that an insult?' I whispered.

'The *worst*,' she whispered back.

Several things then seemed to happen at once. The door was kicked open to reveal Mr Ffoxe, who seemed to have transformed. His eyes were large and bloodshot and his mouth was wide open, revealing sharply pointed teeth wet with saliva. He gave out a dark and forbidding noise from the back of his throat and with his hair rising stiffly on his neck looked about as terrifying as I had ever seen him before – and that *included* the time when he nearly took out my eye. *That* fear, I realised, was just a taster. A cold lump of bile rose in my throat, and Doc's ears went flat on his back.

There was a brief pause as Mr Ffoxe savoured the moment of our terror and then I saw Connie's arm in front of me holding Doc's lark-decorated duelling pistol in her gloved hand. I only had time to register this for a split second as there was a flash, a sharp detonation and Mr Ffoxe's head vanished off his shoulders in an explosion of blood and fur. A fragmented part of his skull actually stuck to the wall opposite, just next to the light switch, and a single yellow eye bounced on the carpet before rolling to a stop near the coal scuttle. The fox then dropped to his knees but didn't fall forward. Rigor mortis, unusually fast in anthropomorphised foxes, kept him on his knees, his arms still upright, making him look not threatening, but *imploring* – and without a head.

'*Sic semper tyrannis*, you contemptible shit,' said Connie.

I stared blankly for a moment at Mr Ffoxe's corpse, the blood bubbling weakly out of his severed neck and running on to his tweed jacket. Connie released her hold on me, and lowered the pistol.

'That was *seriously* risky,' said Doc. 'You should *never* go for the head shot with only one up the spout.'

'I hear you,' said Connie, 'but it was *truly* satisfying, and at that range I couldn't really miss.'

I took my first breath after the pistol was discharged and breathed in the sharp odour of cordite in the room. Doc, Connie and I stared at the headless body of Mr Ffoxe in silence until I found my voice.

'Think of the reprisals,' I said. '*What have you done?*'

'*I* haven't done anything,' said Connie, and she handed me the duelling pistol. 'It's a crime of passion. We were having an affair and you defended me against an aggressor. Your prints are on the weapon, and you're covered in gunshot residue and bits of fox. My husband, eternally grateful, forgives us both.'

'Wait a moment,' said Doc, 'so you were having an affair?'

Constance stared at him for a moment.

'Oh,' he said, 'I get it now. I'm to pretend you were having an affair.'

And that was when the penny dropped.

'Wait, *this* is the intervention?' I asked. 'This is how I make good?'

'As I told you,' replied Constance, 'everyone's repairable. One bad act shouldn't define a person for life, if there is an opportunity to find absolution.'

She smiled.

'And I'm so in love with you right now, Pete. If you get out of this jam you can make a play for me.'

'I knew it,' said Doc triumphantly, 'we *do* get to duel.'

'If I get out of it,' I said.

'True,' said Connie, and she opened her flick-knife, stepped forward and cut off one of Mr Ffoxe's claws. 'Torquil Ffoxe was the true architect of the Rehoming plan, and with him gone, we may have bought some renegotiation time. The Taskforce will be here presently,' she added, threading the fox-claw on to a leather lanyard, 'so the next part of this is really up to you.'

In my short time with the Rabbits I think I understood in the tiniest fashion what a real taste of oppression means. The decision was a no-brainer: a thousand or more rabbits torn limb from limb, or me doing some time for murder.

'You outfoxed the fox,' I said.

'No,' said Connie, '*we* outfoxed the fox,' and she placed the leather lanyard with the fox-claw around my neck, and tucked it beneath my shirt.

'There,' she said, 'you'll never have to buy a round of dandelion brandy ever again. Kent? Bring in the owl.'

There was the sound of footsteps on the stairs and Kent appeared with the owl – the same one that Finkle had delivered to my house.

'Why is the owl here?' I asked.

'You brought it with you,' said Connie. 'Repeat it so you understand that.'

'I brought the owl with me.'

'All right, then. Good luck.'

There was a screech of tyres outside the house, car doors slamming and the sound of footsteps. Doc, Connie and Kent were suddenly on the ground, three terrified balls of brown fur, sobbing uncontrollably, hearts thumping wildly, ears flat on their backs.

Whizelle was first through the door. He found me standing there, still holding the duelling pistol, Senior Group Leader Torquil Ffoxe dead on his knees, arms still up in the air, a pool of blood slowly congealing beneath him. I didn't notice it at the time, but I had one of Mr Ffoxe's ears stuck to my jacket.

'Oh, Peter,' said the weasel, surveying the scene with a sad shake of his head, 'you silly, silly bastard.'

Flemming ran in the door and stopped when she saw what remained of the Senior Group Leader.

'Shit,' she said, 'oh … *shit*.' She glared at me. 'Knox? What in hell's name are you playing at?'

'I brought the owl,' I blurted out, stupidly.

'Good for you,' said Whizelle. 'Flemming? Search the house.'

Flemming, still staring at Mr Ffoxe's body, issued a curt message on her radio and more Taskforce officers entered, then, upon her direction, vanished to all points around the house – upstairs, into the cellar, living room, kitchen, snooker room. My hands were cuffed and the pistol dropped into an evidence bag. In an unusual move – I would find out why soon enough – a photographer was on hand to make a rapid and comprehensive survey of the crime scene while the Rabbits looked dumb and sheepish and forlorn, their ears drooped, their shoulders hunched. It was an impressive performance.

'All clear,' said Flemming as the agents concluded their search and were then ordered to depart, taking all the Rabbits' mobile phones and laptops with them. Agent Whizelle then told Flemming to escort me to the car and hold me there, adding that 'I needed to learn that actions have consequences'. I was moved out of the building as Whizelle and another agent started to take statements from the Rabbits.

'Mind your head,' said Flemming as she helped me into the back of the Range Rover.

'What was that about actions and consequences?' I asked once she'd climbed in herself.

'Search me,' she said. 'This is the weasel's show. Why did you do it, Peter? I mean, I can understand how you could be so easily bunnytrapped, but from there to taking a gun to a fox? And the Senior Group Leader to boot? That takes a lot more cojones than I'd ever credit you with.'

'Is that a compliment?'

She stared at me in the rear-view mirror.

'It's an observation.'

I sighed and gazed at Hemlock Towers. I'd lived in the house next door my entire life and seen the Towers almost every day for the past half-century. Been inside it about two dozen times under various ownerships, but the visit that ended with a dead fox would be my last.

'He said what he was going to do with her before he killed her,' I said simply. 'I couldn't let that happen.'

'You should have walked the other way,' said Flemming, unimpressed by my reasoning. 'Mr Ffoxe was a vital kingpin. You'll be lucky to get out of the clink this side of your seventieth birthday.'

'Yes,' I said quietly, 'and it will be justice.'

We stayed parked outside for about three hours, and watched as various Taskforce personnel came and went. The fox was carried out in a lumpy body bag after one hour and forty-five minutes, and I half expected Mr Smethwick to make an appearance to view for himself where his loyal engineer of the Rehoming was killed, but he didn't. Finally, after much activity, the remainder of the Taskforce staff filed out and departed. Last of all came Whizelle, and I briefly caught a glimpse of Connie as she closed the door behind him. There was a brief pause, and then the door opened again and Doc placed the owl on the doorstep; it looked around for a moment, blinked, then flew off.

Whizelle took out his mobile and spoke for a couple of seconds, then climbed into the car. Flemming made to start the engine, but he stopped her with a wave of his paw.

'Are we waiting for something?' I asked.

The weasel didn't reply, and instead just sat silently in the passenger seat, his rear paws on the dash, claws scratching the vinyl annoyingly. After about twenty minutes, cars began to arrive. The sort of cars sensible people own. Passats, Corollas, a few Audis, people carriers – some even with child seats in the back and nuclear disarmament stickers on the bumper. The cars stopped, parked up and the people climbed out. Their faces were obscured by the pig masks of TwoLegsGood and they positioned themselves around Hemlock Towers in a slow and deliberate fashion.

'I don't mind rabbits coming to grief,' said Flemming as soon as she realised what was going on, 'but when we start letting thugs do our dirty wo—'

'Just relax,' said the weasel, 'it's what he would have wanted.'

He patted her arm in a soothing manner, his meaning clear. He wasn't just going to allow this, he had engineered it. There weren't going to be any reprisals, but the Rabbits weren't going to be given the benefit of the doubt, either. He turned and fixed me with his small black eyes.

'These are the consequences of your actions, Knox,' he said. 'This one's on you.'

He then nodded to Flemming, who shook her head again, started the car and drove out past the growing throngs of pig-masked Hominid Supremacists carrying glass bottles with rags stuffed in the top. I think I even saw Victor Mallett, who looked pretty much the same with a pig mask as without.

'You're making a big mistake,' I said as the car, once away from the small crowd, picked up speed.

'You're the one who made the big mistake,' he said, 'you and the Rabbits.'

He lapsed into silence, but he had mistaken the meaning of my comment. The mistake he made was taking on someone like Constance Rabbit. If they hadn't already escaped through Kent's tunnel – likely temporarily hidden by the stacked bricks in the basement – then they would do soon enough. If Connie could outfox a fox, outweaselling a weasel would be child's play.

Lapin Flambé & HMP Leominster

TV Prison Trope incarceration was a natural progression from the pioneering Seventies Sitcom Hospitals, where the patients never seemed that ill and the nurses were all ridiculously buxom and spoke only in double entendres. They were, in turn, all romantically involved with the doctors, who were unfailingly handsome, witty, urbane and charming. And male.

I was taken to the Hereford Police Department's central station. Whizelle left it up to Flemming to oversee my processing, probably because the weasel was not well liked by the local police as he was arrested quite often for being drunk, and managed to be offensively obnoxious to all and sundry when he was.

I was handed over to the custody sergeant, who confirmed with me that I was Peter Knox; that I wasn't drunk or deranged; that I could be reasonably believed to be wanted in questioning with a crime; that I understood what was being said to me; that the crime required me to be held in custody; that I was unlikely to harm myself.

Pictures, fingerprints, details, then all my clothes were placed in a large evidence bag, signed and sealed. I was given some freshly laundered clothes to wear – a pair of jogging trousers, a T-shirt and a sweat top. On the whole, the officers were considerate and polite, but then I wasn't causing any trouble and I was human, like them. They even offered me something to eat, but I declined. I wasn't hungry. I thought I wouldn't be able to sleep, but I did, and quite well.

After a breakfast of cereal and tea, I was taken upstairs to meet the lawyer who had been allocated to my case.

'You're in luck,' the custody sergeant told me, 'Spenlow & Jorkins have agreed to supply counsel.'

'Oh?' I said, as the law firm were well known, not just in Hereford, but Shropshire and Gloucestershire, too. On numerous occasions they had defended defendants who had clearly been guilty, and while not *always* getting their clients acquitted, they had certainly managed to achieve a reduction in sentence.

It was a surprise when I met my lawyer, but thinking about it afterwards, I should not have been surprised at the surprise. A small Petstock rabbit dressed in a suit and tie was waiting for me, nervously clutching a briefcase and peering at me owlishly through round, steel-rimmed spectacles. He was white and brown, and his left ear was missing the top third.

'Hello!' he said cheerfully, clasping my hand in his two. 'Lance deBlackberry of Spenlow & Jorkins.'

'Hello,' I said, noting that his missing ear ended in the sort of pattern perforations make once torn. 'What happened to your ear?'

'Oh,' he said in a friendly tone, 'that's easily explained: never duel with automatic weapons. Now: Mr Jorkins *specifically* allocated me to your case as he thought I might be able to offer a unique insight.'

'Ah,' I said, 'and can you?'

'Can I what?'

'Offer a unique insight into my case?'

'Frankly, no,' he admitted, 'this is my first case.'

'First murder case?'

'No,' he said, 'I mean my first criminal case. I graduated only last week from Stanford Law School.'

'Stanford? That's impressive,' I said, feeling relieved despite his lack of experience. 'How did you get to travel to the States to attend?'

'You misunderstand me,' he said apologetically, 'not *the* Stanford Law School, but an online law school based out of Stanford, a small village in Bedfordshire. The course was easier than I expected. It didn't really require much study at all.'

'How long and how much?'

'Two weeks and two hundred pounds. Look.'

And from his briefcase he withdrew a framed certificate that seemed quite badly spelled.

'Don't take this the wrong way,' I said, 'but I think I might need a more experienced lawyer.'

'Not possible. The Attorney General *herself* asked for a rabbit lawyer to defend you. Said it would be fitting and just given the circumstances and would also give rabbits in the legal profession a "chance to shine".'

I sighed inwardly. The establishment was taking no chances on ensuring I was banged up for this, and as a bonus feature would be able to discredit rabbit lawyers at the same time.

'OK, then,' I said, 'where do we go from here?'

'Actually,' he said, 'I was hoping you might be able to give me a few pointers. Have you ever been arrested in connection with murder before?'

'No.'

'That's a shame,' he said, somewhat crestfallen, 'as it might have helped us figure out procedure. But never mind,' he added, 'this is only the interview process, and I've seen a couple of episodes of *24hrs in Police Custody* and *Banged Up Abroad*, so I think you should be saying "no comment" a lot and figuring out who to bribe.'

'I'm not handing out bribes, Mr deBlackberry.'

'It's Lancelot,' he said, 'but you can call me Lance.'

I was interviewed by a non-Taskforce officer, a friendly detective inspector named Stanton, and, ignoring Lance's advice, I denied nothing, and admitted everything. Yes, I had been having an affair with Mrs Rabbit, whom I had known for many years, yes, I did know there was a gun in the house, yes, Doc had earlier shown me where he kept the powder and ball and percussion caps, and yes, I pulled the trigger when Mr Ffoxe threatened to kill Constance.

'So you admit to killing Mr Ffoxe?' said DI Stanton.

'Since I was defending Constance Rabbit against Mr Ffoxe when I shot him,' I explained, 'it should be classed as self-defence.'

'Brilliant,' said Lance out of the corner of his mouth. 'Well done.' But DI Stanton put me right on that point.

'A fox is legally permitted to kill a rabbit, so the self-defence plea doesn't work unless you felt that Mr Ffoxe was going to attack *you*.'

He asked me whether I had felt my life was in danger, and I had to admit that I hadn't.

'If Mrs Rabbit was your property,' said Lance, looking up from a book entitled *Your Rights and the Law*, 'then your actions could be seen as using force to "protect your property".'

'But your response would have to be *proportionate*,' said DI Stanton, 'and I'm not sure the courts would see murder as a proportionate response to someone who *threatened* to kill your pet rabbit.'

'Constance wasn't anyone's property,' I said.

I dictated a confession, signed it and was charged with murder three hours later.

The news about Much Hemlock and Doc and Connie came to me on the morning of the second day, via a newspaper brought to me by Lance. The conflagration that gutted Hemlock Towers was reportedly the 'tragic outcome of a series of misunderstandings', and most papers took the angle of it being 'a spectacular loss for the architectural preservation lobby', who, it seemed, had belatedly regarded Hemlock Towers as an unspoiled rarity.

The 'peaceful and well-intended' rally began quietly, it was reported, when a pro-fox group arrived at the house to hold a candlelit vigil for a much-respected member of the *Vulpes vulpes* community, who had done so much to find a workable solution to the rabbit issue. It was likely, their spokesperson said, that the sight of all those candles must have frightened the Rabbits, who responded with 'many hostile acts' which caused those on the vigil to withdraw to safety, after which an 'unfortunate set of circumstances' took place in which the house was accidentally set on fire. 'We have credible information that the source of ignition could be attributed to the Rabbits themselves,' an unnamed source within TwoLegsGood reported. 'They may have been filling Molotov cocktails and had an accident with the matches. It's impossible to say.'

Despite no evidence to corroborate this and quite a lot to refute it, the news was not strenuously challenged. Reports of people in plastic pig masks were also furiously denied, and it seemed that a series of unfortunate car breakdowns had blocked all access to the house, which meant that the fire brigade were late to the scene, and could only control a fire that was so fully ablaze that it even set fire to the house next door, despite there being a gap of forty yards. Corroboration from villagers as to the circumstances of the fire was limited as most people, it seemed, had been watching the season finale of *Holby City* and either didn't know the fire had happened, or had seen it from a distance, or thought it was kids 'mucking around with a bonfire'.

I wasn't so annoyed about the factual discrepancies and the loss of my house, it was more that no one seemed to care. The *Smugleftie* reported it on page six, but with few facts to go on and the Rehoming filling most of the rabbit column inches, the attack on Hemlock Towers story was dead in under twenty-four hours.

My story, however, was emphatically *not*. Mr Ffoxe had been described as 'a much-loved and respected civil servant and decorated war hero' by *The Daily Fencesitter*, and 'a fox of considerable drive and resolve who had tirelessly committed himself to species integration' by *The Actual Truth*. *The Briton* went a step farther in describing him as 'a true British patriot cruelly snatched from us by a lowly degenerate', and 'a tireless champion of rabbit causes' was trumpeted by *The Ludlow Bugle*.

'The Rehoming,' said Nigel Smethwick in a speech at Mr Ffoxe's memorial service, 'will not be derailed by the tragic death of a good friend and loyal servant of the Crown, whose sole purpose was to assist rabbits in their quest to find a way to a joyous and workable homeland. In memory of Mr Ffoxe's good work, we will be accelerating the MegaWarren project: rabbits will start being forcibly rehomed in a month's time if they have not volunteered. Their level of compliance will dictate the level of force.'

I was driven across the road on the afternoon of the second day to make a brief appearance at Hereford magistrate's court. There was a heavy police presence as the slaying of the Senior Group Leader had angered many people who were either partly or overtly leporiphobic. I think the least offensive chant I heard was 'Poxie Knoxie', but there were others, based mostly around the graffito previously sprayed on my garage door.

My plea of guilty to murder and a secondary charge of intimate association was entered and my hearing set for a month's time in order to give an opportunity for both prosecution and defence to prepare arguments regarding sentencing. I had to go over the proceedings twice for Lance, who said we should try to get some rabbits on the jury, but I explained to him that since I'd already submitted a plea, there didn't need to be a jury – and rabbits, not being human, were ineligible to serve anyway.

'Yes, I get that,' said Lance, 'but I still think it would be a good idea. Can I yell "Objection"? I've always wanted to do that.'

'Do you have anything to object to?' I asked.

Lance thought for a moment.

'The breakfast at the hotel this morning wasn't very good.'

After an hour of paperwork I was driven to HMP Leominster in a small van with only one window high up and heavily tinted. I could see the top of articulated lorries, telegraph poles and bridges as we drove along, but not much else.

Once I had been processed again, given my kit and watched the prison's theatrical society perform a short but amusing play about the best way to avoid being stabbed in the showers, the governor himself turned up.

'Hello!' he said in a jovial manner. 'Quentin Pratts, the prison governor. You can call me "Guv". Take it from me that all inmates here are treated with respect and dignity, and utterly without prejudgement. It's Peter "Bunnyshagger" Knox, isn't it?'

'Just "Knox" will suit me fine, Guv.'

We walked off in the direction of the wings, a prison guard walking behind, but at a discreet distance.

'I run a peaceful prison,' said the governor, 'and since your stay here was precipitated by a certain fondness for rabbits I have to ask if you feel you need to be segregated for your own safety?'

I had thought long and hard about this, and although it *might* be safer, I wasn't too happy about the company I would have to keep. It was mostly bankers in the segregation block, talking fondly about collateralised debt obligations and credit default swaps. In a turnabout that no one expected after the 2008 crash, the second-largest group in prison after rabbits was now sociopathic investment bankers, corrupt representatives of ratings companies and dodgy corporate accountants.[59] It wasn't company I relished. I'd take my chances on the wings.

'No, sir.'

'Good man. We have some Hominid Supremacists doing time for some harmless high jinks that have been deemed illegal for some reason, and given your history you'd be wise to avoid them. We also have about six dozen rabbits,' he added, 'troublemakers, every one of them. I don't want to see any cross-species fraternisation of any sort. The bunnies keep to themselves, and that's the way we like it. Get it?'

'Got it.'

'Good.'

We stepped on to 'D' wing, where the central area was taken over by a seating arrangement, the kitchen and several ping-pong tables. There were two tiers of cells, and on the upper-tier balcony I could see prison guards leaning on the rail, twirling their keys and watching us carefully.

'This is the first in an experimental Media Tropes prison,' said the governor, 'designed in order to make inmates feel that they are not being brutalised by a barbaric and outdated system of incarceration, but involved in something more along the lines of a reality TV show.'

'I've heard of this,' I said, looking around curiously.

'The layout on the wings is just one of the many TV Prison Tropes that are promoted here at HMP Leominster,' said the governor. 'You'll find the prison is pretty much as you'd expect: the guards are generally mean and unpleasant – except one who is meek and easy to manipulate. The prisoners, instead of being those with a shaky grasp on the notion of consequences, mental health issues or having the misfortune to belong to a marginalised minority, are mostly pastiches of socio-economic groups mixed with regional stereotypes. And rather than fume about the vagaries of providence that got them here before descending in a downward spiral of depression and drug addiction, they prefer to philosophise about life in an amusing and intelligent manner.'

---

59. If only life were like this.

'Does it work?'

'Recidivism has dropped eighty-six per cent,' he said, 'so yes, it seems so. It's certainly a lot easier on the prisoners unless you get caught up in Gritty Realism Month when it all gets dark and dangerous and we have riots and people end up getting shivved. That's just been, so you're fairly safe for another ten months.'

'That's a relief.'

'Don't count your chickens. Understated violence that counter-points a wider issue in society can break out at any time, and we have the biennial Prison Break Weekend in eight weeks, so if you want to be part of that, you have to prove yourself with the right crowd.'

'Thanks for the tip.'

'My pleasure. The rabbits are over in "R" wing and you'll mix at outdoor break – mostly serial burrowers,[60] which offers us a unique set of challenges. They'll probably want to make friends, but the rabbits in here are different to the rabbits out there. They'll pretend to be your friend over the whole fox-killing issue, but don't get mixed up with them and never accept any carrots. Once you owe them a carrot, you're in their pocket, and you don't want to be in a rabbit's pocket. Well, cheerio.'

I had been carrying my things all this time – blanket, tin cup, roll of loo paper – and the prison guard who had been tailing us showed me into my cell.

I was relieved to find that I wouldn't have to share it with anyone.

I arranged all my stuff, had a pee then lay down on my bunk, expecting to feel anxious. That I didn't was probably due to my attendance at a terrible public school which I now realised had furnished me with useful transferable skills.

I ventured out of my cell an hour later for dinner, and after fetching my tray sat on my own. I was not alone for long, however, as two

---

60. The sentence for burrowing-related crime was never more than a year, but Smethwick's manifesto promise of 'six holes and you're out' rule ensured repeat offenders were banged up for life.

men approached my table. They looked utterly respectable and were chatting in educated accents about how they missed their Agas and their Volvos and badminton and the opera. They also had '*shallow and extremely transparent*' tattooed on their forearms, which related to a much-repeated quote that Beatrix Potter had made about rabbits. It didn't occur to them that it might have been self-referential. In any event, the tattoos marked them out as TwoLegsGood.

'You're Peter Knox, aren't you?' said the first as they sat down either side of me.

'Nope.'

'Sure you are. The one who killed Mr Ffoxe, right?'

'Look, I don't want any trouble.'

'Understandable,' he replied, leaning closer, 'but we don't like people who side with rabbits. Humans have been improving themselves in a continuously unbroken chain of evolutionary advancements from the moment life first flickered into being, and are now the high point of evolutionary perfection. That achievement was hard won, and we will defend that struggle against all comers.'

I didn't think it was the right time to point out the fatal logistical flaw in his argument, but instead repeated something that Pippa's friend Sally had once said:

'All life is one, and there is no objective truth that suggests we have a greater right to life than a lichen.'

They both stared at me and blinked a couple of times.

'That's bullshit, Mr Knox. This is our planet, and we'll do with it what we wish. You're just an … apostate of your species.'

'I'm not sure that word works outside a religious context, you unbelievable *twat*.'

I'd have liked to boast that I'd said that last line, but I hadn't. It was said by the larger of two *other* prisoners who'd just turned up. They were muscly, bald, bearded, and both looked as though they could comfortably strangle a tractor. Their tattoos – of which they had many – were not Elmer Fudd-related or anti-rabbit slogans, but normal sort of stuff: Celtic thingummies, skulls and the dates of their children's births. Significantly, they were both staring at the fox sympathisers in a way I emphatically would not like them to be staring at *me*.

'Another time, Knox,' said one of the supremacists, and they left, grumbling about how they never served quinoa in the canteen, and how much they missed the *GQ* lifestyle awards.

'Upper-middle-class entitled parasites,' said the first new arrival as he sat down. 'Tristran Reeves there is doing six years for rebadging Rayburns as Agas and flogging them off to unsuspected buyers, and his associate, Jeremy Fink-Grottle, had been forging National Trust membership cards.'

'Ah,' I said, 'middle-class crime.'

In another inversion of generally accepted stereotypes, the heavily tattooed prisoners with what would be termed back in Much Hemlock 'a rough manner of speech' had no issue with my friendship with rabbits at all.

'My sister was seeing a rabbit until they rescinded his work permit,' continued the prisoner, whose name I learned was 'Razors' McKay, on account of his hobby of collecting seashells. 'Nice lad and looked after our Stacey well. Don't see the harm in it myself – love is love – and to be honest, anything that knob Smethwick is against is totally fine by me.'

'Yeah,' said his friend in a Liverpudlian accent, 'we'll see youse all right, man. Friend o' the rabbit is a friend of ours.'

His name, I learned, was 'Bonecrusher' Malloy, which related to his previous employment making bonemeal for the pet food industry. They were both inside for employing undocumented rabbit labour, and then illegally paying them above the maximum wage. They'd both been warned six or seven times, and prosecuted twice each. They'd carried on regardless and eventually were given custodial sentences.

After I found all that out, we got on really well. For the most part they were curious about what had happened to me, agreed that, yes, twenty years was likely for murder and intimate association, then asked me what it had been like.

'Killing a fox?' I asked.

'No,' they said, 'the other thing.'

The first three days were relatively uneventful, but on the fourth I lost both my thumbs to Reeves and Fink-Grottle, who came to my cell, gagged me with a towel and then removed both thumbs with a bolt-cutter. I only remembered them cutting off the first; I was unconscious by the time they took the second. I was found an hour later in a pool of blood and rushed to hospital.

The Trials of Lance deBlackberry

Only three rabbit lawyers were ever called to the bar, the longest
serving for sixteen years until anti-rabbit legislation forced her to quit.
'If things had been different,' ex-Attorney General and pro-rabbit
advocate Lord Jefferson said, 'she would have been the finest judge this
nation would ever have produced.'

By the time of my trial, my hands had more or less healed. My
assailants had flushed my severed thumbs down the toilet, so the
surgeons had suggested a series of operations that would have put a
little finger or toe where my thumb had been, but success was not
guaranteed, so I asked them to make the repair as neat as they could
and that would be it.

Lance enquired several times whether I wanted to postpone the
sentencing. I asked him whether that would change anything, and
he said that it probably wouldn't. The story of my lopping had got
out, and while hardcore leporiphobic fox-friends saw it as my just
deserts for killing Mr Ffoxe, most thought it was a cruel and unusual
punishment, given that I was already facing a life sentence. The only
upside to my incarceration was that without me, the *Buchblitz* overran
twice in a row and had to be placed in 'special measures'.

My hearing was held in the Gloucester law courts. I'd heard
nothing from Pippa as the mobile phone masts around Colony One
had been disabled, along with all the landlines. She did manage to
get a message out to me, though. A scribbled note hidden inside a
hollowed-out carrot left in my cell exhorted me to 'be strong' and
informed me that she, and everyone else, 'were fine'.

In the news, the refusal of the rabbits to move out of Colony
One was causing something of a headache for Smethwick and the
Taskforce. A vixen had been appointed the new Senior Group Leader.
She was named Jocaminca fforkes, with two *small* 'f's – as if having

two 'f's wasn't pretentious enough – and the papers had reported 'tensions' within the upper echelons of the Taskforce. Prolonged and heated discussions had taken place amongst the elders of Colony One, the Rehoming team, Smethwick himself, fforkes and the Grand Council of Coneys.

The failure to reach an agreement on the Rehoming was blamed on the rabbit's intransigence, while rabbit spokespeople cited 'a litany of broken promises' in past human/rabbit negotiations, which Smethwick defended on the grounds that 'we may have been lying then, but we're totally telling the truth now', and since that particular gambit had always worked on humans, then it was reasonable that rabbits should adopt it also. The impasse was all set to evolve into an escalation, as the fifteen hundred foxes and several thousand Compliance Taskforce personnel were currently billeted in and around Colony One. The enforced curfew, instigated the day before Mr Ffoxe died, was still very much in place: no one in, no one out.

'Good news,' said Lance as we sat together on the defence bench, the morning of my sentencing. 'I found a boxed set of *Judge John Deed* in Oxfam and have watched the entire series twice and made copious notes. Let me tell you,' he added in a confident manner, 'there is *nothing* I don't know about procedure within the British legal system.'

'OK,' I said, not sharing his confidence. 'You do know that *Judge John Deed* is actually one of the *least* realistic British TV courtroom drama series?'

'Is it?' said Lance, genuinely surprised. 'That might cause a few problems with your defence – but I'm sure we'll muddle through. Now,' he said, 'which one is the judge?'

'She's not in yet. You'll know it's her because she'll be wearing a wig and you'll be asked to stand.'

I took a deep breath and looked about. The public gallery was full, but there were only two rabbits, neither of whom I recognised.

Once we had stood for the judge and were all then reseated, the usual legal preamble went backwards and forwards while Lance doodled a picture of a carrot on his legal pad. When asked to confirm the plea I had entered earlier, he suddenly stood up.

'I would like to put forward a motion that all charges be withdrawn.'
The prosecution barrister also stood up.

'The prosecution will vigorously oppose any downgrading of the charge to manslaughter,' he said.

'You didn't hear me,' said Lance, 'we do *not* seek a reduction to manslaughter, but a dropping of all charges. My client will also change his plea to not guilty to intimate association, for which the court will have to furnish compelling evidence beyond the testimony of witnesses who are either dead or can be demonstrably proven to have anti-rabbit bias by belonging to TwoLegsGood, a membership list of which I will enter as defence exhibit A. Regarding my client's confession, we will come to that later when I outline how, although not coerced by police, my client was nonetheless coerced.'

There was a stunned silence as Lance deBlackberry finished his short speech. The clerks looked at one another and shrugged, and the two prosecution barristers stared at Lance incredulously.

'I have to say I'm intrigued but not convinced by this, Mr deBlackberry,' said the judge, 'but I will hear your arguments.'

Lance thanked the judge and continued.

'The crime of murder can only be committed between two humans. Since we know that Mr Ffoxe was of dual taxonomic status and is to be considered a human for the purposes of this trial, it is this status I challenge. Since he was in that house to kill rabbits then it follows that on the evening of his death Mr Ffoxe should be defined as a fox – if he wasn't, then he would legally *not* be allowed to murder a rabbit, any more than a human is allowed to kill an anthropomorphised rabbit. The law affords us that protection.'

He paused.

'So if the victim was legally a fox, then my client's act becomes simply a man shooting a fox, which he is legally permitted to do under the 1854 Destruction of Countryside Pests Act.'

The prosecution lawyer stood up again.

'While we concede that legally Mr Ffoxe was required to be a fox to kill rabbits but a human to be a victim of murder, we contend that Mr Ffoxe was legally a human when killed as he had not yet done anything that would define him as a fox in the eyes of the law.'

But Lance was not yet done.

'This is not a question about when my learned colleague decides – arbitrarily – that a fox is a human or a fox; this is a question of intent. If Mr Ffoxe entered the Rabbits' house with the sole purpose of terrifying and killing the Rabbit family then he would be very much defined as a fox, and that being so – he cannot be murdered.'

'Defence counsel may be technically correct,' said the prosecution, 'but since we have no sense of Mr Ffoxe's intent when he entered the Rabbits' house, then it cannot be proven that he was there to kill rabbits. He may have been wanting to interview them, or offer a warning. Or simply request a glass of water.'

'A fox does not go into a rabbit's house with any other intent,' said Lance, 'but I concede that his state of mind is unknowable. But will prosecution counsel agree that the victim's intent has a direct bearing on his taxonomic status?'

'We do, Your Honour,' said the prosecution barrister.

'Good,' said Lance, 'then I would contend on the basis of that notion that the *perpetrator's* intent must also have a direct bearing on the victim's taxonomic status. My contention is that since Mr Knox was in that house to do a little fox-hunting, then by learned counsel's arguments, Mr Ffoxe must be classed taxonomically as a fox – and can therefore be legally killed by a human.'

The prosecution seemed more amused than annoyed by Lance's words.

'Does learned council,' he began in a haughty tone, 'honestly expect this court to believe that his client was engaging in fox-hunting? I need hardly remind him that this is not a court of conjecture and fantasy, but one that depends upon burden of proof. The defendant's confession makes no mention of being out for a little fox-hunting, and it seems a stretch for the court to accept this line of reasoning. In none of the photographic evidence can the defendant be seen having a pack of hounds, a horse or a hunting horn, nor was he even dressed in Pink.'

There was a ripple of laughter around the court at this, but not from the rabbits in the public gallery, who had been hanging on Lance's every word.

'Ah, yes,' said Lance, 'the confession to which I alluded earlier. Mr Knox was in fear of his life from the Hominid Supremacist group TwoLegsGood, who are well known to despise rabbits and are not keen on anyone who kills foxes, and there is strong circumstantial evidence – despite the stories you have read in the media – that it was they who burned the Rabbits' house down, set fire to Mr Knox's house, and murdered the Rabbits in their own home. Furthermore, they threatened Mr Knox with a punishment that is well known to be one meted out to those humans who are reputed to side with rabbits – the removal of the thumbs, usually with a bolt-cutter. A threat, the court can see, that was carried out, despite Mr Knox agreeing to confess to everything. His confession, therefore, is unreliable, and should be deemed inadmissible.'

There was a short pause, and someone entered at the back of the courtroom, walked forward and handed a note to the more junior of the prosecution barristers. He read the note, then stood up.

'If it pleases the court,' said the prosecutor, 'I have just received a shocking communication that is pertinent to the proceedings here today. To the effect that opposing counsel, Mr Lance deBlackberry, does not have any professional credentials qualifying him to practise law and has thus fraudulently misrepresented himself, and should be immediately removed from the courtroom pending criminal charges.'

I had seen the junior barrister texting under the table as soon as Lance started to speak, and realised what was going on. Lance had cultivated a sense of incompetence for a very good reason.

'We would also,' said the senior prosecutor, 'move for an adjournment of the proceedings until such time as Mr Knox can be properly represented.'

Lance, however, was not fazed in the least.

'My legal diploma,' he said in a loud, clear voice, 'was sent to the court, which had ample time to review my credentials, but did not. My presence here is simply to undermine my client's case and ensure Mr Knox be jailed for the maximum time possible. I was permitted and encouraged to represent Mr Knox only so I could fail.'

I expected the judge to intervene, but she did not.

'But in light of my learned colleague's accusation,' continued Lance, 'I would apply to this court to represent Mr Knox in a lay capacity as a McKenzie friend.[61]'

'Ridiculous,' said prosecution counsel. 'Mr deBlackberry's status and qualifications should be reviewed separately, and I must once again request, in the strongest possible terms, that these proceedings be adjourned.'

There was silence and we all watched the judge, who stared at Lance and prosecution council in turn.

'The court is dismayed to learn that Mr deBlackberry is not legally permitted to speak,' she said, 'and since he has done so in the capacity of defence counsel, I find that he is in contempt of this court, and the court will fine him a solitary one pound, to be paid to the clerk before the end of the day. As regards his plea to become a McKenzie's friend, I see no reason to deny this, and every reason to permit it. I should also warn prosecution counsel that I have taken note of Mr deBlackberry's concerns, and will direct my staff to make enquiries. If the concerns prove justified, I fully intend to bring charges against anyone who has attempted to pervert the course of justice. Do you understand me?'

'Yes, Your Honour,' said the head prosecution barrister.

'Good,' she said. 'Mr deBlackberry? Please continue.'

Lance cleared his throat and summarised what he had said so far: that I had been coerced and threatened to confess – something that was apparent by my thumbless condition – and that I was actually in the Rabbits' house to indulge in a little fox-hunting.

'Yes indeed,' said the lead prosecution barrister, 'the thorny fox-hunting issue. Would learned counsel care to demonstrate to the court just how he can prove this ridiculous suggestion, given there were no horses or hounds?'

There wasn't any laughter this time around, and Lance drew several evidence photographs from a folder.

'I draw the court's attention to crime scene photographs 8, 17, 34,

---

61. A non-legally qualified person who may assist a litigant in court. See *McKenzie* v. *McKenzie*, 1970.

26 and 38. In all of them an owl can clearly be seen. I would also like to draw your attention to photograph 78, in which we see Mr Knox's burned-out house the following morning, in which an aviary is, again, clearly visible. I also have a signed receipt, here entered as defence exhibit B, to show that said aviary and owl were delivered to Mr Knox the week before.'

He paused to take a sip of water.

'The Hunting Act of 2004 clearly states that a bird of prey may be used to flush a fox, and a bird of prey – brought by Mr Knox himself – was there in Hemlock Towers when Mr Knox was doing what the law permitted: legally destroying vermin. Once again I appeal to this court to dismiss all charges and release my client.'

'None of this was in discovery,' said the prosecution barrister, 'and shows a flagrant lapse in procedural rectitude.'

'Agreed,' said the judge. 'I find Mr deBlackberry in contempt again, and fine him another pound. As for dismissing the charges against Mr Knox, I find Mr deBlackberry's argument plausible, and given the grey areas regarding Mr Ffoxe's taxonomic status, I no longer believe there is enough evidence to satisfy this court that Mr Ffoxe was human when he was killed, and I therefore dismiss the charge of murder. As for the "intimate association" charge, I find that Mr Knox's confession, in light of the personal attack upon him in prison, should be regarded as tainted, and is also inadmissible. Without it, I cannot see any likely chance of a conviction, and dismiss this charge also.'

There was a collective sigh of annoyance from the humans in the public gallery, and three 'huzzahs' from the rabbits. The judge directed her next comments to Lance.

'Mr deBlackberry, I have been as impressed with your qualities in this court today as much as I have been disappointed by prosecution counsel's attempt to undermine the rule of law. I will warn you, Mr deBlackberry, that in future you should not misrepresent yourself in court as other judges may not be so tolerant. Consider this a reprimand. Mr Knox, you are free to go.'

The judge then stood up, the court stood up, and ten minutes later I found myself blinking on the steps of the courthouse.

'My client has no comment at this time,' said Lance as we made our way through the phalanx of reporters to a waiting RabCab, in this instance a charmingly ugly 1973 Ford Gran Torino.

'Nffiffr hrff niffrh?' asked the cabbie, who was an old flea-bitten buck with a single hole in his left ear that was so large he must have duelled with a howitzer.

'Colony One,' said Lance, 'and step on it.'

The cabbie did indeed 'step on it', but only in a strictly relative way: he ramped it up to a heady 40 mph, only 12.62 mph below the all-time self-piloted rabbit land speed record. I think I realised then how they made their cars last so long.

'Is that wise?' I asked. 'I'm probably the last person who should be seen anywhere near the May Hill colony.'

'You need to be there,' said Lance.

'Why?'

'Because Bunty has foreseen that the endgame is near – and we need all the help we can get.'

Rabbit Colony One

A three-dimensional mapping of the warrens beneath Colony One revealed a labyrinthine network of tunnels that were, astonishingly, more tunnel than soil, and instigated a new branch of mathematics that was later used to greatly improve shock-absorbing foam.

We sat in silence as we drove up and out of Hereford towards Ross-on-Wye, and I didn't speak until we were past Harewood End.

'That was really impressive in court,' I said. 'Thank you.'

'Don't thank me,' he said, 'thank the Venerable Bunty and Mr Finkle. It was their overall plan. I just spoke the words, trippingly off the tongue.'

'Are you going to study law for real?' I asked.

'Maybe,' said Lance, 'but it'll take more than just rabbit lawyers – we need rabbit judges to see our point of view. When every legal system on the planet is skewed against any non-human animal group, it's almost impossible to make any headway. We'd have liked to help – the Rabbit Way has a lot going for it – but maybe humans just aren't grown up enough to be able to share the planet quite yet.'

'Why help me out at all?' I asked. 'I mean, you could have just left me to my life sentence and it would be no down off anyone's ears.'

'That's true,' said Lance, 'but the second circle of Lago is about restorative self-justice. Responsibility for one's errors, choice-consequences and transgressions. You didn't kill Mr Ffoxe, so you shouldn't go to prison. Luckily, it's relatively easy to outfox the British legal system. Your billionaires do it all the time. The way we see it, London is just one massive money-laundering scheme attached to an impressive public transport system and a few museums, of which even the most honest has more stolen goods than a lock-up garage in Worcester rented by a guy I know called Chalky.'

We chatted for a while and I learned that Lance's appearance in court had only been his first *criminal* case, but not his first civil plea. Although there was not yet a ruling, the civil case revolved around whether a receipt from a pet shop for Blackberry, Lance's Petstock forebear, could be considered proof of pre-Event residency, and if so, did that count as documentation and thus make the fifty thousand or so rabbits who carried the deBlackberry surname legally British.

'Will it work?' I asked.

'It's legally sound,' he said, 'but with UKARP's shifting legislative goalposts, probably not.'

The cabbie had the radio on as we drove, and I featured prominently on the news. The general consensus was that a 'shady rabbit lawyer' had 'exploited a loophole' to 'get me off', a loophole which fox legal minds were currently trying to close – and there was even talk of appealing the judge's decision as she had clearly promoted 'an appallingly biased anti-human and pro-rabbit agenda'. Either way, it didn't appear as though this was over.

As we approached Colony One we could see a huge military build-up had occurred. There were lorries and tanks parked amongst the trees, with artillery pieces positioned in the surrounding fields, gun crews at readiness.

'This is as far as this old rabbit goes,' said the cabbie, as the access road to the colony had been barricaded about a mile from the main entrance. There was, in fact, a good-sized crowd of humans present and a peace camp seemed to have been set up. Banners proclaiming equal rights for all animals and support for vegetarianism and sustainability were prominently displayed, and several others which were only passive-aggressively anti-fox, as it really wasn't wise to piss them off. The police were present also, leaning on their riot shields and looking bored, while groups of foxes sat around on deckchairs, listening to Caruso on a wind-up gramophone, sipping Chianti and playing cribbage.

'You need to take this in with you,' said Lance, handing me a sealed cardboard box about a foot square.

'What is it?'

'Oh, just supplies,' he said, 'but vital for the effort.'

'OK,' I replied, now uneasy. 'But how am I going to get in?'

'Go straight in the door,' he said. 'My guess is they won't dare touch you.'

I squeezed his two paws with my two thumbless hands. It actually felt more comfortable and connected, as though our hands/paws interlocked more fully and completely, and with them, an understanding.

'Goodbye, Peter,' said Lance with an air of finality, 'it's been a lot of fun. I may see you on the other side.'

'What do you mean?'

'You'll see.'

I climbed out of the car, which drove off without urgency, and walked up to the barrier, where several police officers were talking in a nervous gaggle. For the most part, they stayed separate from the Taskforce. When mud gets thrown around, the further you are away, the less likely it will stick.

'Sorry, sir,' said the policeman in charge, a superintendent, I think, 'no entry to Colony One at present.'

'My name's Peter Knox,' I said, 'I need to speak to the fox in charge.'

The superintendent either hadn't followed the breaking news, didn't see how it might be relevant or couldn't care, so he simply repeated what he had said a little more forcefully: that the colony was closed.

Luckily for me there were also military personnel standing just a little way off and the ranking officer, a brigadier, strolled over and asked the superintendent for a word. It was several words in the end, for they were chatting for five minutes, and eventually the superintendent made a call on his mobile, nodded several times and then walked back to me.

'You're allowed in,' he said, 'under military and not civilian escort. They're sending a car for you.'

He then leaned closer to me and said in a quiet voice:

'Off the record, sir, but if I were you I'd turn around and go back where you came from. Don't look back, don't hesitate, don't stop until you are back safe with your family.'

'I don't have any family. Not out here, anyway.'

'Then I suggest you find some. What's in the box?'

I looked down at the cardboard box Lance had given me.

'I don't know.'

He took it off me and then gave it to an officer who opened it, had a look and then resealed it and returned it to me.

I stood there until the car arrived, a military four-by-four with two armed men in the back who looked like Special Forces, or how I *imagine* Special Forces to look – draped with weapons as a Christmas tree is draped with tinsel. But they weren't moody or philosophical, they actually sounded quite chirpy.

'It's Peter Knox, isn't it?' said the first, indicating my hands. The dressings had been off for a week, but the skin was still pink and the scars, stitched up finely at A&E, looked like thin red zippers.

'That's me,' I replied.

'Outfoxed the fox, I heard,' said the second. 'Hats off to you. What's in the box?'

'I don't know.'

I turned to look back at the checkpoint we'd just left, and noticed that the police were hurriedly withdrawing to their vehicles and the military were moving in to take their place. I could see where several tanks had just fired up their engines, as large clouds of black smoke erupted from where they were parked.

'We're go for Operation Cottontail,' said the first soldier, who had been listening to his earpiece.

'Cottontail?' I asked.

'Forcible Rehoming,' said the soldier, and gave me a wink.

'In what?' I said, looking around as we drove into the large car park outside the main entrance to Colony One. There wasn't a bus in sight. Not up here, not farther down the road. With a shudder, I realised that there wasn't going to be a Rehoming, and that had never been part of the plan. I felt a sudden chill, even though the evening was warm.

The four-by-four pulled up beside more armoured vehicles – personnel carriers this time, manned by foxes – and, more ominously, several bulldozers. I was escorted towards a massive tent with *Forward Operations Post* written on a sign outside. As we walked, I could see more civilians and police officers getting into their cars to leave, while just behind the forward OP there seemed to be a junior officer throwing papers on to a fire inside an oil drum. I was escorted into the tent, the cardboard box Lance had given me was checked and returned to me again, and I was told to wait. I took the opportunity to look around. There was a large map on the wall of Colony One with an overlay of the warrens beneath the ground, so far as they were known. In a small gaggle I could see Nigel Smethwick talking to several foxes and a few high-ranking military officers. The fox who seemed to be in charge looked across at me, then beckoned me to approach.

'Jocaminca fforkes,' she said, shaking my hand. 'Your outfoxing skills compel me to grant you the smallest amount of respect.'

To me, there wasn't much physical difference between her and Mr Ffoxe – shorter by an inch, perhaps, and a little redder. In a helpful nod to assist in gender identification, vixens wore a flower behind their ear that I could have sworn was identical to the ones you could buy in Claire's Accessories for under a pound.

'You dodged justice this time,' said Smethwick, 'but this isn't over by a mile. What are you doing here?'

'I was asked to be here.'

'Why?'

'To help out, I think.'

Ms fforkes and Smethwick looked at one another.

'You can *try* and help out,' said Smethwick with a unpleasant smile, 'but if you go in there and it all kicks off, you – along with all the other humans inside – will be deemed to be unlawful combatants in that you offered material support to an illegal insurrection, where extreme violence was perpetrated upon a taskforce eager only to assist in a legal Rehoming.'

'You're going to kill them all, aren't you?' I said, with a surprising amount of bravado. 'All one hundred and fifty thousand of them.'

'We'd so *hate* to do that,' said Ms fforkes without an atom of sincerity, 'but once Colony One has fallen, the other four will soon fall into line. Rabbits are like naughty children, Mr Knox, and occasionally need to be punished. MegaWarren is a social and economical win-win for all concerned, and it *will* be implemented.'

'Dear Jocaminca can be a little fearsome at times,' said Smethwick.

'Policing actions like these can be very confusing to the man in the street, and although the UK's citizenry is generally on our side, public opinion can be a fickle beast. Do you think you can get the rabbits to return to the negotiating table?'

From what I'd learned about rabbits over the past two months, the answer was a resounding no. But I wanted to get in there, and this seemed as good a way as any. I was kind of flattered, too, that he thought I might somehow be a player.

'I can give it my best shot.'

'Excellent!' said Smethwick, passing me his card. 'If I've not had a call from you by twenty hundred hours then I'll hand over control to the foxes. I am sure you can appreciate what this means, given that foxes have a historically loose relationship with the concept of restraint.'

He patted me on the shoulder, then tapped the cardboard box I was carrying.

'What's in the box?'

'Something for the rabbit, I think.'

He beckoned over a Taskforce officer, who removed the box to a small table, had a look inside, resealed it and then brought it back.

'So,' said Ms fforkes as she walked me across the open area in front of the main gates, 'what exactly was Torquil Ffoxe doing in the Rabbits' house that evening?'

A single sentry was guarding the twin gates of the imposing main entrance, but the admin buildings either side were dark and empty. I checked my watch. It was just past six. There were two hours to go until Operation Cottontail began.

'He thought Constance Rabbit was involved with the Underground and would know of the Bunty's whereabouts.'

'Did she?'

'Probably not.'

'We'll have the VB in custody by dawn,' said Ms fforkes, 'you have my word on that.'

'You'll never catch her,' I said, 'she's been three steps ahead of you every time. I didn't outfox the fox, she did – and she'll do it again. Your days are numbered, just like Mr Ffoxe's. And you know what? You'll never see it coming.'

For a fleeting instant, somewhere deep beneath the brash confidence of a well-evolved carnivore, I saw a glimmer of doubt cross Ms fforkes' features. A sense of … *mortality.*

'Balls,' she said, her confidence swiftly returning. 'Do what you can to bring about peace. The attack would be a lot of fun, and the per capita death payments would make all of us wealthy beyond our wildest dreams – but in the broader picture, a culling benefits no one.'

'That's an oddly charitable viewpoint for a fox.'

'Not at all. A culling in Colony One will only strengthen the rabbit's resolve in the other colonies, not weaken it. So we'll have to kill them, too. And if this all goes to Smethwick's plan and we cull the lot, do you really think that humans will welcome us into their society and offer us a cosy retirement package? No. We've only been invited to top table to do the dirty work, and if things go tits-up – which they eventually will – there is a convenient bogeyman at which to point the finger. Human guilt, as always, will be abrogated to foxes, or circumstance, and eventually to history.'

'Is that really Smethwick's plan?' I asked. 'To eradicate them all?'

'If the Rehoming doesn't work out and there's a general strike, then yes. But listen,' she continued, 'I like to kill rabbits as much as the next fox, but compliance rather than eradication is the winning business model for us. So oddly, yes, I want you to try and achieve a peace. You've got two hours. Good evening, Mr Knox.'

After checking through a peephole, the guard threw the bolt and opened the small wicket door set into one of the large double gates. I took a deep breath, paused for a moment and stepped for the first time into Colony One.

Endgame

It was dubbed 'a battle' to make it sound as though the opponents had been equally powerful and that there had been some sense of doubt over the outcome. A more realistic word would have been 'slaughter' had the engagement gone the way it had been intended.

But it didn't.

I paused inside the gate, suddenly aware that I had stepped into a world that until recently had been closed to me. I still felt a stranger, and knew I could never belong, but I also knew that somewhere close by would be Connie and Pippa, and that I was not alone.

I looked around, expecting to see a massed group of rabbits or something, all armed with whatever was to hand, but there was nobody. The area between the first gates and the second, a place usually reserved for where articulated lorries brought components in and trucked completed goods out, was deserted. I walked towards the second set of gates, which I noticed were ajar.

'Hello?' I said as I put my head around the door. There didn't seem to be anyone around so I stepped inside. To my left and right were the call centres and factories, and straight on was a single thoroughfare that led on to rows and rows of allotments under which there would be a network of tunnels. Beyond this the ground rose to the top of May Hill itself, where a circular grove of trees punctuated the skyline. On the air was the heady scent of meadow-field stew, and on the breeze I could hear the distant strains of jazz.

'Is that Peter Knox?' came Doc's voice from somewhere close at hand. 'Your shape and walk give me only a 42% cenrtainty.'

I said that I was indeed Peter and he stepped out of the shadows.

I smiled, but instead of shaking hands/paws, he gave me a hug.

'You got out of Hemlock Towers, then,' I said.

'Singed a few whiskers when I went back for the Kyffin Williams painting in the downstairs loo,' he said. 'Nearly forgot. What a twit. But otherwise no ill effects. I heard they took your thumbs?'

I showed him my hands.

'That's what comes of playing with scissors,' he said, grinning broadly.

'Is Pippa here?' I asked.

'Safe and well. We followed your court case on the wireless. Lance deBlackberry has quite a mind, hasn't he?'

'The best. He said you wanted my help.'

'Yes indeed. Follow me, and bring the box.'

We walked towards the Lago meeting house.

'When are they planning on attacking?' asked Doc.

'Eight o'clock.'

'Yes, we heard the same. So long as they attack first and we are defending ourselves, then everything is fair game.'

He flicked his incisors with a claw and they pinged like expensive porcelain.

'They have guns,' I said, 'big ones.'

'I know,' he said. 'None of us have high expectations of the outcome, although that's not to say Constance and the Venerable Bunty don't have a few ideas up their sleeves. Smarter rabbits than I, those two. Which reminds me,' he said, 'there is still the question of our duel. Constance said it was OK, so do you want to challenge me, or shall I challenge you? It's traditional as the appropriating husband for you to do it, but I'm flexible.'

'Is this really the time and place?' I asked. 'Besides, nothing happened.'

'Even if it didn't,' he said with a sigh, 'I've seen you look at each other in *that way*. You think it might be doing no harm, but when you've lusted after bacon and eggs, my friend, you've already committed breakfast in your soul.'

'That's amusingly deep.'

'It was C.S. Lewis,' mused Doc. 'Terrific writer but for one thing: did you know there's not a single talking rabbit in all of the Narnia series? He didn't think we were deserving enough, clearly. And don't get me started on Gus Honeybun or the Duracell Bunny: demeaning stereotypes and patronising beyond belief. Br'er Rabbit and Bugs Bunny are about the closest you'll get to a genuine rabbit, although in film and theatre, Harvey is the gold standard. Just the right mix of compassion, erudition and insouciance.'

'I didn't know that,' I said, glad that, for the moment at least, the subject of duels seemed to have slipped his mind. 'What about Roger Rabbit?'

'My uncle? Runs a hookah den in Ross that specialises in readings of Voltaire.'

'No, I meant the film.'

'Ah – the jury's still out on that one. Rabbit psychologists hold entire conferences based on him, and we still have no idea what he saw in Jessica. So, do you have a duelling pistol, or do you want to borrow my spare?'

'It's less than two hours before you get hit with every fox RabCoT can muster, backed up by thousands of Compliance Officers and the British Army,' I said. 'Is this *really* the time to be duelling?'

'*Mais oui*, my little furless friend. You're in love with my wife so it's about you and me making this right. Don't be afraid, I'm an excellent shot: you fire, you miss really badly, I fire, I miss by a hair. Honour is restored, simple. Here.'

He opened his jacket to reveal his duelling pistols, both stuffed inside his belt.

'Loaded,' he said, 'and since it's my challenge, you get to choose.'

I looked at the pistols. One had a silver crocodile on the handle, and the other a mother-of-pearl rabbit elegantly set into the stock. *The gun with the bun has the aim that is lame, but the shot'll hit the spot if you've a croc on the stock.* If I hadn't been a good shot myself, all of this would have been academic. But I'd won prizes at school with a .22 pistol, and once represented the county and got a bronze.

'Is this why you wanted me in Colony One?' I asked.

'Unfinished business,' he said, 'so yes, partly.'

He was right in that I was in love with Connie. I think I always had been, and I think she felt the same. But she was a warrior and so was Doc – fearless and focused, utterly committed to the cause.

They belonged with each other. But Doc was a good rabbit, and I would have to go through with this for the sake of his honour, so I chose the gun with the bun, the aim that was lame. If I was about to lose a duel, I needed Doc's marksmanship to be as good as possible.

'Wait a minute,' I said, realising that to win a rabbit duel one has to hit the opponent's ears without actually killing them, 'I've got no ears – well, none to speak of.'

'I thought of that,' said Doc, handing me a folded chef's hat from his jacket pocket.

'If it's OK with you,' he said, quite enthused by the idea of a duel, 'we'll dispense with the foggy heath at dawn and just get on with it. Twenty paces sound all right?'

I put on the chef's hat and we stood back to back, paced off and then turned to face one another. A .22 pistol has very little kick, but a duelling pistol – which I'd never fired – would be loaded with heavy ball, and the kick would make the shot run high. Plus I had the gun whose aim was lame. I couldn't possibly hit him.

'You first!' yelled Doc, holding his pistol at his side. He was almost in silhouette, his ears tall and erect, his stomach quite large.

I pulled back the hammer, aimed just above Doc's head and fired. The muzzle of the pistol erupted in a ball of fire but, annoyingly, the charge was weaker than I expected and my aim not as errant as I'd thought. I saw a nick appear in the very top of Doc's right ear where the ball just caught it.

'Good shot, sir!' cried Doc. 'My turn.'

I held my breath as he pointed the pistol in my direction, then, at the very last moment, he pointed it to the left of me, and fired. The ball thudded harmlessly into the door frame of a shop that sold second-hand hookahs. He lowered the pistol and smiled.

'Honour is restored,' he said. 'Connie is yours. Pick up your cardboard box and let's get you to the meeting house. We have some vital work we need you to undertake.'

I ran to catch up with him as he strode off.

'What was that all about?' I said. 'You *deliberately* shot wide.'

'I most certainly did not,' he said in a shocked tone, 'and to suggest I had would impugn my good name. Besides,' he added, 'I volunteered to lead first wave against the attack this evening and it will all end for me tonight. Some of us won't get to go home.'

He stopped and turned to look at me.

'There are unsuitable bucks about, and I'd rather you and she had a chance. I know she loves you, always has, and she'll want you to go home with her. She'd like that, and I'd like it too, knowing she was in good hands.'

He put out his paw and I passed back the pistol.

'I worked at the Taskforce for fifteen years,' I said. 'I enabled their appalling work. I'm not a good person.'

'But you proved that you *can* be,' said Doc, 'and that's what's important. You took the heat off Constance, and a thousand rabbits were spared. You're repaired, Peter. Not everyone gets that. Count yourself fortunate.'

We had reached the door of the circular Lago meeting house.

'OK,' he said, 'this is where we need your help.'

'You want me to address the Grand Council of Coneys?' I said. 'And try and broker some sort of eleventh-hour deal? I can take offers back and forth to Smethwick, and even, perhaps, have a few ideas of my own.'

'Perish the thought,' he said, finding my comments somehow amusing. 'Better rabbits than you have tried and failed on that score. You're not here to help us, rescue us, lead us to freedom or otherwise give us the benefit of your wisdom. We're not going to see any hoary old "Hominid Saviour" bullshit this evening, thank you very much – we've got troubles of our own.'

'Then what am I here to do?'

Doc opened the meeting-house door to reveal a large room with about two hundred rabbits inside, all either elderly, young or infirm. There was also a smattering of humans, but Pippa was not amongst them. The tables were arranged seven long in five rows, and in the centre of each table was a huge pile of sliced bread. On the table in front of each workstation were tubs of dandelion-oil margarine, and the air was full of gossip in English and Rabbity.

'You're on sandwich-making duty,' said Doc. 'It's important everyone gets to eat before the attack.'

'You wanted me in the colony to make cucumber sandwiches?'

'Each contributes according to the level of their abilities. Besides, we were getting low on doilies. You can't serve cucumber sandwiches on a plate without doilies.[62] It's just not the done thing.'

I opened the box Lance had given me, and it was indeed full of doilies. Quite nice ones, too. Plain white. Ornate.

'Hello, Mr Knox,' said Kent, who seemed to be in charge, 'you can be on cucumber-slicing duty. It's more efficient with fingers – even without thumbs you're more dexterous than us. We can slice, but not slice *thin*, and that's the secret of really good cucumber sandwiches.'

I turned to say goodbye to Doc, but he had already gone. I think he removed himself quietly on purpose. The dialogue between us was done, our understanding was complete. I wouldn't see him again, nor ever know what happened to him, although it was likely he faced his death with more courage than I would ever possess. I took my place next to a young woman who was also missing her thumbs, and she nodded politely, gave me a sharp knife and I started slicing, although not without some difficulty. I'd only recently lost my thumbs and it was the first knife I'd handled since getting out of custody.

'You came prepared,' she said with a smile.

'I'm sorry?'

'The chef's hat.'

We were, I learned later, only one of twenty-six work gangs making cucumber sandwiches, the snack of choice for rabbits when nerves need to be calmed and the future is in doubt. Carrots are more for pleasure and everyday eating, dandelion leaves for when you just want to shoot the breeze – equivalent to a cup of coffee and a Danish. Radishes are for a hangover, parsnips for when you need a boost, turnips when there's nothing left in the larder. There were gallons of tea, too, but that was handled by someone else.

I worked for ninety minutes, and must have sliced several hundred cucumbers. The finished sandwiches – once given a sprinkling of salt

---

62. In case you're not conversant with teatime etiquette, a 'doily' is the round ornamental mat cakes and sandwiches are served upon.

and with the crusts cut off – were taken off by waiter rabbits who
plied backwards and forwards between us and the troops with the
sandwiches on trays. It all worked in a rota system, so everyone got
to go outside and offer words of encouragement, and to say their
farewells. The news that filtered back was not good. Numerous drones
had been seen overhead, and more artillery pieces had been observed
moving into position and then waiting at readiness. Tanks and bulldozers were massed at the main gate, and infantry had moved up
behind the tanks in case the rabbit had weapons of which they were
unaware. And everywhere, ahead of everything, *were the foxes*, hundreds
and hundreds of them, grunting and howling and yelping in their
excitement, a murderous carpet of orange-coloured hate.

Most of this I found out much later on when researching for my
book. It was Smethwick who had first encouraged, then begged the
use of flame-throwers to clear the warrens, as rabbits, he said, 'are
full of surprises'. The ranking army officer, to his credit, told
Smethwick that 'if you want to do that kind of shit, old boy, you
can get your own people to do it. There'll be no unnecessary suffering
to rabbits on my watch. I'm not sidestepping the ICC[63] on taxonomic
grounds only to be collared by the RSPCA. It's conventional force
only. Any overreach is on your shoulders – and don't you forget it.'

Although I was busy and quite swept up in an odd shared sense
of destiny, at the back of my mind was also survival – which involved
surrendering to the first human I met. A fox, I knew, would probably
be after revenge. They'd know who I was, not least because of the
fox claw that was still around my neck.

63. Evidence suggests he was referring to the International Criminal Court and
not the International Cricket Council.

The Battle of May Hill

The rabbit's 'Circle of Lifefullness' has since been adopted by humans, and the movement is growing. Some say it was what the rabbits were here to do in the first place, to deliver a new faith, a new way of doing things. I try to adhere to the Five Circles as much as my human wiring allows, the same as the rest of us.

'Take a break, Mr Knox,' said Kent when I was down to my last cucumber. 'Why not take a tray up to Mum? She's with the Venerable Bunty and the commanders at the top of the hill.'

I glanced at the clock. It was half past seven. Thirty minutes to the attack.

I loaded up a tray, dispensed with the chef's hat and made my way out of the meeting house and into the colony. All seemed quiet, the only movement from those who were wielding trays piled high with cucumber sandwiches and offering up refills of tea. The rabbits seemed to have lined themselves up ten deep around the entranceways, ready to defend themselves, wherever the first wave of foxes would arrive.

I walked to the top of May Hill from which there was a commanding position to view the battle. It took me a while to get up there, and it was five to eight by the time I arrived.

'I brought up some refreshments,' I said once there was a suitable lapse in the conversation. I noted that they were all does, all Wildstock, and all speaking in Rabbity. Connie noticed me and walked over to help herself, accompanied by the Venerable Bunty.

'Just the ticket,' said Connie, eating several sandwiches in quick succession. 'Glad you could make it. Lance did a good job, I hear.'

I told her he had and then thanked them both for leaving a back door from which I could escape. The Venerable Bunty told me it was the least they could do, but when I said I would leave them to their battle, Connie asked me to stay.

'You need to be here,' she said simply. 'Did you and Doc duel it out?'

I nodded.

'And?'

'He let me win.'

'I thought he might.'

'This battle,' I said, 'can you win?'

'In a traditional sense, no,' said Connie, 'but sometimes, when the long game is played, you can lose a battle and still win a war.'

'Did killing Mr Ffoxe actually make a difference?'

'It showed that foxes could and should be subject to justice. Mr Ffoxe killed over three thousand rabbits that we know of, and wouldn't have stopped.'

'But wasn't he just the shill?' I asked. 'Shouldn't Smethwick have been the target?'

'We needed to delay and escalate things all at the same time. The timing had to be just right. You'll see.'

They went back to talking tactics and I stood there, feeling spare and useless.

'Hello, Dad.'

It was Pippa, the billiard-smooth grass of the hill no impediment to her movement.

I gave her a hug and she said she was with Harvey, who waved to me from the communications table set up under an oak tree. He had a dozen or so field telephones in front of him which rang occasionally and were answered by a clerk, who then wrote down a report on a piece of paper and presented it to the Venerable Bunty's aide-de-camp.

'They can't win,' I said to Pippa.

'I think they know that, Dad – but then much depends on your definition of winning.'

'But you're OK?'

She looked across at Harvey, then back to me, and smiled the most radiant of smiles.

'I have never been happier.'

I was about to tell her that I'd wanted to hear that for a long,

long, time, but I was interrupted by a large explosion as one half of the entranceway collapsed into a pile of rubble. The attack had begun. There was a loud rasp of coordinated artillery fire as a volley of shells flew into the colony and exploded amongst the cucumber frames and runner-bean poles. I heard the revving of tank engines as they advanced through the damaged gateway behind the bulldozers. More chilling than all this, however, were the whoops, cries, yelps and barks of the excited foxes, and the screams of terrified rabbits.

As we watched and listened, the smoke now drifting up and across the hill, there was a second explosion at the northern gateway, and another volley of artillery fire that tore up the gardens, revealing the lights in the tunnels beneath.

I could see Connie staring out across the swirling smoke at the rich fertile land of Gloucestershire. Soft earth, and abundant grass. The summer was not yet over, and there were still long evenings for rabbits to gambol. On the horizon the rim of the rising full moon was just beginning to show. Connie turned to the Venerable Bunty and they both nodded in agreement.

'I'm going to complete the circle before we have too much suffering,' said Bunty. 'I thought our presence would at the very least give humans pause for reflection, but it seems not, or at least, not yet. It may happen, we live in hope. Best say your goodbyes.'

Connie turned to me.

'It's not working out for us, Pete. Driving cars and talking and having TV was kind of fun, and clothes and eating out totally rock. But the hate, the fear, the greed. *It just doesn't make any sense.* You're trying to run a twenty-first-century world on Palaeolithic thoughts and sentiments.'

'I think it's in our nature.'

'I disagree,' she replied. 'Humans have a very clear idea about how to behave, and on many occasions actually do. But it's some-times disheartening that correct action is drowned out by endless chitter-chatter, designed not to find a way forward but to justify petty jealousies and illogically held prejudices. If you're going to talk, try to make it relevant, useful and progressive rather than simply distracting and time-wasting nonsense, intended only to justify the untenable and postpone the real dialogue that needs to happen.'

Sometimes it takes a non-human to say what it is to be a good human. In the ultimate hypocrisy, Smethwick and UKARP and 2LG and all the others that accused the rabbits of unsustainable overpopulation should have turned the accusation on themselves. The rabbits weren't the rabbits – we were.

'So what circle are you completing?' I asked as the meeting house suffered a direct hit and erupted in a ball of fire.

'We're going home,' she said simply. 'We've done about all we can for the moment.'

I looked at Pippa, who had her arms wrapped tightly around Harvey, and I knew then what their play was. Whatever had given them their humanness could just as easily remove it. The anthropomorphised rabbits were indeed going home, back to the way they were.

They'd seen enough. *They were going to revert.*

Connie clasped my hand tightly in her paws.

'Why don't you come with me?' she said. 'I can't guarantee that it'll be intellectually challenging and there certainly won't be any scones and raspberry jam and *Panorama* and Coen brothers movies, but there will be gambolling in the meadows, lots of it, which is kind of special – and you and I will be together.'

I looked around. The rabbit were retreating from the forward positions as they sensed the circle was about to close, and I saw the first of the tanks come into view. It paused for a second then fired, and a shell whistled above our heads and ripped through the treetops.

'I'm not sure I'd make a very good rabbit,' I said. 'Besides, I've not done enough to earn it. I didn't kill Mr Ffoxe; all I did was take the rap – and there's nothing brave, noble or exceptional in doing the right thing. I could have done more earlier, and of my own free will. But I didn't.'

'You did *something*,' said Connie. 'Incremental change comes from incremental action.'

'Incremental is enough?'

'It's the most most people can do. We're not all revolutionaries, but enough people challenging the problem can make a difference. So, you coming?'

'Someone has to tell this story,' I said. 'You're going to have to go home on your own.'

'Then maybe another time?'

'Yes,' I said, 'maybe another time.'

And she smiled, and she kissed me, there amongst the smell of cordite and the whistle of projectiles as they flew over our heads. The mortars had just started, and the *whompa* of exploding shells filled the air.

'Goodbye, Peter,' she said, glancing towards where the full moon had risen above the horizon. 'I'll come and find you. Might take a while, but I shall.'

I opened my mouth to say goodbye, but she and all the other rabbits had already gone. Not *entirely* gone, of course, just back to the part of themselves they had chosen to be, rejecting everything that made them human. I looked down at my feet, and there she was – a small brown-furred field rabbit no bigger than a cat and now covered by a draped mass of mud-streaked summer dress, the same one, in fact, she had been wearing when she turned up in the library all those weeks ago, blinking innocently and asking for a copy of *Rabbit and Rabbitability*. She looked startled and ran away, zig-zagging as though her life depended upon it until she was lost to sight within a furry carpet of other panicked rabbits eager to escape. The attack faltered as the Taskforce quickly realised that the enemy had gone, and they were now simply using their power and might against field rabbits. I stood there feeling empty and lost and broken. Everything I had thought I was, everything I thought my nation stood for, had been wrong. I wasn't anything special, I hadn't ultimately made a difference. I had been complicit in crimes against rabbits and betrayed my own sense of natural justice. *I thought I had been one of the good guys*. I hadn't been forgiven, I wasn't repaired, I was the same flawed person I had been before Connie chanced back into my life. The only difference between the me now and the me then was that I had achieved a sense of awareness, and the measure of Peter Knox was what he'd do with that knowledge in the months and years ahead. I stood there for quite a few minutes, listening to the confused yells of foxes, and the artillery quieten and stop.

'Knox?' said a fox I didn't recognise who had just run up the hill, searching in vain for rabbits. 'Is that you, the one that killed Torquil?'

He was with five others. They were stripped to the waist, the orange of their fur accentuated by the fires now blazing in the colony.

'Yes,' I said, no longer in denial, 'Peter Knox, ex-Spotter, RabCoT office, Hereford.'

They started to move towards me, but I didn't budge. There would have been no point. I knew how fast foxes could move.

'We are so going to enjoy *this*,' said the first fox, grinning fit to burst, his fangs wet with saliva. 'I've always wanted to know what killing a human felt like. But don't feel bad. It's not simply payback for Torquil – but for all those hunts.'

I didn't think I'd mention that I'd never been on a fox hunt, and instead murmured 'guilty on all counts' and closed my eyes.

The circle hadn't only been completed in Colony One. Every single anthropomorphised rabbit had gone home by the time the full moon had risen. Despite this, Nigel Smethwick ordered the attack to continue, just in case it was some sort of a rabbit trick. It wasn't, and the press mocked him for his 'war on rabbits' before they moved on to other matters, such as the shock cancellation of *Casualty*, whether the new Dr Who was as good as the old one, or reporting on what someone on Twitter said about someone else who was also on Twitter. By the end of the month all the colonies were smoking ruins, the network of burrows mined by the Royal Engineers. In a year the land had been cleared and returned to farmland.

As a parting gesture and to refute detractors who said that rabbits had no sense of humour, the rabbits took the foxes with them. The timing was, for me at least, impeccable. My five foxy executioners reverted within one pace of me, and swiftly ran off into the hedge-rows, confused and nervous. But unlike the rabbits, the foxes retained memory traces of their former life and made repeated attempts to sneak into exclusive London restaurants and hotels. The Savoy had to employ a gamekeeper who killed fifty-eight of them in a single six-week period, and foxes can often be seen at Glyndebourne, staring wistfully at the performers from the safety of a near by wood.

Not all animals reverted. Firyali Elephant was sworn in as Kenya's president three years later, a job she has done spectacularly well over the past sixteen years – the model for elephantine governance that is currently transforming Africa. Back in the UK the Dalmatian and the badger were untouched by the deEventing, and last I heard were still doing their 'Spots and Stripes' comedy routine, which remains unfunny, but still unique, to this day. The surviving guinea pigs were released on licence after a decade, reoffended in under a week and are now back inside. Adrian Whizelle changed his name to Arthur Bulstrode, but it didn't help: he, like all the other weasels, was found dead in suspicious circumstances by the time the year was out. The caterpillar is still in the Natural History Museum and s/he has yet to change into a butterfly. And the bees? No one has any idea what happened to the bees.

Aftermath

The Reversion created as many questions as the Event, and as the years
went by, the possibility of another Event filled the imagination of all
those who understood the quiet simplicity of the Rabbit Way. With
each full moon, there is hope of another. We watch, and we wait.

– *Event Rabbits* by Peter Knox, 326 pages, Hodder & Stoughton,
first published Oct. 2028

Without rabbits to be the focus of his hatred, Nigel Smethwick
directed his ire at 'anyone different', and the followers of UKARP
followed suit, using a simple word substitution to change their party
constitution and mission statement quickly and efficiently. He was
defeated at the next general election, his message of Hominid
Supremacism diluted by the loss of the rabbits. He retired from
politics but remains active as a talk-show pundit. The language of
division can always be monetised.

The Rabbit Compliance Taskforce was disbanded, the employees
made redundant with generous payouts. Owing to an oversight, the
paperwork regarding my firing hadn't gone through, and I was paid
off like the rest. I never went back to Much Hemlock, but I understand it's much the same. Wing Commander Slocombe took over my
Speed Librarying duties and is the new Mr Major. He still uses my
system of codes, for which I am grateful. To this day, Much Hemlock
have still not won a Spick & Span award.

I took the insurance payout from my burned house, sold the plot
and moved to Rhayader, where I purchased a large house with
grounds that overlooked the old MegaWarren site. I took to chron-
icling the fifty-five years of the Event in some considerable detail,
and seemed the person best positioned to do so. Of all the humans
who were living in the five colonies at the time of the Reversion,
seventy-six decided not to go. I interviewed sixty-eight of them for

my book. The number of humans who had decided to go with the rabbits was around four thousand, but estimates vary. They were officially declared 'missing, whereabouts unknown'.

Patrick Finkle and Pippa were amongst them.

When the MegaWarren site was sold I bought the entranceway, admin buildings and forty acres of warren, from which was developed the Event Museum, now in its ninth year, and currently Mid-Wales' fifth-most popular tourist attraction. The reopened branch line, now a steam heritage railway, is the first.

It took Connie two years to find me and take up residence in my orchard. I could easily identify her by the mismatched eyes – one bluey-violet, the colour of harebells, one as brown as a fresh hazelnut – but if she retained any sense of what she had once been, I didn't see it. She acted just like a wild field rabbit. Harvey joined her a week later. He was easily identified by the lack of any ears, and with him, *always with him, always together*, was a smaller rabbit, a female, who would have been indistinguishable from any other rabbit but for a single ear stud on her right ear, a present from me on her eighteenth birthday, and never removed. She moved uncertainly, but well enough to forage amongst the food I left out for them, the muscular strength of her forelegs making up for any shortfall. I missed her terribly, but it was her choice to stay with Harvey and fully embrace the Rabbit Way, and I respected that.

The rabbits were curious, but never really tame, and the colony remains there to this day. The one who I once knew as Constance lived the longest. She used to come on to the patio and stare at me quizzically as I made breakfast, but would run away if I opened the door.

It was to be expected. She was, after all, only a rabbit.

Acknowledgements:

I am indebted first of all to my agent Will Francis and my Editor Carolyn Mays, who interpreted a very troublesome first draft of *The Constant Rabbit* in a positive manner and were sufficiently bold to see that the core idea was sound, and that something good may come out of it.

The many references to *The Court Jester* are in deep homage to an iconic movie, but it should be noted that the duelling pistol ditties are an adaptation of Martha Raye and Bob Hope in 'Never Say Die', itself a precursor to the 'Pellet with the poison' routine. I also borrowed a line from a Spike Milligan short story and a Mel Brooks film - two titans of comedy whom I hope will forgive me.

Rabbit information was supplied via Wikipedia and Lockley's excellent *Private Life of the Rabbit*. My apologies to anyone in Herefordshire who have battled tirelessly to attack inequality in this world and feel they might have been in some small measure maligned. I had to set the book somewhere.

My thanks to the team at Hodder for their endless support, especially Lily Cooper, and my thanks go also to the eagle-eyed Sharona Selby and Olivia Davies.

The frontispiece was drawn by Bill Mudron of Portland, Oregon. Other examples of his work can be found at https://www.billmudron. com/ and he will gladly discuss commissions.

And lastly, Ozzy, whose mention will be no surprise to my readers. Although slowing up in the stick-fetching department, he still shows enthusiasm for walkies to a dog half his age, and whose companionship I value beyond that of many humans.

Jasper Fforde,
February 2020